BETWEEN US

CHEYENNE CIERRA

all of us

TRENTON

I wanted her the first moment I saw her. I was only eight, but my heart's been set on her ever since.
I don't know what to call my fixation on her, I don't know if it's just lust. I don't know if it's pure infatuation, or even love. But whatever it is, it's strong.
It's unconditional…it's unrefined…but it's unrequited…
It's unlawful.
And still, no one could convince me that she isn't the one.
She is the one. She's the only one.
I wanted Aubree. I had to have her, but I had to wait.
There's always been a wedge between us. A thick line that's never meant to be crossed.
But sometime after my eighteenth birthday I took the first step over it.
Nothing between us now—except for the guilt over seducing my best friend's mom.

AUBREE

I don't know how we got here.
In Roger's office. My husband, who I won't see for a week. Who'd kill us both if he knew what we'd been doing, and where we'd been doing it.
Trenton stares at me patiently, but the shine in his eyes is urgent. He's waited who knows how long for this, and now he's looking at me like he needs it. Me. Like an obedient puppy who's been told not to eat, waiting for the second he's allowed to devour the food in front of him. The robe falls off my shoulders, gathering in the bends of my arms before I lower them and let the rest of the pitch black silk fall to the ground.
He lets his eyes run down me slowly, taking second looks at the more obvious places. Eyes outlining my every curve and fine line I keep hidden from the world. Jaw tightening, tongue peeking past his lips before his teeth lightly graze his bottom lip like the sight of me pains him. Like not touching me pains him.
I don't know how we got here.
Me, standing completely bare in front of him. Savoring the rush it gives me when I'm under his observation.
Seconds from sex he begged for.
Seconds from sex I've promised him.
Seconds from dissolving the now fine line we've been filing away at since the day he told me he wanted me.
I don't know how we got here.
But I don't want to go back—we couldn't even if we wanted to.

Youth condemns; maturity condones.

- Amy Lowell

PLAYLIST

Got Friends - *Goldlink*
Weekend - *Mac Miller*
Party All the Time - *Danny Brown*
F**k Love - *XXXTENTACION*
Freak In You - *PARTYNEXTDOOR*
Disrespectful - *Trey Songz*
Drama - *Roy Woods*
To the Moon - *Phora*
Nikes - *Frank Ocean*
Better Now - *Post Malone*
Wake Up - *Travis Scott*
Yours - *Alina Baraz*

PROLOGUE

Eight Months Prior

"THAT BARBECUE I TOLD YOU ABOUT. SOLANA INVITED *ALL* OF US two weeks ago." I glare at Diesel, my seventeen—almost eighteen—year old because I already know what's going to come out of his mouth before he's even spoken a word. Defiance.

My dark brown eyes veer over to Trenton as he emerges from the kitchen. "Hi, Mrs. Cooper."

I assume he's helped himself to whatever's in our fridge because he's smiling at me through every chew.

Trenton's my son's best friend—and for the past year, the boy who makes me question my sanity. I use the term *boy* loosely because just like my son, Trenton's soon to be entering manhood and he doesn't let me forget it. Ever since he turned seventeen, he shot up from five seven, to six feet and now towers over me. He went from bright eyed and bushy tailed to brooding and beguiling, and that would be fine if he didn't make me feel like I was soon to be on another episode of *To Catch a Predator*—*in my own home.*

"Hi, Trenton." I only smirk at him for a second before he gives me that look he always does. The one that used to be boyish and adorable and make me laugh, but now it fills me with the deepest feeling of shame because underneath the makings of facial hair, his smile makes me weak in the knees.

"Well, I forgot—we already have plans."

Plans means they're going to sit in the backyard and remind the neighbors how much they hate us for the constant weed smell that drifts into every yard in the vicinity.

"Trenton can come too. She has a couple of cute nieces around your age," I say, as if that'll sweeten the deal.

"Nah, we'll pass, Mom. I have a girlfriend, remember?"

I wince. "That's on again?"

"Anyway—"

"Solana has has a big pool, a hot tub—there'll be lots of food… and it's summertime, it'll be fun."

I hate that I have to resort to *selling* my son time to hang out with me, but I guess that's what no one told you about having a teenager.

Diesel begins to walk away, letting me know for certain that I'm going to this thing alone. Until Trenton opens his mouth.

"Well, wait a minute." He sets his hand on Diesel's shoulder and I know he's going to do his best to convince him. He was always on board when I offered to take them out somewhere Diesel didn't want to go, I knew I could count on Trenton to talk him into it.

I turn my back to them, applying my lipstick in the corridor mirror. I watch as they chat behind me in the reflection. My eyes drawn to Trenton's full bottom lip as he drags his tongue over it while speaking.

It's like it just hit him over night. He looks like an *actual* man. Feels like yesterday I was still taking them trick or treating, and now he gives me heart palpitations whenever his shirt is off. What a mind fuck.

Trenton mutters something along the lines of trying to score with one of the 'cute nieces' I brought up, and Diesel's a loyal wingman so that's really all it took.

"Alright, we're going," Diesel announces, heading toward the garage. I turn around, catching Trenton's satisfied smirk as he follows after him.

Solana's been my friend for years. We met when we were thirteen and I haven't been able to shake her since, not that I want to.

She and I grew into complete opposites, took totally different paths in life. She serves as a big reminder of who I could have been if I hadn't made the choices I made, but I don't dwell on it. Instead, I admire her free spirit. I envy it.

It's a beautiful day out. Her pool is more intricately detailed than ours, but not by a lot. She just had her backyard re-landscaped after separating from Lawson—her husband of three years—and this is sort of a celebration of her freedom.

I mingled with some of her family members who I hadn't seen in a while, chat with a few old but mutual friends, and made my rounds through her backyard just soaking up all the social interaction because I really don't get out much.

I finally stopped to make myself a plate. Her dad barbecued and just finished the last round of burgers, and I needed to eat something in order to soak up all the drinks I indulged in.

"Aubree, where've you been hiding?" her father, Bernard, says to me, sliding a patty onto my bun. He says that like he knows more than he's willing to admit, but I'd account that to Solana's big mouth. "We don't see much of you anymore."

"Yeah, I've just been really busy with Diesel..." I nod as if to make it more convincing.

I haven't been busy with Diesel since he were a kid. Since before he decided he didn't want to be in basketball anymore. Before he was too cool to go to the movies with me. To go anywhere with me—I mean, God forbid he ever be caught at dinner with his mom.

He's been all about his friends or his father since his voice started to crack and I've been starving for his attention ever since.

"Go long, T!" I hear Diesel shout as I go to the condiment table.

I blink only twice and by the third, a football's hurling toward me.

A lone voice shouts for me to watch out, but it's coming too quick for me to react, all I can do is shut my eyes and brace.

With my eyes clenched tight, I hear the impact, but I don't feel the pain that accompanies the sound.

That's because Trenton's caught it single handedly right in front of my face. I swallow hard as he cups the ball in both hands, noticing he's lost his shirt, like always, and his skin is still a bit wet, indicating he'd been in the pool quite recently.

He holds his arms up and yells across the yard, "Diesel, what the fuck, man? You almost hit your mom!"

Diesel shrugs in the distance and Trenton turns back to look at me. His bare skin radiant from the sun shining down on us, the small beads of water glistening on his shoulders. But I beg my eyes not to indulge in the sight any more than I already had earlier. Sneaking peeks of him when he was far enough away from me.

"Careful, Mrs. C. Your face is too pretty for the nasty bruise that would have left you." He gives me a small smile before ambling along the edge of the pool, not stopping until he's returned to the group of teens on the far side of the yard.

My lips part as I take in his words. *Did he just call me pretty?*

"Alright, so he clearly has a thing for you." Solana appears beside me, a red cup in her hand as she joins in my gaze across the pool. The boys begin chucking the ball again, Trenton's arms demonstrating their strength with every throw he makes while every catch flexes his biceps.

"Trenton? No." I chuckle. "He's just messing around."

Solana's silence is like an invitation to look at her, her perfectly arched eyebrow raises in discontent before she scoffs at me.

"What?" I say.

"Are you really that in denial? He hasn't taken his eyes off you all day, and any time I've ever seen him he's buzzing around you like a fly."

"Okay, well so what if he does have a little crush on me—"

"Not a crush, sis. He clearly wants to fuck."

"Solana!"

"He does!"

I take a breath, straightening my shoulders as I take another glance their way. Trenton smiles at me again and my eyes quickly dart away from him.

She's right. She's so right.

He's always been a flirt, but not like this. Not the way he has been lately.

Her brow ticks and she takes a drink from her cup. "He's cute…"

"He's a teenager," I say as a reminder to both her and myself and it makes her roll her eyes.

"Girl, if you only knew how many 'teenagers' I hooked up with this year."

"That's gross." I scowl at her.

She clicks her teeth. "I'm not talking sixteen year olds. They were legal, and so is he."

"He's seventeen."

"He'll be eighteen in what? A few months?"

"Yes. He's a teenager and I'm a married woman."

"Yeah, a married woman who's neglected by her husband and needs to get laid by a hot guy who looks at her like she's the fucking sun, that's what you are."

"Does he really look at me like that?" I get another glimpse of them and it's like Trenton knows when my eyes are on him because he answers my question with just one look. The clear mesmeric gaze he has on me, like I'm entitled to all of his attention. Like I own it.

I've never seen a look like that in Roger's eyes. I'll chalk it up to the fact that he and I are eighteen years deep and any mystery there was has long fizzled out. He treats me like the boy behind the check out stand at our local liquor store. He only ever mutters a few words to me without making any physical or eye contact—like I'm just anyone.

And Trenton looks at me like I'm *the only one.*

But then again, this is a teenage boy.

This is probably puppy love—a crush. Lusting after the older woman. Maybe even just a fantasy of his.

Trenton's eyes drop from me only when he realizes she's looking and she giggles. "All I'm saying is, you're in for trouble with that one around."

ONE

Aubree

PARTIES WERE SO DIFFERENT WHEN I WAS A TEEN.

I mean, we still drank, we still smoked, we'd still experiment, but a birthday party was still a birthday party. Meaning there were decorations, food, family, games, and gifts.

These kids are literally in my backyard laughing and smoking to rap music.

There is no cake, there are no balloons, no streamers. Nothing indicating this is a birthday celebration whatsoever. I'd throw in the fact that no one's dancing, but I guess grinding counts.

A few months ago, Diesel asked me if he could throw his friend a birthday party at our house. I like this friend and I know he's good for it as he's been by my son's side for over a decade now, so it was hardly a question. But now as I watch them from my second story bedroom window, I'm feeling a slight pinch of regret.

Having a bunch of wild teens over is a lot of liability and I'm currently reminded as to why I told Diesel to cool down on the parties in the first place. They're getting older now. They value being reckless over being good. And I'm hardly an authority figure here, it's never been my strong suit.

But I tell myself it's just for tonight and then not again until Diesel turns eighteen next year, so I'll just have to deal and pray that no one passes out and bangs their head on the concrete out there.

I bite my finger nail as I watch some teenage girl grind against Trenton's lap in her high waist Levi shorts and worn out checkered vans. Her hands pressed to her bare knees and making me curious of what it feels like to be in her position.

He couldn't look more bored, so maybe it doesn't feel like much of anything.

Or maybe he's just so high, he makes it come off that way.

Trenton looks up at my window and I freeze. His teeth graze his bottom lip before turning into a wolfish smile that makes my stomach flutter wildly. My breath hitches and I let the curtain fall out of my fingertips as I back away from the glass.

Trenton Laguna. The neighborhood heartthrob, Diesel's best friend since elementary school, and the boy who never leaves my house. He's charming and funny, and witty and sweet. Every word that boy speaks is qualified as sweet talk.

My son's the total opposite. He's an asshole just like his father, but that doesn't stop all the girls from swarming him. Only thing that does is the little snob, Chloe, who he's been on again, off again with for the past two years.

She started off sweet, then sometime after the third break they took, she came back suddenly comfortable enough to eye roll and scoff anytime I told her it was time to go home. They're lucky I even let her over at all. I know what they're doing when they're locked up in his room, and it's not 'just watching tv'. But, I do feel safer knowing they're doing it at home with condoms available, and not spur of the moment somewhere where they figure one time won't hurt anyone, because it can. I learned that the hard way.

"Mrs. Cooper, you didn't wish me a happy birthday yet."

While my back is turned, I squeeze my eyes shut. My hand draws back from the unopened bottle of Merlot I was reaching for in the hopes it'd help put me at ease tonight. Because let's be honest, I'll need it if I'm going to be able to ride out the rest of this party.

I clutch my black, satin robe shut at my breasts before turning around to face him. His light brown, almost gold, eyes are glossy from all the smoking they'd been doing out there, but his crooked smile is just as strong as always.

"Happy birthday, Trenton." I smirk.

He always looks at me like that, like he's so stimulated by how uncomfortable I get when he catches me alone. And he *always* catches me alone.

I turn back around to put the long stemmed glass back in the cabinet, pushing all the others back neatly like I've just gone through and polished them instead of having had plans to run one up to my room and lock myself in. "I figured you were busy out there," I add, "you know how Diesel gets when I step in on his parties. I didn't want to get in the way."

"Nah, you could never get in my way. I actually wouldn't mind if you were in it more."

I let my brows bunch, but my smirk stays. I don't know what to say to that, and I hope that if I keep quiet he'll leave me alone and go back out to his party.

Where he belongs.

With all the little teenage girls who've been drooling over him all night.

It's kind of hilarious to watch actually. They all fling toward him like stretched rubber bands, forming a circle around him and the other boys while they smoke or do whatever. Diesel seems to always love the attention, but Trenton's different. He has a complete 'no fucks given' attitude and I think it only makes them want him more.

"I'm eighteen tonight," he says and I can tell he's come closer, but what I can't tell is if he's reminding me or if he's just that excited about his age. "A legal adult now."

I raise my eyebrows as I pivot back around and let a playfully smug look take over my face. "You don't say? And here I was thinking Diesel was throwing you a sweet sixteen."

"Ha-ha. Hysterical as always, Mrs. C." He tilts his head to the side, coming closer to me until nothing's between us but the cold beer in his hand that I keep eyeballing, but plan to say nothing about.

I know it's not the right thing to do, but I've always tried to be the cool mom. Both to Diesel and his friends. Roger gives me a lot of shit about it, but I'd rather know they were safe, drinking at home where I can check on them and limit what their friends smuggle in the house. I always do a check at the start of the night. Diesel hates it, but come on. I give him a lot more slack than any of their parents do.

Especially Trenton's mom. She wasn't always, but she's gotten so overly strict over the years. I wonder how it's all going to play out now that he's a *legal* adult.

I scolded the boys once around the time Diesel had just turned fifteen. They stole two beers from Roger's stash in the garage, got a couple more slaps on the wrist when they did it again the same year. Now I've declared an unwritten accord that they've both agreed to follow. As long as no one drinking drives, and the party is limited to no more than twenty-five people, I allow it.

So far they seem like they aren't all complete idiots and they value their lives, so they abide by it. Most of them usually just stay the night in the pool house and sleep it off anyway.

"I already opened all my gifts and noticed on top of you not wishing me a happy birthday, you didn't get me anything this year. That's not like you." He pouts and my heart leaps, making me suddenly antsy enough to know I need to get away from this boy. Now.

I squeeze past the small space he's left between our bodies and go to another cabinet to pull out a random mug for no reason other than to seem busy. It's red with Santa Claus's cartoon face on it. The last gift I got from Roger's mother—three years ago. On my birthday.

I exhale a calming breath. "I thought allowing you to have your party here was a good enough gift, no?"

"I mean, yeah it's awesome of you to let Diesel do this for me. But I mean, nothing beats a physical gift." I see him bite his cheek, and somehow without me even having noticed him move, he's in front of me again and this time I don't think I've got a way to squeeze through as I realize I've stupidly walked myself into a corner. "Like…something you can hold in your hands."

He puts his beer down behind my back, setting both of his hands on the countertop only millimeters away from my sides.

I'm locked in between his arms. Face to face. I'd be breathing the same air as him if I could get myself to start breathing again. How could I when he's hovering over me? Lingering in front of my face like he's daring me to breakaway.

Like it means something that I haven't yet.

"I owe you then," I say in a breath, blinking as I look anywhere but at him. He smells like a mixture of weed, spicy cologne, and young masculinity and I'm fighting the urge to breathe deeply into the crook of his neck. Especially with the way he's looking at me right now, like he knows it. Like he's challenging me to.

I'd never.

We hear the sliding glass open and he steps away from me. Not quickly, like if he were trying to hide the fact that he was deep in my personal space, but enough so that it's still a question if he was. Trenton's never cared how blunt or obvious he can be at times. His eyes are still roaming over me like they've got a warrant to.

"Ay, Trent!" Diesel calls from the living room. *Thank God.* "You still in here?"

"Yeah, I'll be out in a minute," Trenton barks back and I admire his jawline as he does. He licks his lips, swiping his beer from behind me. His arm brushes against mine and I can feel how solid it is for just a second. "Well then, Mrs. C," he takes a breath, "let me know when you're ready for me to come collect."

He backs away from me, smiling as he sips from his bottle and then finally disappears behind the wall.

I pinch my lips between my fingers, releasing the breath I was holding.

When the sliding glass is shut again, I quickly pour myself a glass of wine before taking the entire bottle with me upstairs.

I figure my best bet is to hang out in my room and catch up on my naughty novellas while I supervise from the window. Since Roger's taken on this new position at his job, I've been reading a lot more. He's out of the house for weeks at times, and although I was upset about it when he first told me he was considering the position —because that meant I'd be all alone with my teenage son who listens to his father over me—now that I've experienced the first few days alone, I'm fine with it.

I mean, is it bad that I feel sort of relieved that he's gone? It's like the black fog has cleared and now everything's a lot more lax around here.

I know the boys are happy because if Roger was here they definitely wouldn't be outside partying. Instead, they'd be downstairs playing a game of UNO to ring in Trenton's coming of age. No drinks, no girls, no loud music. A curfew of eight P.M.—and that's generous for Roger.

I hear a big splash and jump up from the grey, tufted chaise I was curled up on. *Dammit, I said no swimming!*

I set my book down and rush the stairs, my long, silk robe flying open as I catch wind from the descend. I clutch it closed again before I reach the sliding glass and pull it open.

"No pool, guys! We agreed that you'd either have drinks or have pool time."

Diesel's laying back in a pool lounge with the hood of his sweatshirt covering his eyes until he wriggles in his seat and squints at me. "Why do you gotta talk to us like we're fucking babies, Mom?"

"Diesel," I warn through gritted teeth. I'm seconds from ending this shit altogether and the look I give him makes him straighten up and realize that.

"It's hot out, Mrs. C," says Trenton, rising up the pool steps and slowly revealing his impressive abs. He rubs his hand over his dripping wet stomach, further drawing my eyes there—as if they hadn't already slingshot to that region as soon as he spoke.

I cross my arms over my chest and quickly look away.

"But I'll get out, if you want me to," he adds with a smile.

I hold my palm up to him. "No. Stay in. Whatever. Just, wrap it up in an hour. It's getting late."

Diesel rolls his eyes and I slide my tongue over my teeth as I refrain from grabbing him by his collar and embarrassing him in front of his friends. I'll save his scolding for tomorrow morning.

"You look hot," Trenton says above the music playing and the sounds of a couple of girls still splashing behind him.

I look at him sideways, keeping my eyes from lowering into a focus on the water that's still glistening down his chest. "Excuse me?"

He returns the look and chuckles. "I said you look like you're hot too. Why don't you get in with us, Mrs. C? It'll cool you down."

"Yeah, come on *Mrs. C,*" Gio drawls out my name, swimming over to the edge. His shoulder length hair slicked back. "I know you've gotta be bored up there all alone. We're good company." He winks before resting his arms on the pavement.

It's different when he does it. It's different when any of the others do it, because I can tell they're joking. They're trying to get a rise out of Diesel. But Trenton? He flirts with me in secret. He hems me up all alone when no one's watching and he does it to get a rise out of me.

"I'll pass, guys, but I do appreciate the offer." My sarcasm only makes Trenton laugh. "One hour—And please just stay here if you've drank too much."

"They've all got rides, Mom." Diesel speaks like he's been repeating himself to me all day and has gotten tired of it. But he hasn't. He hardly speaks to me throughout a day at all.

But I toss my thumb up as I whisk myself back through the sliding window. I'm staying in the rest of the night.

TWO

Trenton

"I'M GONNA BE YOUR STEPDAD SOME DAY, BRO. BET ON IT," I SAY, drying my face off on a pool towel.

"Fuck you." Diesel laughs before driving his fist into my side.

That's been the running joke since we were preteens. Since the three of us hit puberty and realized Diesel's mom was a fucking delicacy. A rarity, considering everyone else's moms' looked like, well...moms. Often sporting messy buns and tired eyes. They smelled like rose perfume and Aqua Net. The kind that curled their bangs and wore baggy scrubs most of the day, then white bath robes and rollers in their hair the rest of the time.

They were the kind of mom's that force fed our friends just because they were at the house, the kind of moms who'd never, ever let us drink or party on their property. They called us sweetie, or honey, or baby. But Diesel's mom, she never uttered those words—they wouldn't sound so innocent coming from her.

Mrs. Cooper's just, different.

She walks around the house in a silk lounge robe and wears her hair in long waves like she's just done print shots for a Victoria's Secret catalogue. I always wondered what she wore underneath the thin fabric. The death grip she has on it every time she's around me makes me guess it's either lacy underwear or nothing at all.

I always had a little innocent crush on her when I was a kid, but when I turned thirteen, things changed. When her tits bounced, it was captivating. And anytime her shirt rode up, it was like all eyes were summoned for a peek at any inch of bare skin that made itself known to us. She was hot, and she's still hot. She's always been hot.

It's fact.

Even Diesel knew it, and he hated it.

But he can't deny that having an insanely attractive mom has gotten him out of a whole lot of shit, not to mention the fact that it's gotten him the majority of his friends over the years.

Everyone wanted to hang at Diesel's house because his Mom's the hot housewife that stays home all day and walks around in leggings and crop tops. *Fucking crop tops.*

My eyes rise up to her window again. I love catching her watching me. She can't deny the joint attraction there is between us, but she does because it's unorthodox. I can tell she beats herself up about it, but fuck is it sexy to see her get all hot and bothered when I get too close.

Diesel smacks my thigh with the back of his hand as a billow of smoke flows out of his mouth. "Marina's here."

"Fuck," I mutter and he laughs.

Marina's the cute, petite blonde we grew up with. She's always had these golden doe eyes and her long wavy hair is never not braided or twisted in some way around her hairline. I crushed on her for a short while, and then the feeling soon disappeared like I never did.

I see the box she's come in with as she shuts the gate and feel a little bad for not wanting her here for a second. And it's not even that I don't want her here, I just…I don't know.

She smiles up at me as she walks into my open arm. "Happy birthday, Trent."

"Thanks." I squeeze her into my side, feeling her small hand wrap around my torso.

"Aw, you guys are cute." Diesel crinkles his nose at us and I get the compulsive visual of drawing back my fist and launching at his jaw. He's been pushing for us to get together for a couple of years now and it's annoying.

I open the box, revealing a giant chocolate cupcake with a candle shaped like the number eighteen sticking out of the top of it. She's smiling at me, flicking the lighter in her hand.

"We're singing happy birthday!" Diesel shouts. "Rina didn't come to fuck around!"

"Shut up." She rolls her eyes, still smiling as she leans toward me to light the candle.

Everyone in the pool swims to the edge while the others huddle around us. All mouths open in unison before they're all bellowing out the happy birthday tune as obnoxiously as they can, and all I can do is stand there awkwardly with a giant cupcake in my hands as Gio takes video of the whole thing.

"Happy birthday dear Trennnn—tonnnn! Happy birthday, you douche!"

I laugh at their hardly clever remix, glancing up at Mrs. Cooper's empty window once more before Marina places her hand on my forearm and tells me, "Make a wish."

I let my eyes fall from her face and to the lit candle before I blow it out in one big breath. As the group cheers, Diesel stands up with his clenched fists at his sides and a devious smile cinching his cheeks.

"Don't even think about it," I warn him, seeing a couple of the other guys catch on and adopt his same stance.

"But you're eighteen, man," says Gio, his brow arching up at me. "It's tradition."

"Fuck tradition." My voice wavers as I run my eyes over all five of them, waiting on one to get bold and throw the first punch.

They all exchange happy glances before their fists start flying at me, tenderizing my bare skin. I hold my arms square in front of me to block, but the hits to my back are brutal. I endure their pounding until eighteen hits have been made, but I swear it had to be about thirty. Once they back off, I have to talk myself out of jumping on one of them as I'm still filled with adrenaline over it all. Bastards.

Marina smiles up at me from one of the patio chairs as I grab my beer and down the rest in an attempt to keep cool. "You guys are idiots."

"Hey, eighteen for eighteen," says Diesel, catching his breath as he falls back onto a pool lounge. "I don't make the rules."

"Yeah, as a matter of fact," Gio lifts his finger, "Trent did."

I squint at him. "I didn't make that shit up."

"Yeah you did. Once upon a time, it was my twelfth birthday and you said it was something you saw on tv. Long story short, you guys gave me a black eye, and since then it's just something we do," he explains, matter of factly, taking the blunt from Diesel.

"You idiots don't have to do everything I say."

Marina giggles and my eyes veer onto her. I give her a smile, but only to be polite. I'm reminded once again why I'm not into her hanging around anymore. She used to be this chill tomboy who'd get dirty with us, wrestle, or whatever the hell we were all in the mood to do, and now all she does is stare at me like a weirdo and watch us talk.

Maybe if she had a drink she'd loosen up.

I waltz over to the cooler and pick out one of the lame girly drinks Diesel's girlfriend brought over. As I lift the lid, I glance over at Chloe as she wades through the water in her tiny thong bikini.

They're a weird couple. They break up every month, and when they are together, they're either hot or cold, meaning they're either fucking all day or ignoring each other. Tonight, they're cold as fuck. She hasn't said a word to him all night. She sat with the other girls for a few hours, drinking and making all of us rub our ears from her overdramatic shrieks while they gossiped. Then she started giving us the stink eye—probably because she was talking shit about Diesel or me—until I jumped in the pool and she got in with the herd like the sheep she is.

I only did that because I knew Mrs. Cooper would run out of the house all frazzled. She thinks she's going to come outside tomorrow morning to a water graveyard if one of us even looks at the pool while we're drinking. She's fucking adorable, really.

"Rina," I call, holding up the bottle of pink liquid so she can see it.

She shakes her head coyly, still smiling.

"Okay…well, do you want a soda or something? Water?"

"I'm okay, thanks Trent."

I bite my cheek as I set the bottle back in the cooler and head back over to have a seat on the edge of Diesel's pool lounge. He's lying there spaced out and I know Mrs. Cooper would be pissed if she knew he was this fucked up.

"Welp…" I look down at my wrist, my Apple Watch screen lights up, revealing the time. *10:47.* "Time to wrap this shit up, eh?"

"No, fuck no." He groans.

"Man, you're about to fall asleep anyway." I tap his cheek with the back of my hand. "You need to go drink some milk or something."

"Whatever, *Dad*," he mocks, but then pauses when he realizes what he's said.

I wrinkle my chin, shrugging smugly like, *what can I say?*

"Don't say another word or you're sleeping on the fucking pool float," he tells me, sitting himself up.

I did that once and woke up with a bad sunburn, but it's only the toe end of spring so I'm not that opposed to it.

Diesel rounds the guys up, and everyone else leaves the pool. All towel drying themselves and getting dressed, booking their ride shares, discussing the costs to split the pay and who's taking what leftover drinks home with them.

The music stops and I see Chloe unplug her phone from the speaker as I sit down next to Marina at the table.

Diesel comes toward us, leaning against the arm of my chair. "So, when are you guys going to stop playing around and date each other?"

Marina eyes me curiously as if the decision's all mine. It probably is. Marina's blatantly proved she's into me time and time again, but we never really get time alone. Diesel would love it if I finally found a girlfriend. Any girlfriend. Especially one that would hang out with us.

That way I couldn't really joke about hooking up with his mom without feeling like an asshole.

I open my mouth to either tell a lie or steer around the question, I really didn't think through what I was going to say. Most times it's a game of roulette, especially when I'm drinking, but luckily Gio slams his hand on my shoulder and cuts in.

"You know what I was just thinking about?"

I respond with a lifted hand because I know he's probably going to say something stupid, but I'll give him the go ahead to tell me anyway.

"You're eighteen and you still can't do shit. You still can't buy a pack of cigarettes, you can't buy weed, can't buy alcohol—"

"I can think of some things I'm gonna try to do." And it's not until the words leave me that I realize I was speaking more to myself than anyone else. Thinking about the fact that I simply have the adult stamp on me now. The fact that I'm not considered a minor anymore and won't be treated like one. That's the only thing I've wanted for the past five years.

"Whatever you're thinking, I can assure you it's illegal," says Gio. "The only thing you can do is get into eighteen and over clubs and gamble at some casinos, but even that's limited to all the shitty ones."

I shrug, glancing over at Marina who's got her eyes on me already, just like I figured she did.

Gambling, legal drinking, buying cigarettes and weed? I'm not concerned with any of that. Getting into clubs or bars? The only place I'm trying to get into is Mrs. Cooper's bedroom, and I'm definitely of age to do that now.

THREE

Trenton

AFTER SCHOOL I ALWAYS GO TO DIESEL'S HOUSE. HONESTLY, I always go to Diesel's house period. After work I go to Diesel's house, after going to my house, I go to Diesel's house—after being at Diesel's house, I go back to Diesel's house.

My mom used to complain about how often I was over and that I needed to be home with *family*, but she finally got over it when I turned seventeen and ever since then it's like I live here. Most of my stuff is here, only thing I do go home for is dinner, because that's the one thing that is sacred to my mom. Ever since my dad left, I figured the least I could do was sit through dinner a few nights a week with her and my sister.

Diesel returns to the room, dressed and reeking of cologne that wafts in from the doorway. "Well, ready to go?"

"Go where?" I keep my eyes on his flat screen, my finger steadily hounding the *R2* button on the controller in my hands to trigger rounds of shots in this first person shooter game.

I like Diesel's house for a lot of reasons. Besides him being my best friend, there's minimal rules here compared to at my house.

Sure, Roger's annoying, but he really doesn't ask for that much. Just to pick up after ourselves and occasionally to *turn the fucking music down*. Besides that, they've got everything here. A pool, hot tub, sixty inch flat screens in every room, and they pay for all the cool streaming services so Diesel has access to whatever movies or shows he wants.

When I'm here, I mostly play video games. Every birthday, Aubree buys him whatever new system or game is out. He's spoiled to the max, but the way they let me hangout here all the time, I sort of am too. Only difference is, I know how to say thank you.

"I'm going to Chloe's," he states, his hand resting on the door knob. "You're going home."

"Really, man? You're making me leave just because you got a booty call? We all know you won't be gone longer than thirty minutes. If that."

"Fuck you." He rolls his eyes. "Come on, or you're walking home."

And Diesel got a car for his sixteenth birthday. I'd be jealous, but he's been my chauffeur for the last year and a half so it's cool.

"I'll just stay here." I lift my eyes briefly at him. "Yeah, I'm on a killing streak. Don't fuck this up for me."

I hear him sigh. "Fine. I'll be back later."

"Cool. Later."

He shuts the door behind him and I keep playing until I hear his car take off. I could care less about a killing streak or anything else they have in this house. Let's be real. The main reason I like being here is because of Mrs. Cooper, and ever since Roger started leaving on business, it's been easier to get time alone with her.

I peek out the window to make sure he's gone before leaving the room.

The light is on in the den and I know she's in there. It's sad, she spends all this time at home by herself. Roger never takes her out unless it's to some lame ass business party or something, which she always gets dressed to the nines for. I bet he walks her around like she's some kind of trophy. I mean she is, but she should be more than that.

He doesn't deserve her.

I step into the wide entrance of the den, standing beside the wall watching her for a moment. She's sitting on the couch with her kindle reader in her lap, legs curled up and a blanket draped over her thighs, but hardly covering anything or providing her any warmth. Her arm's outreached for her glass of wine when her eyes lift onto me, and she pauses before taking a sip.

Her head tilts as she returns her glass to the coaster on the coffee table. "Where'd Diesel just run off to?"

"He went to his girlfriend's."

"And you stayed here?" Her brow arches and she lowers her kindle. "Why aren't you at your girlfriend's?"

"Don't have one." I take a seat on the farthest end of the couch. "I'm cool here."

"What about…" she snaps her fingers as if the word is on the tip of her tongue. "Marina? Diesel said you guys had a thing."

I shake my head. "Nope. Absolutely, definitely not."

"Why do you have to say it like that? She's cute." She giggles and I sink deeper into the sofa at the sound of her laugh.

"Yeah, she's cute. I'm just not into her like that."

"Well, why not? If she's cute, what else do you need, hm?"

"She's just, she's gotten kind of weird over the years."

"How?"

"Well she hardly talks, she stares at me all day, she doesn't eat, doesn't drink—and I don't just mean alcohol, I mean like, liquids. I haven't seen her consume anything in like four years. I don't know if she even breathes anymore."

A laugh rises from her throat and I can't help the involuntary smile that sets in on my face over the fact that I'm responsible for it.

"Well first of all, she obviously likes you. She's probably just nervous or a little self conscious because she wants you to like her back, that's why she doesn't eat in front of you."

"I don't care if she eats."

She giggles into her glass. "Girls think you do." She shrugs. "I know it sounds stupid, but give her a break. She's a teenage girl."

"A teenage girl I'm not into."

"Hm…" She cocks her head at me like she's challenging my

statement, but I don't twitch. I mean what I say.

Marina's been trying with me for at least four years, but it's easy to brush her off when I've got Mrs. Cooper to take up all my free headspace.

"No parties tonight either? It's Friday." She says that like it's supposed to mean something to me.

"I'm sure there are, but like I said before, I'm cool here."

"You really like being at our house." She chuckles.

Not so much that I like being at your house, as much as I like watching you strut around here like you aren't aware of how much of a goddess you are.

"I can't believe you're already eighteen," she adds, with a small huff. If I didn't pay such close attention to her, I probably wouldn't have noticed it.

"I know. Time flies…" *But not when you're counting down the days to adulthood in the hopes that your best friend's mom will be down for casual sex.*

"Geez, come to think of it…" She adjusts to sitting on her knees. "You and Diesel have been friends since you two were practically babies."

I scrunch my nose at the thought of her visualizing me as a baby. "I was like eight."

"You were a baby." She grins.

"Well, I'm not a baby anymore."

She brings her stylus up to her lips and bites the end of it, my cock hardens under her gaze like it's been called to attention and I lean forward to hide the evidence.

"True. You're both becoming men." Her brow ticks. "Crazy."

After a few short moments of silence as she picks at her pink manicured nails, I will my dick down and feel safe enough to sit back against the couch. I rest an arm up on the back of the couch as I examine her. She pulls her knees up and the blanket falls off of her, exposing the rest of her thick, bare thighs. I can smell her sweet fragrance from where I'm sitting and it's killing me that I can't be closer.

"You know, I was really young when I had Diesel…fifteen. Only a couple years younger than you boys. Definitely not ready for what was coming, but I didn't have a choice. My family was against... methods that could have gotten me out of being a teen mom, but looking back on it now I'm glad they were. Diesel's a brat, but I can't imagine life without him."

I nod, lost in the patterns her lips move in when she talks. So smooth and plush, I've thought about how they'd feel closing around my dick for years. The thoughts turned to wishes, and now the wishes are hopes. I want her so badly. I promised myself that once I'd turned eighteen I'd tell her. I'm just waiting for the right moment. Timing is important.

"And that's how I know it's time to put the wine away." She stands up and I watch her walk into the kitchen before following after her. Admiring her figure in the grey dress that fits her body like a rubber glove.

I lean against the wall. The glass is set on the counter and she's gazing at the bottle in her hands with her back to me.

"When I've started rambling about my life to my son's friend, I've probably had enough, huh?..." she huffs at the thought and I hate that she has to continue to remind me who I am. To remind herself who I am and the imaginary boundary we have between us. A reminder to me that I may never be able to separate myself from being Diesel's friend, and that's what fucks everything up.

I notice the three open bottles on the counter beside her and pick through them before realizing they're all empty. "Did you drink all of these tonight?"

"Maybe." She looks up at me and I can see the haze in her eyes.

"You didn't used to drink so much, Mrs. C...."

"What do you know about how much I used to drink?"

"I pay attention." I shrug just as the front door opens.

Fuck.

After a second of listening to movements in the living room, I realize it's not Diesel. It's Roger. There's something about the way he slams things down when he's here, he's really heavy handed and even shuts the door hard.

"Babe?" She calls, and I roll my eyes while she isn't looking at me.

Sounds like a set of keys drop on a hard surface almost like a slam, only validating how heavy his movements are. You never know if he's being noisy because he's in a bad mood or if he's just being his usual self. There's hardly any difference.

"Do you want me to heat up your dinner?" She continues, crossing through the kitchen in a few steps, but not leaving the room. She gets so tense when he's around. Even if she did gulp down three bottles of wine tonight, she seems sober now.

Roger finally makes his way into the kitchen and I step back to get out of his way. He passes me like usual. Without saying a fucking word to acknowledge me. He proceeds to the fridge, grabbing a beer and popping the cap off right there.

"Roger," she says to him more urgently.

He holds his palm to her and takes a hearty sip before leaving us alone again.

"Asshole," she mutters once the bedroom door shuts.

"I'll take his plate." I smirk at her playfully, tilting my head down at her until she giggles.

"He'll probably want it later, but I can make you one." She turns around to open the fridge. "I always wait on him to come home before I eat dinner, but I usually just end up drunk on an empty stomach instead."

I praise the back of her as she prepares my plate and places it in the microwave, searching for a panty line that I can't find, which only makes me even more curious.

We end up sitting in the backyard at the patio table under dimly lit string lights that wrap around the yard. Moths swirl the bulbs, crickets chirp around us, and the air is brisk but has just the right amount of warmth in it to be comfortable out.

She's changed out of the tight dress she was wearing and now I'm left to wonder what color panties she's slipped on underneath that robe.

I sat across from her while I ate my food. A blanket's around her shoulders, and she's mostly staring down at her phone, only making brief glances at me while I eat.

"Your cooking's always A1, Mrs. C."

"You're such a fucking kiss ass." She chuckles. "What do you want now, Trenton? I mean, why are you really here? Normal people don't hang out at their friend's house without them."

I lick my lips, chewing the last of my food. "It's just that…I don't know. It's stupid." I lift my shoulder and purse my lips which seems to only make her more interested.

"What?" She puts her phone down. "What is it, Trent? Stop being so weird."

"Just…if I tell you, I'll be crossing a line I can't come back from."

She stares at me blankly and I back at her. I can tell the pieces have come together in that beautiful mind of hers, but just to make sure, I think I'll mess with her.

"I'm worried about Diesel."

She frowns, pulling the blanket closer over her chest as a wind chill blows over us. I see a million things flash behind her eyes and I know for sure knew what I was getting at and is now totally confused.

"Why?"

"Just, him and Chloe…" I shrug. "They're…trying for a baby, Mrs. C."

Her jaw drops and she rocks her chair. "WHAT?"

I fall back into my seat and laugh. Two of her worst nightmares, Diesel getting anyone pregnant, and more specifically, Diesel getting Chloe pregnant. I don't blame her, I hate Chloe too. "I'm kidding, I'm kidding."

"You little shit." She narrows her eyes at me, but I see a small smile underneath her scowl.

"But really, there is something I did have on my mind." I bite the inside of my lip, seeing her eyes drift back up to me, waiting on me to speak again.

This feels like the right time. I've got her complete attention after Roger's proven to be the asshole he is once again. Diesel's gone and I've got her all alone. The only thing I'm afraid of is coming up empty handed after waiting all this time.

This woman has been the base model of all my fantasies for years. If she denies me, I don't know what I'll do. I've always been optimistic, thinking by the time I turned eighteen I'd look more like a man than I do. Thinking I'd feel more like a man than I do. Honestly, I just feel like a really tall sixteen year old, and that's the way she seems to look at me too.

In her mind, I'm just another stupid kid, but I'll be damned if I don't get that out of her head soon enough. I'd settle with being just another stupid man if it meant she'd finally give in to me.

"Trenton." She blinks, seeming completely serious.

"It's about the birthday gift you owe me."

She lets out a breath, scooping her hair to one side and my eyes run along her bare collar bone. "Well, what do you want? Cash? An Xbox?"

I huff out a small laugh. "I'm more of a Playstation kind of guy, but that's not where I was going with this."

"Then? What do you want?"

"Something pretty and wrapped in black satin."

Her face tenses up and I see her grab the sash on her robe.

"Have you ever…wondered why I never have a girlfriend, Mrs. C?"

She nods. "I thought maybe you were gay and still figuring things out."

"Pfft." I cross my arms and she chuckles. *Always with the jokes.*

"All the pretty boys usually are."

My brows raise and I wrinkle my chin to keep from smiling. "Oh, so I'm pretty?" I would have preferred a different adjective, but I'll take it.

"Shut the fuck up." She laughs, but doesn't deny a thing. "Well, continue."

"*Well*, it's because I'm a picky guy. I only want one person. One person who's always been off limits to me. Now that I'm eighteen, I figure she's less off limits than she was before, even if it's only a little bit."

"Trenton," she says, sternly.

"I want you, Aubree."

"Trenton!" She groans. "I'm like a second mom to you, stop it."

"Not at all." I snort. "Not even close. You're closer to being Diesel's hot older sister than his mom."

I see how bothered she is, how quickly her thighs slammed together and how tightly her arms crossed over her chest. How her eyes strictly roam everywhere but on me, how she suddenly keeps grazing her teeth over her lips because she's nervous and doesn't know how to respond.

"Come on, when's the last time you've even fucked? I can tell Roger hasn't touched you in months. The whole neighborhood can see that."

Her eyes widen and she stares out at the dark yard. "I'm not discussing that with you. And what do you mean the whole neigh—"

"All I'm saying is, I think you're hot as fuck and I'd chop both of my legs off with a butter knife if you'd take my virginity."

She drops her face in her palms and laughs deliriously, but I swear I can see her blushing. "I cannot believe you're saying this to me!" She lifts her face and her red-violet tinged skin gives me validation. "Are you serious?"

I lean forward, my elbows on the table that separates us. "Just think about it. No one has to know. We can keep it between us. One and done."

She looks up at me and I widen my eyes at her as if to show I'm serious. But I can already tell she's contemplating everything I've just said. She looks me over like she's able to see under my clothes and I know she's considering it, even if just a little.

"Take a few days to think about it." I rise from my seat. "Maybe it'll be easier to decide when the General's out of the house."

Her lips part in shock and I snicker, grabbing my empty plate and cup from the table.

"Thanks for dinner, Aubree."

FOUR

Aubree

"SO…HOW ARE YOU AND ROG DOING?" LYSSA'S ALMOST GRITTING her teeth at the question as she asks it, knowing how Roger and I have been surviving on a tiny thread for about a decade now.

And Trenton was right, it's no secret to anyone.

I live in a neighborhood full of married couples who like to pretend their husbands aren't stepping out behind their backs, but equally like to gossip about the Cooper's. They've made bets on how much longer they think we'll last, and which one of us will be the first to wave divorce in the air like a surrender flag.

Yep, we're a hot topic thanks to supporting acts, Diesel and Trenton, who are always responsible for any mischief that happens around here by default. Whether they are or not, all fingers point at my son as soon as something happens in the neighborhood. I'll admit, he does slip up from time to time—as teenagers do—but he's not the one behind every single instance of crime that happens on this perfect, quaint little block.

But I like Lyssa. She's one of the only other housewives I can tolerate around here. Everyone else is about as phony-fake as their *designer* bags.

"Oh, he's been a delight. Everything's picture perfect at our house." I let my eyes arch over her and smirk, the steam from my chai tea latte drifts up toward my face as I wait on it to cool down.

"You know, I actually think his new schedule has made him even more of a grouch than he was before he started flying across the country every few weeks. *So that's nice.*"

She laughs. "And how are you transitioning into your new found freedom? Lonely yet?"

"I thought I would be, but I mean, Diesel and his friends are always home and it's never a dull moment with them around. We just threw his friend a birthday party the other day—the first of the crew to turn eighteen." I twirl a finger as I go to take a sip and cringe as I scorch my lip.

"Oh, right. Marina did say she stopped by for an hour or so. Trenton, the Laguna's kid, right?"

I nod.

"I do not get what she sees in that boy."

I do. And if I were her age, I'd be just as obsessive over him as it sounds like she is. Ugh, I wish I didn't have thoughts like that, but it's the truth. I feel less guilty now that he's of age, though—as silly as it sounds. He's still old enough to literally be my son, but damn these last couple of years have been hard. Pretending I didn't notice him suddenly bloom into this six foot sweet talker who is well aware of the effect he has on women.

"I mean, he's a good looking kid," she adds, "but I wish she'd listen when I tell her there's got to be more to a man than his looks."

I frown, slightly insulted for Trenton because I don't think he's that much of an idiot. He'll probably go on to get a decent job and a nice apartment within the next few years—he's a go getter that way—but I also agree because Roger was my Trenton at one point in time.

The good looking boy who made me weak in the knees when his eyes were on me. I wanted him so badly, I couldn't think straight most times. I mean I clearly didn't, because if I had I would have ran for the hills instead of having signed up for a lifetime dosage of neglect.

She swirls her stirring stick around in her coffee mug. "And nothing against Diesel, but I wish she wouldn't hang around that crowd sometimes."

"No, I hear you. If I had a daughter, I wouldn't want her anywhere near Trenton." I blink, thinking about how that's because I'd want him for myself. "And Diesel is just…I just hope he gets his act together soon. I feel like I'm lecturing him about his grades every week."

Her lips slant in dismay. "He will. They all do eventually."

I sat with Lyssa, enjoying this warm afternoon at our local coffee shop, hoping her words would rid my mind of thoughts of Trenton. But she could only serve as a temporary relief. I know that once I leave I'll have to worry about who's waiting on me at home, and more than likely if anyone was, it'd be Trenton.

"We need to do this more often, Aubree." Lyssa looks at me with a sad smile. "We've let our lives get too busy."

What she really means: *I've let my life get too busy for my friends, but I don't want to make you feel bad for being the lonely housewife who's trekking a nasty divorce and chooses to forget about it by spending her nights chain reading steamy sex novels—so I'll just pretend you've been busy too.*

"I know." I smile at her before she pulls me into a hug.

And maybe I do need more friend time. Or just more busy time, period.

We go our separate ways, and I envy her briefly for having a so-called life. Lyssa's a PTA mom, soccer mom for twin boys who are also in the scouts, hosts a book club—which I'd join, but I'm not into fantasy—and has her own party planning business. It's really slow and mostly throw away money for her, but the point is, she has a lot going on.

Diesel used to be on the basketball team before his grades started to go south, so he ruined that for me. I hate dealing with other PTA mom's so that's a definite no. And I don't think I'm very crafty, so a makeshift business of any sort is probably out of my ballpark.

When I step inside my home, I hear the guys talking and shrink when Trenton's laugh echoes through the house. He's gone from making me roll my eyes hard when he hems me up in a room with him, to making my heart pound from the sound of his voice.

I never in a million years thought he'd be bold enough to ask me not only to have sex with him, but to take his virginity while I'm at it. And him? A virgin at eighteen? All the girls he has on his back all the time and he's a virgin?

Obviously I was completely flattered because I'm thirty-two with a husband who doesn't even look twice at me anymore. And here I was thinking Trenton was just naturally flirty, when all this time he's been that way for a reason.

The whole thing is still incredibly mind blowing and now I find myself flustered like a teenage girl every time he's around.

"Hey, beautiful." Roger comes toward me and kisses me on the corner of my mouth. I see Trenton's jaw tense as Roger places his hand on my lower back.

"Hey." I smile. "What are you guys up to?"

"Just catching up with the boys."

I almost breathe a sigh of relief at the fact that Roger seems to be in a great mood today. There was something I wanted to talk to him about later and that's already half of the battle.

"Hey, Mrs. C," Trenton says quietly, his eyes staring into me as if he's hoping to remind me of the insane conversation we had last night. *Like I could forget that.*

"Trenton." I nod at him, then walk off and toward the kitchen to get his eyes off of me. "Hey, what did you guys want for dinner?"

I set down my purse on the counter. The way expensive, unnecessary Gucci bag Roger gave me for our anniversary. I get a new one every holiday, including birthdays, and I really don't care for them, but with this being the thirty-sixth bag I own, I think it's too late to mention it.

Lasagna it is, I tell myself, resonating on the words *pizza* and *spaghetti* being shouted at me.

I hide in the kitchen as I cook, indulging in the newest edition to my kindle shelf just so I don't have to face the music. The three of them are in the living room playing video games—loudly, I might add

—but I know as soon as Trenton finds a way, he's going to get me alone and I'm not ready to deal with that.

I mean, what did he expect me to say last night? *Yes, I'll take my son's best friend's virginity?* The kid I've known since he was running around in tighty-whities?

The same kid who cried every time he spent the night because he was homesick after only being over for a couple of hours? I'd hold him on my lap while he called his mom, and she'd assure him he was okay and would talk him into staying because it was late and no one wanted to drive over to pick him up.

I watched this boy go through it all. Growth spurts, voice changes, the weird skateboarder haircut phase that went well with all the scrapes and bruises from doing stupid and dangerous dares that had me pulling out my hair. I was there when his parents were going through their messy divorce when he was fourteen. I tried to show him I cared about him and that he was always welcome at our house. I knew it was hard on him and that he'd rather be anywhere else but home with two people always shouting and throwing dishes at each other. His smile was non existent and all he wanted was to be with Diesel.

And now he expects me to just forget all that and make his teen fantasies come to life?

It's not even a question.

Roger rubs his palms together as I serve the plates around the table.

I'm so glad he's not being a grumpy jerk today. I already have enough on my mind and that just makes everything so much easier. Having both him and Trenton glaring at me from across the table would be too much. And that is exactly what Trenton's doing as I eat.

With him watching me, I've barely touched my food. I'm slowly turning into a teenage girl.

"Eat, baby," Roger says with a mouthful. He squeezes my thigh under the table. "What's the matter? Aren't you hungry?"

"Yeah, Mrs. C. You seem, self conscious or something." Trenton takes a bite and smirks as he chews his food.

I look at Roger. "Yeah, I'm just not as hungry as I thought."

Diesel's got both earphones in and I know if Roger were in one of his moods they'd have been snatched out of his head already.

Phones at the table are only a problem when Roger feels like they are. He's got his eyes down on his right this second, but I'd account his carelessness to his apparent good mood.

My phone vibrates in my pocket and I lean forward slightly to pull it out.

Trenton: *You look nice today.*

Keeping my head down, I look at him through my lashes before quickly shooting a reply.

Me: *Don't text me at the table.*

Trenton: *Why not? He doesn't notice. Neither of them do.*

Me: *Because I said not to.*

Trenton: *Well, we need to talk sometime, don't you think?*

Me: *No. And to answer your question from the other night, that's also a definite no.*

Feeling him looking at me, I lift my eyes only to lock with his. His brows ridge like he can't believe I'm saying no. If I wasn't who I am, I wouldn't believe it either.

Trenton: *Seriously?*

Me: *Seriously. So drop it.*

He gets up from the table, taking his plate with him into the kitchen and I hear the water run. I finally begin eating my food, glad I can eat in peace.

FIVE

Aubree

"I MISSED YOU," I BREATHE INTO OUR KISSES. ROGER'S HANDS ARE running up my body for the first time in weeks and I need this. All those stories I've been reading had me wound up tight, and with Roger gone, I had no outlet.

"I missed you, too." He pulls back, holding my face in his hands. "I think this new schedule is just what we needed."

"How's that?"

"I mean, we're usually around each other all day. I think the space has made us appreciate each other more. Like that saying—"

"Absence makes the heart grow fonder?"

"Yeah, that's the one." He nods, dipping back down to place his lips on mine again.

I grasp the hem of his shirt and slide it up his body. Roger's husky with broad shoulders and thick hair. Light skin that makes for a brilliant contrast to mine when my body's against his. I'm bronze in the summer and olive the rest of the year. Roger's either pale, slightly pink in the sun, or tomato red when he's mad.

He tosses his shirt beside our feet before peeling my dress off of me and lifting me into his arms. My back drops onto the bed as he continues kissing my neck, his hand playing with the band of my panties.

Roger stops to look at me, like *really* look at me. Maybe he's right.

Maybe that saying does hold true and all we needed was time apart for him to really appreciate me.

"I want to have another baby." The words shoot out of me so fast, I'm surprised myself. It's been on my mind for months and I wanted to bring it up tonight, but now that it's out in the universe, I can't help thinking that was the wrong time.

He shuts his eyes, pushing off the bed and then begins to pace in a small circle with an annoyed look on his face.

"Another baby?" He chuckles, stopping still to look at me as I'm lying almost naked on the bed. "Aubree, that ship has sailed, babe."

I sit up, the tips of my toes touching the ground as I cover my breasts with my arms. "What do you mean it's *sailed*? I can still have babies."

"I can't." He raises his brows at me to emphasize his point.

Roger had a vasectomy when Diesel was thirteen. We'd agreed that another kid wasn't in the cards because Diesel was such a piece of work at the time, he made us come to the conclusion that all kids were demons sent straight from hell and that we'd never do it again.

"You can reverse it, Roger."

"I don't want to reverse it. I like things the way they are. Diesel's about to be eighteen, and once he's out of the house we can finally travel and go on trips like we always planned to do."

"We can still do that after the baby is born—"

He shakes his head as he walks to the bathroom and I follow him. He turns on the faucet and grabs his tooth brush from the holder.

"I mean, didn't you ever want to have another? A daughter, maybe?"

He pulls the sudsy brush from his mouth and spits into the sink. "Not really. But even if I did, who's to say it's even a girl this time."

"That's what's fun about it." I grab a hold of his arm as he begins brushing again. "You don't know what you're going to get. It's a gamble."

He stares at me, mouth open while he brushes his back teeth, leaning his hip against the sink.

"Remember when we used to talk about having another baby? You wanted one at one point, why not now when we can actually focus all of our attention on this new person?"

He rinses his mouth out before turning around to dab his chin on a towel. "Aubree, I didn't get a vasectomy just for the hell of it."

"And you won't be reversing it just for the hell of it either." I shift my weight to my right leg, leaning against the door frame. "I think this is what we need."

"I think that's what *you* need. I don't need another baby. I'm fine with the seventeen year old one we have." He brushes past me and back into our bedroom. "Christ..."

There goes his good mood, and my outlet.

I climb into bed beside him as he begins flipping through channels on the television, and I lay my head on his chest but he doesn't touch me.

"Another fucking baby." He scoffs. "We'll be in our fifties when the kid's Diesel's age. We'll probably be fucking grandparents by then."

"Forget it. Forget I asked." I shimmy myself under the covers and roll the opposite way.

"Great. Now you're going to be mad at me for how long over this? A month? A year?"

"I'm not mad. I'm just, disappointed."

"Well, *you* disappointed yourself. I didn't fucking disappoint you."

"Okay." I roll my eyes.

The wall in front of my face stops flashing and I know he's finally settled on a channel. Either reruns of Seinfeld or Frazier. I can't tell the difference with my back to it all.

My phone vibrates on my nightstand and I reach for it with no hesitation.

Trenton: *So it's for sure a no then?*

This kid is something else.

Me: *It's for sure a no.*

Trenton: *I can't change your mind?*

Me: *No.*

Trenton: *Alright. Goodnight.*

Me: *Night.*

"What does he want?" Roger grumbles.

I gulp, locking the screen before setting it back in its spot and plugging in the charger. "Oh uh, he was asking about another party."

He huffs out something similar to a laugh and I feel him shift on the bed. "And you want to have another kid who's just gonna try to throw more parties and trash the backyard with their stupid fucking friends?"

"I'm done discussing it, Roger. If that's how you feel then, fine."

"I mean, there's your second kid right there." He gets out of the bed and I roll over to look at him. "Trenton's here all the damn time. We feed him, we practically take care of him. I spend my hard earned money on him every damn day."

He stares at me and I don't respond. What do I say to that? Trenton likes being around us. He likes our family. He's practically apart of it. It's not news that he spends at least six out of seven days a week under our roof.

I see Roger's face redden under the television light right before he bolts out the door.

"Roger!" I jump up out of the bed just as fast and throw on my robe, tying it tightly around my waist. This is my fault. He was in a good mood and now I've aggravated him instead of just keeping my mouth shut and having a nice night. "Roger!" I fly down the steps until I see Roger's burly stature barging into Diesel's bedroom.

"Trenton, time to go," he barks, wiggling his two fingers in a come here motion.

I peek in and see the boys sitting up from where they were laying. Diesel's in his bed and Trenton's in the futon against the opposite wall.

Trenton's eyes dart to mine and I shake my head to let him know it's not what he's thinking—and thank God for that. Had he been more specific in those messages, this could have gone a whole different direction.

"Why? What'd I do?"

Roger grabs him by his shoulders and lifts him to a stand. "You're here way too fucking much. Go home for once. Don't you have your own family to mooch off of?"

"Dad!"

"Roger, stop it!" I grab him by his strong arm in an attempt to coax him off of him, but he swats me away and continues dragging Trenton out of he futon.

"Dad, stop!"

Trenton finally yanks himself out of his grip with a solid scowl on his face. "I'll fucking go! Whatever!" He leaves me with one last glare that makes my chest ache before he grabs his phone and backpack and heads down the hall.

Diesel gets out of bed and walks past us. I hear his keys jingle before the door slams and I hang my head in my hands.

Roger blows out a heavy breath, his face blotchy with anger. "I'm sick of people just doing whatever the fuck they want around here."

The next morning I got up at six A.M. to go for a quick run like I usually do every Sunday. I pulled my long waves—which were yesterday's curls—into a high, messy bun and put on a purple, camouflage sports bra and matching leggings.

I run three miles in a complete circle around the neighborhood. Everything from the past few days floods my mind as the cool wind blows against me and stings my skin. Roger's anger is getting out of control. He'd never been one to put his hands on anyone, but last night I saw an entirely new side to him. I think we all did.

Trenton looked at me like I betrayed him, and thinking back on it now, I feel like I did. I'm supposed to step in when Roger gets out of line and I froze. I couldn't do much to stop him. I'm to blame for the reason his mood did a one-eighty, anyway.

I slow to a stop as I see Martha stepping out of her blue Prius in front of my home. Looking both ways, I jog across the street, gaining her attention.

I pause my music and pull my earphones out of my head to present her a smile despite the way she's looking me up and down like I'm out here in lingerie.

"Hey, Martha—"

"Listen, Aubree. I didn't come here to be friendly with you or catch up." She shakes her head. "Do. Not. Give. My. Son. Alcohol. Do you hear me?"

I raise my eyebrows, stunned by the way she's coming at me. "I didn't give Trenton alcohol." My voice comes out hard and dull as I cross my arms over my chest.

"He came home late last night, so drunk, he passed out as soon as he stepped in the house." She places a hand on her hip and I notice the thick, white tipped acrylics she's wearing. "He was at your house last night, wasn't he?"

"Right, but I wasn't aware of them drinking, Martha. Diesel drove him home, I wouldn't have let him get into his car if I thought they were drinking. I don't condone that."

"From what I hear, there's a whole lot you do *condone*." She cocks her head at me. "Your son treats you more like a friend than a mother. I wouldn't be surprised if you were up drinking with them last night."

"That's definitely not happening." I scoff. "But fine. I won't let them drink at my house just like I already wasn't." A bold lie, but she doesn't need to know how much I let them get away with.

"Better yet, keep my son out of your house. Period."

"He's an adult. He can make his own decisions."

"He's hardly an adult."

"Well, he's finally old enough to get away from you for good."

She huffs as I begin walking up my driveway. Before I reach the doorstep, her door slams and she speeds off.

SIX

trenton

"COME ON, MAN. MY DAD'S COOL NOW. HE WAS JUST IN ONE OF his moods. You know how he gets," Diesel tells me.

"Fuck that. I don't wanna be around that type of moody shit. He's like a light switch." I clench my lips around the end of a fresh cigarette. My hand swirls around in my pocket for my lighter.

I don't smoke much anymore, but after the past couple of days, I feel like picking the habit back up. Especially after my mom spent all morning bitching over the fact that I blacked out in the living room.

Last night after Roger kicked me out, I had Diesel drop me off at Gio's and we drank until I was completely numb and couldn't see straight. I took a Lyft home and that was the aftermath; me lying face down on the tile in front of the front door while Mom tried everything she could to get me up.

"Yeah, I know…he'll be flying out to New York in a couple of days, though. You know my mom's cool with you being over."

I watch as a perfect ring of smoke leaves my lips. I don't even want to think about Aubree. What the hell was that, last night?

Because of the fact that Roger didn't kick my ass, I'm assuming he doesn't know I asked her for sex, but what the fuck made him snap at me unless she said something?

"Hello?" Diesel's got his phone pressed to his ear, stretching his legs out in front of him. We walked to the park a block down and have been sitting on a wooden bench for about thirty minutes. My mom wouldn't be okay with me smoking anywhere near the house. She doesn't like Diesel either, so I didn't even think about bringing him inside.

Diesel smiles and his eyes swerve onto me. "Yeah, we're down for that."

I shake my head, cutting my fingers back and forth across my neck which is meant to indicate I am not cool with whatever Marina has planned. I know it's her. He always looks at me like that when she's concerned.

"Alright, we'll meet you there tonight..." He chuckles. "Alright, bye, Rina."

"No. Fuck no." I suck the end of the cigarette again and breathe out the words, "I'm not in the mood."

"Look, I know you're mad over my dad and stuff, and I feel really bad about it—but listen, Marina's invited us to go with her to this party and I think tonight's the night."

"For what? For her to finally eat something?"

"For *you* to finally eat something." He grins and I sock him hard in the arm. "No, but seriously. I think tonight's the night you make your move on her."

I sigh, dropping the cigarette butt and dragging it under my shoe. "Nah."

"You need to fucking get laid already. You're too uptight."

Yeah, I do. "Not by Marina."

"Then fucking who? I'll call one of Chloe's friends for you. Whoever you want, they're all lined up for you anyway."

I wave my hand at him. They're all a bunch of ditzy, melodramatic nightmares. "Nah. I'm probably just gonna go home."

He stares at me and I clasp my hands together, squinting up at the sun as it beats down on me. "Fuck no. Stop being like this. What the fuck's wrong with you?"

"I don't know. I'm a little hungover I guess."

"More reason to go get fucked up." He wrinkles his chin.

"Fine. I'll go. Whatever."

He laughs, smacking me on the shoulder and we leave the park. I head back home to get changed. Diesel agreed to come back and pick me up when he's done getting ready at his house.

I'd been avoiding my mom all afternoon after this morning, but now I don't really have a choice. She's home from work and I know she's just waiting on me to walk through the door.

When I step inside, Joselyn's sitting cross legged on the couch with her phone in her hands and her earphones in until she tugs them out and sits up. "Mom's so pissed at you."

I roll my eyes, shutting the door. "So what? When isn't she?"

She brushes her bangs out of her eyes, exposing both of her light green irises, and shrugs like she knows it's true.

I never did anything right according to my mother. Every chore was never complete or thorough enough for her. My grades— although I kept them at a solid B average—weren't satisfactory enough. My friends were shit. The few girlfriends I did have were shit. Anything I ever had to say was shit.

Diesel's house was an escape, and thanks to his dad I now have no where to go to get away from my mother's suffocating personality.

As soon as I turn my doorknob, I hear movement in my mother's bedroom which is right beside mine.

"Fuck…" I mutter, shoving the door hard to get inside. My bedroom door is even shit. It gets stuck all the time. Only door in the whole house that stays jammed.

"Trenton?"

I let the door swing, leaving a small crack because I anticipate her making her reveal any second. I pull my shirt off over my head as I walk to my closet to flip through whatever's hanging there. All my good clothes are at Diesel's so I don't know what I'm going to put on.

"Where are you going now?" She stands in my doorway, but I don't look at her. I'd rather not stare disappointment in the face.

"A party."

"Where?"

"I don't know. Down the street, probably." I pull out a striped tank top and put it on.

"Trenton, I don't want you over Diesel's anymore."

I turn to her. "Fine. Whatever."

"Whatever?" She frowns. "What went on over there last night?"

"Nothing, Mom." With my eyes shut, I pinch the bridge of my nose in frustration. "Whatever you want me to do, fine. But I'm going out tonight."

When I open my eyes she's got her arms crossed, leaned against the doorframe. She's looking at me like she's got a bad taste in her mouth, but that's how it's always been with me. Joselyn is the favorite. She's the good girl who doesn't sneak out, smoke, drink, or apparently have shitty friends. Probably because I do all of that abundantly enough for the both of us.

I start unbuttoning my shorts and trade them for a pair of jeans.

"I spoke with Diesel's mother this morning."

Gulping down the mention of Aubree, I pause. "Why?"

"I went over there to warn her."

"Warn her about what, Mom!? Nothing happened!" I shout, arms raised.

"She's a pathetic excuse for a mother, allowing teenagers to drink and party in her backyard. She dresses like she's a teenager herself."

"Stop talking about her like that." I slip my feet into my nikes, knowing in a moment I'll be running out of here.

"Why? It's the truth. She's obviously having a mid-life crisis or something."

"She's not that much older than me, Mom. And she's definitely not as old as you."

I see my mother gasp and her arms tighten. It's true, and I'm tired of everyone making it seem like just because she has a son only a year younger than me, that she's in a totally different age group.

Diesel sends me his *I'm here* text and I couldn't be more glad to get out of this house.

"I'll see you later, Mom."

She says nothing as I walk past her, and I wave at my sister as I rush out the door.

I slow to a stop as I get closer to the car, his music bumping out the speakers and rattling my chest the closer I get. Chloe's blonde hair is reflecting the sun as it shines through the open crack in the window.

"Get in the back," I tell her.

She looks up at me and laughs. "*You* get in the back. I know you like to think you're Diesel's girlfriend, but that's all me."

I look at Diesel and he purses his lips and shrugs like he can't argue it. Like he won't suddenly decide he wants nothing to do with her in a couple weeks from now.

"Get in the back, man."

I groan as I open the back door and slide into the back seat. I try to ignore them as they argue about something stupid Diesel said months ago that Chloe found necessary to bring up right now. It's that on top of the loud music that's giving me a throbbing headache.

My thumb's scrolling down my phone screen. Social media feed, but I'm barely even processing what I'm seeing. Girls posing in their bathroom mirrors. Duck faces. Peace signs. More bathroom mirror shots. Drunken group photos. And different angles of Gio's motor in the car that he still hasn't fixed up enough to the point that it's actually drivable. *Fascinating.*

After about fifteen torturous minutes, we finally arrive at a culdesac in a neighborhood I'm not familiar with. Seems like a big party so it may not be too much of a bust. I'm up for anything at this point, especially if it's lit on fire or burns my throat going down.

Chloe and Diesel hold hands as we walk up to the house. I notice Marina coming toward us when I finally look up from my phone and I have to do a double take.

The front of her hair is braided and clipped on the side, curled loosely on the ends, and she's wearing pink lipstick to match her form fitting dress that stops at her mid thigh. It's strapless and reminds me of something Aubree would wear. Only thing different is that Aubree would swap the sandals for heels.

Diesel and Chloe tell her hello and give her hugs before she returns her focus back onto me, smiling up at me with her twinkling eyes.

"Hey, Trent."

"Marina, you look pretty."

She drops her gaze as her smile widens. "Thanks. So do you—I mean, you look good."

"Thanks." I chuckle, noticing Diesel and Chloe have began again toward the side gate of the house and we walk beside each other, following closely behind.

There's a few seconds of silence as Diesel unlatches the gate hook.

I lean down toward her and hush my voice. "Whose house is this?"

"My friend, Jessica. Her parents are out of town for the weekend. Just something to kick off spring break, I guess."

"Cool." I hold the gate open for her and she smiles at me as she walks inside.

The yard's like a petri dish of girls I've either hooked up with or was talking to before I became disinterested like the snap of a finger.

"Trent," says the glossy lipped ring leader of a group of them, dressed in barely-there tops and tight jeans, eying me hard as they breeze by. I take that as a clear invitation for me to come find them later. Too bad I'm just not interested. Other than scoring free drinks, I don't want to be here.

As I continue through, a few others sending me their hopeful smiles, giggling into their cups while I pass them because they're too shy to shoot their shot, I realize no one could hold my interest like Aubree could. She's the only one I never got bored of. She's the only one who never gave me the opportunity to.

Diesel immediately attacks the drinks while Chloe shrieks over the fact she's run into some girls from school—like she didn't just see them in class on Friday.

I sat with Marina for a while, sipping a strong drink while we exchanged a few words.

The music's good, the drinks are strong. Diesel's clearly having the time of his life—as he does anytime he's not home.

There's a lot of people here and it looks like it'd be a good time if I was in the mood for it, but I have a lot on my mind.

I feel like I've invested a lot of time into hoping something would happen that didn't. Like I've wasted years of my life betting on Aubree to give me this one thing when I turned eighteen only for it not to pan out.

But that's my own fault.

I don't know who I was kidding, thinking she'd ever stoop as low as to not only cheat on her husband, but fuck her son's barely legal best friend. It was a dumb dream that I'd convinced myself was possible until it proved not to be.

But Marina's real. She's possible. She's standing in front of me. She's pretty and nice and she likes me, no doubt about that.

She catches me staring at her and bites her lip to suppress the smile she's been wearing since I got here.

I place my hands on her arms and swoop down to her ear. "Stop being so shy. I like you."

When I pull back her smile's finally dimmed down and she stares at my lips. I can see the want in her eyes and how badly she's holding back from hopping up on her toes and fulfilling it, so I do it for her.

I move my hands to her small waist and kiss her.

I'm even more impulsive when I drink than I am when I'm sober.

The second our lips touched I wondered why I made that move.

I don't know why I kissed her. I don't know why I even said what I said. I mean, I do like Marina. She's not what I want, but I like her.

My hands pull her closer as the kiss deepens and all I can taste is her strawberry flavored lip gloss and I'm sure it's all over my chin, but whatever. I'm pissed off, I'm horny and I can tell she is too.

"Oooohhhh!" Chloe cheers, killing the moment. We break apart as Diesel comes at me with two red cups and his mouth opened wide like he wasn't pushing us toward each other for the past four years.

He tosses his head back. "Fucking finally!"

Marina chuckles, her hand sliding into mine. The realization sets in as our hands link together. That kiss was like *crossing a line that I can't really come back from.* Now that we've crossed it, things will be different. She might think we're together now, she might think it's worth defining what we are now that we've taken that step. She'll have expectations that I already know I'm not willing to meet.

But whatever. What else do I have going for me?

I roll my tongue over my lips, licking the remnants of gloss off.

Diesel hands me a cup and normally I'd ask him what was in it, but instead I clink it against his and we down both of them together.

He nods at me before Chloe clings to him, swaying to the music as his arms go around her waist.

Marina pulls me down to her side and asks in a tone I'm unfamiliar with, "Let's go somewhere?"

I nod and let her pull me wherever she wants. That drink was strong and it's hitting me just that quick. Whatever it takes to get Aubree out of my head.

Marina's leading me up the stairs and as I follow behind her, pulled by the hand, I trace the small frame of her body. She's petite with a slim waist and toned legs from years of softball. It's not that I'm not attracted to her, because I am. It's just that after crushing on Aubree for so long, it's hard to stop comparing everyone else to her. My standards are sky high.

I know it was all in my head because I've never touched her more than a hug, I've never seen her naked. She could practically be imaginary. My idea of the perfect woman that I've crafted in my mind.

Marina opens the door to a room that's only lit by the moonlight coming in through the open window.

She doesn't shy away this time. Her hands are on me, sliding my shirt up my stomach as I walk her backwards to the bed, my tongue spiraling in her mouth on the way.

I lay her back, hovering over her. She finally gets my shirt up over my shoulders and as soon as it's off, I move my hand to her thigh, quickly slipping my fingers underneath her dress and rising up to the hem of her panties.

"Trent, Trent—Wait."

I stop, pulling back to look at her. Her eyes are wide and her lips are still parted from my tongue slipping past them. "What's wrong?"

"I…I never did this, before."

I lick my lips and push myself up to sit beside her body.

"I didn't say I didn't want to do it." She sits up. "I just never have."

My phone vibrates in my pocket and I stand up to slip it out as I come to terms with what almost happened just now.

Aubree: I just wanted to apologize for what happened last night. I feel really bad about how that went and I just wanted to check and make sure you were okay.

A little late, but better late than never, I guess.

Me: I'm fine.

Aubree: You know you're still welcome at our house. Nothing's changed.

Nothing's changed. I scratch my head, tucking the phone back into my back pocket.

Marina's sitting quietly behind me and Aubree's etched herself back in my head. The idea of her thinking of me makes that single sliver of hope return.

I'm an idiot, yes.

"You know…I don't really feel right about this." I turn back around to face Marina who's sitting with her arms crossed and clearly seeming more uncomfortable than usual.

"What do you mean? Because I'm a virgin?"

I let go of a breath as I sit by her side. "Yeah...I can't be your first, Marina."

She grabs my hand and holds it in her lap. "I want you to be. I've always hoped you would be."

I weakly smile at her as her eyes dance over my face. I can't. I can't do it. If I do I'll feel like I'm just using her for sex because after tonight, I don't know how I'm going to feel about her. And she's still my friend, even if things have been weird between us for a long time.

"Trenton..."

"I just don't want things to move too fast, you know?"

She drops her eyes from me, but then nods.

I lean toward her and give her another soft kiss, noting the fact that I get absolutely nothing from the feeling of her lips on mine. It's dull. The only thing I do feel is how she practically vibrates every time I touch her.

"I should go," I whisper onto her mouth. "I have curfew."

She knows all about my mom and nods like she understands. "I'll walk you out."

Aubree

"Fuck Roger," says Solana. "He's dead weight, just like Lawson was for me. He always thought he could control me. He always tried to find little things I did and hold them over me for leverage. But little did he know, I've never been a shameful girl. I didn't give a fuck about getting caught talking to guys on Plenty of Fish. Maybe had he been a better husband, I wouldn't have been on there in the first place."

I rub my lips together, spreading out the pink lipstick I applied three hours ago to salvage what little is left of it. I told Roger I'd be going to the mall and then to dinner afterwards. And we did stop by the mall so that I'd have a purchase to prove I'd gone, but Solana really just wanted to do a club run, so now we're here, indulging in drinks and conversation. Mostly, her talking about her husband like they aren't still married. Like they don't split every couple of months just so that both of them can have an excuse to see other people.

And she's pissed because we can only stay for an hour or else Roger's going to start blowing up my phone.

"I feel so free without him. I don't know why I ever got married in the first place..." Her eyes land on me. "And I really think you can relate to everything I'm saying, but you're so deep in the clutches of denial, you can't get out."

"No, I know exactly why I got married." *Literally for everyone else, but myself.*

"To be in a sexless marriage and sit around at home all day?"

I inch forward to bring my glass to my lips. This strawberry daiquiri is a nice change to all the red wine I've had running through my system lately.

Trenton didn't reply to my text and although the little *I'm fine* he sent should have put me at ease, I still feel like he's upset with me. Solana's irritating words are the only thing keeping me from sending another message.

"You could do so much damage, Aubree. You'd easily find another guy, a better guy. You are wasting your beauty on a man who doesn't even touch you."

I draw in a breath, regretting keeping her up to date on my sex life. When she asked me out tonight, I didn't think it'd be a lecture on how my marriage is dead and how my life is withering away because of it. "I had a talk with Trenton last weekend."

Her eyes widen and look like blue marbles. "And?"

"He asked me if we...if I...would have sex with him."

She stares at me intensely, frozen and mouth agape until she grabs my wrist and laughs. "I knew he wanted you! Oh my God, did you? Please tell me you did."

"No," I speak in a hiss. "Of course I didn't."

"Why the hell not?" She drops her head back like she's fed up.

"So many reasons that you are already well aware of. I'm Diesel's mom for fucks sake—and I'm too old for him."

"Okay." She rocks in her seat like she's about to hit me with the facts of life. "First of all, you're a fucking vampire! You. Don't. Age. Forever 21 was made because of bitches like you!"

I laugh, mostly at her mannerisms.

"Second—finally! A young guy who isn't stupid! The boy has eyes and he sees how hot you are—just because you've got the *mom* tag on you, doesn't mean you're an old hag."

"Fine. I'm hot, whatever. But I'm still too old."

"You act way older than you actually are." She goes to raise her glass to her lips, but pauses. "Really, what's a fifteen year difference anyway?"

"A huge difference! Maturity, development, wisdom—"

"Oh please. All those vary no matter what age a person is. I know forty year old men who still do the things Diesel does—including living at home with mommy—and a twenty six year old who has his shit together and is so book smart it's not even funny."

I stare at her, my back pressed to the booth seat as the colored lights flash over her face. "I can't cheat on Roger. I won't."

"Aubree! Are you serious?!" She scolds me with her eyes. Solana knows it all, she knows everything about Roger, about our relationship, about our marriage. She was there for me the day Diesel was conceived and the day he was born. Her perspective means something to me, but I still can't wrap my head around what she's saying with a clear conscience.

"Yes. I want things to work out, Solana. Our marriage has never been easy, but I don't want all of this time I spent with him to be for nothing."

She lifts her almost empty glass. "It already has been."

"Diesel needs a stable family."

Her eyebrows furrow and her lips twist. "You two have never been stable."

I suck up a breath. Solana's brutally honest, but she's right. The only reason I take her opinion for truth is because she speaks the same words the small voice in the back of my head does. She validates me when I need it. And lately, I've needed validation for these thoughts I've been having regarding Trenton.

"And Diesel's a man, damn near. He'll get over it if you guys split."

"Split? And do what? Start fucking his best friend? Date him? This is insane."

"But you're thinking about it," she sings with a grin on her face. "Take a walk on the wild side, Aubree. You'll love it. I bet Trenton's a beast in bed, I don't even care that he's only eighteen. He looks like he knows his way around."

"He's a virgin."

Her straw falls from her lips and she looks at me. "A what? You mean a *Virginian* right? Like he's from, Virginia. I know that's what you meant to say."

I laugh. "He's a *virgin*, Sol. He told me. More specifically, he said he'd cut off his legs if I'd take his virginity."

"A guy like that? A virgin?" She blinks. "That changes everything."

"I know. I can't, right?"

"No, now you have to! It all makes sense. I bet he's been saving it for you, I mean why else would he still be a virgin if he wasn't dead set on giving it to you?"

"No." I shake my head.

"Yes." Her eyes glow. "I bet he's just been waiting on the day to finally pursue you as a man. He clearly wants you to be his first, you have to."

"I definitely can't."

"Think about it. You get to be worshipped by this hot guy who's probably been wanting to fuck you since his balls dropped."

"And? What's the incentive?"

"That's the incentive. I mean, how hot is that? Having sex with a virgin—it's like witnessing magic." She stares at me, not blinking like she's holding her breath for my response until she realizes I'm not going to give her one.

That sounds disastrous, but still appealing underneath it all. Trenton's great looking. If I were his age again, he'd be out of my league—just like Roger was.

"I mean, he'll come quick, that's for sure," she adds, "but more than likely he'll make up for it by *going alllllll night.*"

I let out a steady exhale and that's all I can give her in response to that. This conversation is insane. The fact that it's even a discussion is insane.

"Ugh." She pouts. "Sometimes I wonder if you'd be any less uptight if you were getting any."

SEVEN

Trenton

DIESEL TEXTED ME THIS MORNING LETTING ME KNOW ROGER WAS leaving this afternoon instead of the following day, so I headed over. Chloe was already hanging out there, so I figured there wouldn't be a sequel to the other night. He's not comfortable enough around her to act out, so I'll be stuck side eyeing the phony, average dad role he plays when company is around.

We sat outside at the patio set, Diesel snuck puffs of a blunt while we watched his parents walk through the house as Roger got ready to go.

At this point, I think Diesel just gets a rise out of being defiant. He could wait the thirty or so minutes for his dad to leave so that we could all smoke together, but instead he'd rather risk one of them walking out here and detecting the obvious scent in the air.

Aubree's wearing leggings and a shirt that ties in the front and shows a sliver of her bare midriff. Her hair is in long waves like she's just come from the beach. Her tan suggests that she probably did. Radiant and glowing like a bronzed angel.

I'm tired of her being so perfect all the time. She's making me hate her for it.

"So, when are you going to give us the details?" asks Chloe, sitting diagonally from me with her legs propped up on Diesel's lap as he traces circles into her skin. "You haven't said a word about last night and we all know you didn't take her up to Jessica's room just to talk."

"Uh…well." I shrug. "We made out a little bit, that was it."

"What? All those years of build up just for a weak, little make out session?"

"She's a virgin."

"So?" Diesel arches his brow. "If she wanted it, it's cool."

"Nah. I didn't want her to get like, attached to me or something."

Diesel clicks his teeth, fanning away a big heap of smoke as if that'll really make the evidence disappear.

"No, I think he's right." Chloe sets her feet on the ground and pushes her chair in closer to the table. "Diesel was my first and I'm pretty sure that's why I can't stop coming back to him."

"That's bullshit." Diesel's lids are suddenly heavier. "I don't even remember my first. Who cares."

"It's different with girls." She says it like it's fact, and maybe it is. Something's keeping Aubree with Roger despite how badly he treats her. Maybe he was her first.

But dammit, I'll be her last. I swear.

I stare through the glass and see them in an embrace. Their lips are moving and she's smiling like he's said something sweet. Bullshit.

"Put it out, put it out," Chloe says in a sharp whisper as Diesel frantically pinches the lit tip of the blunt and seals up what's left in a plastic sandwich bag.

I shake my head, knowing the evidence is in the air. Roger's not stupid, he'll know as soon as he steps outside, and I swear if things escalate and he puts his hands on me again, I'm fighting him this time.

Roger knocks on the glass, gives us all a tight smile, and waves. We all awkwardly wave back before watching him leave through the window.

"That was a weird goodbye," says Chloe.

"Nah, he'll be back tomorrow. He has a quick meeting. Nothing to hug about."

He's probably just avoiding me because he's a pussy and doesn't want to apologize for being a dick to me the other night.

Looking in, I see Aubree combing her hair out of her face as she disappears into the kitchen.

"So, going back to the previous discussion, Trent," says Chloe, "you didn't have sex with Marina just because she's a virgin?"

"Well, yeah."

"Are you sick or something? When has that ever been a problem for you?"

"I mean, both of our first times can't be with each other."

Their eyes bulge out of their heads and my jaw twists. I never talk about my sex life with Diesel because I pretend I'm too picky to have one. He's bought it for as long as I've told it, but now I think I've said too much.

"What do you mean, both of you?" says Diesel, staring hard at me. "You're a virgin?"

"No way you're a virgin." Chloe scoffs. "I have so many friends who've told me explicitly how they hooked up with you."

"Yeah, and I'm sure in those stories they told you I touched them but never mentioned touching me."

"But..." Diesel squints. "What the fuck, why not?"

"I didn't fucking want them to. That's all."

They exchange looks and I snatch the blunt from Diesel's fingertips. I take three hits as they stare at me like they don't know who I am anymore. I don't even know who I am anymore.

I should've just done it. Marina wanted me to and it's probably about time I give up on the whole celibacy thing since Aubree's made it clear that nothing will ever happen between us. But truthfully, I just don't want anyone if they aren't her.

"Trenton Laguna is an eighteen year old virgin..." Chloe says under her breath. "Unbelievable."

I hand the blunt back to Diesel before getting up from my seat and heading inside. They were annoying me and I needed a moment alone to relax. Soon enough, Chloe and Diesel would probably be kicking me out of his bedroom anyway, so I figure I'll hang out in the den until Chloe finally goes home for the night.

Aubree's reading spot is my favorite. She's the only one that sits in the very corner of the sectional and it smells like her shampoo where she lays her head.

I lie there, scrolling through social media feed while sending vague replies back to Marina. She's been texting me since last night, asking me how my day was going, who I was with, what we were up to, my plans for later tonight. I can tell what she's getting at, but I'm not planning on asking her out any time soon.

Aubree walks by the wide double doors of the den, and I sit up when I notice her slow down as she spots me.

She crosses her arms in a way that keeps her robe from accidentally opening. It's killing me that I don't know what's underneath it and that she makes such an effort to keep it unknown.

"Hi." She speaks softly, coming toward me.

"Hi." I swing my feet off the couch and onto the floor before hunching over to run my fingers through my hair. Her white polished toes come into view before she sits beside me.

"Trenton, I'm sorry. Roger's been hard to deal with lately…"

"He's been hard to deal with for as long as I can remember."

The room goes silent until Chloe's giggles fill the air and both her and Diesel bypass the doorway without even noticing us.

"I don't want you to think you aren't welcome here…that's far from true." She looks at me sadly. "You know you're like a son to me —and Roger, even if he doesn't act like it sometimes."

"I hate when you say that."

"What?"

"That I'm like a son to you when you don't look at me any way close to how you look at Diesel. You don't talk to me like you talk to Diesel."

"Trenton…"

"Can you just tell me why your answer is no? I think I'm worth an explanation at least."

"Why do you think? I mean, the main reason being that I'm married."

"But do you feel like you're married? Does Roger make you that happy?"

"He's my husband, Trenton. I took a vow, made a commitment. That's what marriage is. I'm not just going to throw away my family for a one time fling."

"Even though he already has?"

"I know you're mad at him, but you don't know anything about our marriage so don't speak on it like you do."

"I know more than you think, Aubree."

"You've been eighteen for three days and you think we're on a first name basis now?"

"That *Mrs. Cooper* shit's gotten old, don't you think?" I narrow my eyes at her. "Besides, I hate calling you by that fuckers last name. I'm not doing it anymore."

She stares at me again, her fingertips touch her lips and she says, "You know exactly why it's a no, Trenton. Even if I wanted to, I couldn't."

"I know you want to. I wouldn't have asked if I didn't think you wanted to."

Her eyes hold on mine, hardening in a way that makes me want to leap from my seat and kiss her the way I've been dying to the past five years. But before my impulsivity can make me act, she leaves me there.

I sit in the quiet space, listening as her steps ascend until they're right above me. Up in her bedroom.

EIGHT

trenton

I WOKE UP AT NOON, FLAT ON MY STOMACH ON DIESEL'S FUTON.

He wasn't anywhere in the room. He didn't even wake me up this morning like he usually does when he's up before me.

I took my time sitting up, ruffling my hair as I checked my phone for messages and emails.

Marina: *Good morning.* *heart emoji*

Marina's a sweet girl. So sweet, it makes me want to keep my distance from her even more. A guy like me doesn't deserve a sweet girl. A guy like me isn't good for a sweet girl and I can't be responsible for killing someone's innocence.

I send her a *good afternoon* back with a smiley face emoji before I finally get up and stretch. I dig through Diesel's closet and pick out some of my clothes to wear, brush my teeth, and then head down the hall to see where everyone is and why no one woke me up.

"I just...I don't get it. How could you let this happen..." says Aubree, her voice breaking like she's on the edge of tears. "After everything I've told you. Everything I expected from you, you still..." she sighs and I imagine her palm covering her face.

I assume she's on the phone with Roger. He's probably finally told her he's leaving her or cheated or something. Nothing to be surprised about. It's about time.

I slow my pace, stopping beside the kitchen wall to listen in.

"I don't know." Diesel breathes out his words and I draw my head back in surprise that he's the one she's talking to.

"I tolerate so much from you, Diesel. All I wanted in return was for you to have a chance at having a good life. For you not to do something stupid and ruin it before it's even gotten started."

"Is that how you felt about me, then? That I ruined your life before it started? That I kept you from a good life?"

"No. Never. I've never regret you, Diesel." She speaks frantically as if she can't say it quickly enough. "Never. That's not what I meant."

"That's what it sounded like."

"What I mean is, you've just made your life a whole lot harder because of this. This isn't going to be easy, for you or Chloe." She breathes in a way that convinces me she's crying or on the verge. "How am I going to tell your dad?"

I drop my eyes, wondering if I should interrupt this with a joke to lighten the mood. Probably not. I know how Diesel sounds when he's pissed, and his mood is unredeemable from the sounds of it.

"I'll tell him myself," Diesel grumbles.

"No. It'd probably be better coming from me."

"I can handle dad just fine on my own."

I hear the chair creak and turn to step away, but I feel him behind me as soon as my foot hits the ground.

I swallow thickly as I turn back around to face him. Waiting for the inevitable to leave his mouth.

"Chloe's pregnant."

I tilt my head, staring at him in dismay. "A—are you…sure it's yours?"

He scoffs like he isn't in the mood and storms down the hall, slamming his bedroom door behind him.

Before I can take a step in his direction, already mentally preparing myself for all the groveling I'm going to have to do to get him to come out of his room, I hear Aubree's small sobs from where I'm standing.

I'm conflicted, but my body takes me to her before I can even make a mental decision on who to console first.

As soon as she sees me, she turns her face away.

"Hey…" I come toward her, seeing her wipe her cheeks before presenting herself back to me like she wasn't crying at all.

"Did you hear any of that?"

I nod. "Yeah."

She blows out a heavy breath. "I cannot deal with this right now. I just can't."

There's so much pain in her eyes. She's so worried. I hate the look on her face, it's killing me.

"I'll deal with Diesel. Don't worry about it."

She leans against the kitchen island, biting her thumb nail as she stares thoughtfully at the ground. Almost like she didn't hear what I said.

"Aubree." I stand in front of her, my arms opening up hastily, but she walks right into my chest and hugs me. My chin rests on top of her head that's pressed against my body.

I haven't hugged Aubree since my fifteenth birthday. Our hugs were always one armed and quick. Needless to say, those times never felt like this. So natural. My arms closing in around her shoulders as she shudders against me. Holding me back.

"Trenton?" I heard Mrs. Cooper call out for me and wedged myself further back against the corner of the room. I watched Diesel fall asleep on the couch and sat there next to him until the tv timed out, casting a blue glow across the room because the screen hadn't shut off. The dark creeped me out when I was a kid, feeling alone creeped me out even more.

So I panicked.

I'd been sitting there in the dark for a while, crying for no reason. I wanted to go home, but at the same time I didn't. Especially not at this hour.

"Trenton?" She whispered, sounding louder like she's only on the other side

of the couch. I remember wondering how she knew I was awake. How she knew I was in the middle of panicking.

I peeked out from beside the couch as another sob came and a tear rolled down my cheek.

"Hey, what's wrong?" She hurried toward me with a frown. "Why are you crying?"

She crouched down, reaching for me as I crawled out from the small space, holding me by my arms in front of her, rubbing them as if I were cold. I sniffled up the rest of my tears, admiring her pretty face. That was the first time I really noticed her lengthy, dark eyelashes and how sheen and long her hair was. The dots all over her face—also speckled scantily on her shoulders—were something I'd never seen on a person before her. Beauty marks that later served as map markings of places I'd want to kiss.

She placed her palm on my cheek and wiped my face dry with the soft pads of her thumbs. Her hands always smelled like strawberries and I always inhaled the scent deeply.

I felt so helpless at that age. So alone. Home life was confusing. The hate was thick, the house was quiet—until it wasn't. Until someone lashed out.

Thinking about it made another wave of tears hit and I shut my eyes tight before feeling her arms envelop me.

"Aww, Trenton. You're alright." She spoke softly as I laid my head on her chest. "Let's call mom? Maybe that'll make you feel better, hm?"

She clasped my hand in hers and I glanced at Diesel, sound asleep as we passed.

She sat down at the kitchen table, grabbing the landline as I stood by, antsy, while she dialed. We probably shouldn't call mom, *I thought. It was dark out and although I still hadn't gotten the hang of reading a clock, I knew her and dad were usually not their happiest around this time.*

But Mrs. Cooper smiled at me, spun me around and leaned me against her lap with her hand on my shoulder, making me feel like it would be okay if we did.

"Hi, Martha—" I heard mom's tiny voice come out of the speaker before Mrs. Cooper switched the phone to the ear farthest from me. "Oh, I just… Trenton's having a little trouble sleeping and I…"

I didn't even care that my mother was unconcerned with me at the time. I expected it. I was unconcerned with her too. My focus was on watching Mrs. Cooper speak, wondering how a person could be so pretty. I was only eight, but I knew I'd never again in my life find someone that caught my gaze the way she did.

Her hand pat my back, making me remember I was upset a moment before, squeezing anxious tears out of my eyes. But that was all gone now that I was with her.

"I just thought he might feel better if he spoke to you."

She takes a breath before placing the phone on my ear and I sniffle as my mother speaks. "Trenton, what's the problem?"

"I…I don't know," I said timidly as all reason left my mind. But I was a kid. That was a kid thing to do, to not know what the cause for your actions were. But those tears were always justified. My anxiety was always justified and to her, it should have been.

"Well, no one can pick you up. Dad's taken the car and I don't know where he's gone. Understand?"

That meant they fought and he was probably going to be gone for another week, only to call me every other night and speak to me for five minutes before rushing off the phone.

"Kay."

The call ended immediately, the dial tone blaring in my ear before I could even hand the phone back to her. It was clear to me that it was another one of those nights at home and although five minutes before I wanted to go back there, I didn't anymore. I was glad I was here. It felt safer than home.

"Everything's fine, Trenton," Mrs. Cooper assured me. "You're safe here, don't be scared."

I swallowed, blinking at her nervously. I'd only been that close to Mom before, never any other woman—besides Grandma or Aunt Kate. And no one that beautiful and nice.

And then her eyes brightened like she'd just thought of a good idea and she said, "I know what we need."

Mrs. Cooper held my shoulder as she guided me into to the kitchen. She lifted me up and set me on the high bar stool that we usually aren't allowed to sit on because Diesel always rocked them, but since he was asleep, it was our secret.

She opened the freezer and took out two fudge ice creams, handing one to me. Diesel was begging for one all day—he kicked his feet and had a full blown tantrum while I blinked at him—but since he'd gotten caught in Mr. Cooper's office earlier, she wouldn't allow it.

"Don't tell anyone." She placed her finger over her lips as I blinked away the very last of my tears.

I studied her smile as she peeled the wrapper open and took a bite. A long time ago I'd noticed the way she'd bite into her ice cream, because I always thought was weird and sadistic since it hurt my teeth if I ever did. She never even got a brain freeze or anything.

"You're not supposed to bite it, Mrs. C., you're supposed to lick it." I smiled, tearing the wrapper from mine.

She chuckled. "Well, I guess I'm just breaking all the rules tonight, huh?"

I breathe into the top of her hair, closing my eyes as the tropical scent fills my lungs. Her arms tighten around my back, and I can tell she wants to stay like this just as much as I do.

This year has been off to a wild start and I have a feeling it's only going to get worse.

At some point, Aubree came to her senses and we broke our embrace. She thanked me for being a good friend to Diesel and told me she knew I'd stick by his side through this and that she was glad I was there. I nodded, taking it all in. It was all superficial words to me anyway.

Things we already knew.

There's no doubt I'd be there for Diesel. Whatever he needed, I'd give it to him if I had it. That's how it's always been.

And am I surprised that Chloe finally got knocked up? No. Only thing I'm surprised about is that it didn't happen sooner. Diesel always bragged about his pull out game—which apparently isn't as good as he thought it was.

I may be a virgin, but at least I'm not tied to someone I can't even keep a steady relationship with. Whatever. I've got his back either way.

The Cooper household was too tense for me after that conversation, so I headed home. I hadn't been there in a few days and wanted to be home tonight for dinner, anyway.

I don't know if my mom's still mad at me or not. She usually just needs time to cool down after we fight like that, and then she doesn't bring it up again unless we get into another argument regarding something wrong I did again.

"You know, I almost forget I have a brother until you finally decide to show up at home—where you live," says Joselyn, leaning over the kitchen counter. Earphones in and phone in her hands as always like they're extra limbs.

I smirk at her, blowing a breath out as I join her in the kitchen. "What are you listening to?"

"Music."

"No shit?" I raise my brows to emphasize my sarcasm.

She laughs. "So, why are you home this afternoon? It's weird seeing you in the daytime."

"Drama at Diesel's house." I reach into the pantry for the box of pop tarts. "It got too heavy. He locked himself in his room, his mom was crying. It was a whole ordeal."

She wrinkles her forehead, pressing pause on her earphones and setting her phone down completely. "What happened?"

I take a bite of the frosted pastry, crumbs falling onto my shirt. "Keep your mouth shut?"

She nods.

"You know Diesel's girlfriend, Chloe?"

"Yeah." Her eyes shift back and forth in her head.

"Three positive pregnancy tests this morning."

She gasps. "Oh no."

"Oh, yes."

She clenches her teeth. "Yikes. That's going to be a bummer on your bromance."

I watch her open the fridge and toss her light brown hair back before she grabs the big liter bottle of sprite. The top hisses under her palm as she opens it in front of the open fridge.

"Nah. That's not going to affect us." I huff, tapping the countertop.

"Well…" she pulls a clean cup from the cabinet. "Babies are twenty-four hour jobs." The soda sizzles as it fills the cup. "Not to mention the fact that they may decide to move out together, or she might even move into Diesel's house, which is probably more likely since neither of them have jobs. There won't be any room for you anymore."

My face constricts in denial. "No. That would never happen. Aubree—Mrs. Cooper hates Chloe."

Joselyn narrows her eyes at me like she catches the fact that I called Aubree by her first name, but doesn't say anything about it as she returns the bottle to the fridge.

"But now she's not just Chloe—She's the mother of Mrs. Cooper's grandkid. And Mrs. Cooper is a sweet person from what I remember, so I doubt it'll be hard for her to change her mind about her just to keep the peace between everyone."

I take a breath, placing my hands flat on the cool surface of the marble countertop.

"Whoops. I worried you didn't I?" She takes a drink from her cup.

I ignore her as I reflect on all she's just said. I didn't think about any of that, but she's right. This mistake is going to change everyone's lives. This is going to upset their whole family dynamic and now I get why Aubree was so upset.

I should be too.

NINE

Aubree

I AM SO DISAPPOINTED.

Actually, disappointed is probably an understatement.

Here I was thinking he'd at least make it out of high school without an unwanted pregnancy, but there he is. Seventeen with a girlfriend who is already eight weeks in.

We just found out how far along she is today, a week after he told me. I can't help but to wonder if this is what I wished for, coming to me in the least desirable way possible. My mother used to tell me all the time, *be careful what you wish for, Aubree.*

I was always a wisher. I'd wish for the best, instead of hoping for it. And in a way I'd always gotten what I asked for, even if it wasn't the way I intended on receiving it.

Diesel hasn't spoken much to me since he told me. Today, he went with her to the doctor and returned with an ultrasound photo that just tacked on weight to my already heavy heart.

I won't say I'm not happy in a sense, because I am. I've always visualized becoming a grandparent, but this just does not feel like the right time. Especially with the way Roger's been acting. He's been stressed over who knows what, and I know this isn't going to help at all.

"Your dad's coming home tonight," I tell Diesel, stopping him before he can leave me alone in the kitchen.

"Are you going to tell him?"

I look up at him as I shut off the sink, shaking my wet hands over the steel. "I can, if that's what you want."

He nods subtly, slipping his hand in his back pocket as he leans against the wall. *I guess he changed his mind.* "I'm going to stay over Chloe's tonight, then."

I blink, dropping my eyes from him. As much as I think he should be there when I tell his dad the news, I also wonder if it's better that he isn't.

I don't know how Roger is going to take any of this. I know it won't be good after the conversation we had when I asked him about bringing another child into this family, but all I can do is wish for the best, I suppose.

"Okay. I'll let you know what he says."

He swallows before turning away and heading back down the hall.

Maybe Roger was right to be against us having a second baby. I don't think I can go through the possibility of this happening again, especially if I'll be in my fifties by that time. This whole thing has me on edge. I wonder how Chloe's parents are taking it.

Roger texted me hours ago letting me know he was boarding his flight home. Since then, I've escaped into the pages of one novella and polished off three bottles of wine.

In a spur of the moment decision, I cleaned the house, as if that would do anything to change the possibility of Roger throwing a fit over the news I'm going to tell him. I don't think anything can soften the blow I'm going to take for my son, but I guess this all started with me in the first place.

Me falling for a man that didn't think anything more of me than another notch in his belt when we were teens. A man who took advantage of me, a fourteen year old girl, when he was days from being seventeen. A man who didn't think enough of me to wear protection. He didn't care. *One and done.* Or that's what I was supposed to be.

I hate that phrasing.

And maybe that's what turned me off most about Trenton's proposition, the fact that he termed it that way. Am I ever going to be more than someone's quick fling?

I mean, I'm a wife, but I shouldn't be. The only reason I am is because I won the game of Russian roulette Roger was playing. At the time, I convinced myself that I was lucky because he did propose to me. Because I was the one he *chose*.

Looking back on it now, I wish he would have just left me alone.

The door opens and I jump as the sound breaks my thoughts. I hear Roger's keys slam on the entryway table, and although he normally sounds like a bull in a china shop when he's home, I can tell a difference in the noise when he's in a mood.

I shut my eyes, taking a deep breath. Willing myself not to break down right here on the couch in the den.

He needs to know, and he needs to know now.

"Roger?" I call, rising from the sofa. I hear the fridge open and slow to a stop as I remember I've done everything except for make dinner.

It didn't occur to me earlier through the fog of my anxiety that I still needed to prepare something even though Diesel wasn't going to be home for dinner. It's easy to mix it up now that everyone's out of the house all the time. Even Trenton's been infrequent all week, and I actually miss him. He was a dash of bright light in our house.

"You didn't cook anything?" He growls as I take a few steps into the kitchen.

"Diesel went out tonight, I didn't think about it."

"You didn't think I'd want to eat when I got home?" His voice is hard and menacing and I know he's going to hit or slam something. "What the fuck were you doing here all day?" His arm swings the fridge door so hard the entire thing wobbles.

"I'll make you something right now."

"Fuck it. I'll just go pick something up." He raises his arms and lets them thud against his thighs. "I wouldn't want you to overexert yourself. I know you're probably tired from all the reading and wine guzzling you do all day."

I cross my arms over my chest and bite my cheek. If there was any worse time to tell Roger, it would be tonight, but if I don't it'll only crash down on me harder when he finds out later on.

"I need to talk to you."

"About what now, Aubree?" He narrows his eyes at me. "You wanna hound me about how I never gave you a daughter again?"

"This is something serious," I say bluntly.

"Fine. Go ahead. I can tell you right now, whatever it is, it's a no."

"This is something that doesn't need your approval."

"What the fuck is it, Aubree?" He sets his huge hand on the countertop and leans over it, staring at me with furled brows and defined lines warping his forehead.

I gulp, taking a breath as I feel anxiety slowly rushing in. The dreaded sentence chants in my head, nudging me to gather up enough nerve finally force it past my lips.

"What? Say it."

"Chloe's pregnant…Diesel got Chloe pregnant."

Roger blinks at me, then his top lip puffs up as his tongue runs underneath it. His hand tightens into a fist and he bangs it on the table, not once but three times in a row.

I let my lids fall shut and another breath drags in to keep me from crying again.

"Son of a fucking bitch, Aubree." His fist covers his lips and he stares blankly at the wall ahead of him.

"I know. I know you're disappointed, but there isn't much we can do. We just have to support him."

"Support him? I support him realizing his mistake and taking her to a damn clinic."

I frown at him. "She doesn't want to and she doesn't have to, Roger. They knew what the risks were when they made the decision to have unprotected sex, and unfortunately they weren't lucky enough to get away with it without facing the repercussions."

He waves his hand at me. "Fuck all that. I wish someone would have forced me not to go through with it when it was me, but no one did and now I'm here."

"What's that supposed to mean?"

"Exactly what I just said." He stares at me and my lip twitches. "Come on, don't act like you suddenly don't think the same thing, Aubree. We both know how much you hated—"

I raise my hand and the words leap out of my throat. "I hated nothing!"

He gives me his pitying eyes and I know the next thing to come out of his mouth will be so tsk-tsk I'll have to bite my tongue. "I could've sworn you did. I very blatantly remember you hating life at one point, am I wrong?"

"Yes."

His brow raises and he takes a few steps through the kitchen, his hands finding solace in the pockets of his slacks.

I did hate at one point in my life. For the first time in my life, and certainly not the last. I hated the decisions I made, or didn't make. I hated my naivety. I hated myself. But if Roger's going to stand here and insinuate that I blame the baby we made for the reason we are where we are now, he's absolutely wrong.

"Our lives are nothing like we wanted them to be." He stops still. "And that's because we didn't think for ourselves. Just did what everyone told us to."

"And that was the right thing to do."

"They told us all the wrong things."

"And you think guilting him out of it is the right thing? You think revoking his freedom to choose on his own, without you persecuting him is the right thing? Telling him that baby is going to ruin him just like his existence did for us, is the right thing to do, Roger?"

His mouth widens and I know his voice is going to raise to an ungodly volume. "The right thing to do for two kids who hadn't even graduated high school was to get rid of the mistake they made and learn not to do it again."

"It doesn't have to be a mistake, Roger!"

"It will always be a mistake, Aubree! Nothing can make this right! Getting married, pretending they wanted the baby, nothing will ever make it right!"

He drives those words into me by staring me dead in the eye as he shouts them in my face. I hear him loud and clear.

Diesel was a mistake.

Marrying me didn't make it better.

Staying with me, building a life with me.

Mistake, mistake, mistake.

He hates it all.

I shut my eyes and a small sob leaves me without any tears falling.

"It's the truth. You know it and I know it," he adds. "Why let him follow in our footsteps, hm? Don't we owe him that much?"

He glares back at me as I glower at him. My eyes prickling and face radiating waves of heat.

Something flickers in his eyes before he walks past me. I follow him into the living room, seeing him swipe his suitcase and keys from the spot he tossed them in by the door.

"Where are you going?"

"Somewhere else. I'm not staying here tonight."

"Roger," I say, urgently with tears lining my eyes.

"I'll be back when things make more sense."

TEN

Trenton

I'VE STAYED HOME THE PAST FEW DAYS. DIESEL'S BEEN SPENDING more time with Chloe and just like Joselyn predicted, there isn't enough room for me in that equation.

We hung out a couple of times after school and I slept over one night after work, but he's just been so dull. I can tell this is weighing heavily on him. It really set in for me when he showed me the ultrasound photo. Even though I had no idea what I was looking at, I knew it meant this was really happening.

And suddenly he's been hard to reach. I've been texting him all day with no reply. It worried me, so I braved up and headed to the Cooper house—despite knowing Roger should have come home tonight, and the fact that I could be walking in on world war three.

But the house is quiet as I walk up the dimly lit steps. Roger's car isn't parked in the driveway, so the coast must be clear.

I use my key to let myself in and hear the familiar sniveling that broke my heart last week. I follow the sound into the kitchen and see Aubree crying quietly beside the fridge.

"Hey," I say, gently.

She viscously wipes her face dry before taking another sip from her glass. I don't even want to know how much she's drank tonight, but I'm sure it's both not enough and too much. Her lips quiver as she forces a smile and raises her glass to me.

I know this is where I'm supposed to chuckle at the fact that she's trying to be humorous while she's in complete distress, but I don't find anything funny about walking in on her like this.

"Where's Diesel?"

"Chloe's..." She nods glumly.

"What's wrong?" I cringe internally as I hear the words leave my lips. Like it isn't obvious. I know what's wrong.

Everything.

She thinks I know nothing about her, but truthfully I'm the only one watching. I know how much of a dick Roger is, I see the way he treats her. I knew Diesel was going to fuck up, and I know she was just waiting for the day. I know she's lonely. I know she's full of regret. I know she coddles endless bottles of wine because she doesn't know how to get out of this. Because she doesn't want to think about it. She doesn't want to stare reality in it's red, angry, ugly face. I know so much more than she thinks.

"Nothing." She presents me a faint smile. "What? A girl can't cry and sip a glass of wine in her spare time?"

"You look fucking miserable."

"No." She shakes her head. "This is just normal housewife behavior, Trenton. I swear."

I tilt my head at her, smart enough not to fall for her shit. Caring enough not to take her nothings for an answer. She has no idea how much I really do care about her. I've been with Diesel and walked in on her doing this plenty of times, but he's never noticed anything wrong with her. He's never asked her how she was doing. He's never talked to her more than to ask her to leave him alone or what's for dinner.

"Bullshit." I let one corner of my mouth rise an inch or two as I come closer to her, seeing her pinch the front of her robe together to hide the small bit of cleavage that was peeking out. *Too late, I already noticed.* "But even under all the misery, you still look beautiful. How in the hell do you do that?"

"Okay, Romeo." She rolls her glossy eyes before a genuine smile plasters on her face and she dabs the inner corners of her eyes with her fingertips. "Anyway, Diesel's not coming back tonight. Sorry to disappoint."

"I'm not." I shrug. "I didn't really come for Diesel."

"Then what'd you come for?"

"To check in with the house. To make sure everyone's okay."

"How noble of you." That sarcastic tongue of hers darts out to wet her bottom lip and she drops her eyes down at her glass.

"Where's the colonel?"

She swallows hard and bats her lashes like she's taking a moment to think. "You just missed him. I don't know when he's coming back —if he's coming back."

"You told him, didn't you?"

She frowns like she's beginning to cry again, but sniffles the urge away. "I did."

I stand at her side, setting the heels of my palms on the edge of the counter as I sigh. I don't have anything to say because ultimately I know nothing can make this hurt any less for her. I can't do anything to take her stress away—unless she lets me, which she made clear wouldn't be happening.

I'm hardly of any importance in her life, so anything I say is just trivial. All I can do is be present.

"Can you stay here with me, tonight?" Her wide eyes look up at me and I purse my lips to keep myself from smiling at such a bad time.

"Of course. Whatever you want."

"Thanks, Trenton. I wish Diesel could be more like you sometimes." She smiles sadly before finally setting down the empty glass and leaving the room.

Aubree hemmed herself up in the den, silently reading. I know that's the only thing that seems to relax her—or take her mind off things—so I left her alone while she was in her own world.

While she was busy, I went to the store. I picked up some groceries after seeing there was literally nothing to eat besides some expired pop tarts and a bag of stale chips I think I remember seeing Diesel leave open last week when he got another Chloe booty-call.

When I returned, I heard the tv on in the den and figured she must have finished reading and was ready for a new distraction which I was fully ready to be for her. I think.

I'll be honest, for the first time in ever, I'm nervous to be alone with her. This is the first time I'll actually be hanging out with her. Without any real dividers.

Real or imaginary.

She knows how I feel about her, and she still asked me to stay here, alone. With her.

I mean, I assume that when she asked me to stay she wanted company. I'm all up for taking her mind off things, whether that be watching tv in silence or making her laugh at my stupid, desperate jokes, I'm fine with whatever.

After I put away the groceries, I met her in the den. She's sitting in her usual corner spot on the sectional with her favorite thin blanket draped over her legs. She's staring at the tv, but not watching it, until she sees me come in.

I've already been beaming off the fact that she asked me to stay for an hour now, but then she smiles at me, causing a warmth to ignite in my chest and fuck, it feels good.

"Popsicles!" She chuckles as I sit next to her.

There's a possibility that the reason behind her smiling at me like that is because I came in with ice cream, but either way I made it happen.

When Diesel and I were kids, Aubree used to have fudgesicles stocked in the freezer like a convenient store. Eventually she swapped the ice cream for wine sometime when things between her and Roger got noticeably rocky.

She slides the paper down and as soon as her lips form an *o*, I realize I made a poor choice. Not for her sake, but mine. I froze as I watched her suck the tip of the ice cream, her eyes stagnant on the tv screen.

Only Aubree Cooper could make me solid from watching her eat a popsicle. Twirling it between her lips as she drives it farther into her mouth, knowing her tongue is just swirling over it inside.

She pulls it out and I force myself to drop my eyes, unwrapping mine.

We eat them while the tv runs, not saying a word until mine's gone.

"You guys used to love these. You especially." She looks at me. "Only thing that helped you get over being homesick."

"You know…" I sigh. "I wasn't always homesick…I mean, the first few times I was, but after a while I just knew if I cried you'd find me and I sort of just liked hanging out with you."

She lets a slow smirk creep on her face. "I know. I figured that out somewhere around the tenth time it happened."

I smirk back at her, slightly embarrassed. Like I said, my mouth's a loose cannon. I never know what's going to come out.

"But," she adds, "I liked hanging out with you too. You were such a sweet kid, always helped out around the house. Always kind and giving, and so funny. You were the second son I never had."

I drop my head back and roll it so I'm facing her, playfully wincing as she returns the half of the popsicle to her lips. "I really wish you'd stop saying that. Especially when you're…sucking on that."

She bites off what's in her mouth and chews it like the psychopath she is. "I'm being honest. When I say it, I mean that we're close. It's not meant as anything other than a compliment, Trenton." She's laying her head back just like I am, face turned to mine and we're only inches apart. Just far enough so that I can comfortably see her entire beautiful face.

"I know, but I really don't want to be a son to you," I say in a hushed tone.

"What do you want to be?"

Under you. Inside of you. Yours.

My tongue peeks out to lick my lips as I stare into her dark eyes.

I'm convinced. She's the most beautiful woman I've ever seen in my life. That's it. No one tops Aubree Cooper. No one.

"I want to be kissing you right now." *Loose fucking cannon.*

And for the first time, she doesn't tense up. She doesn't press her thighs together and remind me that she's wrapped in an invisible caution tape. She doesn't quadruple knot the sash around her waist. She doesn't run away.

"You're so beautiful. So, so beautiful." I speak the words as I lean toward her, our lips touch and a surge of heat rushes through me like my veins are pumping gasoline and she's the fire that's set it all to flames.

Her tongue pushes past my lips and it takes everything in me not to rip the robe off of her. My fingers cinch the slippery fabric and that's about as far as my self control goes.

Her lips are like suede and she tastes like chocolate frosting with a hint of red wine. She tastes like all of my dreams and goals intertwined. She tastes like reaching the finish line. A mile stone. Like I've won.

Her dainty fingers curl around my neck and crawl up through my hair, sending chills down my spine and cause me to fucking dry hump her like a prepubescent boy. But fuck, I don't even care and she doesn't seem to either. She lets out the sexiest breathy moan and I wonder if it's because she imagined for one second I was bare against her entrance and that was the thrust that broke the thin line of a boundary we had left.

I almost want to shut the tv off so I can hear every sound of her desire, but I don't. My body is hot against hers, her back to the plush couch and I don't want anything to break us out of this moment.

My fingers are desperate to feel what's underneath the damn robe she teases me with every night and my hand scrambles for the sash until she grabs me by the wrist like she's come to her senses.

"We can't, we can't, we can't—" Her words are coated in her soft breath and I never knew a rejection could sound so sexy.

My breathing's heavy and I'm so turned on, I press my forehead to hers for a second as I process what the fuck just happened while also ordering myself to calm down.

She sits up and I stay between her legs, her hand clasped in mine.

"Aubree, it's okay." I lick my lips, staring her in the eyes, aching to taste her again. I bring her hand to my chest, holding it in between us as she battles both her mind and her desire. "No one's here. It's just us."

She blinks nervously, staring at the doorway like she's expecting someone to walk in.

And then she grabs me by the front of my shirt and pulls me back in. We kiss so deeply, I feel like I'm going to explode. My hands are drawn to her robe again and I pull one long strand until it's unknotted.

She looks up at me, perfect and waiting. But I want this reveal to be slow. I want to savor every second I see her body for the first time, because it may just be the last.

My fingers weave into the spot between her warm skin and the thin satin and I gulp as I slowly slide the fabric over. I barely get to the see the sculpted crest between her tits before her hands are wrapped around my wrists again.

"Trenton." She shakes her head.

I let out a sad breath before my teeth sink into my bottom lip. "Why not?"

"There's no way I'm going to have sex with you while you're still in high school."

"I graduate in May." My voice perks up in hopefulness.

"Then wait until May."

"Really?"

She nods. "I guess you should get your butter knife ready."

I only allow myself to smile for a second before our lips link again in what's got to be the hottest kiss I'll ever have.

ELEVEN

Aubree

I OPEN MY EYES AND INSTANTLY REALIZE I'M NOT IN MY BED. I'M on the couch in the den. As I slowly rise, I hear small snores below me and look down to see Trenton asleep on the floor. The memories from last night come to me in a big rush of visuals.

I made out with Trenton for hours. *Hours.* Not just a few minutes at a time like normal people do, we sucked each other's lips for literal hours. Mine are actually sore as I drag my tongue between them. Time just sped when we he was on top of me, or holding me. Tasting me so desperately, I almost did give myself to him.

I hang my head in my hands as the shame drops on top of it all like a cartoon anvil.

Honestly, it took everything for me to keep my robe on last night. His impulsive thrusts against me, his hands in my hair, his soft touches to my skin. Ugh, the desire I felt for this boy last night was unreal. And it's still there now as I look down at his sleeping body.

The front door opens and I panic. We're caught, red handed. I don't even stop to listen for hard or soft movements because I need to pretend like we didn't fall asleep in here together after laughing over episodes of sponge bob like we used to when he couldn't sleep at night.

"Mom?" says Diesel from the front room.

I tighten my robe like Trenton never loosened it to kiss my bare shoulders last night and drape the blanket over his body, but he opens his eyes, staring up at me with a smile like he didn't forget what went on last night at all.

I don't want to, but I melt over his sleepy gaze. His hair is a wild mess, but I believe that's more due to my hands coursing through it than a case of bedhead.

"Good morning, Mrs. C," he whispers.

"What…the hell?" Diesel appears beside us, frowning as he waits for an explanation as to what's going on.

"Hey Dees…" Trenton sits up, slowly. His smile hardly fading and I could kick him for being so obvious.

"Hey man, what are you doing on the floor? What are you doing here, period?"

"You know this is my second home." Trenton speaks it so confidently, I let out the breath I was holding. "I was waiting for you to come back. Thanks for ignoring me all day, dick."

"I wasn't ignoring you. I shut my phone off yesterday."

"Why?"

"In case my dad tried to call me." His mouth twists and he glances at me. "If he did, I didn't want to know, so I shut it off…but when I turned it back on this morning, I saw that he never did so I was just worried for no reason, wasn't I?"

I tangle my fingers together at my waist. I don't know what to tell him, and I was much too busy with my tongue down Trenton's throat last night to be a mother and decide on the words I was going to use to tell Diesel his father left aggravated without a real explanation as to where he was going or when he'd be back.

The thought of it is bringing a throbbing tension to my chest. He won't take it well, no matter how well I sugar coat it.

I glance down at Trenton who's staring up at me, biting down on his thumb nail with that same smile on his face. He's such an adorable idiot.

"Well? Where's he at? He clearly isn't here." Diesel's hands fall against his jeans. "I'm assuming you told him last night and he was so pissed, he walked out."

He knows his father best. By the way he says it, I'm sure he was expecting it to go that way and that's why he stayed away. Leaving me to take the brunt of the heat.

But I nod, leaving it at that. What else is there to say? I'm just as disappointed as Roger is, but I wouldn't walk away from our problems. We're supposed to come together on this. Be a unit. But who knows where Roger went that he thought was better than being home, discussing ways to get prepared for this baby.

"Of course he did." Diesel chuckles, scratching the side of his nose. "That's just classic dad, you know? Never fucking there for me when I need him."

"Diesel…"

"No." He holds his hand up, his lips tighten and I'd swear he's close to tears, but I'm not sure. "You know, I thought he'd come looking for me last night? I thought maybe he'd show up at Chloe's even if it was just to yell at me. I would have taken it, but fuck." He shakes his head.

Trenton finally stands up as he's probably realized he's no help sitting on the floor like a goofy idiot with a pair of swollen lips I'm sure he's proud of.

"It's fucking bullshit, mom. He doesn't give a fuck about us. I bet he's the happiest when he leaves out of town. What do you think?"

He stares hard at me, but after seeing that I'm not going to egg on his anger with an answer, he leaves the den.

"Diesel," Trent calls, brushing past me to go after him. I stand there a few seconds, shutting my eyes as I endure the head spinning brought on by the overwhelm of stress.

There's a lot that Diesel doesn't know about his father. That he doesn't know about me. That he can't know about either of us because we've hidden it so well and so long it'd wreck everything we barely have now.

A pair of fingertips grip me by the jaw and my eyes open right as Trenton plants his lips on me. I open my eyes to his sweet smile as he pulls back.

"Don't worry about it. I'll take care of him."

Trenton leaves me there, but I can still feel his touch even after he's gone. It's like a vibration on my skin. A vibration I've never felt before in my life and I'm not sure how to feel about it.

I drop my face in my hands as I hear the door to Diesel's room shut. I'm a terrible mother, but Trenton is such an angel.

An angel I need to keep the peace around here.

TWELVE

Trenton

"WELL, WELL, WELL…LOOK WHO'S BACK." JOSELYN SMIRKS AT ME from the couch. Her legs folded up in front of her. Her skinny jeans look extremely tight, so I'm not sure how she's pulling off criss-cross apple sauce. "Is this gonna be an ongoing thing for you now, coming home?"

"At least I leave the house, unlike someone…" I flop on the couch beside her.

"If mom would let me," she mutters. "What are you doing here?"

"I can't come home?"

"It's just weird that all of a sudden you've been home a lot."

"Well, I already told you Diesel's issue."

"The baby isn't here yet." She speaks in a duh tone.

Like that matters. Even if the baby isn't physically here yet, it's still *here*. It's still a big part of Diesel's life already and he's so scared, he just hasn't been himself.

"It's just different now, so I'm home. Deal with it." I reach over and shake my palm on top of her head so that her hair fuzzes and gets all staticky, and she squeals like a pig.

"Stop, dummy!"

Even though I'm an adult and she's definitely not a kid anymore, we get along like we both still are. I don't think that'll ever change. Joselyn's too fun to mess around with. Especially now that she thinks she's all grown up since coming to the end of her first year of high school. Poor kid has no idea, she's got a long way to go. I wouldn't redo those days for anything, especially since I'll be done in less than two months. It was all worth the wait.

"So what's going on with you? I mean, come on. Aren't I finally old enough—at the ripe age of fifteen—to finally be in the loop?"

"You are in the loop." I poke her on her squishy, babyface. "I told you about Diesel."

"No. I'm talking about the dumb smile on your face. You're dating someone."

"I'm not smiling." I am. It's deep and it's dimpled. And it feels fucking permanent as long as what went on last night is reality—and it is.

My dick's been hard all day because I can't stop replaying the vivid memory of it in my head. The way her weight felt against me, the way her body moved against mine, like confirmation to every assumption I had about her. I knew she wanted me. I knew the attraction wasn't only one sided.

As much as I wanted to have her completely, right then and there, I am totally satisfied with the promise she made me.

"You are, you big cheesy idiot!" She laughs, shoving me, hopping onto her knees. "The last time you were even a little bit like this was when you were dating Thea Mahoney."

"How do you know about that?"

"Because I did my best nosey little sister detective work."

"You were like fucking twelve."

"I still knew how to get on your phone and snoop around."

My jaw tilts and I say nothing, turning my attention to the overly dramatic teens she watches on MTV. I still feel myself smiling a little bit every time I touch my lips with my tongue.

"You've got it bad. Geez, you can't even stop." She crosses her arms and I avoid eye contact with her. "Who is it? Do I know her?"

You definitely do. "Uh…" I stretch my legs out in front of me as far as they can go before the coffee table gets in the way.

"Oh, just tell me! I'm not going to say anything to mom if that's what you're worried about."

"Alright. You know Marina Benson?"

Her jaw drops. "You're seeing Marina?"

"Yep."

"And she didn't tell me!?"

Fuck me. Me and my inability to make one good decision. "What? Why would she tell you?"

"If you were around more maybe you'd know she was my friend too." Her brow curves.

"Since when?"

"Since I started ninth grade. She spends the night all the time. You didn't know?"

I mean, they've always known each other because Marina would come around often, but suddenly she's friends with my sister? Friends enough to spend the night at my house? I wouldn't be surprised if she went through my things after midnight and rolled around in my bed.

"It's still new. We're in the texting stage."

"Hm. That's kind of unbelievable. I didn't think she was your type."

"And what do you know about my type?"

"Enough to know you like your girls a lot less modest than that."

"Marina's…cute."

"Yeah, but—I don't know, I can't see you guys together." She clutches the couch pillow over her lap. "Lucky for you though, Mom loves her."

"So?"

"You can bring her over without worrying if Mom will be okay with it, because she will."

Great. I just started a whole new problem.

I'm already plotting the fake break up to our fake relationship.

"Hi, Trenton. Didn't expect you back this early." Mom glances at me with a small smile as she makes her way to the kitchen.

"Hey mom." I rock myself up off the couch and when I get into the kitchen she's retrieving pots and pans from the cupboard. "What are you making?"

"Chicken and rice."

I nod, noticing the bags under her eyes and the way she keeps her head down as she works. Back and forth from the fridge to the cutting board.

"How's work been?"

"I just got off a double a couple hours ago."

That explains it.

I watch her fingers move fast as she chops the vegetables before I finally leave her alone. I haven't had a very close relationship with my mom since I was a kid. A young kid. Probably since Dad was around and she didn't need to work herself to death.

As soon as I graduate I'm going to work full time so she doesn't have to anymore. Maybe then she wouldn't be so exhausted all the time.

We all sit around the table, making a clatter as we set down dishes and forks and bowls. When dad was here, there'd be a lot of talking at the table. A lot of Mom laughing and a lot of Dad cracking jokes and even more of Joselyn telling stories about things that happened in kindergarten, but now it's just a lot of the refrigerator humming and even more of the silverware scraping the dishes as we eat.

"Me and Jessica decided we're going to prom together," says Joselyn, twirling her fork in her rice.

Mom looks up at her under her heavy lids. "How much are the tickets?"

I hold my phone in my lap, my eyes widening a few centimeters at a sudden message from Aubree.

Aubree: *Thanks for talking to Diesel. You're the best. Really.*

"Like seventy dollars," says Joselyn.

Me: no problem.

I hear a big breath drag in before Mom asks, "Is Jessica going to pay for you?"

"No..."

Mom sets down her fork so hard it clanks against the plate. "I can't dish out seventy dollars, Joselyn. Not right now." She rests her hand on her forehead. "Why didn't you decide on this earlier? Prom is when? Next month?"

"Yeah..."

"I don't have the money for it. Not to mention the costs of a dress. Just wait until you're a senior and go one time like everyone else does."

My phone vibrates in my hand again.

Aubree: Are you coming over tonight?

My teeth graze my lip as it pains me to say no, but I have no reason to go over other than the fact that I want to relive last night.

It was too close of a call. We were almost caught. Had I not rolled off the couch at some point in the night, we would have been. I swear I fell asleep with my arms around her.

"Maybe I can do some chores around the house for the money? Or I can come to the office and help out like I used to? I can wear my eighth grade graduation dress. It still fits..."

Diesel: Coming through tonight?

I chuckle as I type yes to both of them. When I look up, both Joselyn and my mother are staring at me like they're waiting on me to explain what's so funny.

"What are we talking about?"

"How I can't afford to go to prom with my friends. I never get to do anything." She sulks, pushing her rice into a pile. "First, you didn't let me go to Jessica's party, now this."

"How are you, a freshman, going to prom? It's only for juniors and seniors."

"Marina, a junior, invited me," she quickly corrects me and I wrinkle my chin like she just snapped her fingers in my face. "And I'm sick and tired of having to tell my friends no to everything because Mom never lets me out of the house."

Mom scoffs, staring at her like she can't believe she's having this conversation with her. "You don't need to go to prom this year, Joselyn. No one goes to prom their freshman year. Besides, I just scraped up the money for you to go to homecoming."

"Everyone's going to prom, Mom!"

"Why don't you ask your father then, hm?" Her chair slides out and hits the wall behind her and she takes her plate away. A door shuts and I know she's went to her room.

That shouldn't be as controversial of a sentence as that always is in this house. Our father is unreachable. On my sixteenth birthday he finally sent me a card in the mail after three years of silence. If it weren't for his name and address written on the envelope, I wouldn't have known who to thank for the twenty dollars mailed to me, as if that's even covered any expenses in my life since he left.

"How much is prom, Jos?" I ask.

"Too much, apparently."

I stand up, pulling out my wallet. Quickly, I count out eight twenties and walk them over to her. "Here. I'm not going, take my place. Now when I get asked, I'll have a nice excuse instead of looking like the dick who just says no to every girl who comes at me with a *prom-posal*." The word grates off my tongue as I say it, grimacing.

I've been asked six times just this week and said no every time. It's a hard thing to do when these innocent girls are surprising me with candy and banners with lyrics from my favorite songs written in glitter. The hallways fill up with onlookers only to watch me reject yet another one, but most times I don't even know these girls. And with my reputation, they're really taking a shot in the dark.

"No, Trent. I'm not taking that much money from you."

"Like I said, I'm not going. Take it. You're welcome." I let the stack of bills fall on the table in front of her.

"Gio's going."

"How do you know Gio's going?"

She rolls her eyes. "Marina's going too. She's probably gonna ask you."

"I hate stuff like that so I'm not going. You be her date." I return my wallet to my back pocket as she flips through the cash. In a quick, swift movement, she stands up and hugs me.

"Thanks, T."

I let go of her just as quickly as she threw her arms around me. "Alright, alright. It's not that big of a deal."

"Fine." She rolls her eyes and chuckles.

"I gotta go."

"Mhm, I figured. I'll see you in a week." She raises her brow at me, stuffing the cash into her jeans.

I raise my brow back at her. "Apologize to Mom for being a brat."

"You never do."

"Jos," I warn.

She disappears into the kitchen with her hardly touched dinner plate in one and hand and my empty one in the other. I'm sure she's only cleaning up after me due to the fact that I gave her money.

Mom's obviously stressed, Joselyn's entering her selfish teen stage and doesn't get it, and I have the money so why not throw her some cash to do something fun? It also helps that I'm due to spend another night under the same roof as the woman I'm completely infatuated with and I'm in a great mood because of it.

When I got to Diesel's house, I met him in the backyard. I would have figured he was out smoking, but the loud smell reeking up the back of the house told me before I could even make the assumption.

I sat with him at the table in complete silence until he finally said, "The sex was never worth any of this shit. I wish I never did it. I wish I never met her."

"Don't say that, man."

"It's the truth. I always figured when I did get someone pregnant it would be because I was in love with them. I don't love Chloe. At all." He takes a hit. "I actually think I hate her."

"That's just tonight. You guys do this all the time. Tomorrow you'll be back at her house, fucking around like everything's fine."

"Nah."

"Trust me, dude." I rub my eyes, chuckling at the ridiculousness of their relationship. "I think you guys just need to have a serious talk."

"Have you ever tried talking to Chloe? She's incapable. She always flips shit around in her fucked up head whenever she feels attacked instead of just owning up to her faults."

"Well, I don't know. But you need to sit down and talk to each other."

"My fucking dad…" he blows out a stream of smoke, passing to me and I take a hit. "He won't even talk to me. How do you expect me to talk to Chloe?"

"You can't just do what your dad does."

"I already am." He chuckles, leaning his head back against the chair he's in. "Too. fucking. late."

I watch him, pursing my lips on the blunt again.

"Might as well just go all in, huh?" he adds. "Maybe I should leave Chloe. Or better yet, maybe I should stay and just cheat on her…Work a job where I don't have to see her more than twice a week…Make the kid feel like shit for existing…Like he ruined my life so badly I can't even look him in the eye. Then I'll buy him gifts to make up for the fact that I know nothing about him. What do you think?"

"Diesel…" I let out a dry sigh.

He doesn't say anything else. His eyes bat shut and once his head rolls over his shoulder I know he's out. I could wake him, but he's let me sleep out here during winter before, so I leave him there and head back in the house.

Obviously, I search the house for Aubree. She isn't in the living room, kitchen, den. The front patio.

I look up the stairs, knowing her room is right up there. The door directly in line with the flight of steps. The one place I'd never been because upstairs has always been off limits.

There's only Roger's office and the master bedroom. Both places I've dreamed of christening.

Mainly Roger's office.

I'd set her down on the desk that I've only seen once and fuck her until its surface is drenched in her juices, dripping down the dark wood.

That might require some convincing, but fuck I'm hopeful. I imagine leaving the evidence for him to find later, especially when he's all pissed off after work, but I don't really want to die over it, and Roger would definitely kill both of us.

Oddly, that makes this so much better. The fact that I know Aubree has morals, but that she's breaking them all for me.

She wants to be a good wife, and she has been. She puts up with all of Roger's shit and she doesn't get enough credit for it.

I've seen her put her all into her marriage to the best of her ability. I know, because my mom didn't. I watched my parents fall to pieces like the broken dishes I've cut my fingers on when I went to clean up after their fights. I was the only one who cleaned up those messes because Mom would lock herself in her bedroom and dad would run straight to the bar. But if I didn't, it was either Joselyn hurt herself on broken glass and shards of porcelain, or me.

I chose me.

I take my time going up the staircase. My hand dragging along the rail the entire way. I know she's in there. The block of light beams underneath the door and outlines its entire shape like it's the doorway to paradise.

I knock twice, gently because I still have manners—and because I know she'd be pissed if I walked in on her naked, even though I considered bursting through the door in the hope that she was.

I hear movement behind the door before it opens, shamelessly revealing the most alluring thing to ever grace my sight.

My jaw falls open as my eyes glaze her body. The black robe is open and she's wearing black, lacy panties that hug her hips and accentuate her waistline with a matching bra that cradles her tits so perfectly I could cry.

"Holy…"

She giggles, her cheeks tinged in what's becoming my own signature hue of blush as she grabs my hand and pulls me inside.

The door shuts behind me and I can't believe she's letting her guard down like this. Diesel's fucking asleep outside in a damn lawn chair. The spring chill is probably going to wake him up if a sore back doesn't first.

But she has both of my hands in hers and I'm completely mesmerized and a little bit afraid because I didn't expect this. I'm not prepared if this is happening now.

"Fuck. Take this off."

She laughs again, stopping my eager hands before I can slide the fabric from her shoulders. "Graduation."

I throw my head back as if it physically pains me to hear that. I've waited five years for this. For all of this. "I can't wait anymore, you're gonna fucking kill me."

I brush down her bare stomach with the back of my hand before she grabs both ends of the sash and stares me in the eye as she covers herself up.

She's a tease. I knew it.

I groan as my dick throbs under my jeans, threatening to break through the fabric, and I can see the satisfaction in her eyes. She loves this. *Sadist.*

I watch her strut over to the window, peeking out at the back yard. She must have known when I'd be coming up because she has a clear shot of the table from this spot. "What were you two talking about?"

I rip my eyes off of her. "What?" I squint. "I can't even think straight. What'd you just ask me?"

She giggles. "You and Diesel…what were you talking about? He looked angry."

"He's mad about Roger." I walk to her, placing my hands on her hips. "He hasn't called him about this whole thing and he's pissed about it. Feels like Roger doesn't care about him."

She sighs sadly, but I bring her closer to me until I can feel her heat coming through the two layers of fabric between us, lowering my head to nuzzle my face in the crook of her neck.

She slides her hands under my shoulder blades as our breathing synchronizes.

"I'll talk to him again about it later, but right now…" I lick my lips. "Let's talk about something a little more positive."

"Positive?"

"Yeah. Like, you plus this robe on the floor. Positive."

She smiles but doesn't show her teeth, then cutely shakes her head. "Not yet."

"Well, you've gotta give me something. You can't open the door looking like a goddess and expect me to just be cool with it."

Her cheeks rose again and she drops her head. Her smile's in full bloom and I'm shining down on it like I'm the sun that made it blossom. Maybe I am. I haven't seen her smile so much, ever, but I know I want to be the one responsible for all the times she does from now on.

I place my fingers underneath her chin, lifting her face to the sky before my lips land on hers. Our tongues eagerly break through the barrier our lips create between us and the back of my shirt crumples beneath her fingers.

We're chest to chest, so close that nothing's between us but our clothing, and still I need to be closer.

Soon, only kissing her won't be enough for me. It barely is now.

"Fuck, Aubree." I bite down on my bottom lip as she stares up at me, and I know she's feeling it too.

This isn't just a crush I have on her. It never has been. I don't even think it's infatuation anymore.

We have a bond that neither of us understand yet, but damn is it strong.

THIRTEEN

Aubree

ONE MONTH. FOUR WEEKS. THIRTY DAYS. SEVEN HUNDRED AND twenty hours. That's forty three thousand, two hundred minutes that Roger hasn't spoken to me.

This is by far the longest we've gone without contact. I'm beginning to think he's finally left me—and so is the neighborhood.

Lyssa's sitting in my living room, listening with wide eyes and a glass of wine as I take her through the journey that has been my past month and a half—leaving out big details regarding what's gone on with the boy her daughter has an obsessive crush on, of course.

Trenton and I have kept it PG. Our clothes always stay on every time we're together, and although he begs me to let him see more of me, I don't give in. I meant what I said. I'm not having sex with a high schooler. I can't believe that's the only thing stopping me and not my damn morals, my marriage, or the fact that he's my son's best friend. I guess Roger makes it easy for me to act on this guilt free, but if our little arrangement gets out, I don't know what'll happen.

I mean, I'm sure Diesel will hate me, but that's the least of my problems considering the fact that I'm already his least favorite person. Even though Roger walks around like he doesn't have a son, I'm still the one on the back burner. And I don't even want to think about what Roger would do if he knew about this, though I'm sure it would cover all bases of slow, torturous, psychopathic homicide.

But—and I can't believe I'm going to say this—Trenton is becoming a habit. A bad one...*but when is a habit ever a good thing anyway?*

Habits are repetitive, addictive, frequent.

My body is becoming reliant. My mind is trained by both his voice and his scent and responds to it. I'm beginning to crave him.

When his arms are around me and my reflection is in his eyes, everything makes perfect sense. And it also doesn't.

I don't know why I keep running into his arms. If they weren't so wide open for me, would I still? Would I still seek comfort in him if he weren't the only one offering it?

When we talk we're always on the same page. He tries so hard to make life easier for me, however he can. Mediating between me and Diesel, being my emotional support. But sometimes I can't tell if he really understands me, or if he's only acting that way because I promised him I'd be his first.

And I will. I want this to be one strong jab against Roger, even if I do keep it secret. He'll never know about it, but I will and it will satisfy a part of me that's seemed insatiable since I became Roger's wife. Once this is over, it's over.

I can't possibly keep this up, we both know that.

"Have you tried calling him?" asks Lyssa.

"Yeah, I've tried it all. I've contacted his office and they've left him countless messages from me, so he knows I've been trying."

"All because Chloe's pregnant? I mean, that's hardly either of yours problem. That's Diesel's problem. It's unfortunate, but it's not really your responsibility. Above all, it's your son's."

"Well, that's true, but our son is hardly a responsible person, so in turn it's all bound to fall in our laps." I stare down at the ground until I hear Trenton's laugh outside and my thighs clench together.

"The boys in the backyard?"

"Sounds like it."

Trenton does his little howl that used to irritate me, but now it's suddenly the strangest turn on. She shakes her head and chuckles, going to perch her glass on her lips.

"You know, I've got a dilemma of my own." She sighs. "I mean, nothing compared to what you're going through, but it's really been bothering me."

I frown, reaching for my glass. "Like what?"

"Marina. I overheard a conversation between her and a friend the other day, apparently things between her and Trenton are blooming. Quickly."

I blink as the sentence slam dunks into my head. "Trenton and your daughter? They're dating?"

"I don't know. I heard her talking about how she went to some house party and they almost had sex," her face constricts in disgust, "but thank god the boy had some sense and told her they were moving too fast. Maybe he's not as bad as I thought."

I let out a breath and a chuckle. Relieved. "Yeah, maybe not."

"Come on Roger…" I pace my bedroom floor with my cellphone against my ear, glancing down at the fresh pink polish on my toes from the pedicure I got earlier in the day. He hasn't revoked my access to our shared bank account yet, so I figure that's a good sign.

I guess Chloe's pregnancy really did just catch him by surprise. It's not an excuse for him to disappear, but maybe all he needs is time to process it.

For me, it's almost like reliving the days we went through in this exact situation. Except I was much younger, and Roger was hardly by my side, not anywhere near the way Diesel is with Chloe. Either way, I think it's safe to say Roger's probably reliving it too.

I want to assume he said things he didn't mean that night, but his words were so sharp, surely they were meant to be weapons.

"You've reached the automated voice messaging system—"

"Dammit," I mutter as I toss my phone onto the bed. My fingers go straight through my long, beach waves, but stop mid length when the doorbell rings.

My brows drop over my eyes as I wonder who it could be. Diesel's out for the night and Trenton would definitely just let himself in. Roger's not even a consideration. And it's nine P.M. I can't imagine who'd be at the door right now.

I jog down the steps and straight to the door without checking through the peephole. For a split second I almost hope it's a mass murderer who's polite enough to knock on the door before taking me out of my misery.

I swing the door open without even a second thought, and Chloe's staring me in the face. I haven't seen her since before it was announced that she was pregnant. My eyes fall down to the bloat-like bump that's only enhanced by the tight, pink shirt she's wearing.

"Mrs. Cooper. I need to talk to you about Diesel." And then she breaks down like the snap of a finger. Her face constricts as fat tears run from her eyes like she was holding it all in until she made it to my doorstep. "I really need to talk to you."

"Aubree, what are you doing here? Roger's out with some friends, I'm sure you knew that."

"Mrs. Cooper…" I sighed, twisting a bunch of my fingers in my other palm. I was nauseas and didn't know if it were because I was about to tell her something she didn't want to hear, or if it was solely because I was pregnant.

She stared at me, her eyes examining me as I fought to force words out of the dry well that was my throat. "Aubree."

"Can I come in?"

Her brows bunched, but she let me inside. Walking fast ahead of me like she wanted to make whatever this was quick.

It was never a secret that she disliked me. She seemed not to like anyone who was interested her son. I didn't get it at the time, but now I know it's just because she never deemed anyone acceptable enough to have him. Her standards were so high for that boy, and me, a pregnant fourteen year old girl, I had no chance at changing her mind.

I sat down at the sofa in the living room I'd been in only once before. The living room where this all began and ended. Only a few months before, the Cooper's were out of town for the weekend. A couples retreat or something. Who knew if that was even the truth? Roger would say anything to get a moment alone with the girl he was fixated on for the moment.

She returned to me with iced tea. I thanked her, but I didn't want to touch it because I was scared that as soon as it went down my throat, it'd shoot right back up and splash all over her carpet along with my lunch.

"So, you're here to discuss your options." She crossed both her arms and legs. "I'm assuming you came to your senses—let me grab my check book." She stood up from her seat, but I let out a breath that made her sit back down.

Camille Cooper wanted my baby gone. She wanted it gone from the moment we told her. She hoped to groom me into wanting it gone too, but my parents were so different from Roger's. I came from a caring family who all huddled up and cried when I told them, but held me and told me everything would be okay. That the decision was ultimately mine, but if I kept it, they would be with me through the entire thing. And I believed them, because they were my parents. I knew they meant that.

Mrs. Cooper stared at me with dark, beady eyes. Her skin was leathery from years of tanning bed use—and probably all those tropical vacations—but she still kept up the habit. Her hair was thin, but she thickened it with extensions that were a shade off from her natural light brown. I may have been biased because of her snarky attitude toward me from the start, but she wasn't a pretty woman. She tried to be. Mounds of make up that got caught in the aging lines in her face wasn't enough to mask her attitude. She was thin, but unnaturally so for her age. Her skin was loose, fragmented, especially in her face. Crows feet she desperately tried to keep filled with injectables. She was a mess.

"I have and I'm keeping it," I spoke.

Her face hardened and her spine straightened, I felt threatened, but not much more than I did initially. "You're a fool. You don't know what's best for you, Aubree, but I promise you, my son and this child are not it."

I took another breath, choosing to ignore that. "I was hoping to speak to Roger first to tell him that this is my decision, but he's been ignoring me. That's the only reason I came here."

"Well, do you blame him?" She inched forward, her eyes jumping around on my face like I make her as sick as I feel. "You've trapped him. Girls like you have always thrown themselves all over my boy, but you know why he doesn't settle with any of you? Because he knows he can do better. So much better."

I stared down at the ground, the lump in my throat hardening and swelling up to the size of a golf ball.

"And now you have to get married." She crosses her arms and my eyes widen twice their size because of the word. "Our business is our legacy. It was built on morals and family values and we aren't changing a damn thing just because you two children are having a baby out of wedlock. You'll have to act like this was all intentional. That you weren't just his one night of recklessness. Are you ready to put on a show for the next eighteen years, Aubree?" She spoke at me, but I knew she didn't want me to answer her. "Roger isn't going to be happy. He won't be happy at all." Her head drifts toward the open window. "But I hope you are. You wanted him that badly, you opened your legs and tricked him into impregnating you." She huffs out a dry laugh. "I hope you're happy that you got him. That's all you wanted, isn't it?"

I pulled Chloe inside and she sobbed all the way to the living room. I sat her down on the couch before I poured her a glass of cold water while she searched for the will to stop crying, which took about ten minutes.

And I know exactly how she feels, without her even saying a word. I see the fear and the anxiety. The regret, the uncertainty. I went through it all.

"What's going on, Chloe?"

"I don't think Diesel is going to be around for the baby."

I clasp my hands loosely over my knees, leaning toward her. "No, no. Why would you think that?"

"Because he was really drunk and he told me..." she pauses as she shudders from incoming tears, "that I'm better off without him. That the baby is better off without him. That he can't do any of this and doesn't want to."

"When did he say that Chloe? Where is he?"

"About an hour ago, he left my house before I came over. I think he went out with some friends. That's how the argument started. He wanted to go out and I asked him to stay with me because I've been so sick and just wanted him there."

"Don't worry. Diesel isn't abandoning you or this baby as long as I have anything to do with it." I place my hand on her forearm and she grasps mine tightly in her palm. "I'm here for both of you."

She nods, dropping her head to choke out another sob. But the idea of my son out drunk and upset makes my stomach spin.

I leave her to continue crying on my couch and grab my phone.

After listening to Diesel's straight-to-voicemail greeting twice, I cave and call the one person I'm sure he's with.

Trenton.

FOURTEEN

Trenton

IT'S BEEN A WILD MONTH. I'VE GOTTEN QUITE A FEW WICKED cases of blue balls from all the alone time I've had with Aubree, but it's all worth it because in just a few weeks my fantasies will finally come to life.

In order to keep the suspicion down to a minimum, I've spent more time away, meaning after school I head to work and then home instead of straight to the Cooper house like I had been for the past ten years. Diesel's too wrapped up in Chloe to notice, but I've honestly missed all the time I used to spend at their house. My room at home is small, bleak. The house is quiet besides Joselyn's television constantly playing marathons of teen mom—as if we all don't get enough of that around here. My mom's always coming or going. Unless she's going to bed or cooking, I only see her in her scrubs these days, but she seems happier now that I've been home more, even if it's just a little bit.

Diesel: *Come to Gio's.*

I squint from the brightness of the screen. It's fucking nine o' clock at night and we have school tomorrow morning. Now, that never used to be an issue for me. But it's like ever since I've turned eighteen and can now see the light at the end of the tunnel, I've lost interest in that. Maybe it's just the fact that the void I had has finally been filled, but I couldn't care less about partying straight through the night. It's not worth the risk of being expelled from school for showing up hungover.

Me: nah. It's late. Catch you guys on the weekend.

Diesel: Stop being a fucking lame ass.
Diesel: Come on, fucker.

I roll my eyes, taking in a breath as I stare up at the popcorn ceiling right above my bed.

Me: Can't man.

Diesel: I miss you bro. Please.

I frown at my phone, sitting up. "He's fucking shit faced," I mutter.

There are two things Diesel would never tell me unless he were drunk: I miss you or I love you. And that's not only exclusive to me, he won't even say the words to his parents unless he's had too much to drink.

Me: Fine. Don't go anywhere. I'm coming.

I call a Lyft and get down there in less than fifteen minutes. All the way from the driveway, I can hear his voice belting out as I get out of the car and I know this night is going to suck. I'm going to be out late as hell, dragging this idiot home—or trying to. Aubree's going to be pissed, but fuck, best case scenario is me sleeping in her bed tonight with my face buried in her tits.

Diesel's shouting slurred obscenities and all the usual suspects are here cheering him on with their drunken laughter as I come through

Gio's back gate.

And to think, this was once my idea of a fun night. I'd sit here with these guys, one of us would get crazy and break something, Gio's mom would run out, screaming at us in both Spanish and broken English until she realized Gio's dad was out here drinking with us. Sometimes Diesel would start fist fights because he's such an asshole when he's drunk and I'm just easy to trigger. It's a wonder how we're all still friends. And alive.

"Finally!" Diesel spots me, taking another big swig from a bottle of clear liquid.

"Dees, what the fuck, dude. You're fucking gone."

"Yeah I am. Gone from that bitch Chloe's house." He sets his heavy, clammy hand on my shoulder. "And I'm not going back. Fuck her. She thinks she can break me? Nope."

The guys laugh, but I don't find it funny at all. He shouldn't be here right now. He shouldn't be talking about her like that. He should be owning up to his actions, not drowning his liver in straight vodka.

I take the bottle from him and he stumbles into me.

"Fuck." I shake my head, holding him up. I keep my voice hushed to avoid the rest of the guys hearing me. "That's it, you're done. We're going home."

He stands up straight, still swaying until he knocks his fists into my shoulders in an attempt to shove me. "Fuck you, I'm not going anywhere."

"You're going home, Diesel."

"Hey, let's play would you rather!" he shouts, rotating back to get the group involved. There's about five guys I don't know sitting around a table with Gio and the rest are a few that I sit with during lunch at school. "I've got a good one!"

"Stop, Diesel—"

"Trenton, who would you rather fuck? My mom, or my fucking mom?"

I grit my teeth. "Shut the fuck up."

"What? It isn't funny anymore? A couple of weeks ago you

thought it was the funniest thing ever, what changed?"

"Lets go." I grab him by his elbow, but he shoves away.

"Is this your attempt at being my step dad, bro?" He tilts his head at me, smiling and looking at me through slitted lids. "You're never going to be my dad, Trenton. No matter how much you want to be, or say you'll be. Is that what you're here to do? To bring me back to my mom, hoping you'll get a pat on the head for doing a good thing? You're so fucking desperate for her attention, it's almost sad."

Desperate?

"You're talking out of your ass." My hand grasps him by the back of his shirt, knowing he's seconds from falling over and hitting his head on something.

The guys have gone quiet, watching us like we're acting out a play. Honestly, probably waiting on Diesel to get violent like he usually does when he's hit this point.

I notice a few new faces. People I don't know, people I'm not even sure Diesel knows. He more than likely doesn't, and I don't trust them. The way they're looking at me makes me feel like they know more about me than I'd like them to. That's just more reason for me to get both of us out of here.

"That makes two of us, eh?"

"Shut the fuck up and give me the keys," I rasp, my face tensing because he's only pissing me off now.

My phone's vibrating in my pocket, but the way Diesel's swaying in my grip has my hands full and keeps me from answering it.

"I'm not leaving, Trent. Just get the fuck out of here if you're gonna be a buzzkill."

I reach for his pocket to grab his keys, but he musters up some kind of coordination to shove me. Just as sudden as his hands jet into me, reflex drives me to slam him against the wall of the house and snatch the keys off of him.

"We're fucking going!" I shout with no remorse.

He and I are staring at each other in a way we never have. There is suddenly a layer of hatred that's never been there before. His eyes are boring into me, glossy, but menacing in a way that isn't like him.

"Fuck off, Trenton! Leave me alone!"

Metal chair legs grind the pavement behind me. "Hey, T, why don't you just chill and have a drink with us?"

I hear Gio's voice, I hear his steps as he moves closer to me, but I can't break the glare Diesel and I have on each other.

I always wondered if we'd remain friends into adulthood. I always wondered how things would end up with him still being in high school a year after I graduate. With me being a year older than him, from a different background and upbringing. I always knew Diesel was different from me, but for a short while we were the same. Two kids who felt neglected by the people we craved acceptance from the most.

But at some point, you've gotta grow up. You've gotta let all that go and just accept the cards you've been dealt.

I don't know who the fuck I'm looking at right now. It's Diesel, but it's not. *He's drunk, Trenton. This isn't him. Just take him home.*

"Because I came to get him," I say.

Another chair grates the ground and a new voice speaks. "He clearly doesn't want to leave, so maybe you should just take yourself home."

That did it. That got me to disconnect from Diesel. I turn my back to him to see who decided to speak up.

"And who the fuck are you?"

I'm staring at a pale faced kid who looks a lot more familiar up close, but I still can't place my finger on it. He doesn't matter enough for me to know him by name or remember where I'd seen him. My eyes land on the hoop piercing he has in his nose and I almost hope we do fight so I can snatch it out.

We take a few steps toward each other until we're almost chest to chest. He angles his head at me and it's instant hate. I don't even know this guy, but I know I don't like him and I don't want him around my friend.

"Who the fuck are you?" He sputters. "You're the one who came here fucking up the vibe."

"You should stay out of shit that has nothing to do with you."

"Alright, let's calm down." Gio stands beside us. "It's getting a little too serious. Go have a seat, Manny."

Gio sets his hand on Manny's shoulder, but neither of us move. I'm pissed, and if this guy makes any sudden moves, I'm striking him in his fucking face. The muscle that flexes when his jaw clicks at me, I'm aiming there.

"You want to take Dees, then take him," Gio tells me. "He's fucked up, you're right."

I shift my eyes onto Gio and nod just as he releases Manny from his grip.

I take a step back, Diesel's keys still firm in my hand, when a laugh bubbles up from the guy's throat.

"Fucking pussy." Manny spat out the words, arms spread out at his sides with a sickening smile on his face that screams *knock me the fuck out*.

My fist clenches around the bunch of keys, stabbing the inside of my hand, but I barely feel it when my knuckles collide with the side of his face.

One hit was all I needed to knock him down. But I didn't stop there, the keys flew out of my hand at some point, but I got several more hits in before I was thrown on my back, and not by Manny.

A blunt pain shot through my side as soon as my back hit the pavement. I rocked in an attempt to get up, until it happened again, knocking the wind out of me this time. I curled up, gasping for air as I took another hit on the other side and the pain prompted me to open my eyes only long enough to see the four legs swinging at me on both sides.

FIFTEEN

Aubree

TRENTON DIDN'T ANSWER ME OR EVEN RETURN MY CALLS. CHLOE left an hour ago, I assured her I'd handle everything and that put her enough at ease to leave. She hugged me for the first time before walking out the door, and that was one good thing to come out of this.

After glancing at the clock above the oven, both hands on twelve, I go to reach for my phone again when the front door opens.

I walk past the wall to see Diesel hanging from Trenton's shoulder, but my jaw drops when I see how battered Trenton is. His eyebrow is split, blood crystallized before it'd ran straight down his cheek. The blood vessels in his left eye have burst and the skin around it is bruised.

My hand covers my mouth as I rush to help him set Diesel down at the dining table.

"What the hell happened? Where were you two?"

Diesel collapses on the tabletop, face down, and I sigh into my hands.

"He was at Gio's." Trenton brushes past me and straight to the fridge, holding his side, but his obvious anger masks the pain he's in.

I watch him guzzle a cold water bottle before leaning his back to the counter, staring blankly at the sink in front of him.

"Who did this to you?" I reach for him, placing his hot face in my hands.

He doesn't answer me. He doesn't look at me. His chest is still rising and falling in a way that indicates he's still coming down from an adrenaline rush.

"Trenton," I say, hoping to snap him out of the fury trance he's in.

His eyes lift to mine and he softens in my palms.

I gently lift up his shirt by the bottom hem and expose the deep v on his lower abdomen, raising it up until I can see the spot he's had covered by his hand all this time.

I sigh at the tender bruise that takes up a pancake sized patch over his ribs.

"I'm alright," he says softly. My eyes veer up to him to witness his smile. The smile that's only ever been for me. The one that plays with his eyes and displays my clear reflection in his widened pupils.

After making Trenton a sandwich bag icepack, coaxing Diesel into drinking a glass of water, and then into his bed, I return to Trenton who's standing silently against the hallway wall just outside the door.

He snags me by my waist, grunting from the pain of his movements, but that doesn't change the look on his face or the fact that I'm right up against his bruise.

His forehead presses to mine.

"What happened?" I ask against his lips.

"I got my ass kicked," he whispers, "but to be fair, I was jumped. You should still see the other guys."

I pull back to look at him, my motherly concern toward Trenton coming out to play for the first time in weeks. "Poor baby," I whisper back.

The corner of his lips rise as his hands lower. "I'm okay. Diesel was being a fucking dick, but I brought him back to you. That's all I was trying to do."

He stares down at me, his face busted, holding me through the pain he's feeling and I am completely enamored by him. He is slowly piercing his way into my heart and it both hurts and feels so, so good.

In a sudden rush, our lips connect and he lifts me into his arms. A subtle groan leaves him as I wrap my legs around his waist, but he carries me up the flight of stairs anyway. Suddenly he seems like he never got into a bloody fight at all, whisking me up to my room like I'm light as a feather.

"I've gotta have you, Aubree," he breathes in my mouth before our lips seal together again. "I can't fucking wait anymore."

He hovers over me, feathering kisses down my neck and sliding down my robe so that my collar bone is exposed before kissing me there, making my breath catch in my throat.

He begins biting and sucking on my neck and filling me with a sensation I'm finding so hard to fight away, but the realization sweeps over me like a dust storm. I can't let this passion turn into visual evidence. A hickey appearing on my neck when Roger hasn't been home in weeks will be obvious to everyone.

I gently nudge him and he instantly stops, aggressively rolling onto his back and making the mattress bounce beside me.

"I'm sorry, Trenton. We can't."

"Will we ever? Or are we just going to keep making out forever?"

"We really shouldn't even be doing that." I return the slick fabric over my shoulders as common sense wrings my wrists.

"Is that what you want? After I've spent the past three weeks with my tongue down your throat, you want to stop?"

"Well—we can't keep doing this. We shouldn't be doing any of it. My son, your best friend, is right down stairs."

"So, what then? The whole graduation thing was bullshit? You've just been leading me on this whole time?"

I frown, sitting up from the harshness in his voice. He's got his arms crossed over his face, but I can see his jaw and it's tight like he's trying to hide how upset he is, but failing to do so.

"I haven't been leading you on." I crawl closer to him, sitting on my knees.

He raises his arms up so I can see his eyes staring up at me.

"Then what? You were down with everything a week ago and now you're clearly changing your mind again." His brows bunch. "Makes me wish I wasn't so damn *desperate for you.*"

His accusatory tone is hard to miss.

"Desperate? Who said anything about that?"

"I mean, isn't that what I am? Just this desperate idiot who fucking begs for your attention?"

I shake my head. "No. I've never thought you were desperate, Trenton."

"Then why do I have to beg you? I know you, Aubree. You wouldn't have let things go this far if you didn't want them to. You don't say things you don't mean. You go back on them after they're said, but you mean them."

I roll my tongue between my lips, gathering a taste of what's left of him on the moist skin. "You know this isn't easy for me, but I'm still doing it. I'm still spending time with you, I still want…you." *But I shouldn't.*

"Why?" He sits up on his elbows, wincing as he does. "Why do you want me?"

"I don't know. Can that just be good enough for now? The fact that I do want you and that I'm admitting it?"

"Then you're keeping your promise?"

"When have I ever broken one with you?"

He swallows, his eyes running down me like a bad habit. "What's going to happen to us after graduation?"

"You said it'd only be once, Trenton," I remind him.

He huffs, looking remorseful. "Yeah, I did say that, didn't I?"

I cross my arms loosely in my lap, watching him run a million thoughts through his head.

"But that was before I spent time with you, Aubree. That was before I even thought any of this could really be possible. I'm getting…attached to you." *Attached.* There's something about the way he says the word that seems to make it unfit for that sentence.

I purse my lips, my eyes falling from him because I can't stand to see this look on his face. Trenton always means everything he says and I can hear the sincerity in his voice.

"Trenton…"

"No, Aubree. Stop trying to talk your way around everything. Let's be real for once. How do you feel about me?"

"I care about you more than you'll ever know. You are such a special and important person to me and the family—"

"How are you going to say that after we've done all that we did? Like I'm just another fucking cousin to you?" He groans as he pushes himself up to a stand. His intense eyes drill into me while he drags his hand over his chin. "I need you to tell me right now if I'm wasting my time with this."

"Wasting your time? What do you expect to happen?"

"I don't know, maybe I don't want it to be a one time thing anymore. Maybe I want it to be a long term thing…Maybe I want to be with you." He speaks like he's only just realizing this for the first time in front of me. "Yeah. I want to be with you. I want you to leave Roger, and be with me." He nods, taking a breath.

"Roger's my husband, I'm married. I'm thirty two years old—"

"I don't give a fuck about your age." He shakes his head, dismissively. "And you hate your husband, you hate your marriage, but you like me. You want me."

I stand up like the bed is on fire. "You don't know anything about my marriage!"

"Enough to know your marriage is shit."

"You are so out of line!"

"Only thing out of line here is me and you. Us. Things are different between us, there's something there now. Something real and I know I'm not the only one who sees it."

There is something there, something I don't want to acknowledge. Something that's easier to brush off as nothing so that once this is all done, we can resume life as normal. But I forgot how persistent Trenton is. I forgot how bold and resolute he is with anything he's passionate about. I forgot to remember that he'd never let this go if this was something he wanted. He claims he's wanted me forever and if that's true, he's not planning on letting me go.

"It's...lust. That's all it is." I shake my head, crossing my arms over my chest.

"Maybe." He shrugs considerably. "But if it isn't—say, it's possible I actually just know what I want—would I be wasting my time if I went after you?"

I see him gulp as I sit in contemplation. The fact that I even have to think of an answer to this scares me deeply. The position I've put myself in scares me *deeply*, and I can see that he feels the exact same way by the look in his eyes.

He isn't supposed to want more than a night with me. I'm not supposed to want to give him more than that, either. But this can't be more than that. We can't be more than that.

"Yes."

SIXTEEN

Trenton

SHE CHASED ME ALL THE WAY DOWN TO THE FRONT DOOR THAT night, but she didn't go any further. God forbid any one of her nosey ass neighbors hear her screaming my name in the middle of the night.

I walked home in the complete dark. In the dead of the night. During the most dangerous time of night to be caught alone, but I was so depressed and defeated, I didn't care. I'd been beaten both inside and out and the physical pain was the only thing that could combat the ache in my chest. But not quite.

That was brutal.

Even though my body healed since then, my heart was still raw.

It hurt for her. I've never wanted anyone as badly as I want her, I've never even wanted her as badly as I want her now. I made a big mistake making moves on a woman I knew would never cross the bridge that separates us, but damn was it worth the try.

It was worth me being the fool who thought for a split second that I could change her mind.

I've screened all of Diesel's calls since that night. It's been a couple weeks, but everything's still fresh in my mind. I got tired of being so *desperate*. I can't be that person, and for her I'm the most hopeless person to exist.

"You girls look so beautiful." Mom gushed behind the lens of her camera. She's the only person I know who still buys the disposable cameras with the blindingly bright flash that need to be rewound after every shot.

This is the first time I've seen her smile like this in a while. She still has those tired eyes, but her smile enriches her face.

Joselyn, Jessica, and Marina are all standing against the beige wall of the living room, arms linked as they pose for pictures. They all have similar styled mauve dresses that flow down to their feet. Sparkly jewels halo their necks and the crowns of their heads. There's more makeup than I've ever seen on my sister, but she really does look pretty. It almost makes me sad to see her look so grown up.

I'm standing beside Mom, the corners of my mouth risen as I snap some shots on Jessica's phone. It's a nice distraction from what's been spinning around in my head the past two weeks.

Marina did ask me about going to prom with her—as did a few more girls at school—but she just about melted when I told her I gave my sister my opportunity and couldn't afford to go anymore. It was obviously a lie since I do have a stable job, but I'd rather lie on the ground while Gio's new asshole friends pummel me again than go to prom.

Not that I'm against the idea of going with her, it's just that those types of events just aren't my thing. Sending my sister in my place was better for everyone.

If I'd gone, it would've been with some guys who'd surely smuggle in alcohol. I would've been drunk alongside them when we all got caught with it. That would have been a for sure expulsion, weeks before graduation.

Speaking of, I don't know if I even care about graduation anymore. The warehouse I work for doesn't even require me to have a diploma. Besides that, my main incentive feels like it may have been zapped right out of my hands. Aubree hasn't dared to contact me since I left her house that night, which lets me know everything I was beginning to assume was true.

She doesn't feel the way I do at all. She wouldn't keep backing down every time things got intense. Every time she got close to giving in before her mind was ready.

But I know she's scared. Terrified. And I try to understand because I know she's dealing with a lot, but it's hard because I know like the drop of a hat, she could just back away from me completely.

"Wait, one more. One more." I smile holding the phone square in front of me. "Try to keep your eyes open this time, Jos."

Joselyn scowls at me before they all smile. Both their eyes and teeth sparkle as the flash beams at them.

Jessica thanks me as I hand her back her phone and she begins flipping through the pictures with my sister. Marina walks up to me and it's clearly back to square one with this girl. The shy smile, the timid stance. I wonder if she regrets that night we had the way I regret every night I've had with Aubree.

"Trenton…" she smiles without showing her teeth.

"Marina. You look stunning tonight." I return the smile to her, watching her cheeks blush. "Keep my sister out of trouble, please."

"I will."

I scratch my head as I realize I've caught my sister's attention with the last of my words.

"What do you mean? I'm not the one who goes to parties and gets into fist fights."

I narrow my eyes at her. She doesn't know the half of it, so I won't bother rising up at her. I know she's just trying to be snippy to get on my nerves.

It's just her job as my little sister.

"You should be going with us," she adds. "This is your prom and you're missing out on it."

"I'm living vicariously through you," I say, dully. I don't give a fuck about prom or anything that has to do with high school unless it's me running the fuck out of there on May seventeenth in a cap and gown.

A horn honks outside and the three girls exchange gleeful looks with each other. They're kind of adorable.

116

I'm glad I could do this for my sister. Someone in this house should be excited about life.

"That's the guys," says Jessica, not looking up from her phone.

"The…guys?" I scowl.

Joselyn scoffs, wrapping her hand around Jessica's wrist. "Yes, we have dates."

"Um, no one said anything about dates, Jos. You said you were all going together."

She opens the front door, grimacing. "Whoops!"

"No one said there'd be guys!" I go after them as they all slip out the door.

"Trenton, she's fine," Mom says behind me.

From the door step, I watch them all run off in their heels to the car parked at the curb. I can't see any faces inside, but I don't have a good feeling about her getting in the car with *guys*.

I slide my tongue over my teeth as they veer into the street.

Diesel: *Are you really still mad at me?*

Diesel: *I don't know what I said. I can't remember anything that happened that night, but based on what Gio told me I'm sorry.*

Diesel: *you know I didn't mean it.*

Diesel: *So please just talk to me. Come by the house or something. We can do whatever you want.*

I draw in a breath and release it just as slowly as the screen goes black before I push my phone back into my pocket.

SEVENTEEN

Aubree

OUT OF SIGHT, OUT OF MIND. *Out of sight. Out of mind.*

More like out of sight, now I'm out of my mind.

Two weeks ago when Trenton stormed out of here like the Tri-State tornado, he awakened a feeling in me that I didn't know was still there. Roger didn't disturb me in that way anymore. Whenever he stomped out of the house, I let him and even though it bothered me, it didn't hurt me. But watching Trenton rush down my stairs, clenching his side after dragging my boy home to me because he knew that's what I'd want, it tortured my insides like I'd run toward an oncoming truck until it struck me.

I still feel it. Knowing he's so upset with me that he hasn't been to the house or even spoken to Diesel, it makes me sick to my stomach.

Last night I squeezed in some Solana time that I desperately needed. She's got her own things going on so we hadn't seen each other in a while and it was nice to catch up. I got her up to date on everything, to which she responded simply and with hardly any instance of surprise over the fact, "Please just fuck him already." Of course she backed up her claim with a valid and convincing argument on why I should, and I confessed how good Trenton was making me feel. How he was making up for what was lacking in my life, and now I just want to make things right.

I hurt him so badly, I tore away his hope—but I had to. I can't promise him something like that. Something that can't happen.

"Nah, it's cool, Dees." Trenton's voice is faint and hearing him somewhere nearby makes me clutch the edge of the kitchen sink. "Just remember I got my ass kicked because of you."

"I know, I owe you for that," says Diesel. "I promise."

My eyes search for him and I see him pass by the kitchen window as the two of them enter the back yard.

I need to talk to him. I need to tell him I'm sorry—something that can make this right. Normal. I don't know.

But it may be too late to be able to make things right, or to even pretend like we didn't end up here. Knowing the texture of each others lips, the tastes of our tongues. The feeling of his kisses on my bare skin, and mine on his.

Ugh, we can't go back. Not even if we wanted to.

And I don't want to. All I want is to see him. To touch him. To be next to him.

I hear the glass open and Diesel passes the kitchen as he goes toward the hall. Leaving Trenton outside by himself.

I toss the soapy sponge on top of the dishes and rush through the kitchen. Through the sliding glass, our eyes link as soon as he's in my sight. Sitting right in my line of vision at the backyard table, an unlit cigarette placed in between his lips, and I wish it were me.

The doorknob jingles viciously and I stop, dead in my tracks when the door opens up beside me and the big, hulking man of my nightmares tosses his briefcase and pulls me into his chest.

"I'm back, baby. Things make sense. I'm going to do right," he whispers in my ear, but my eyes are still on Trenton. He's risen from his seat, lips parted in shock and an intensity in his eyes that looks a lot like the last night I'd seen him.

I shut my eyes because I can't handle it. I can't physically ingest his heartbroken stare anymore. He shouldn't have that look in his eyes. He shouldn't be so jealous any time Roger touches me. Roger's my husband and Trenton's just a boy.

A loud crash from outside prompts me to open my eyes again. The table's on its side and Trenton's hands are in his hair like he's just lost himself to a fit of rage.

"I'm sorry." He mouths to me. "Fuck."

Diesel appears beside us, standing there until Roger opens his arm for him and pulls him into our embrace.

"I'm sorry, Diesel. I'm sorry I was gone so long, but I'm not leaving you like that again. You have my word."

I feel both of their arms tightening around me and it's just enough to take the sting off my chest. Can this work? Can we be the family I've desperately been trying to stitch to life all these years? Can Roger be both a husband and a father? Can we be…normal?

"We're going to figure this all out," Roger says. "I promise."

I shut my eyes hard as the tears flood in. I'm a mix of a hundred emotions, all bubbling up at once. I want to fall to my knees, I want to beg Roger to leave, but also kiss him for saying those words. I want to tell Diesel we don't need him, but also tell him I'm glad he's come back for us. I want to tell Trenton I'm sorry. That this is what we need, but that he's all I want.

He's all I need.

But I can't possibly do that when the front of my shirt is wet by Diesel's tears and the only reason we're all still hugging is because he wouldn't dare show the world his emotions. My boy likes to pretend he's made of steel, but really he's a walking dart board. He takes all these hits and lets it all build up, and now he's finally letting go.

Who am I to get in the way of him and his father? Especially if Roger means what he says, and I think he may.

I stare out the window, the sheer curtain clinging to the back of my hand. The boys are out back. It's dark now, but the glow coming up from the pool lights them enough that I can see two figures sitting at the table. Diesel's mood has completely flipped since Roger's come home, and so has Trenton's. He's just zoned out and Diesel's reverted back to his normal, chatty self.

Happy, maybe.

I'm supposed to be happy. My husband's returned with a clear head, speaking sensibly. Here with a plan to save our family, and I don't even know if I want it anymore.

My mind is so preoccupied with this boy who should be out of bounds to me, but I can't stop thinking about him. Yet, I pushed him away—but for all the right reasons.

Roger's hand glides around the front of my stomach, slipping underneath my robe and stimulating my skin with his warmth.

"Do you hear me?" He kisses my cheek. "I said I'd never leave you." He grabs me by my hips and spins me to face him. "You should know that, baby."

"I don't know anything anymore."

"Well I'm telling you. You don't ever have to worry about me leaving either of you." He drops his head, massaging my sides with his big hands. "I don't know what's been going on with me lately—stress over this new position, probably—but I'm sorry. I realize I've said some things that I didn't really mean—"

"It all sounded like things you really meant. Things you wouldn't have just threw into the air unless they'd been fermented in your mind."

"It wasn't. I don't regret you, Aubree. Really."

I turn my head away only to be caught in his fingertips and brought back to look at him.

"Listen. I don't regret you, sweetie. I love you. I love you and Diesel so much."

Maybe, but are you in love with me? I stare up at him with the question in my eyes, but his answer isn't in his.

My lip trembles and I see his eyes cushion instead. "Then why don't you act like it? Why don't you talk to our son? Why don't you talk to me?" I sob. "Diesel thinks you took this position because you don't want to be here, and I'm starting to think the same thing."

He shakes his head before gently guiding me to his lips, kissing me sweetly. My face heats under his breath, cooling the rush of tears that are leaving me in mass amounts.

"I'm sorry. I'm sorry. I'm sorry."

Grateful to hear those words, I sling my arms around his neck. His hands are so big it feels like he's covering my whole back with just his palms.

My eyes jet onto the bed, reminiscing on the two instances Trenton was in it beside me. One night he spent holding me and making me laugh, and the other making me feel like a terrible person for wringing his heart dry.

He can't mean that, can he? That he wants me to leave Roger for him? He's just a teen boy in lust. He doesn't know what he wants. Does he?

In an instant of me being focused on my inner thoughts, I didn't notice my sash untie until Roger pulled back to drop my robe from my shoulders.

I let it fall on the ground, my eyes flying to his to see his response to me. Tonight I wore my new favorite maroon set, it's embellished in satin ribbon and the color makes my skin look more cocoa than usual.

Roger looks me over once, but doesn't say a word. He never does. I got into the habit of wearing sexy underwear underneath my robe whenever I knew Roger was going to be home because I never knew when he'd be in the mood for sex, but I was always in the mood to try to seduce him. Until now.

Now that I see the difference between being cherished and not.

Roger doesn't admire me even a fraction of the way Trenton did when he saw just a piece of me.

Roger walks me to the bed, laying me down as he removes his shirt. I watch him unbuckle his belt, completely unfazed by him. It's strange. I always thought Roger was the sexiest man I ever laid my eyes on, but now I'm so null to him.

His hands are rough in a sandpaper way and it doesn't help that his movements are anything but graceful. He moves quick like he can't wait to be inside me, lifting my hips like he's hoisting up a heavy wheelbarrow as he pulls my panties off.

I hear the seam pop and know he's ripped them—that should be hot, but instead I'm just mad because this was my favorite set.

I gasp as he drives himself into me and I realize I am no where near as wet as I should have been for a thrust like that, but I take it anyway, running my hands up the length of his arms in an attempt to enjoy this—because I should. This is what I've wanted for months now. Intimacy. He hasn't touched me in so long, I should be in pure bliss.

But I'm not.

He lowers to kiss me and I shut my eyes as his tongue barges into my mouth, despite me not being quite ready for that either. I'm still trying to get into it, and in trying I think back to the night I was underneath Trenton in this very spot. He fought himself through hard breaths to keep his hands from roaming me the way he wanted to. He did only what I let him, but then there were the few small moments where he lost control of himself and his hand cupped my breast and gently squeezed, or his groin grazed the soft spot between my legs, showing me how hard he was for me.

I'm drenched just thinking about it, my nails digging into Roger's back as I lift my hips to match his every movement.

Roger breathes in my ear and I imagine Trenton's subtle groans of desire, letting me know how badly he wants me. His desperate tongue tasting every corner of my mouth in an attempt to satisfy the deep thirst he has for me and all the while I wish that tongue were between my legs.

"Oh my God!" I gasped as I came harder than I ever have before.

Roger growls, picking up his speed while I quake beneath him, coming down from the intensity. My face flushes and my entire body feels warm as I imagine Trenton's soft, pillowy lips kissing me gently on mine one last time before I have to return to reality.

My eyes open to Roger's reddened, blotchy face as he violently arrives at his climax. He's sweaty and radiating a suffocating amount of heat. As soon as he's done, I roll off the bed and head straight for the shower.

EIGHTEEN

Trenton

DIESEL KNOCKED OUT SOON AFTER WE SMOKED. I KNEW HE
would, I was counting on it.

The moment Roger came in, I lost it. Right when I thought she
might have been coming to talk to me—right when I thought maybe
I meant more to her than she claimed—he comes through the door,
ruining things like he always does.

I'm pissed, and what makes it worse is that I don't even have a
right to be. Sitting on the third step on the stair case, I stare down at
my phone before my fingers fly across my keyboard.

Me: Come down stairs.

Aubree: No, are you kidding? Roger's home now, Trenton.
Aubree: We can't do this tonight.

Me: Come downstairs, now.
Me: Please.

I waited in the den, my knee bobbing in front of me serves as an
outlet for my anger. I've never hated anyone before, but with Roger I
come pretty close. I just don't get how someone so vile can manage
to keep someone like her. Aubree is sweet and loyal—or she was until

I came in and corrupted her. But you can't corrupt something that doesn't want to be corrupted, not even a little bit.

She came downstairs in loose pajama shorts and a tank top that I really wish I'd see more of around here instead of that damn cover-all robe.

The double doors shut behind her, but she doesn't sit down. She stands in front of me, arms crossed and clearly antsy enough to run back upstairs without warning. "What?"

My nostrils flare and I bite down hard on my jaw. What does she mean what? Like I didn't just listen to her moan for fifteen minutes while that asshole drove his fake apology into her.

"What was that about?" I speak in a hard tone, but still manage to keep my voice down.

"What are you talking about?"

"I saw the way you ran to the door when he got here. You're just going to forgive him after all that? After the way he treated both you and Diesel like dirt?"

"I wasn't running to the door, Trenton. It was just bad timing."

I cross my arms, my heel bouncing quicker. "I heard you up there. You fucked him."

"Are you really mad at me for having sex with my husband?" She sits down, finally.

"Yeah because he doesn't deserve to. He doesn't deserve a fucking thing from you, Aubree." I scoop my hair back with my hands and sit with my back flat to the couch.

"Would it make you feel better to know I thought of you the whole time?"

My eyes taper at her. "Bullshit."

"I did." She stares down at her hands, almost ashamed but not quite. "I imagined he was you the entire time. I felt you. I felt, us. It was amazing."

The tension leaves my face and I stare her over, noticing how her nipples have made themselves known through the thin grey top she's wearing. And as if her physical composure, her rosy cheeks, her glossy, licked lips and her hazy eyes that are locked on me aren't proof enough, I say, "Prove it."

"How?"

I widen my legs and pat my thigh, an invitation for her to sit on my lap. I don't even care that he just had his filthy hands on her, soon enough I'll wash it all away with my cum. I'll mark her in bites and hickeys, I'll mark her in me.

"I can't. You know I can't."

"Then I don't fucking believe you, Aubree. It's hearsay. Convince me that I'll make you sound just like that when it's my cock you're bouncing on."

"Trust me."

"With my life. Just tell me how it went." I swallow. "In your head. What did we do?"

She stares at me as the beginning of a smile leaves its traces on her face. Her hair frames her cheeks and a few strands fall over her eye as her head tips to the side.

I want to know every detail. I want her to map out every touch, every movement, every moan, and every beg. I've imagined it countless times in my head, but somehow it seems so much better coming from hers.

"Am I not worth the wait?"

"Of course. Fuck." It's no question. I wouldn't still be in this, torturing myself by hanging onto the thread of hope she leaves me with.

I reach for her face, my fingers gliding along her soft skin. Her eyes flutter shut and I bite my lip as the pads of my fingers trace the space just above her chin.

"Then you'll hold off until your graduation night. Just a few more days." She crawls toward me and I'm paralyzed by the sight of her on her hands and knees, her bedroom eyes penetrating me, lust radiating off of her in enchanting waves. "The real thing will be so much better."

I'm fucking convinced.

And then her lips crush mine and I can't control myself anymore. My hands go straight to her tits and her tongue burrows into my mouth, making me lose my breath for a second.

She grabs my hands, removing me from her and her absence from my grip is almost painful. "Goodnight."

NINETEEN

Aubree

TODAY IS THE DAY.

The day I promised Trenton would happen. The day he's waited on for who knows how long. The day he's begged for, that he's practically guilted me into, and I couldn't be more nervous.

I didn't think I'd be nervous, it doesn't even make sense that I am. He's the one who *should* be nervous, but he's so filled with elation over the fact. He's been smiling all day long, prominent pep in his step like he can't wait for the ceremony to be over with so he can claim me in every way he's ever desired to.

And that's what I want. I want Trenton to do whatever he wants to me. No more boundaries. If we're doing this, we're doing it right. If I'm cheating on my asshole husband, it's going to be worth it.

One and done, then I can go back to repairing my family.

He's a teenage boy. Once we do this, he'll be over me and onto the next girl. I'm fine with that as long as my life returns to normal and none of this comes back to haunt me.

"Trenton Laguna," says a man in a black cap and gown into the microphone in his hand.

Down below us, the crowd roars so loudly for him, I laugh at the unexpectedness of it. Seeing how many people love him and are cheering on for him and how happy he looks. I think I'm…proud of him.

From where we're standing, Trenton looks like an ant, but his personality is huge. He runs up on stage as a mass of students and now graduates begin chanting his name. He smiles for pictures and my heart palpitates.

How is it that this all has worked out perfectly? That Roger's been called back to New York and he leaves right after this ceremony?

Diesel and Chloe have been getting along flawlessly since he and Roger finally sat and had a three hour heart to heart conversation about fatherhood and his experience through it all. For the first time in a long time, Roger treated him like a son, guiding him through something he knew about all too well. I saw the ease in Diesel's eyes the moment after they'd finished talking and it gave the entire house some relief.

He most likely won't be home tonight and Trenton's smiling that hard because he knows it. He knows neither of them will be and he knows as soon as the festivities are all over with, he's going straight to my house to lay me down and cash in on my debt.

"Life begins now, Trenton," Roger tells him as he shakes his hand. Trenton's still got that happy smirk on his face, despite his obvious hatred for Roger. It gives me anxiety. "No one's going to give you a slap on the wrist anymore. No one's going to give you second and third and forth chances. I know these school's baby you kids, brainwash you into thinking the world's fair, but it's not. It's every man for himself. Remember that when you're out in the real world."

"Yes sir." Trenton nods and Roger whacks him on the back, but in a friendly way.

"And, listen, I'm sorry I can't make the party, but I left Aubree in charge of your gift. She won't disappoint, don't worry."

I place my palm on my cheek as Trenton's face brightens. *Dim it down some, idiot.*

"Thank you, Mr. Cooper. I know she won't."

Roger stares out at the parking lot, his hand over his forehead like a sun visor, like he's looking for a sign of where he parked his car. Trenton uses the moment his eyes are away as an opportunity to wink at me, bouncing on the balls of his toes and looking like a million kinds of adorable.

I'm so sick.

My eyes widen at him as if to say *cut it out* and I feel like I'm scolding a young kid again.

A thin layer of regret cloaks me as Roger brings his attention to me. He kisses me on my lips and says, "I'm leaving now, but I'll be back next Friday. I promise."

I nod, my hands held over his on my arms.

None of that matters. That he's leaving, that he won't be back for a whole week, his promise. I just don't care.

"I love you," he says softly. And that doesn't matter either.

I blink, finding it slightly hard to breathe. Trenton's watching us from the corner of my eye, and it's getting to me.

Why does he have to be so adamant? He's so clearly jealous, his flexing jaw during any type of affection that's made between us gives it away. I'm not even his and he's acting like he has a problem with every interaction I have with Roger. *My husband.*

"I love you," I say back. *But do I?* Can I love him when I'm planning on wrecking his favorite bed sheets with the teenage boy who's been plotting on having me since his hormones kick started six years ago?

I don't know.

I watch Roger say goodbye to Diesel, noting the happiness in that boy's eyes at the relief of his father finally being a father. Giving him his approval and attention. Loving him and befriending him. Diesel loves his dad, he loves our family when things are good—that's clear. Yet, here I am about to spit all over it in an attempt to get even with Roger for all the hurtful things he's said and done to me.

Trenton's frolicking around the big lot, taking photos with groups of girls in their caps and gowns. Their long shiny hair contrasts against the colorful leis around their necks. They hold balloons, and flowers, posing with their empty diploma cases while playing off the wobble from standing in high heels. He's hugging them, smiling down at them. Girls who look at him with nothing but desire in their eyes. Girls he should look at the same way. Girls his own age. A pinch of jealousy hits my stomach.

You can't have it all, Aubree.

I can't be disloyal to my family, and expect not get caught. I also can't have a one night fling with this boy and then get jealous when he moves on to girls in his age group, which I will. Which he will.

This whole thing is ridiculous and as much as I want it over with, I can't wait for it to happen.

I hadn't seen Martha since she told me off in my driveway that one Sunday morning. The feeling she had toward me clearly hasn't changed. She's still staring me down like a mad dog and I almost think it's because of my choice of outfit.

I wore a dress to Trenton's ceremony. Form fitting, solid maroon with thin straps. I've always had a rule. If my husband didn't have a problem with me wearing it, it had to be appropriate. Roger rarely told me I looked distasteful, in fact, he picked out the majority of my clothing, so now I'm thinking it may actually be due to the fact that she sees the way her son looks at me. She pays enough attention to notice.

Over the years, Martha's turned into this overbearing mother. She's all over him, wiping his face, brushing down strands of his hair, adjusting his collar. And he obviously hates it by the way he's always wriggling away from her, telling her to stop and the familiar grumbled, "I'm fine, Mom."

And maybe in a way he feels like sex with me, an older woman, would be liberating. That it would make him feel like the man he so gravely wants to be.

Martha put together a nice graduation party in their back yard.

There's a big tree out back that provides a good amount of shade, but the house is also open to us too. The front room is decorated with a big *Congratulations Trenton* banner and a cutely decorated box for cards placed beside his portrait.

I waltz over to the big, framed senior photo of him and admire his handsome face with a blue envelope in my hands.

"See something you like, Mrs. C?" Trenton says, his cup to his lips as he appears by my side.

My throat knots. "Oh, so we're back to Mrs. C?"

"It's just a formality." He shrugs, his eyes so still on mine I almost forget to breathe. I don't know how an eighteen year old boy can have this affect on me, but it's a sore reminder of how deeply sunken I am. "And it's kinda hot."

I gulp, breaking eye contact with him to remind myself why I came this way in the first place. It was to put this card in the box for him.

Roger told me to gift him five hundred dollars, which I'm still surprised about. I know he's a little indifferent over Trenton, but that's an awfully generous gift to give to someone you aren't crazy about.

Since he's here next to me I may as well just hand it over.

"Well...congrats, Trenton." I hand him the blue envelope before hugging him. "You know we're all so proud of you."

I feel his hands slowly drop to my lower back, his fingertips only grazing the very curve of my ass and making me swallow hard to keep from focusing on the hard bulge pressing into my stomach. *Is he going to be hard all day? Can he be?*

And then in my ear he whispers, "Thanks for the card, but hearing you moan *congrats* with my tongue between your fucking legs tonight would have sufficed."

He lets me go, his smug smile adding to the sudden rush of wetness between my thighs. He winks at me again and it's all over. I'm putty in this boys hands and I've never been so grateful, or so turned on.

"You look fucking stunning, by the way." He lifts his cup and I watch him go back out to the back yard, completely stunned by his confidence.

He makes me feel so small, yet so important. So wanted.

But I, myself, am so confused. I'm empty, like I've created a new void that needs to be filled. And he's the only one who can fill it.

Trenton

Graduation day. The one day every senior in high school waits on. The day they all claim will be the best day of their young lives. The day *life begins*, according to Roger. And for me, that's exactly what it is and more.

It's the day that changes everything.

I can sense Aubree's nervous and I love it. I love that I affect her that way, it means she actually fucking cares what I think. If I can recall correctly, she's *self conscious* because she wants me to like her back. And the way she stared at me like her knees were going to give out after I hinted to her what tonight would entail is making me ten times harder than I'm comfortable being around all my friends and family—I don't want to be hard around any of them, but whatever. It's worth it to walk around a little stiff when that one's around.

I saunter over to Diesel and Gio, but not without noticing the weird change on Diesel's face. Chloe probably texted him something to piss him off.

Yeah, that's what he looks like. Pissed off.

"Your pockets are gonna be so fat, dude," says Gio. "You've probably got over a thousand dollars in that box. When my sister graduated, we counted out about two grand."

"Who?"

Gio has five sisters and I never know who he's talking about because he never calls them by name. I'm not sure he even knows who he's talking about sometimes.

"Genesis. She didn't have a lot of friends, but we have a lot of relatives so she still cleaned up. I'm expecting to double that when it's my turn."

I shrug, looking back Aubree's way as she comes out the house. My mom's been staring her down all night and it's pissing me off. I just hope she doesn't try to get bold and say anything to her. I never know what's going on in her head these days.

It's probably her appearance. She snags everyone's eyes whenever she passes them, walking so gracefully in heels. I can't help but to check her out again for the hundredth time. That fucking dress she's got on is phenomenal. I wonder if she wore it purposely. I want to believe she did.

Diesel socks me in my side before standing in front of me. "Stop, fucker."

"Stop what?" I frown at him. "What the fuck are you talking about?"

"You know what I'm talking about."

I wrinkle my chin and shift my eyes from him. Obviously I know exactly what he's talking about, but damn, I didn't know I was getting sloppy. I usually time it to where it's not obvious that I'm gawking, but maybe I got a little greedy that time.

"You, fucking staring at my mom like that. Stop."

"I'm not staring at her, Dees. You're tripping." I lift my cup to take a drink, but he pushes me all the way inside the house and shuts the glass door behind us before I can even reach my lips.

"I'm serious, man." He stares me in the eye and I wrinkle my chin again in an attempt to convince him I'm still oblivious to what he's getting at.

"I'm not even looking at her."

"I saw you talking to her a minute ago. What were you telling her when you two were in here?"

"Nothing—I just thanked her for the card."

Diesel stares at me like he wants to believe me but isn't convinced. I guess I have had my guard down today, but it's hard to pretend I'm not fucking ecstatic about tonight.

"Well, don't hug her like that—and you know what I'm talking about. Watch your damn hands."

I finally take the sip he prevented me from having when he shoved me in here, wondering how long he's noticed. Knowing him, it only just hit him. If he'd noticed sooner he would have confronted me then. He doesn't play around when it comes to Aubree, but neither do I.

TWENTY

Aubree

Trenton: *8:00*

THAT WAS THE TIME WE AGREED ON HOURS AGO WHEN I LEFT THE party. Except now, I'm standing in the kitchen listening to Diesel and Chloe's giggles in my living room, serving as a sign that they're not leaving anytime soon.

There's no way I'm going through with this while Diesel's home. I'm already having second thoughts, teetering the fine line between going back on it or proceeding only because I've already ventured way deep into forbidden territory. I may as well follow through.

I don't think I really have much of a choice now. Trenton's had his heart set on tonight for two months. I'd be terrible to go back on it now.

Me: *They're still here. I have a feeling Chloe's going to stay the night.*

Trenton: *Well, tell her she has to leave. You're the parent here.*

I hang my head. This is ridiculous.

Me: *It's too late for all that. She's already pregnant with my son's baby.*

Trenton: *So what? That was her decision. Kick them both out.*

Trenton: kidding. Throw on Legally Blonde for Chloe and make Diesel some warm milk. He's easy to put out that way.

I chuckle just as Diesel enters the kitchen, but straighten my face up quick.

"Is that Dad?" he asks, coming toward me with a plate of crumbs. I lock my phone screen and place it over my chest in case Trenton texts me again.

"Yeah."

"You guys are doing good." He says it more like a question that he wants me to elaborate on. This is the first time Diesel's ever shown any interest in our relationship—my perspective on it, at least.

"Yeah, we are." I smile at him, my throat knotting. "I'm almost wondering what's happened that made him come back a whole different person."

He faintly smiles back at me, but doesn't respond. Instead, rinses the plate and places it in the right side of the sink before leaving me there.

That's a start to something, I guess.

I peel my phone from my chest and unlock the screen.

Trenton: I'll be there in five.

My breath catches in my throat and I suddenly feel a little bit faint, like every last drop of blood has drained from my body. Five minutes. *Five.*

Except, what I assumed was five minutes is in fact five seconds because the front door opens, making my heart do cartwheels in my chest.

I can't tell if I'm excited or just nervous. Everything we're about to do is all kinds of wrong, but that's not stopping either of us.

I find myself fixing my hair without a mirror in the middle of the kitchen. Adjusting the front of my dress, pressing my lips together to smooth out my lipstick. Primping for an eighteen year old? I've clearly lost my mind.

Trenton pokes his head in the kitchen. "Hey, Mrs. C." Sounding lax, his deep voice makes my face flush and heat up and I know I'm bright red.

"Hi." I breathe out my words, realizing I've completely reverted to my teenage self. He gives me his coy smile before tapping the wall like it'll be my ass later and disappears.

Solana: *Turn on your photogenic memory. I'm gonna need details. *thumbs up emoji**
Solana: *Proud of you.*

I panic for a few more minutes, shaming myself over the countertop while I listen to them chat in the living room until another text rolls in.

Trenton: *Change into your robe and put on something pretty underneath.*

My breath catches in my throat as I clutch my phone to my chest and do as I'm told. I've never been more excited to choose a piece of lingerie before, but I had one in mind. A special set that I didn't even want to wear for Roger because I knew his grizzly hands would tear it to shreds.

After I changed, I took my time heading back downstairs, and I think Trenton heard me come down because he quickly changed the subject upon my arrival in the kitchen.

"Hey, so what was the plan tonight?" he asks them. "I mean, you guys were staying in, right?"

There's a moment of silence and I'm sure Diesel and Chloe are probably blankly staring at each other because neither of them have thought it through. They do a lot of that.

"Mm, I don't know. We're probably gonna go stay at my house for the night," Chloe answers, and I purse my lips to suppress the stupid smile that comes over me.

"Nah, I think I'll stay here." Diesel coughs. "I mean, it's your grad night, man. We can hang in the pool house—I'll call Gio to bring some drinks over."

"Ah, I mean—yeah." Trenton hums. "We could, but I already partied a lot today. I'm a little tired. Probably end up crashing soon."

"Well, since we're leaving, we'll take you home then."

Me: *Let him take you home, I'll pick you up.*

The obvious option to avoid them being suspicious of him being so adamant about sleeping over without Diesel. *Check your phone, Trent.*

"Uhh…well I just got here," he answers.

Idiot. My forehead rests in my palm.

"Well, what are you going to do here by yourself?"

"What I normally do. Watch tv, enjoy not being at home with my dictator mom."

I let go of the breath I was holding. *Nice save.*

"Alright, just stay out of my stash," Diesel warns him. "If anything's missing—"

"I know, I'm not messing with any of your shit. Don't worry."

I impulsively pop open a fresh bottle of wine and pour myself a glass. This is really happening.

It's really happening, and it's totally fine because Trenton is now officially an adult who's graduated from high school. I keep telling myself that in order to rid him of any similarities to my son. That's all that's keeping me in the game.

"See you later, Mom," Diesel says with his cheek against the wall. He waves a hand at me and Chloe comes in to view.

"Bye, Mrs. Cooper." She smiles, arms outreached. This pregnancy is really softening her up and I like it.

I set my glass down before giving her a hug. "You're off to Chloes' then?"

"Yeah, I'll be back later on tomorrow," answers Diesel.

I nod, the corners of my mouth upturned. "Drive safe."

I follow them to the door, and the feeling that surges through me as I turn the top and bottom locks is nothing compared to the intense tingles that fill my lower abdomen when Trenton's hands slide around from behind me.

My breath draws in as he begins kissing me on my neck, pulling my hips back so that he's pressing against me as he grows in excitement.

He spins me around so that my back is to the door and pins me there, holding my hands gently above my head as he finally brings his lips to mine.

"He hasn't even pulled out yet." I laugh in between us. "We're going to get caught."

"I don't care." His desire lies beneath his smile, shining through like a spotlight and it makes me weak. "We've got all night, but that doesn't mean I'm trying to waste any of it."

I place my hands underneath his shirt to feel his bare skin for the first time. To really feel him. He's warm, smooth, and his abs are solid.

"Where are we doing this?" He gently bites my neck and my eyes drift closed before his tongue teases the spot.

"Here," I breathe, "anywhere. I don't care." The idea must excite him because he lifts me off my feet and my legs wind around his waist. My robe opens up outside my thighs almost completely. No turning back now.

"No, I have a better idea."

He carries me up the steps again and I'm not sure how we made it all the way up with our eyes closed, kissing fervidly like two nymphomaniacs, but we did.

The door opens, but I don't open my eyes until I land on a cold, hard surface that's sleek under my fingertips.

We're in Roger's office.

"No, Trenton." I look around, realizing I haven't been in here in a long time. Years. I've never before had a reason to come in, and

Roger made it clear long ago that he'd prefer it if we all stayed out, so I've always steered clear from the room.

He nudges my knees further apart and slides me into him, so close that the satin hikes up my hips. I can explicitly feel his hard bulge through the thin layer of panties I'm wearing and my head becomes about as fuzzy as it does when I've had a long, drunken night out with Solana.

"This is where I've always imagined it."

"In Roger's office? Really?" My eyes project in an effort to get him to realize how risky this is, but he clearly doesn't care. His mind is made up and apparently it has been for a long time now.

"I promise, you won't regret it."

I drop my gaze from his mesmerizing brown eyes to follow his hands as they return to my hips, tugging the sash so that it's untied. I slide onto my feet to allow him to completely peel the smooth cloth off of me, and once it's fallen to the ground, he steps back.

His head subtly dips back, his eyes half mast as he looks me over. "You're just, perfect. You're so, so perfect. Holy fuck."

I let a small smile appear, but I'm too turned on to let this get cute, and apparently so is he. He doesn't let another second go by without his hands on me in some way and after running them along my bare skin, he drops me back down on the flat surface and lowers to his knees.

"What are you doing?" I ask as he removes his shirt from his body. My fluids collect in my panties as I scan him over, loving this angle of him beneath me. Loving the way his eyes lower and how he looks at me through his lashes. He's literally everything.

"Shh." He kisses my inner thigh. "I know what I'm doing."

Things virgin teenage boys have never said.

He slips my panties off like he's got all the time in the world. Like he suddenly doesn't want to rush this like he seemed to before.

He bites his lip, his hands escalating the length of my thighs, teasingly. Getting so close, but never touching the most sensitive spots. "You made a big mistake, Aubree."

"How's that?"

He opens my folds with two fingers and I whimper from his touch. He's licking his lips as he stares at my slick, wet sex like he's completely adorn by what he's seeing.

"Because…I'm going to be so in love with you after this. I can already tell."

Things all teenage boys have said.

I roll my eyes, and they stay fixed up at the ceiling when I feel his soft lips on my clit. He kisses it a few times and the gentle sucks make me clench the edge of the desk.

I feel his tongue widen over it before sliding over the bundle of nerves, back and forth in the most perfect rhythm. I lower my eyes to watch him, eating me like a pro. Like he knows just what I like, but I guess it helps that I'm wiggling against him every time his tongue strokes me just right. "Oh my god," I sigh, my chest drawing in as our eyes align.

"Fuck, you taste so good, Aubree." His voice makes me shudder in a way I haven't in years.

My lips part and a desperate mewl leaves me as I reach for the back of his head.

I gasp, my fingers coursing through his hair. "You're going to make me come…"

His thick locks between my fingers anchor him there, reminding me that *he's* there. That Trenton is the one behind the intense pleasure I'm feeling and the thought both makes me more excited and slightly repulsed. I'm conflicted, but I manage to push back the morals that are trying to ruin this for me.

He pulls back for a second and smiles so beautifully, it gives me butterflies, goosebumps, heart palpitations. All of it.

"That's the point, Mrs. C."

I'd roll my eyes and even address the fact that he called me Mrs. C. while in this position, but the absence of his tongue on me is almost painful, all I care about is putting it back and riding his face until the moment my senses aren't so cloudy.

His arms are weaved around my legs, hands gripping my ass and squeezing harder every time I moan. I set my hands behind me, my head falls back and I rock my hips up and down controlling each stroke of his tongue, but he only allows it briefly before he pins my legs down and regains control. Sucking me in pulsating rhythms and torturing me like he knows I'm on the edge.

I whimper, desperately pushing him away. I don't want it to stop yet, I've never come this fast and I'm not ready, but he holds me down like I've got no choice but to let him finish me.

"Oh…Trent, oh my—" My hips buck when he brings me to a trembling orgasm, my thighs tightening around his neck as he keeps my arms glued down on the desk.

He rises to a stand, wiping my glistening arousal from his chin. I'm still trembling as he firmly grabs me by the back of my neck, as if to let me know he's in control of tonight, and we come into a kiss. But this is so much more than any other time we've kissed. This is so passionate and sensual. I taste myself on his lips, my body tingles all over, my sensitivity is at an all time high and I shiver from his touch. His thumb slips underneath the lacy bra I've worn for him and brushes over my nipple, making my toes curl as the second wind of pleasure comes over me.

"You picked this for me?" He pushes his finger underneath the band and slides it smooth across my chest, feeling the bare skin underneath.

I nod, suddenly shy like some bashful fifteen year old girl.

"I love it." He kisses me and I feel validated. "But I want it off." He reaches behind me without breaking our lips apart to unhook my bra, and he does it so swiftly, I'm almost certain he lied about his lack of experience. I couldn't care less in this moment, I just want him inside of me.

"You're gonna drive me fucking insane." He leans down to kiss my breast, feathering down to my nipple where he bites me, then sucks the sting away. "I'll come in like one second."

"That's okay," I persist. "We have all night, remember?"

Who am I? Solana?

In a frenzy, I rush to unbuckle his belt. I drag his pants down, the buckle clinks when it makes contact with the ground, and just as quickly his boxers are down with them, revealing his thick, impressive cock.

Not at all what I was expecting, considering Roger was nothing like this at his age. Not even half the size.

He takes it in his hand, holding it proudly as my eyes take it in.

"Fucking hell, Trent," I breathe, staring at all of its veiny masculinity in shock. "You're definitely not a baby anymore."

He bites his lip in delight and I spread my legs for him, waiting on him to have me the way he claims he's always dreamed to.

By my chin, he tilts my face toward the sky before lowering to kiss me. His thumb pulls my lip down as his tongue dives in and meets mine again. The sloppiest kiss I've ever had, but it's so hot I don't even care how dirty it feels. I need this. I need him.

He rubs the head of his cock over my slit, spreading the pre-cum that I'd watched drip down the tip as soon as he took it in his hand.

I never realized how hot it would be to be someone's first time, feeling how tense he is, listening to his shallow breaths. I'm certain he won't last long, at least not as long as I need him to.

With my hands placed on his chest, I step down from the desk, pushing him back until he's against the wall. Noting the way he didn't resist, I'd say he knew where this was going and didn't mind giving up control for a moment.

I lower to my knees, my mouth salivating when I'm in front of his thick member. He has a pretty cock. I don't think I've ever seen one so solid and symmetrical.

My lips press gently to the tip and his head rolls back, giving me view of his strong Adam's apple that bobs as he swallows.

After a moment of teasing him with long licks up the length of his shaft, he impatiently grips me by the back of the head and pulls me closer. I give in to his wants, taking him all in and he groans up until the last inch.

I bob my head back and forth, watching him breathe and let out the small moans that I can tell he's desperately tried to suppress escape him anyway.

"Shit, you're amazing," he says, looking down at me in admiration, his fingertips brushing down my cheek, to my chin. "Your lips are so pretty around my cock."

I eat up every compliment like I've been starved of them, because I have been. Trenton's got this way of making me feel so beautiful, so perfect. Like I could actually do nothing wrong and as much as I know that's a complete lie, I let myself believe it for a moment. All I want is for him to come down my throat so I can drink him down the same way I consume his words.

I place my hand at the base of him, matching the strokes with the motions of my mouth and it drives him wild. He gathers my hair back into a makeshift ponytail and breathes more raggedly, letting me know he's racing to his orgasm and it's only a matter of time before he explodes into my mouth.

"Don't stop, don't stop."

I wasn't planning on it. I meant what I said, I wanted to do everything tonight. I pull back, but don't stop stroking. "Come in my mouth."

He nods like that's all he has time to do before shoving my head back down and shooting his hot liquid down my throat with one last grunt that makes my juices run down my inner thighs.

"What. the. fuck." He sighs, grabbing me by my hands and helping me to a stand like a gentleman. "You trying to make me fall in love with you, or what?"

I shake my head with a small smile as he places his palm on my cheek, staring at me lovingly.

"You can't suck my dick like that and expect me not to."

Take those words with a grain of salt, Aubree.

He lifts me up and plops me back down on the desk like I weigh nothing.

"You trying to ruin Roger's desk, or what?"

"Don't say that name right now." He grins before kissing me, but I can tell he's hardly joking. Bringing him up just then wasn't really a good idea. It was actually distracting, until I realized he was already ready for more.

Our lips lock as he positions himself at my entrance, but he's not quite where he needs to be. Maybe he really is a virgin.

He slid the length of himself between my lips as I prepped the condom, meshing all of our fluids together as he kissed my neck. We were slippery and our flesh was sensitive and wanting, both of us just ready for what's next.

I could tell he was seconds from going for it raw, but I stopped him to slip the condom on as quickly as I could. I guide him where he needs to be, his fingers entwining in my hair at the back of my head. Our foreheads press together as he begins sliding himself into me. So slowly, so selfishly.

I gasp as my walls adjust to him, and in response he lets go of a desperate breath before briefly connecting our lips again.

"Oh fuck, Aubree."

He begins a slow pace, our breathing pairs and I swear our hearts are matching the same rhythm.

"Is this okay?" he asks me, looking into my eyes for approval.

I nod and then breathlessly, I say, "Faster."

I thought it'd be rougher, rushed and distant. I thought I'd feel like a sex toy, like one of those rubber torsos Solana and I laughed at during our last trip to the local sex shop. But his eyes are on mine, locked and daring me to break away from him…and I can't.

It's just so perfect, it's so intimate.

It isn't the raw fucking Solana swore I'd get when dealing with an eighteen year old. We're making love and I didn't realize how badly I needed it until now.

I feel him losing himself, his cock twitching inside of me, the look of restraint on his face, but he's losing.

And I find it so sexy that I can measure every ounce of desire he has for me. That he's worshipping my body, but also surrendering to it.

His hand slides around to the front of my neck, gently, but firmly grasping a hold of it as he places warm kisses on my lips, not stopping the swing of his hips as he rams into me. "You are the fucking girl of my dreams. I'll never find anyone like you."

I feel myself blush as a small whimper falls from my lips.

I've never been told a thing like that before, it made my heart swell, my clit throb, and strangely it turned me on ten fold and I clutched onto him, our chests pressing together with every thrust.

We fed off each others energies until we came together. *Together.* Our lips melded, our moans muffled, bodies hot and hypersensitive.

As we come down, I wrap my arms around him like it's a habit. Like I need to keep him from leaving me. It's not until a few seconds after that I realize he doesn't want to. He's not Roger. He's nothing like him.

Trenton makes small touches to my skin, caressing me gently, kissing me lightly, holding me back. Like we've forgotten that this was all about lust and spun it into something unintentionally sweet.

We've just bonded in a new way and I don't know how to feel about it. He lays his head on my chest and wraps his arms around me, stilled inside of me as I run my fingers through his hair.

I've never had someone look at me the way he does. Touch me the way he does. Cherish me the way he does.

This isn't just spiteful sex. This hasn't been just a long time crush he's had on me. I don't know what it is, but it's scary because it's unlike anything I've ever had with the man I married.

The two of us ended up on the floor of the office, I'd made a run to the shelf outside the door for warm blankets we could lie on before we went for round two and three—and five. I forgot how much stamina a boy his age has. Hell, I didn't know I had this much in me. Roger never, ever went this long.

It was strange, but I was sort of glad we did it in the office, a place I never step foot in. A place that stays shut. Any other place in this house would have been too distracting and I would have worried about how memorable it'd be for me later.

"I knew you weren't a virgin," I profess as he traces the curve of my hip. We lay face to face, our eyes in perfect line with each other and neither of us look away for longer than a few seconds.

The way the streetlights shine in through the horizontal blinds cause lines to stack over his face. He's breathtaking. I don't think things will go back to normal, I don't think they can after tonight.

"I was a virgin. I'd never lie to you." He speaks as softly as his fingers float over me.

"Then what the hell was that?" I chuckle. "I wasn't expecting any of that at all."

"I've eaten a lot of pussy, watched a lot of porn." He narrows his eyes at me. "Fantasized about how this would go so many times in my head. I just never wanted anyone to touch my dick—unless their name's Aubree Cooper."

"I can't believe you're telling me that." I roll onto my back, clutching the blanket over my more intimate parts because the free roam his eyes have on me is too much.

"I can't believe you actually let this happen."

I blow out a big breath. "Neither can I." My voice is so monotone, I look over at him to see if he caught it. His lips are pursed, but he doesn't address it and I'm glad. I don't want a repeat of the other night. Flinging *what if's* in the air like we even have any control over our future.

I speak mostly for myself.

I'm really just enjoying this. Laying together in silence, touching each other. His hands haven't left my skin in three hours.

"These little lines you have on your thighs," he says, trickling his fingers over my hip. "I like them."

"My stretch marks? That makes one of us. I fucking hate them."

I scoff, attempting to cover the brown stripes with my palm. "Thanks, Diesel."

I didn't have stretch marks until I got pregnant, and then after Diesel was born, they got worse. Darker. I've always been self conscious of them, probably because I've caught Roger staring at them like they're something to be disgusted with. Just thinking about that rids me of any guilt over lying nude on the floor of his office with another person. Another man.

Trenton pushes my hand out of the way and strokes my skin again. "They're sexy." He comes closer to me, wrapping his arms around me and I feel so comforted in his embrace. So accepted, so connected to someone for the first time. "Trust me."

"I do." I actually do.

I close my eyes, breathing out as he breathes in. Our stomachs moving together in back and forth motions. His skin warming mine.

He kisses the top of my head and I'm at a complete loss for words. We're naked, cuddling on the floor of Roger's office. And the goofy kid who always seemed to pester me for the heck of it turned out to be the sweetest, most gentle, and compassionate man. He's unapologetically handsome and my sexual attraction to him is beyond belief. Our sexual chemistry is beyond belief.

I almost don't want to let this go, but I have to.

We have to.

The wall behind him lights up from headlights shining through the blinds. That would only happen if someone pulled into the driveway.

"Fuck." His voice is sharp beside my ear.

We both jump up from the floor, scrambling for the blankets and I grab my bra and robe as he jumps back into his jeans.

He grabs me for a quick peck before we go our separate ways, which looks like me shutting myself in my room and him hopping down the stairs in twos. I'm plagued with that empty void once more, knowing that was the first and last time we'd ever have a night like that again.

TWENTY ONE

Trenton

I heard Diesel come in his room last night. I was there on the futon where I was expected to be.

My back faced the door in an attempt to pretend I was in a deep sleep and not slightly out of breath from jumping down the stairs.

Diesel's a lot like Roger in the way that he's a loud person whether mad or in a decent mood. But for him to leave Chloe's house in the middle of the night, I'd bet my life the two of them got into a fight over something stupid, now the honeymoon is over—but mine's just begun.

That didn't go anything like I'd always thought it would in my head.

It was so much better.

Her pussy was incredible, the head was incredible, sex was incredible—*ass, phenomenal.* But besides that, just laying there with her. Both of us bare, inside and out. Complete comfort.

Just us.

I wish we could have stayed that way longer.

I wish I could stay here to get a chance to talk to her, to test the waters and see how she's feeling about it—to see if she still wants it to remain a one time deal—but she hasn't left her room yet and I have to get ready for work.

My boss was ecstatic when I agreed to work full-time hours as soon as I graduated, and honestly I was too. I get a pay increase and a better schedule, four tens and then three days off. I've been saving up for a car and with one more check, I'll have what I need to finally make the down payment.

Everything's looking up for me.

I return to Diesel's room to change into a plain black tee shirt and jeans, glancing his way to see him facing the wall, snoring. I'll text him later to see what made him storm home last night.

"Sup, G." I head toward Gio and the rest of the group from our unit, standing where we usually do as we wait to clock in.

A few of them hold coffees, water bottles, or bags of chips from the vending machine—despite it being a little before six in the morning. *The breakfast of champions.*

"You ready for the first day of the rest of your life?" He asks me as we shake hands.

Most people hate this job. I hated it. The hard labor, the long hours. Repetitive movements, long periods of standing. Shit sucks, but the money doesn't, and it keeps me in shape. Who needs a gym when you're lifting hundred pound boxes all day long?

"I don't know about that, but I am ready to get that twenty dollar an hour pay."

"I know. Asshole."

"You'll get there next year." I shake his shoulder like I pity him and then realize I'm still beaming after the amazing night I had. The memories are so vivid and I can't get them off my mind. It's like I still feel her on my skin and even though I showered this morning, I swear I still smell traces of her scent.

"Hey, where'd you sleep last night, T?"

"Diesel's, why?"

"Mmm…" he tips his head side to side like he's thinking of a way to say this. "Dees texted me some weird shit last night."

My brow raises and I unscrew the lid of my water bottle, hearing it snap upon being opened for the first time. "Like what?" I bring the spout to my lips and tilt my head back.

"Like, he thinks you're trying to fuck his mom. Like for real."

My lips tense and the water spills out the sides of my mouth.

"What the fuck?" I drag my arm over my chin to wipe it dry.

Gio's bushy brows lift at me and he smirks like he doesn't believe me. Like he wouldn't be surprised if I was. "I mean, you do talk a lot of shit about how you would, so—"

"Yeah and that's all it is, shit talk. I wouldn't..." I scoff. "Come on, man."

"Alright, alright. Well..." He sucks up a breath before setting a hard hand on my shoulder. "You better set that straight with Dees, cause he's convinced otherwise."

I already knew he was suspicious yesterday when he caught me groping her a little bit, but I couldn't help myself. It was like dangling a piece of meat in front of a dog and then finally saying he could have it five fucking years later.

But I'm not worried about Diesel finding out. Aubree would never let that happen because unlike me, she's still able to think rationally when we're together.

Five hours into work and I'm beat. Usually by now I'd be going home—well, I'd be going to Diesel's because I'd be off shift after five hours. But nope, instead I'm on my lunch break only to do it all again in thirty minutes.

I leave the building to pick up my lunch from the delivery guy who's just messaged that he's arrived out front. After tipping the man and taking my bag, I head back in. On my way to the break room, I spot out a familiar face and have to do a double take.

Diesel's talking to my boss in the middle of the warehouse.

It's clear what he's doing here, but he didn't tell me he was thinking about working with us. I could have gotten him in. I offered time and time again, but it looks like someone else already did by the way my boss is pointing out the different departments to him.

I only watch them briefly before continuing on my way. I only get so long to eat and relax and since Diesel didn't think enough to tell me he'd applied to work at my job, I won't think too hard about acknowledging that he's here.

Aubree: *Hey. We need to talk.*

There it is. The dreaded text no man ever wants to receive, and I never fully understood why until now. When my stomach has turned completely upside down and I suddenly don't want to touch the rest of my tacos, tossing the one I'd just bitten back onto the styrofoam plate with a dry sigh.

Me: *Alright. I'll stop by after work.*

Aubree: *No, I'll meet you somewhere.*

Fuck. This sounds like all kinds of bad, all kinds of Aubree's regretting it, all kinds of she's come to her senses, and all kinds of Diesel's probably ruined fucking everything.

I blow out a breath, stretching my arms up above my head to keep from turning into a trembling idiot.

The rest of my day is me anxiously working with a pit in my stomach. I keep my earphones in in an attempt to drown out my thoughts with music. It doesn't work. Every thought in my head is clear. Nagging. Urgent.

Either we're completely caught, she's done with it all, or both. I can't handle either scenario.

My thumb shakes as I go to press it down on the pad for clock out, and as soon as I'm off the clock, I don't waste any time heading to the destination we agreed on.

Down the street from the warehouse, there's a six level parking garage that's meant to be for the hospital, but the top floor is always empty. Me and Diesel used to do illegal things up there around our fifteenth year of life.

I got there before she did, smoked a cigarette in the dark. Stood alone in the muggy heat that served as a reminder to me that it's the start of summer.

When her car rolls through the empty lot, my nerves splinter and I drop the cigarette at my feet, too bothered to even stomp it out.

She parks right beside me and I get into the passengers seat. I enter thick silence, thick tension. I can feel her regret and it's suffocating.

"Hi," her soft voice speaks, but she doesn't look at me. Her hands are still held on the steering wheel like she's afraid to move.

I drop my hand on my thigh, resulting in a soft thud. "Are you here to break up with me, or what?"

She finally turns to look at me. "We can't break up, we were never together."

I shrug, turning my gaze forward to stare out at the city. Mostly tree tops that are like dark, fuzzy blobs in the night, but the sky above them is a gradient of dark blues peppered by stars, and as a whole it's a nice view.

"I'm just here to tell you, Diesel and I had a conversation earlier that I never wanted to have with him."

"Great. How'd he find out?"

"I don't think he did, but he's suspicious. He explicitly told me he isn't comfortable with us being home alone together, so I wanted to make sure you understood that. I deleted all of our messages and I'm advising you to do the same."

"Advising me? What are you, my guidance counselor?"

She sighs. "I think the best way to transition out of this is for you to spend more time home, and only come by if Diesel's there. Maybe take out that girl that likes you." She shrugs. "Anything to keep this under wraps until it blows over."

"So that's it then?" I look at the side of her face. "We're just going to pretend none of the past two months ever happened?"

"You're the one who said it'd be a one time thing, and I truly think that's best for everyone, don't you?"

"I don't give a fuck about everyone, Aubree. I only care about me and you."

"There is no me and you, Trenton." She lets her head fall on the steering wheel, resting on her knuckles. "I knew I shouldn't have let this happen."

"No one let anything happen, it was bound to."

"No, no it wasn't." She draws her head back until it's against the headrest and crosses her arms like she does when she's arguing with Diesel.

"Let's be real. We've been attracted to each other for a while, it was *bound* to happen."

Her pretty, mauve lips protrude as she glides her tongue over her front teeth. She can't argue that. We've both been set on each other for a while now. I was just the one brave enough to push the envelope. If it were up to her, none of it would have ever happened, and she's looking at me right now like she wishes it never did.

"Well, it happened and now it's done, Trenton. I gave you what you wanted. I won't lie and say I didn't have a good time, because I did. You did. What more do you need?"

I grit my teeth to refrain from telling her that she didn't give me what I wanted at all.

What I wanted was her, all of her.

Always.

I just couldn't see it so clearly until now, when she's threatening to take that away from me.

"I don't know, but that wasn't enough."

"It has to be." She turns to look at me and as if to bluntly pound the words into me she says again, "It *has* to be."

"What if I love you?"

"Are you…is that what you're saying?"

I lick my lips, seeing the stagnant look on her face like she's holding her breath in the hopes that I'm not.

Don't worry, Aubree. I won't say it even if I am feeling it.

If I did, she'd knock down the idea as soon as I spoke it into existence, and there's no way I can let her crush me anymore than she already has today. "No. But…I could."

"Trenton…" She pauses, pinching the bridge of her nose. "You're young. You are so handsome, so funny, so—*everything*. You are the entire deal and more and you have so much life ahead of you, so much time to find a girl who wants everything you want, who is perfect in every way you want her to be. It won't be hard for you to fall in love with somebody else…anybody else."

"I don't want to love just anybody," my voice comes out hard and pained, burning the lining of my throat as I speak. "I just want to love you."

She snatches me by the jaw, my skin sizzling from the feel of her hands encasing my cheeks. And I shut my eyes as I melt under her gaze, even if it is filled with worry and hurt, I just love being near her.

"You do not mean that!" Her words are wrapped with ice, harsh and reprimanding. "You hear me? You don't know what you want, but I promise you I'm not it."

"I do," I choke. "I've known since the day I first saw you, Aubree. I knew it would be you and it would only ever be you."

"You didn't know anything." Her eyes begin to fog. "This can't happen, this can't go on. Do you get that?"

Her hands leave me and I feel like my face is marked by her palms. That's always how it feels after she's touched me, like I've been branded by her. And ever since the first time, I've only wanted to feel that sensation all over me.

Maybe now I never will.

My eyes are still on her, unmoving and hoping she will change her mind. Hoping there's one single ounce of requite in her, until she sighs into her hands.

This never happened in my head.

I watch her ride out the wave of regret I caused her as my chest tenses in pulses. Her hands tightly held around the steering wheel.

I regret it all too. Had I known I'd be sitting beside her as she told me it was all over with before it's even started, I'd have left her alone.

Maybe.

TWENTY TWO

Aubree

THINGS HAVE BEGAN DULLING DOWN AROUND HERE, BUT AFTER that conversation with Trenton last week, I'm still on edge.

He didn't take it well. He didn't want to take it at all. It actually felt like I *was* breaking up with him. I keep seeing the look on his face and the words that accompanied it.

That wasn't enough.

He was right, it wasn't. I didn't feel like I'd gotten enough of him either, but what I did get was still too much and I knew I shouldn't have any more.

Solana and I went out for mani-pedis this afternoon and I gave her the run down of it all.

"Well first and foremost, you blew him," she says, receiving a nosey stare from the woman stroking hot pink gel polish over her bare, stiletto shaped, acrylic nail. "That was your first mistake. Never give a fling a blow job, Aubree. Never." She scoffs as I watch my technician file and shape my ring finger. "You can't just give a guy award-winning head and then expect him to just suddenly respect your marriage and never want to see you again. Don't you know the key to a man's heart is at the back of your throat?"

"That's ridiculous, Sol."

"Is it really?" She turns to look at her technician who glances up at her through the bright light shining down on their hands. "Is it, Helen?"

Helen looks at me and gives me a quick head shake before

continuing the precise gel work she's highly concentrated on.

"Do you know how many teen girls give head, Aubree? Plenty. Know how many give good head? Close to none, and that's why he *loves* you." She raises her eyebrow like that's supposed to explain how I convinced a teenage boy he's in love with me. Or—excuse me— that he *could* love me. We all know what he meant. What he was thinking. Why do men always resort to that? They draw the L word when things go south like it's the wild card in a game of UNO.

"It's not your fault, though—rookie mistake." She shrugs, twirling her finished hand. "I don't blow a man unless I'm drunk or want him around for a while. I learned the hard way."

I blink to myself, turning my attention back to my hand as each nail is coated in white polish.

Roger's returning home today, so I already cleaned the house from top to bottom before I got my nails done. After leaving Solana, I did some grocery shopping to make sure both I and the house was to his liking.

He needs to be in as good of a mood as possible because tonight's a big night for Diesel. We're going out to dinner with Chloe's family to get acquainted and discuss the pregnancy with them for the first time. I think they want to be sure that we're all on the same page as far as their living situation and money is concerned, and I agree. We do need to discuss this all, because they clearly have no clue what they're doing or what they've gotten themselves into.

They have no idea what the road looks like ahead of them, and instead of being like Roger's parents who'd rather force the idea of termination than the idea of preparedness, or my parents who'd rather baby me, pat my head and say, "there, there," instead of making sure I fully understood the big changes both my mind and body were going to go through, we need to break it all down for them and make sure they have their best shot at this.

Standing in front of the vanity mirror, I watch my bedroom door open behind me.

Roger comes toward me with a smile. "Well, hello." His arms

wrap around from behind me as I continue putting in my earrings. "How'd I get so lucky, hm?"

We smile at each others reflections and he kisses my neck.

I narrow my eyes at him. "I ask myself the same thing all the time." Lucky isn't exactly the word I'd use. More like, how did I get, here. Period.

He spins me around to face him and gives me a soft kiss that does nothing for me but take a load of worry off my shoulders. If he'd come home grumpy, dinner would be a sure disaster. I may have even told Diesel to just reschedule instead of risking him hating Chloe's dad on the spot and trying to fist fight him in the parking lot of the restaurant.

But no, this should be a good night.

I settled for a slim skirt and a silk blouse buttoned low to show a little cleavage. I don't want to look too casual, but I also don't want to look old. Roger gave me a nod of approval after twirling me around in front of him.

I started on my makeup while he showered and we ended up ready to go at about the same time. We'll be meeting everyone at the restaurant.

Diesel's been staying over Chloe's a lot so I've been stuck at home alone and it took some serious will power not to send Trenton a text invitation to the house, and instead to do something productive, like read. I hadn't been reading much since Trenton began taking up my free time, and in order to get life back to what I consider normal, I spent a lot of time getting back into it. Only problem was, even that didn't take him off my mind. Instead, he became every male lead I read about and I swooned over him all over again. I'm a mess.

Roger guides me into the building, his hand on my lower back as he holds the entrance door open for me. I've never been a big fan of the Cheesecake Factory ever since the only dish I liked disappeared from the menu. Their low lighting is pretentious, the food is way over priced for what you get, and the tables are way too close together.

Diesel's already coming toward us, arm raised to grab our

attention.

Roger pats him on the back before setting his firm hand there as he greets him and we follow him across the room.

It doesn't occur to me that this dinner isn't just to get us parents acquainted with each other until we enter a banquet room with a huge table that's filled by not only Chloe's parents, but more than a handful of teenagers I hardly recognize without the cloud of marijuana smoke that's usually screening their faces.

And then my eyes lock on Trenton and I stumble over my step before Roger grasps me by my elbow.

"Careful, baby." He smiles at me.

I remove my gaze from Trenton before he can notice me. He's awfully absorbed in the conversation he's in.

Diesel walks us over to Chloe's parents who've risen to greet us. There's quite an age difference in comparison to me and Roger and I can tell it's caught them off guard, but they smile anyway. I feel like I can almost hear their thoughts, something like *teen pregnancy must run in the family*.

"Chloe's parents," says Diesel, blandly. His dry attempt at an introduction.

I give him a brief glare as Roger extends his hand to her father. He's got silvery blonde hair that looks strictly scissor cut based on what I've watched during my hair appointments. He almost looks like a doctor, the really friendly type that seem to reek of empathy. He's wearing a dressy, blue shirt that's tucked into his crisp black pants, radiating warmth and sincerity.

"Patrick Hanes, but call me Pat," he says. "And this is my wife, the lovely Victoria Hanes."

I shake both his hand and his wife's, noticing the way she's staring at me. Like she's trying not to show her immediate disproval, but it's clear as day to me. I know that look, I've seen it a million times. The older women in this city love to glare at me like they've just swatted me on the wrist with a ruler.

I've known women like her. I've hated women like her.

A designer bag clutched firmly by her hip, the contrasting sheen differences between her auburn extensions and her natural hair. Her unnaturally sharp nose and pinched lip. She's fighting for youth and losing.

"Roger and Aubree Cooper." Roger speaks sternly, his arm loosely around my shoulder.

"It's nice to finally meet you all," says Patrick, smile nonfading.

"Should have been sooner, but you two are quite hard to track down, according to Chloe," Victoria finally speaks. It's the exact kind of attitude I would expect from a woman who was more plastic than the Pacific Ocean.

"Hey, Roger what's your poison?" Patrick whisks Roger away with a firm hand on his shoulder like he knows his wife has a loose lip and is bound to piss someone off. "They've already taken drink orders, but I'd be happy to flag one of the staff down for you."

I follow them to the two empty seats in between Diesel and Patrick.

Roger answers him in a gruff mutter. Probably his typical dark-liquor guilty pleasure that he can't resist having on the rare occasion we're out to dinner, but I zone out when I notice how Marina's sitting next to Trenton, giggling at everything he says. I mean he is funny, but can she be more desperate? No wonder he's not interested. Men want what they can't have and she's so plainly available to him.

I glance down the row to say hello to Chloe who looks a bit bigger than she did the last time I'd seen her, but I'll blame the dress she's wearing and the fact that most times she comes around, she's wearing baggy t-shirts.

Trenton laughs and I look his way. He hasn't looked at me once tonight and it bothers me. He usually seeks me out and makes sure he says hello, but now it's like I'm invisible.

Has he thought about me at all? Has he gotten over me just that quickly?

And then he links hands with Marina and my heart feels like it's free fallen a hundred feet.

This is what I wanted, right? For him to move on with someone his own age and lead a normal life. But why does it feel so crippling? Why is my heart wrenching in my chest. Why is there a prick in my eye, and why am I having trouble looking away?

He gives her a quick kiss. When they part, I see her bright eyes staring up at him and I'm so envious and shocked my lips part.

"Mom?"

I look at Diesel, completely flustered as I return to reality. Roger's getting along with Patrick flawlessly, they sound like they're engaged in a conversation that involves many gestured hand movements, but I can't care enough to listen.

"You good?"

I nod, fighting myself to keep my eyes from bouncing back onto the couple down the table. "Yeah, just tired."

He stares at me, but doesn't respond.

"You didn't tell me friends would be here," I add, reaching for my water.

"Well, Chloe wanted to reveal the gender tonight, so we thought they should be here too."

The idea of putting a gender to this baby makes me smile and takes some of my attention off the new couple that are bothering me so much I'm actually ashamed of myself.

I place my fingertips over my lips and put my arm around him, my eyes water and I blink to keep back the tears.

"Don't cry, Mom," he warns, slightly smiling.

"I can't promise I won't."

Chloe reaches for my hand over his lap and we share a moment of excitement.

When the plates are served, the table quiets down a bit, with only a few instances of murmuring coming from between the kids down the row, but not much chit chat going on on our side besides Roger and Patrick's occasional sounds of agreement. I tried listening in on their conversation, but it was so boring they lost me in seconds. Stocks or something.

"So, Diesel," Patrick finally says. "Part of this meeting was to discuss with you and your family how you plan on providing for the baby." Patrick places his fist over his mouth as he clears his throat. "Just curious if you've thought that through yet?"

I'm quickly distracted as I notice Trenton mumbling something to Marina, staring at her like she's the apple of his eye. The exact way he'd spent the past two months looking at me—well, the past five years, technically. Such a damn flirt.

I bite my cheek as I drag my eyes away, but it's hard.

Why do I care what attention he gives to someone else? Someone he claimed he wasn't into weeks ago. I mean, we only had sex a few times, and that's all it was. Casual sex, nothing more. And he knew just as well as I did that it would never be anything more. I'm married, he's a young man who should be entering college and experimenting with all kinds of girls and things while he's there. He has no choice but to move on, the world would only force us to anyway.

I know this, I've told myself this time and time again, but the idea of him moving forward still upsets my stomach.

"I just got a job with PKG Logistics—a warehouse thing," says Diesel, bringing his glass of water to his lips.

I frown, my head snapping toward him. "You didn't tell me that."

"I just did."

I look to my right at Roger who looks pleasantly surprised about the news.

"When did you start?" I ask, my lip thinned as I try to keep myself from looking bothered.

"A couple of weeks ago."

"Great," Patrick chimes in. "And what's the pay rate?"

"Fifteen an hour, but I'll be working weekends and a couple days of the week after school, so I'll average twenty five hours a week."

Roger nods at him in approval, but I'm still set back by the fact that he didn't tell me before now. I'm tired of Diesel treating me like I'm some kind of stepparent or something. Like I don't matter enough to know things as they happen. I get why Roger is just finding out since he's hardly home, but even he could have received a text message announcing that Diesel had gotten a job.

I just feel like he purposely keeps me out of as much of his life as he can.

Marina giggles and I almost hurl my glass at them. I feel like I'm overstimulated. On one hand I'm worrying if Roger's going to snap and suddenly decide he hates everyone and everything, on another, I've got my son treating me like I'm no one, and on top of that, so is Trenton.

"Victoria and I have been talking," Patrick says in a more hushed voice, grabbing both Roger's and my attention, "and we agreed that we would prefer Chloe and Diesel have their own place when the baby comes."

Roger and I glance at each other. This was the first time either of us have thought about this issue. He's been gone too often for that to be a central focus in his mind and I've been busy romancing the teenage boy from hell. I hate teenage boys. Here he is, all over this girl only days after we had sex. I mean, at least wait a month before getting a girlfriend.

Says the hypocrite who's sitting next to her husband.

"Yes, that would be ideal, but there's no way he can afford a place while only working twenty five hours a week," Roger states.

"Right." Patrick nods. "But since he has a job—which is all I was really hoping for as of now—I am willing to cosign for him as long as he keeps the job and pays a good portion of the rent, handles the bills, we can negotiate it all later on."

I look at Diesel and he appears to be just as jazzed about that proposition as I figured he would.

"That would be awesome." He glances at Chloe and they share a chuckle as their fingers entwine. "Of course I'd keep the job, Mr. Hanes."

"Well, I don't doubt that," says Patrick, gesturing his hand to him as if to make that statement believable, "but, I'm leaving the decision up to your parents, respectively."

Roger and I turn face to face, looking at each other blankly. We've never been good at decision making—clearly—but my mind's already made. I just don't want to say what I think in front of everyone.

"We've got at least three months left to decide." Patrick's voice breaks Roger's stare with me, almost like he's just as aware as we are that we have differing opinions on the matter. "So take your time and get back to us."

Roger nods at him and based on the way he looked at me, I can tell it may end up being an argument between us tonight.

As everyone segregates into cliques, talking amongst everyone else, I sit in the middle of it all. Silently watching everything as it goes on around me. Roger and Patrick's animated conversation, Chloe and Diesel neck deep in pre-baby bliss—that facade of happiness that happens at some point during pregnancy—the few of their friends laughing at whatever's on each others phones, and then Trenton and Marina who've apparently used this outing as a date opportunity.

Diesel and Chloe stand up as the cake is brought out. They're going to slice into it and whatever color is beneath the frosting is the baby's gender.

The excitement brings a smile to my face as I watch the two of them, reaching for my phone to get some photos of them just seconds before we make this whole thing even more real than it felt before by assigning a gender. Next thing you know, they'll be deciding on names, I'll be guilty of online browsing for baby clothes, picturing his or her face in my head. I'm only thirty two and months away from becoming a grandmother. This is insane.

Diesel holds his hands over Chloe's as they sink the knife into the cake once and then again before pulling out a blue slice.

Roger sweeps his big hands into a loud clap. "Alright, a boy!"

The table cheers and I laugh into my hands. Victoria hasn't cracked a smile once, but maybe that's because her face will literally crack if she's overzealous.

I get up from my seat, as does Patrick, to hug and congratulate them. I hold Diesel's face in my hands and although I can tell I'm embarrassing him by the way he tries to wiggle away from me, his smile still holds.

"Congrats on creating your very own Diesel junior," Trenton says beside me and my whole body tenses.

I step back and they shake hands.

"Thanks, man."

I find myself desperately trying for his attention, my eyes beaming into his skin, hoping he feels me looking at him. Hoping he'll finally acknowledge me.

"Oh hey, Mrs. C." Trenton looks at me like he's just realizing I'm there.

"Hi, Trenton." I swallow, unsure what to do with my hands, but he doesn't let his eyes stay on me long before he turns his attention back to Diesel like he couldn't care less about me standing here. His eyes didn't graze over me once. He didn't smile. He didn't call me by my name. I feel like nothing to him.

Actually, no. I feel like the fourteen year old girl that's just realized she's been taken advantage of.

TWENTY THREE

Aubree

I GUESS I COULD SAY THINGS ARE NORMAL.

That everything's going just the way I hoped it would—better, actually. Trenton's done with me and I'm done with him. No if's, and's, or but's.

But I'm still not happy.

I never thought I'd be jealous of a teenage girl, but I am. I miss being that close to Trenton, having his eyes on me, my hand in his. He made me feel like the only woman on Earth, and now I just feel stupid for buying it all. *Didn't you learn your lesson the first time, Aubree?*

There was no special connection between us, I was just his coming of age conquest, the forbidden fruit, the *MILF*—as I've been referred to more times than I can count by Diesel's friends—and now I'm just back to being Mrs. C.

We're just leaving the Cheesecake Factory—Diesel and Roger's banter beside my ear has already gotten old and we've only been in the car for about five minutes. Diesel decided he'd come back with us since his father's in town and that seems to be the only time he ever does want to be home these days.

I ignored both of them and fled the steps as soon as we got inside. They couldn't care less. The rest of their night will consist of junk food, video games, and the never-ending round of *would you rather*. Roger never grew up, and now that Diesel's put himself in the same jam his father did at his age, I can only imagine he'll be a teen forever just like him.

I took a bubblebath with a bottle of wine. Old habits die hard.

This is the part where I pick through my lingerie drawer until I settle on a set that I think will finally blow Roger's mind, but truthfully I couldn't be more disinterested in sex—*with Roger.*

Only thing I'm interested in is what dirty read I'm curling up with in the den tonight and how many more glasses of wine I'll need to pass out there. I swear my tolerance is skyrocketing and soon I may have to permanently switch over to hard liquor.

I put on a pajama dress that looks like a long, striped t-shirt, and tied my damp hair up in a messy bun because no one's looked at me since we left the restaurant anyway. As I bounce down the stairs I hear that familiar crippling laugh that makes my ab muscles constrict like someone's brushed a feather over my stomach, and I almost backtrack. *No, I need that damn drink.*

And better yet, I'm not letting Trenton's presence stop me from doing what I wanted to do tonight: get drunk and horny all by myself.

I bypass the kitchen without even a glance at the men occupying my living room, and grab a fresh bottle from the wine rack that I just restocked this morning. He laughs again and I boycott the glass altogether in a rush to get away from him and his charming ways and lock myself in the den.

I picked up a new novel, taking a sip straight from the bottle as I stare at the digital first page. My blanket covers only my feet and I'm almost in the mood to put on a face mask to really kick this lonely party into full gear.

I sat there reading, so consumed in the story I didn't realize at what point the house had finally gone quiet. I glance up at the time and realize it's midnight. *Time flies when you're nursing your self esteem with alcohol and erotic literature.*

I see something move behind the crack between the double doors and shortly after, I hear the living room sliding glass open and I know exactly who it is.

A hasty decision is made during a long swig of wine, but I find myself stepping out on the warm cement, only to inhale a big puff of smoke.

I cough, waving my hand in front of my face and Trenton turns around to face me, sucking the end of what isn't a cigarette at all.

"You wanna hit this?"

I shook my head no, but for some reason I was still intrigued. Maybe it was the way the smoke rose off his lips. Maybe it was the way he was looking at me. Maybe it was the realization that my lips would be right where his were the moment they sealed around the tip of the blunt.

The fact that I was even sitting in my backyard with a seventeen year old as he broke the law—and as I permitted it just because I simply enjoyed watching— was nerve wracking enough. I didn't need to join him.

Be the adult, Aubree.

Pfft. Who am I kidding? The adult left as soon as he lit it and I didn't say a word.

"Have you ever?"

"Once." *I swallowed, watching his lips purse and suck. His eyes on me, like a subtle threat. "When I was hanging with Solana one night."*

"Of course." *He smiled and I got goosebumps. The way the cold air was drifting over us, I was certain my nipples were seconds from putting on a show so I folded my arms over my chest.*

Get a hold of yourself.

"Roger was pissed," *I added.*

His brow ticked and he stared at the smoking tip before holding it in front of me. "Good. Piss him off again."

Our eyes aligned and I felt like I was in grade school, succumbing to peer pressure with my 'just say no' wristband on. But I didn't care. I wanted to, especially when I saw him lick his lips. A reminder to again wonder how soft they are.

"You need it. It can't be easy being such a saint all the time."

He lowered his chin, staring up at me through thick lashes as I took it from him, pinching it between my pink nails. His wolfish smile as I took the first hit in years was like validation to what I was doing. But really, it was validation that he could get me to do whatever he wanted me to.

"Oh, hey Mrs. C."

"Alright, cut it out with that."

He tilts his head, staring at me through slitted lids as a sheet of smoke caresses his lips. "That's who you are. I mean, what do you want me to call you?"

I cross my arms over my chest, unsure of how to respond.

"This *is* what you wanted, correct?" He drops his arm, taking a few steps across the pavement. "Normalcy. You want the Mrs. Cooper and Diesel's best friend show to resume where it left off, right?"

"Well, yeah—"

"That's not true though, is it?" He comes toward me. "If it were, you wouldn't have looked so fucking jealous at dinner."

His jaw flexes as he takes another hit.

"I wasn't jealous!" I say in a sharp whisper. "I just see the game you play. On to the next, right?"

"Game? That's what you fucking told me to do!" he snaps. "Delete the messages, only come over when Diesel's home, date the girl that likes me, totally ignore you. I'm doing everything you wanted me to do."

I guess not. I guess I wasn't sure of what I wanted until it proved not to be what I wanted at all.

He flicks the butt of the blunt onto the pavement as he walks to me, studying my face like he always does. It's so fulfilling to be in his focus. "And you looked so good today, god. I don't know how I kept my eyes off you, you make it so fucking hard."

His eyes fall onto my lips and that's all it takes for me to leap forward, attaching to him like velcro to a soft sweater. We mesh together in a tangle of arms, fingers swirled in hair, twirled tongues, and spiraling breaths. We are the raw passion I spend night after night reading about. The scenes I'd always wished to experience, but never had. Until now.

Trenton is my hopeless romance. The one that's sure to end in tragedy, but all the best one's do usually.

I back us against the wall of the house, deep within the shadows and out of viewpoint from my window. My shoulder blades graze the textured cement, but I ignore the sharp scratches. He hikes me up against the wall and my legs enclose around his waist again in their rightful place.

"Roger might wake up, Aubree," he pants like it's taking everything in him to stop and remind me. "Diesel might come looking for me."

I stare into his eyes, my hands set on his strong jaw. I hope he knows I don't care without me saying it. I can't utter those words out loud, what kind of person would I be? What kind of wife—mother?

Instead I bring him back in, lowering his shorts. His thick cock is so hard, it drives right into my lower stomach and makes me ache in the very spot it touches.

Reaching underneath my dress, he grabs the hem of my panties and I yelp when they rip against my thigh, the quick snap of the threads signals my body's instant response to be ready for him.

And as if he knows, he traces my slit with two fingers, collecting the anticipation that's seeping out of me.

"You're so wet for me, fuck."

I whimper as I watch him taste his fingers like he's licked up buttercream frosting. Roger's never done such a thing, but I've never gotten this wet for Roger either.

"If no one was home, I'd eat your pussy until you couldn't take it anymore." His fingers slip into me with ease, his thumb grazing my clit with every stroke and making my breathing unsteady. "Until you were begging me to stop. And even then, I don't think I could."

"I wouldn't want you to stop." I bite down on my lip as his pace quickens.

I wish we didn't have to sneak around, but either of them could wake up at any minute and I'm just so desperate to feel him again.

In the next second, he's gliding inside of me, our heads pressed together, eyes closed. My teeth sink deeper into my bottom lip, enduring every perfect stroke he makes, pulling out almost completely before driving back into me.

"I missed you," I whisper as he drags his lips across my jaw. "I missed this."

"You...you did?" He breathes into my ear and I nod, my legs tightening around him as he finds that spot he quickly discovered during round three of our one night together. I moan without a care, but his eyes widen and he plants his palm over my mouth, which only turns me on even more.

"As much as I want to hear your pretty little moans, you've gotta be quiet." I hardly believe he cares as much as he wants me to think he does.

Another moan leaves me, muffled by the palm of his hand and he speeds up his pace, thrashing inside of me.

"Fuck, I missed you too," he growls. "You know I don't want anyone else, don't you?"

I don't respond. If I do, it's back to square one, and I've already said too much as it is.

He removes his hand from my face to get a better hold around my thighs. The wall is prickling into my back, but I couldn't care less.

"Don't stop, Trenton," I say in a breath.

Those words seem to have a direct line to his cock, because he tenses up inside me, groans against my neck, and a warmth fills me that I can hardly even handle. I bite down to suppress the sounds threatening to wake the neighbors, wake my son, and my husband.

And he softly kisses me before gently setting my legs down and raises his shorts up to his waist, keeping our lips connected before encasing me in his arms.

"What are we going to do, Aubree?" he asks me, his lips brushing against mine. The question brings on an endless aching in my chest because I have no clue—other than the fact that I'm going to purchase a plan B pill and pick up a prescription for birth control.

TWENTY FOUR

Trenton

"YOU BROKE MARINA'S HEART," SAYS JOSELYN, COMING INTO THE kitchen. She's in her pajamas, has been sleeping all morning, making that the first thing to come out of her mouth today.

I'm leaned against the counter, eating a bowl of cereal as I text Aubree about last night. We had sex in her backyard without a condom and I honestly couldn't give a damn. She assured me that she took a plan B, but the idea of her becoming pregnant with my baby is both eye opening and something that I didn't realize I actually wanted until we had to have a conversation about it.

Other than that, it's been vague responses. She's worried about Diesel or Roger possibly going through her phone and potentially forgetting to delete messages, so we mostly send funny pictures back and forth. Sucks, but better than not having any contact with her at all.

"She'll be okay," I mumble, hitting the send arrow.

"No she won't. She's in love with you, dummy."

I roll my eyes, holding a palm up to her. "Okay, hold it right there. First of all, we haven't been around each other long enough for her to be in love with me. Second, we were on a date. Not *dating*. It's different."

"She's known you for five years. She's in love, I had to listen to her cry about you all night last night. I tried to tell her you're an idiot and not at all worth crying over, but she wouldn't take it from me."

"Hey, I'm plenty to cry over."

She blinks at me before she guffaws in my face.

I shrug. I had to let Marina go. I realized I was wrong to use her as a place holder—or worse, a pawn that would make Aubree jealous. It worked, clearly, but it was wrong of me. I let her down easy, told her I wanted to focus on school. Complete bullshit, but at the time she seemed like she understood. She didn't have any other choice but to.

"Jerk." Joselyn brushes past me and pours herself a bowl of cereal.

My phone chimes as I receive a text from Aubree. One of those relatable posts that are funny because they're true. I huff out a short laugh as I shoot a quick reply.

Joselyn scrunches her nose. "You already found a new girlfriend? Really?"

"No, Jos. Mind your own business."

"I'm telling Marina."

"Fuck! You're even more annoying than you used to be!" I squint at her. "I don't care. Tell her whatever you want, you're the one who's gonna hurt her feelings, not me."

She scoffs dramatically before taking her bowl with her as she leaves the kitchen.

My phone rings and Aubree's name scrawled across the screen brings out a stupid smile on my face. I've been waiting on Roger to finally leave town again so I can stay a few days with her. We've been surviving on quickees in the den way after midnight and a few instances in the pool house, but that felt even riskier. Aubree doesn't know it, but Diesel keeps his stash in there and sometimes wakes up in the middle of the night to smoke.

I clear my throat, ensuring that my voice comes out smooth. "Hey."

"Hi." I can hear traces of her smile in her voice and a warmth erupts in my chest.

"I…I miss you." It's still new to say and sometimes I wonder if it's too much since I know she goes back and forth with herself about what we've been doing.

She huffs out something like a laugh. "I miss *you*, and that's exactly why I called. Roger's leaving around five tomorrow, and Diesel's going to some family get-together with Chloe afterwards, so the house is all ours."

"All ours, huh?" I bite down on the grin that's beaming from me.

"Mhm, and I'm all yours."

Fuck.

"I'm glad you said that because you're gonna say it twenty more times tomorrow."

"Only twenty?" She giggles and it makes my chest warm.

"I was thinking of coming by tonight to hang with Diesel, I hope I get some time with you before tomorrow."

"Mmm, Roger's been acting weird so I can't promise that. It's probably not a good idea."

I take a breath, hating that he's always factor when it comes to us, but I'm still relishing over the fact that she's claimed herself as mine, so it doesn't bother me as much as it should.

"Well, tomorrow then. I'll have a surprise for you, actually."

"I don't know if I like surprises." She chuckles. I can hear the elevator music layered underneath her voice and I know she's at the grocery store or something. She never sounds this relaxed at home, even when no one's there with her.

"You'll like this. Trust me."

"Always," she tells me, and for some reason that makes me feel certain. Like I have her, even though she's really more like sand slipping through my fingers.

I'm still staring down at my phone moments after we've hung up, so distracted in my thoughts, I don't expect it when Joselyn plucks it from my hands.

"WHAT THE FUCK, JOSELYN!" I wrestle her for the phone she now has her fingers tightly netted around.

"WHO IS SHE, TRENTON!?"

"NONE OF YOUR FUCKING BUSINESS, GIVE IT BACK!" I enclose my arms around her like a hungry snake and take her down to the ground. She curls up in a ball, holding my phone to her stomach while I try to pull her arms from her body. "I'M NOT PLAYING AROUND! LET GO!"

She wiggles out of my grip and runs down the hall so quickly I don't even try to go after her. I just accept my defeat, sitting on my knees in the middle of the room and run my fingers through my hair, catching my breath.

She stops abruptly, head down as she looks over the screen. "Aubree Cooper, as in…Mrs. Cooper?" She comes back toward me, slowly.

"No. Not Aubree Cooper, as in Mrs. Cooper." I stand up from the floor, snatching my phone from her hands. "Aubree Cooper, as in mind your own business."

"Really, Trenton?" Her eyes insinuate that she knows I'm lying. "Diesel's mom? You're having a thing with Diesel's mom?"

"Mind your business, already. Fuck!"

I go to my room, banging my shoulder into the door so habitually, I don't even have to try anymore. I hit it just hard enough every time.

"T…"

"What, Joselyn? You want to tell me how wrong it is of me? Lecture me on how Diesel's going to hate me when he finds out? Tell me I'm wasting my time? That I'm going to end up hurt?" I shrug my shoulders. "I already know."

"Oh my god, you're in love with her," she states, placing a hand on her hip. "How long has this been going on?"

"I'm not talking about this with you."

"I'm not going to tell anyone, I swear." She tilts her head at me. "Come on, this is your little sister you're talking to."

"I know. That's exactly why I can't tell you anything."

"Trenton. When have I ever ratted you out to mom?"

My eyes narrow at her and she raises her hand to me before I can go into depth on the million and one times she has.

"This year." She blinks at me. "When have I ever ratted you out to mom, this year?"

I scratch my eyelid. I guess she has proven herself to be less of a snitch than she used to be the past year. She actually covered for me a lot, now that I think of it.

I stare up at her underneath heavy brows. "You better not say a fucking word."

Her eyes are big and wide and she shuts the door behind her with a thud even though mom isn't home.

"I'm not in love with her," I say.

"Liar."

"I don't know. I haven't decided on that yet, but I really like her, Jos. It was only supposed to be a one time thing, but now I don't really want to stop seeing her."

"Well, you have to. I mean, Diesel is never going to accept you with his mom. Not to mention, she's married to her hot husband. Why would she leave a guy like that for, you?"

I look at her sideways as if to say, *are you serious?* More like hot headed husband, and what the fuck does Roger have that I don't? I mean, besides the great job and stability a man his age would have…

"I mean imagine if Diesel was hooking up with mom." She grimaces and I pretend to gag, making a deep laugh rise from her throat.

"I know. I realize everything wrong with what I'm doing, I realize we'll never go any further because she's married…because she's Diesel's fucking mom, Jesus." I rub my forehead as I resonate on those words for the first time. Saying it out loud is like reality banging it's heavy fist on my head. "I'm being selfish, Joselyn. I know. I've thought it all over so many times and I feel like shit about it every time."

She twists her lips, blinking at me as if I'd taken the whole speech out of her mouth. I was aware of it all. I'm aware of the fact that I'm a bad friend, that I pushed Aubree into doing something I knew she wasn't comfortable with.

Just as well as I knew this was bound to happen, I know it's bound to end. I know it's going to hurt like hell when it finally does, that it's going to feel like a fever dream when I think back on it years from now, but I'll enjoy it while it lasts. That's all I can really do.

"She *is* really pretty, I can't blame you." One side of her mouth rises into a half smile.

"She's fucking gorgeous." I purse my lips as my arms cross over my chest. "She's perfect."

"Aww." She sticks out her bottom lip and places a hand over her heart. "Who'd have known the same guy who used to burp the abc's would turn out to be a true romantic?"

"Alright, enough." I stand up to walk her out of my room. "Get out of here, nosey."

Joselyn is a pain in my ass, but I know I can trust her with keeping serious subjects secret and this is a very serious subject.

"*Los cuatros amigos*, back together again," says Gio before guzzling half of his freshly opened beer. We're all sitting around the table in Diesel's backyard for what feels like the first time in forever.

"I know. I missed this," Diesel admits, his eyes mostly focused on me and Marina. "Like what the hell happened to us?"

"Rina turned into a girl." Gio huffs. "That's what happened."

"I've always been a girl, dick."

"Yeah, but you went from this dope girl who wore her dad's tee shirts and mud stained, ripped jeans—who could always outrun everyone, except Trent—to this lame little cheer-squader who only wears short skirts and listens to fucking, Justin Bieber."

"It's called growing up."

"No, it's called trying to fit in. This isn't you, you know that."

I stare at Gio as he speaks, wondering why he's so passionate about the new Marina. I mean, I never liked all of her changes either. She pretty much fell off the face of the Earth sometime when she was fifteen, and then when she resurfaced she suddenly had this huge crush on me and wore butterfly hair clips and pink ballerina flats.

"Alright, alright." Diesel pats his hand on the table. "Let's all chill out. This is supposed to be fun, fun means I break out the bud."

Gio doesn't argue. He's one of the biggest pot heads I know and that word is a tranquilizer for him.

I glance up at Aubree's window, I can tell the light is on by its dim yellow hue. I miss her already. This fling we've been having is so unhealthy, but I can't stop. I don't want to. I'll indulge until she doesn't let me anymore. And when that time comes, I know I'll be on my knees begging to be back in between hers.

A cloud of smoke hits me in the face and brings me back to reality, which is me sitting around a table with two idiots and a girl who doesn't know how to take a hint. It's almost like she wants me to reach my limits. She wants me to have to tell her straight up that I am just not interested in her that way. I mean, I'm sure it doesn't help that I told her I liked her a few times, but I didn't lie. I do like her, just not anything beyond friends. I really just want to go back to being friends.

I feel eyes on me and mine shift onto her. She doesn't even shy away or blink when I catch her staring. She's so shameless with it now, it's annoying.

Diesel passes me the bong and I take a hit, but she's killing it for me by staring so damn hard.

I exhale before skipping over her and passing it over to Gio. She doesn't smoke anymore, I guess.

"Rina, can we talk later?"

She nods with no hesitation and I realize I may have made it seem like we were going to have a get back together talk, but that's definitely not what's happening.

After we migrated into the pool house, it didn't take long for the guys to drink themselves to sleep. They laughed for about an hour straight before that so they were a done deal as soon as their eyes finally shut.

It was then that she took me up on my offer to talk, and we headed back out to the yard.

We walked slowly along the edge of blue glowing pool as I chose the nicest words I could think of to break this to her.

"I just wanted to say…" I lick my lips, finding this way harder than I thought it would be. I'm not a mean person, I don't like making anyone feel bad, and I've already dragged this girl a few times by using her to make Aubree jealous. "I hope there's no hard feelings after the way we ended things. I just want to go back to being regular friends like we always were."

"What? We are friends." She smiles as we lean against the cement planter.

"Good. That's all I—"

"But we're also more, aren't we?"

I take a breath. "No, not really. And that's what I mean." I rub the back of my neck. "We shouldn't have…crossed those lines."

"All we did was kiss."

"But we shouldn't have. I'm sorry."

Her pupils widen as her eyes leave my face. "I…I think you're confused, Trenton. I just don't think you mean that."

"I mean that. I'm telling you I just want to be friends, Marina. I'm sorry if I maybe lead you on in the past, but all I want is for us to go back to the way—"

"Am I not good enough for you?" Her brows bunch at the center of her face. "What is it? What do you want me to be? I can be whatever you want."

"No, you're fine—"

"But I'm not what you want?"

"Marina." I hold my palms together in between us. "It's not that I don't want you, I'm just focusing on myself right now. I'm—"

"Yeah right! That's textbook for 'I'm already seeing someone else'."

"Well, I'm not." I shrug, truly over this conversation. I'm catching glimpses of the spunky Marina we all knew and I'm suddenly wishing she was still scared to eat in front of me.

"I can be her," she says, softly. "I can be just like her."

"What are you talking about?"

She stares me dead in the eyes. "Mrs. Cooper."

How does she know?

I blink a few times, caught off guard. "Why are you talking about Mrs. Cooper?"

"You don't have to pretend with me, Trenton. I know you left me for her."

"You're confused." I push myself up from the ledge, but I feel her following me and it has me unsettled.

Especially when her hand wraps around my wrist and she stops me right beside the pool.

"That window right there," she points over the fence at the house directly behind the Cooper's, "That's my bedroom."

I look up and can barely see it through the trees, but the memory of being in her room and looking out through that very window hits me violently like an electrical current. I turn around to look at Aubree's window and realize she'd have a direct view of what's going on if she really wanted to. If we'd gotten careless and left the curtains open.

"I've seen you in Mrs. Cooper's room. I saw you—"

"Alright, alright. I fucking get it. You saw us." I cross my arms, hushing my voice even lower. "Are you going to tell Diesel? Are you going to be the one that breaks all of us apart, for good?"

"No. I'm not planning to do anything but let it all play out. It's only a matter of time before you realize you fell for the wrong person and come back to me."

"Marina." I drop my head in my palms. "That won't happen."

"Well, I don't know what you think is going to happen, but it won't be a happily ever after, that's for sure."

I shake my head to myself, pivoting backwards with my fingers laced behind my head.

"Think about it, Trent. She doesn't love you. She's married and miserable. Everyone knows what's going on with her and her husband, and that's nothing. I'm sure you're nothing but sex for her and you deserve so much more. She'll never be able to give you anything someone like me could."

"Someone like you?"

"Someone who's loved you all of our lives, Trenton." She scoffs, her eyes beginning to crystallize with emotion. "God, like when will you open your eyes? When are you finally going to get it?"

"Get what?!" My hands flair out at my sides in frustration. "There's nothing to get!"

"That I'm perfect for you—you're perfect for me. We're the one's who should be together."

"No, no, no, Marina. This is all in your head. I don't want that, I don't want you!" I blink at her, we're chest to chest. My angry reflection is in her eyes, and I realize I reached my limit. I've snapped.

"You...you really don't?"

"No." I swallow, stepping away from her. "I'm sorry." I left her there by the shallow end and rejoined the pool house slumber party.

I don't know how she's taking that. Through the glass in the door, I watched her head toward the gate and leave.

It didn't come out the way I planned for it to. I didn't want to be mean. I didn't want to hurt her feelings. But I hope the harshness of my words is enough for her to get the memo.

TWENTY FIVE

Aubree

I'M HELPING ROGER PACK, MAKING SURE HE DOESN'T FORGET A few small items that he can't ever seem to remember for some reason.

Deodorant, aftershave, his mouth guards because he grinds his teeth in his sleep. Crucial things.

Sometimes I wonder how he'd be without me. His life wouldn't be anywhere near as organized as I make it. It would be chaos. He couldn't even feed himself without me because I cook all of his meals. Not to mention, he can't even correctly follow microwave instructions.

He's the kind of man that needs a wife, but I'm realizing I'm not the kind of woman that needs a husband.

Solana: That's so fucking cute. Like a real date!
Solana: Just be careful. You're treading dangerous territory.

Me: More dangerous than fucking him practically every day while Roger's home?

Solana: You know what I mean. You're making this more than just sex and that's not where you want to be if you really want to stay with Roger.

Maybe I don't really want to stay with Roger. Maybe she knows that. Maybe Trenton knows that. Maybe I knew that all along.

But one thing is for certain, this has never fully been about sex with me and Trenton.

Roger's deep voice wakes me from my thoughts and makes me shove my phone into the waistband of my leggings. "Aubree, have you seen my—"

I run my eyes through his bag, double checking his things, when he appears from the bathroom, blinking at me with a stern expression on his face.

"What? What are you looking for?"

He holds up my compact of birth control pills that I thought I'd shoved deep into the bottom cabinet in the bathroom, but by the looks of it, I must have forgotten and left them somewhere easy enough for even him to find.

"What the fuck are you on birth control for?"

I stand up straight, swallowing even though my mouth's already gone completely dry. "Oh—remember? I told you weeks ago my cycle's been irregular."

He raises a brow at me, still looking over the pills. Probably counting to see how long I've been taking them.

"You know how I get when it's thrown off." I turn my back to him, zipping up his bag because I am having a hard time lying while looking into his eyes. "I just wanted to regulate it."

"You didn't mention that."

"I did, you must've not been paying attention." I leave the room, exhaling a hard breath as soon as I've reached the stairs.

He can't argue that. Most times he really doesn't pay attention and he knows it. He misses about seventy percent of the things I say and then is confused about it when I bring it up again later.

And my cycle hasn't been irregular since I gave birth to Diesel. It was spotty for a couple of years after that, but soon worked itself out. That's another thing he doesn't pay attention to, so I'm sure he'll just scratch his head and forfeit the discussion altogether.

But that was sloppy of me. I need to be better at keeping my tracks covered. As much as I love the idea of going out on a real date with Trenton—as well as I am enamored by the sweet gesture—it's risky.

It's almost too risky, but maybe he's worth all the risks.

TWENTY SIX

trenton

One Hour Prior

I SPENT A LITTLE EXTRA TIME GETTING READY TODAY. I GOT A hair cut, showered, dressed in summer friendly clothing. Even broke out a new pair of Nikes because my last check was great—so great that I picked up my car this morning.

When I went with Diesel to pick out his first car, I was jealous. The feeling went just as fast as it came. But now as I sit behind the wheel of my first car, I realize nothing can compare to this feeling. Having worked my ass off, I now know that all the waiting and saving was worth it. Especially since I plan on taking Aubree out tonight.

Somewhere far away from here where no one knows our names or our stories. Somewhere we can just be us without having to hide or put up a front.

Every time I get to Diesel's house, I'm struck with nerves. My stomach quivers, my heart feels like it's trying to burst through my rib cage. As much as I hate the feeling, I love it.

I admire my car once more before hiking up the steps, but before I reach the door, Diesel's already come outside with a look of surprise on his face.

"What! When did you get a car?!" He walks past me and straight to the vehicle. "This is nice, man." He wrinkles his chin as he scopes it out.

Aubree comes outside and my knees almost buckle when I see her smile.

"I got a car, Mrs. C.," I say, rubbing the back of my neck.

"I can see that." She grins, coming toward me. "I'm impressed."

I turn around to glance at Diesel, still walking a full circle around the car.

"This is nicer than my car." He tilts his head as he opens the drivers side door and gets inside.

"You look so handsome today."

"Thank you, beautiful." My smile is wide and the type that's sure to be the reason why my cheeks are sore later. "We're going out, tonight," I say to her in a low volume, keeping it short because Diesel can pop back up any moment.

Her face brightens and I really want to kiss her, but I settle for a subtle touch to her arm. It's crazy how a small thing like the feeling of skin can a give off the same sensation as if we did kiss.

Finding it hard to break away from her, I head down the steps anyway and get into the passengers seat while Diesel's connecting his phone to the radio.

We stayed out in the driveway for twenty minutes as Diesel gushed over my new car. Repeating the fact that he wishes he could trade up for a new one like mine.

When we went inside, Roger was rustling through the fridge, going up and down the stairs in preparation to leave. Aubree looked to be helping him pack, but she was mostly just circling the house like he was.

Diesel and I played video games in his room until it was time for Roger to finally go. He wasn't in the worst mood today, but definitely not a good one.

He peeked in and said goodbye to us, and as soon as he left, Diesel seemed ready to go too.

"You're leaving already?"

"Yeah. Chloe's dad wanted me to meet some family tonight." He wraps the controller around its cord before setting it inside the shelf of his entertainment center. "And I definitely don't want to be here, so…"

"Why not?"

"I haven't really been a big fan of my mom lately." He speaks with his back to me. "She's trying to make everything harder for me than it already is."

"I doubt that's what she's trying to do."

He turns to face me. "And what would you know about anything?" He chuckles to make that sound less accusatory than it does. But I hear him crystal clear. "I mean, Patrick offered to give me and Chloe an apartment and she fucking said no. My dad actually has a brain and argued for it, but I guess he's trying to kiss her fucking ass or something and just went along with what she wanted."

"Well, maybe your mom just knows what's better for you."

"Fuck that. She doesn't know shit, and neither do you." He exits the room and I shake my head as I go after him.

"Diesel," I speak, halting him in his tracks.

He stops in the living room, his keys in his hand. "How's it better for me to struggle, Trenton? You tell me since you seem to know the way my mom's head works all of a sudden."

"I think she just wants you to earn the apartment yourself. You're not going to learn anything if you just keep getting everything handed to you."

"Oh, because she doesn't get free handouts? She gets to sit at home all fucking day, doing her nails and getting drunk on cheap wine."

And that hit me hard. I've had enough of everyone downing her, judging her. She doesn't want to be here. She's miserable, and maybe he'd know that if he took the time to talk to her.

"Don't say shit like that."

"Don't tell me what to say in my own house."

He slams the door in my face, leaving me there to resonate on the growing tension between us. It's clear. Diesel and I are growing apart.

I almost talked myself out of tonight, but I wanted to see her. I felt like shit about how that went with Diesel, and Aubree's the only thing that can make me feel better—even though she's technically the problem.

I feel like Diesel's lashing out at me because he knows. But if he doesn't know, he still thinks he's onto us. He's been different with me, and at first I thought it was just stress, but now I just think he recognizes the attraction between me and Aubree and—of course—he doesn't like it.

I'm not going to keep dwelling on the fact that I put myself in a mess that's costing me my relationship with my best friend, because I'm sitting in the dark, parked in front of Aubree's house waiting on her anyway.

My eyes veer up at my reflection in the rear view mirror before I brush a few strands of hair down.

She opens the passenger door, not even giving me a chance to see what she's decided on wearing before she's shut it.

I don't waste any time before pulling away from the house. This is the riskiest thing we've ever done. The neighbors that Roger plays basketball with at the gym would probably love to report back to him that they saw his wife getting into the car with a teenager—by the way Aubree's looking around the area, I'm convinced she knows this just as well as I do.

We drove the first ten minutes in silence as I replayed the fight I had earlier with Diesel in my head. I don't like the feeling of him mad at me, especially when I know I'm doing something wrong and he has every right to be.

"He'll get over it, you know," she says into the silence like she knew exactly what was on my mind. "You two have had a lot of fights, he always gets over it."

"Yeah, but this is different. He knows something's up."

"He doesn't know—"

"Well he's trying to find out, and who's to say we haven't left enough breadcrumbs for him to figure it out soon enough? Is this worth him hating me?" I'm mostly speaking my thoughts out loud, but as soon as the words leave my mouth, I regret them. The silence she's sitting in sends a chill down my spine and I know I shouldn't have questioned us.

"I don't know, Trenton." I see her shake her head in my peripheral. "That's something I've been asking myself this entire time."

The drive is silent. There's moments of me holding her hand in between us when I don't have to shift gears, and that's more satisfying than speaking.

Four cities over, we arrive at an Italian restaurant. She's always making spaghetti or some type of pasta based dish with weird sauces so I figured she must like it.

I run around to her side before she can even take off her seat belt and open the door for her.

Seeing her emerge from my car, dangling from my hand like a queen, is enough to make me snap out of the shitty mood I was in. Especially knowing that we're far away enough from home that we don't have to worry about how we look at each other, or how much physical contact gives us away.

I cup her face in my hands and say, "You're worth it all, Aubree." I lower my head and kiss her like I mean it, right here in the middle of this parking lot.

She's mine, even if it's just for tonight. Even if the world around us is threatening to rain on everything we have. Even if our clock is ticking. She's mine for now.

We link hands and enter the restaurant. A slim hostess sits us down at a booth under dim lighting that makes her eyes look even more radiant than they always do.

I hold her hand over the table, unable to let her go now that I have the freedom to be as affectionate with her as I want to be. We're given glasses of water with lemon wedges split over their rims and our order is taken, leaving us alone. On our first date.

"What made you choose Italian?" she asks.

"You make lasagna so much I just assumed you liked it."

She giggles. "Well, fun fact—my grandma's Italian—Italian's all I really know how to make."

"Oh," I say, intrigued. "Part Italian—no wonder why you're so fucking hot."

"Mhm. My parents are all mixed up. My dad's completely Trinidadian, and my mom is Italian and a quarter German."

"It all makes sense."

"So, what's Laguna anyway? I never met any other family by that name."

"It's Spanish, my dad's side is all straight from Spain. My Mom's just…European…American."

"So, white then?"

We share a laugh and I nod.

"I barely remember my dad's face, but I know he had these swampy green eyes and almost, golden tan skin like my sister. I'm the only one in my family who missed out on those traits."

"You don't need it. You're handsome either way."

This feels unreal. She was my impossible, and now we're here doing the impossible. I fell for her like a snap of a finger, just falling deeper every day I'm with her. *God, this is going to hurt when it's over.*

It already hurts now.

"Trenton…when's the last time you saw him? Your dad?"

I release her from my hand, blowing out a breath, surprised she asked me. I don't talk about my dad, he's dead to me. But if I were ever to start, she'd obviously be the first person I told.

"I'm sorry, I…I shouldn't have asked."

I shake my head. "No, I don't mind that you asked." I swoop back my hair with one single hand stroke over the top of my head. "The last time I talked to my dad, I was…" I stare down the aisle as I bite my inner lip in thought. "Thirteen. That was the last time he left, that was it. I didn't have any contact with him except for two birthday cards he sent. One on my sixteenth, and the second…I just got on my eighteenth. It's funny because, I think I knew he would. I had a feeling I'd get another card this year. Words written in his sloppy writing. *His attempt at fatherly advice*." I huff. "I don't want advice from him. I don't want to be anything like him."

She stares at me with so much care in her eyes, I reach for her hand again. "I'm sorry."

"It's okay, now. When I was a kid, I was really fucked up over it, wondering when he'd be back. *If* he'd be back. It took me a couple years to accept that he wouldn't be. You just never expect the important people in your life to just leave so easily like they can go on without you without even a second thought."

She nods, her thumb swiping over my fingers.

"Joselyn didn't know him like I did, she was young. He could've been anyone to her—but shit, I guess I really didn't know him like I thought I did either, huh?" I arch my brow, reaching for my water and taking a short sip. "One thing I can say though, he taught me something. He taught me that a good parent puts their child first. For him, alcohol came first. Later on I learned that other women came second…He was selfish…Maybe he thought he was better off without us.

Maybe he thought we slowed down his life, I don't know. I've tried to figure it out for years. There's no concrete answer." I let my other hand rest on top of the table. "Even fucking Roger hasn't left Diesel and he's a terrible dad, but he sticks around so I respect him for that."

Her eyes are suddenly glossy and I squeeze her hand in mine.

"But you, Aubree? You are such a great mother. You do everything for Diesel and I don't know why he doesn't see it. He's stupid—spoiled, naïve. He takes you for granted."

She blinks her eyes until they aren't so shiny. "Well, that's because it's Diesel, and he only sees all but what's right in front of him."

"Yeah." I huff out a small laugh. Our eyes lock and she smiles at me sullenly. I didn't plan to get so mushy and sentimental tonight, but something about this setting is making it all pour out of me like honey.

"Aubree, you got me through the hardest time of my life."

Our fingers intersect without either of us thinking.

"Your house was my safe haven," I tell her. "You always made me feel welcome, you always knew when I needed you. I was just some kid who'd made friends with your son, but I felt like you loved me then."

"I did. Not like I do now, but I really did."

"I knew that. And I'm so grateful for you, because I don't know how I would have turned out if I didn't have you to lift me up all the time."

"Is that why you fell for me?"

"No, that's why I love you. I would have fallen for you anyway. That was a given."

She smiles at me, her glimmering eyes have returned.

I smile back at her, caressing the top of her hand with my thumb. I look down and notice her wedding ring is gone for the first time and it prompts me to take a deep breath.

She looks down at her empty finger as well, seeing that I've noticed, her hand shies away. Loosening from my grip before she sets it in her lap. "This is the first time I've taken it off."

"I like you better without it." My lips find my straw and I take a sip of water.

She smiles again, but suppresses it half way.

Her mouth opens to speak, but our waitress drifts over to us and sets our plates down on the table. The woman leaves just as quickly as she came over and Aubree returns her eyes to me as I pick up my fork.

"Trenton, I think…Roger's seeing someone." She looks at me like she's gauging me for my reaction. Like whatever she says next only depends on the response I give her.

But all I can think is, *no fucking kidding.*

"Really? What makes you say that?" I twirl the fork in the middle of the steaming Alfredo noodles and take my first bite.

She stares at me blankly, almost like she's disappointed. "Well, you don't seem surprised."

"Honestly, I'm not." I shrug, watching her slice up her chicken. "But if he is, what are you going to do?" I swallow, about to ask something I don't really want to know the definite answer to. "Are you going to leave him, or stay and keep pretending you have no idea?"

"I don't know."

I scratch my head, briefly looking down at the table. She's supposed to say she'll leave him—and not for me, but for herself. For the sake of her own integrity and dignity. She's supposed to leave Roger because when he's not treating her like a human Barbie doll, she's more like a low paid housekeeper he's secretly fucking than a wife.

"So, Trinidadian, huh?" I let out a breath and smile at her, gently changing the subject to something lighter because I really don't want to kill this date before it's even gotten started.

After we ate, we parked by the beach. The air was warm and salty, the sand was even still warm from earlier like it absorbed the eighty six degree heat. We walked hand in hand along the shore. Her heels dangled from her hands as we ventured into the chilly water until it reached the tops of our ankles. And when she wouldn't go any further, I picked her up over my shoulder as she screamed for me to put her down and carried her until the water just caressed my knees.

We laughed and we kissed, I held her under the moon and we watched the tide crawl further every time it rolled back in.

It wasn't until it came up above all the sand that we knew it was time to go. We ran back to the car, hands linked until I had her back against the passenger door. We're like magnets at this point, neither of us can get enough of each other. The rest of the world doesn't matter, she almost makes me wonder if it ever had.

Tonight, it's like the only thing that does matter is us.

It's always been us, but it won't always be us.

Back at the Cooper house, we run up the steps through the thick of the dark, her hand in mine. We haven't bothered to turn a light on because who has time for that? Our relationship feels like an hourglass, and we're just watching the sand slowly trickle down until it runs out.

I don't want to know what happens when time does run out. I don't want to think about it. All I can focus on is the way her body looks standing over the dress that's pooling around her feet.

I lay her down, our lips connected, hot, and swollen as I place myself between her legs. Every touch she makes ignites my bones.

Her head rolls back as I make that first thrust inside of her, and she moans so beautifully, I lose myself. I lose myself every damn time.

She is everything.

She will always be everything.

Aubree's the only thing that's ever made me feel like a man. Not a birth date on my ID card, not assuming the man of the house role after my dad walked out on us. Not my job, not my car. Just her.

"I love you," I breathe, going harder. Her eyes widen at me, but she's so deep in her senses, she doesn't respond.

The next moment, we're in complete bliss together. She's trembling in my arms and I'm holding onto her like I'm going to lose her forever.

"I mean it, Aubree." I brush her hair from her face, still hovering over her. "I—"

"Trenton!" she warns, pushes me off of her, rolling off the bed into a stand and going straight to the bathroom.

I charge after her, making it just in time to block the door from closing with my fist.

She looks up at me through the cracked door and the regret in her eyes is agonizing. I'm tired of seeing it. I'm tired of great nights turning into fights about what's right and wrong.

"Don't, Trenton." She shakes her head subtly, her eyes suddenly glowing. "Don't say that. You cannot love me, you're not supposed to. This isn't how this was supposed to go." She drops her head, her shaky fingertips touching her forehead as a small sob comes out.

"But I do…I do, and I just want you to know that."

She tries to push the door shut again, but I overpower her with one hand until she finally stops trying and breaks down in tears. I open the door, pulling her small body into me before I kiss the top of her head.

"You weren't supposed to fall in love with me," she cries. "This wasn't supposed to happen."

I comb my fingers through her hair, holding her head straight up at me. "I've always been in love with you, Aubree. Nothing was going to prevent that from happening, I've loved you for a long time. Feels like forever…and I'll love you forevermore."

She cries harder, her tears running down onto my palms.

I brought her back to bed, holding her long after she stopped. And when she finally did, she uttered the words, "I love you, too."

TWENTY SEVEN

Aubree

I AWAKE TO THE MID SUMMER SUN BEAMING HARD THROUGH THE sheer curtains in my bedroom. Beside me, Trenton's small snores remind me he's there. That we made love for hours, that he told me he loved me, and that I told him I loved him back.

My eyes itch as I stare down at him, the urge to cry setting in again. Every wall I had up for this boy, he's torn down with a sledge hammer. I get up from the bed, trying to be as quiet as I possibly can, but then I hear his body shift, and when I look back at him he's smiling at me.

It's that just-woken-up smile he wears so well.

The one that makes me want to curl up against his chest for a few more hours, but I shouldn't because I honestly don't know when Diesel's planning on coming home.

We should really be getting ready to resume real life.

The life where he's just a boy my son grew up with and I'm only a lonely mother looking for a purpose, a way to get my husband to notice me and my son to love me.

Trenton reaches out for me and I can't resist. I crawl back into bed with him, tucking myself in as he encases me in his strong arms.

"Good morning, pretty little thing."

I grin like an idiot, my arms tightening around him and locking at his mid back. "Morning, Romeo."

"Still Romeo, huh?" He pulls back to look at me, his sleepy eyes making my heart beat quicker. "Mm, that's cool. He gets the girl in the end, right?"

"He dies in the end." I say into his chest. "They both do."

"Fuck." He chuckles.

"Yeah, they kill themselves." I lift my head to look at him. "Didn't you read Romeo and Juliet this year? Did you pay attention in English at all?"

He lowers his chin, crinkling his nose as he looks down at me. "It was never my favorite subject." Our fingers meld together. "But, if you were my teacher, that would've been a different story."

"I can be your teacher." I wiggle up to his lips before placing a kiss there. "I've already taught you a lot, haven't I?"

"Mm, yeah you have…but I'd rather you be my little school girl." He kisses me. "You can put on one of those little plaid skirts for me, and some long white socks that come up to your thighs. We can play detention in Rogers' office, I'll have your ass all over that desk."

He growls against my cheek as a throaty laugh leaps out of me. "Oh God! You'd love that, wouldn't you?"

"Fuck yeah, I would!" His arms tighten around me before he wrestles me around on the bed, making me laugh like a little kid who's too small and too weak to break out of his grip.

When he stops still I'm lying on top of him, face to face. Staring into his sleepy eyes that only look back at me with love.

Trenton is perfect. My idea of it, at least. And for the first time since last night, I resonate on the very words I spoke to him before we fell asleep, wrapped in each other.

The long overdue *I love you*.

I'm in love.

I fell in love where love shouldn't have existed. He planted a seed in the driest soil and I watered it until it bloomed into a picture of a life with him. A life where I wake up to him a million times. A life where he holds me like this, where he makes me feel safe and secure like this. Where we're in our house, in our own bed. Like this.

And as if he hears my thoughts, he speaks.

"I want to wake up to you everyday," he whispers into my hair.

My eyes slam shut as I feel guilt stabbing me in my stomach. "Everyday, for the rest of my fucking life…but that's not reality, is it? That's just not possible, right?"

My eyes water, prepping me for a crying fit that I cannot allow myself to have, so I blink away the tears that are threatening to run down my face. I kiss his shoulder in an effort to make this sweeter than it is. "We have to get up…"

He sighs as I wriggle from his arms and go straight to the shower. I step out of my tank top and underwear right as he enters the bathroom and I catch his eyes glazing over my naked body while I step behind the glass. The steam has slowly began filling the room as the hot water first shocks my skin.

Trenton's hands slide around me, not stopping until he's got both breasts in his hands. He sucks on my neck, shortening my breath with the sensation.

I turn to face him, staring up into his eyes. Water streaming down his skin, tiny beads of liquid sit on his eyelashes and bring more of a shine to his eyes.

"I'll never, ever get enough of you," he says to me before kissing my lips.

He's holding me in his hands so delicately as if I'll break or shatter if he grips too hard. Like I'm rare and fragile and something to be admired, but also something he won't have forever.

Something he can't have forever.

I swear my legs are going to give out, but I stand strong while melting in his arms. Melting until something flips a switch in him and he spins me so my back is to him.

He grabs my wrists and places my hands flat against the shower wall before sliding my feet further apart.

"Never?" I ask him.

"Never, baby. You're it for me."

My breath hitches as he brings my hips back into his erection. He's hard as a rock, sliding his slick rod between my legs, tauntingly.

"But, how do you know that? How are you so sure?"

I feel him breathe on my neck as he slips his hand down my stomach, not stopping until the pads of his fingers circle my clit and I shut my eyes.

"Trust me?"

I nod, sighing as he slowly rubs the sensitive spot between my legs. I don't know why, but I do trust him. I trust him more than anyone at this point. He's never done anything to make me feel otherwise. I guess I don't need an explanation. There isn't one. He's sure of me because he just is. There's no reason for it, just like I'm sure of him because I just am.

I love him. I want him. I need him.

He's the one.

A single quick thrust sends him deep inside of me before his hands return to my hips. The water splashes between us with every pump, slapping the glass walls and only slightly masking our sounds.

He grabs me by my jaw, angling my head so he can kiss me, not stopping his strokes as he does. I can barely catch my breath as I match his every move, my hips driving back into him every time he pulls back.

I'm drowning in him and it's the most liberating feeling there is.

To be this consumed by someone who's just as consumed by you. It's everything I was missing and more. It's everything I'd never have with anyone else.

He finishes inside me and then backs me against the wall before crouching down and lifting my leg over his shoulder.

I don't know what's better, his tongue or his dick. It's a close competition, but his mouth always has me in awe over what it can do.

I come with my hands in his hair, with his fingers tight around my skin.

He's hard all over again, his erection noticeably throbbing against my stomach as he hugs me. This could easily go for three more rounds, but we're on a time limit and we both know it.

Reluctantly, we wash the sex off our skin and step out of the shower. Wrapping towels around our bodies, hardly able to see each other through the mist after being in so long.

He pinches my chin before placing a kiss on my lips that produces my bittersweet smile. It's almost time for him to go.

"*Mom*." Diesel's voice is loud and clear like his face is right up against the bathroom door.

My heart splits and shatters and Trenton and I stare at each other, both panicking with no where to go. *Is this it? Is this where it all finally ends? My crash and burn finale that declares me the worst mother in history.*

Trenton shakes his head at me like he's accepting his defeat, like we have to go out there with brave faces and fess up to what we've done. Like he's thoroughly prepared to do that. I know that's only because Trenton wants the world to know. He wants us out of the dark, but I can't let that happen.

I shove him back into the shower, hiding him behind the foggy glass in a desperate, last ditch effort at hiding him.

"*MOM*," Diesel calls more sternly. I know exactly what that tone means. *You're caught.*

I open the door and squeeze through the crack before shutting it firmly behind my back. Diesel's forehead is ridged as he looks me over in only a towel, my face probably plastered in guilt, despite me forcing calm thoughts through my head.

"Who's in there?"

"No one. It was just me."

"I heard someone in there and I know it's not fucking Dad." He reaches for the doorknob, but I grab his wrist before he can touch it. "You've got clothes on the floor by your bed. Also not Dad's. Who's in there, Mom?"

"No one is in there, Diesel!"

"Then why are you holding my arm like that? If there's no one in there, let me go. Let me open the door to see no one, even though I swear I heard a guy talking to you."

I purse my lips, fighting off the trembling that's making my body feel like it's on vibrate mode.

"Come out, pussy!" he shouts over my shoulder before grabbing me by my arms and moving me out of the way, but when I spin around, Trenton's already opened the door and is looking at both of us like he's admitting to it all, hands held up like he's surrendering, yet there's not one ounce of shame in his eyes.

If I didn't know better, he wanted this to happen.

Diesel's face drops and the look pains me so badly, I bend at the waist. "I fucking knew it." Diesel stares at him with a hatred in his eyes I can't even recognize. He looks at me. "What the fuck? You hate Dad, fine. I figured you'd been cheating on him anyway, but of all the people to do that with, him? My best fucking friend who you've practically helped raise, for fucks sake?"

"Diesel," I say sternly, tears racing from my eyes, but there's nothing I can say to make any of this make sense. We're completely wrong and completely caught.

"No, everything's always your fault, Mom. You ruin fucking everything. You've ruined Dad's life and now...you've ruined mine. I hate you."

"Alright." Trenton cuts in, a stern hand held up. "I'm not going to let you keep treating your mom like shit! You have no idea what she puts up with to keep you happy, she fucking bends over backwards for you!"

Diesel stares up at him in disgust, nostrils flared like in a split second he could wring his neck. "Well, she does a lot of bending over for everyone, doesn't she?"

Diesel shoves Trenton hard enough for him to stumble backward, but in the next instant Trenton shoots back, pinning Diesel against the wall, his arm pressed down on his neck.

"Fuck you! I'm done putting up with your moody bullshit, Diesel! You're just like Roger—right down to being an irresponsible fuck who can't keep his dick in his pants!"

"STOP!" I shout so hard my throat feels like it's ripped from the size of the sound.

Diesel's face turns an alarming violet red as I beg for him to let him go. It's not until I pull at Trenton's arm that he comes to his senses and releases him.

I cover my lips with my hands as Diesel coughs violently, staggering out of the room. I go after him, clutching my towel as I fly down the steps, calling his name.

He finally stops at the front door, but only seeming to do so because he's so winded.

"Diesel, are you going to tell your dad?"

He whips around to face me, rubbing his throat. "That's what you care about right now?"

"No, I—"

"I should," he speaks over me. "I should call him right now...but I won't. This is your fault, so it's your problem. Tell him yourself. You've always been better at handling him, right?"

I bite my thumb nail as he walks out the front door, my nerves completely frazzled. When I spin around, Trenton's coming down the steps, clothed. His hair's still damp, sloped to the side and hanging over part of his forehead, droplets of shower water glistening over the back of his neck.

I think he's coming toward me until he makes a sharp U-turn, swinging around the stair rail and heading down the hallway, straight to Diesel's room.

I make my way after him to see him grabbing his clothing from the closet and shoving it all in a backpack that I swear I haven't seen since they were in middle school. It's over stuffed, but he seems not to care.

"He says he's not going to tell roger...I believe him."

He pauses, releasing a breath before returning to shuffling through the hung fabric again.

"Just, go talk to him, Trenton. Tell him we won't see each other anymore. You and me, we can work something out so that we can still—"

"Wait wait wait." He shakes his head as the heels of his palms rub his eyes. When he removes them, he looks at me in utter disbelief. "No. You're saying you want to keep this up? To keep sneaking around? More lying? I just put my fucking hands on Diesel, Aubree. That's something I never ever thought I could bring myself to do, and I did. There's no way we can keep doing this."

My lips part, but I can't make a sound, clutching the ends of my towel in my fist. I watch him zip the bag up as far as it will go before carrying it out of the room.

"I can't do this anymore, Aubree," he mumbles, knowing I'm on his heels as we make way to the front of the house. "I'm not going to."

"So that's it? You want to just end everything?"

"I mean, after that, it's ended itself." His hands fall to his thighs. "You're never going to tell Roger you're done with him. That you don't want this life anymore, I know you won't." He looks at me with a stare that could slice me in half. "And Diesel hating me is only worth it if I'm the one you choose."

I can barely hear him over my mind as I replay the words, '*I hate you*' in Diesel's voice. Those words shattered my heart. They knocked into me like a wrecking ball. They're words that I never in a million years wanted to hear come out of his mouth.

But on top of those loud I hate you's, my mind is echoing my favorite '*I love you*,' and it's Trenton.

And that's why I'm standing here, torn to shreds.

Begging him to stay, but knowing he needs to go. This is the part where I lose one of them. This is the damned part I was dreading.

The part where I choose.

"Don't do this, to me. Don't make me pick between you two." *Because Diesel wins every time. Every. Damn. Time.*

"Not between me and Diesel, but between you and Roger. That's what this has always been about. You choosing to be happy, or to continue being a puppet for him. A puppet that keeps up the life he's brainwashed you into living."

I shake my head. "You know it's all so much more complicated than—"

"Bye, Aubree."

"N-no, no—don't go!" I catch him by his arm before he can leave me. But I don't look over the fact that he could've easily gotten away if he really wanted to. "Please, Trenton. I love you."

"I didn't believe it the first time you said it and I don't believe it now."

My eyes widen at him. "Seriously?"

"Seriously. If you meant it, we wouldn't be having this conversation. You wouldn't still be his. You'd only be fucking mine."

"So, what then?" I gulp, taking my time because I'm afraid of the answer he'll give me. Because his foot is down for once and I know he's strong. He's stronger than me, someone who goes back on their words sometimes. Someone who second guesses themself. Someone who doesn't know their self worth well enough to leave a situation that's hurting them. "You don't want to…see me anymore?"

"Not if it means we're having an affair." He slings the bag strap over his shoulder. "Not if it means I'm still second best and that we're back where we were. Keeping secrets again with no chance at anything, real."

"But there's no other way around that…"

"The way I look at it, we have two choices here. The obvious being that you leave Roger, you get a divorce, let Diesel hate both of us and hope he can get over it in time."

"And the second choice?"

He scoffs like he didn't expect me to ask. "We go our separate ways, meaning I never see you again. *Meaning,* I get on with my life and you get on with yours."

Tears rim my eyes, but don't fall. The way Diesel stormed out of here just now is engraved in my mind. Every word, his face, his hate.

I'd say my choice is obvious. It always has been.

"The choice is yours, Aubree. It always has been," he reminds me like he's heard my thoughts.

I drop my eyes from him and see him shuffle his feet like he already knows what I'm going to say before I've even made a sound.

I am wrong.

I am absolutely wrong.

This never should have happened. We never should have ended up here.

I wasn't supposed to fall in love with him. I was never supposed to be in this position.

I've hurt two people I love, and now I've got to be the bigger person and fix it. Even if it kills me inside.

"And my answer has always been the same. Diesel's my son. This is my family."

He hangs his head and a small breath leaves him. "You're choosing your broken family? You should have decided that before you told me you loved me, Aubree! Before you let me love you!"

"You're right. I shouldn't have done this and I can't let Diesel hate me, Trenton. I can't let him hate you. We need to make this right." I feel the first tear run halfway down my cheek. "I cannot be the reason his family is broken. You cannot be apart of the reason."

"Diesel isn't a baby anymore. He's starting a family of his own, he doesn't need you to stay in a marriage that doesn't even make you happy."

"My family makes me happy," I say, dully.

"Roger makes you happy? You look forward to seeing what kind of mood he's going to be in when he comes home? Wondering if today's the day he's going to finally snap and put his hands on you?"

I turn my head. "Stop…"

"Why do you stay, Aubree?" He looks at me with glazed eyes. "Besides Diesel, why have you stayed with him this long? There's gotta be something else. He treats you like shit." He pauses, his hands raking through his hair. "He's been cheating on you for fucking ever and you're just now realizing it."

"What?"

"Everyone knows what goes on in this house. It's no secret. You're the only one who's been in the dark, here."

"No one knows a damn thing about what goes on here." I take a few steps away from him, focusing my eyes out the sliding glass window.

"You know it's the truth. Think about it. Where do you think he goes all week? Conferences? It's all bullshit. The only conference he's having is between someone else's legs. Open your fucking eyes."

I scoff. "I knew you had an asshole side to you."

"So, I'm an asshole because I'm the only person in this damn city who's willing to tell you the truth? Or because you know it's true and didn't think anyone knew?" I don't answer him. The subject of my marriage has never been up for discussion with anyone. Definitely not him. "Aubree, you deserve better. You deserve whatever the fuck you want."

Change this, Aubree. Make him leave. Make him leave for good. For his own good, because nothing good will come out of this love in the end.

You've hurt him enough.

Just hurt him one more time. One more time that counts.

I pivot around to face him. "And what do you think I want?!" I snap, glaring at him the way he's been eyeing me since he came downstairs. "You? You really think I want you, of all people?!"

"After you said you loved me, yeah."

I fold my arms without saying a word. Although I know I need to take that back now, shoving those words back in is even harder than when I finally got them out last night.

"Don't say you didn't mean it." He shakes his head. "Don't even stand here and say that it wasn't true. That suddenly you don't want me. Really, I think you've wanted me for longer than you're willing to admit."

Smart boy.

"I used you!" I shriek. "I used you to fulfill what was lacking in my life Trenton!" My eyes burn as I keep from crying. The look in his eyes as he takes in my words is comparable to being slowly stabbed. "Don't be so fucking full of yourself!"

"No." He shakes his head, but there's clear question in his voice. "That's not true."

"It's true. I never had intentions on being anything more. You just wouldn't let up, but I liked the attention so I kept stringing you along. It was just...fun."

"Fun? That's just bullshit, Aubree." He frowns. "You're lying because you know I'm who you want and should be with, but you're scared."

"You don't know anything, Trenton. You're just a kid." I shrug. "You're a fucking kid who knows nothing about anything."

"And I'm also the kid that gives you multiple orgasms, makes you fucking hyperventilate and scream like you couldn't give a fuck about Roger. Admit it. He's never gotten close to making you feel the way I do."

"This was a mistake." I hold my hands up in surrender. "I should have never let anything come between me and my family."

"Fine, don't. Tell Diesel I'm gone—tell him whatever you want. That I lured you into it, that it was my fault. I don't care anymore. Continue kissing Roger's ass to keep up the 'happy family' image that everyone already sees through." He opens the front door. "And at the end of the day when you're crying into your third glass of wine, remember me. Have a nice life."

TWENTY EIGHT

Trenton

MY EYES BURST OPEN AT THE SOUND OF THE FRONT DOOR opening. I reach out from under my blanket and grab my phone to check the time. A few minutes after midnight. Mom's probably just getting in.

I lay my head back down, only to be startled by the sounds of small sobs before Joselyn's door opens.

"What the fuck?" I say under my breath, leaving my bed.

I go to her door, listening in for it again.

She's clearly crying, and although my sister is normally overemotional, there's something disturbing about this cry—there's something even more disturbing about her coming home this late.

"Jos?" I tap my knuckle on her door.

"I'm fine, Trent."

"You don't sound fine. Open up."

She cries harder, but doesn't open the door.

"I'm coming in."

I take her silence as a go ahead, and open the door to see her sitting on the edge of her bed, head down at the floor.

"Where'd you just come from? Does Mom know you were out this late?"

She shakes her head. Of course she doesn't. Mom's at work, she has no idea.

"Where were you?"

She snivels to herself, but doesn't answer.

"Joselyn, where were you!"

"I was out with someone!"

"Who?"

"…*Someone.*"

My nostrils flare, but I try to keep from losing it. I know what *someone* means. It means she doesn't want to tell me because she shouldn't have been with them. It means she snuck out to see someone she had no business seeing.

"Who were you with, Jos?"

"A guy, okay?"

My jaw clenches at the phrase and I feel a nervousness in the pit of my stomach. "What the fuck happened? What'd he do?"

She pulls her knees up to her chest and hugs them. "I don't want to talk about it. Just leave me alone."

"I'm not going to just leave this alone." Kneeling down, I grab her by the shoulders then turn her head towards me so I can get a good look at her. Checking her face for any markings, then her arms which are red around the wrists. "What the fuck did he do to you?"

She shakes her head, her eyes shut tightly to force out more tears but force back an answer.

I don't need her to answer, I can put it together myself. The thought of someone hurting her makes me want to drive my fist into the wall, but she's so fragile right now, I'd rather go out and find the asshole.

"Tell me," I speak softly. "Tell me his name and where he is."

I went straight to the house she told me this *guy* was at. Lucky for me, I knew the bastard first hand. More specifically, my fist. The moment it clashed against his cheek.

As soon as she uttered his name, my hatred for him returned.

Manny. The asshole who can't handle his own battles. The guy who went down in one hit and needed his hoard of friends to get me off of him.

That explains why he seemed like he knew me. He did, I bet he was fucking around with my sister all this time. If I'd have known, that would have never went on. This would have never happened.

I feel guilty. Joselyn doesn't poke her nose in my business just to be annoying, she does it because she cares. All this time I had been respecting her privacy, hoping she'd do the same for me, but maybe I should have been more like her. I should have looked deeper. I should have paid more attention and I should have been home more than I was.

I'm seeing red as I enter the back gate to a house I'd never been to before. I'm driven by fury. By the fact that he touched my sister with his filthy fucking hands. I pray I don't kill him.

"Yo! Trenton finally came out of the shadows!" I hear beside me, but I don't bother to stop and chat. I've got one goal in mind, and that's retaliation.

"Trenton." Gio's voice is riddled with concern, but like before I keep moving. Searching for that despicable face. "Hey, man what's going on?"

"Where's fucking Manny?" I continue walking, shoving whoever's in my way.

"Stop for a second, wait." Gio's hand grips me and forces me to stop in my tracks.

"My sister was here and you didn't tell her to take a hike? You know how I feel about her being out."

He shakes his head dismissively. "She's old enough to—"

"She's fucking fifteen!" I shout, but the music still masks my voice and doesn't cause a stir. Everyone's still in their own worlds, drunk, dancing and hardly aware of what's going on around them. "He hurt my fucking sister, Gio. I can't let him get away with that shit."

Gio's face falls like he didn't realize that was the result of her being here. He points to a big group, all of them sitting in a circle at the far end of the yard, and I spot Manny out like it's target practice and I'm locked and loaded.

My vision tunnels as I proceed his way, until I'm shoved and lose my footing. Diesel appears right beside me, glaring at me like he's ready for a fight as much as I am.

"Get out of my way, Diesel!" I jerk him back by his shoulders hoping to stun him enough that he lets this go, but he doesn't. He shoves me again.

"What the fuck's your problem!" I snap.

"You! You're my fucking problem!"

I loosen my grip, remembering this is Diesel and not some random person I don't care about. *He's not Manny, don't take your anger out on him.*

"Look, you want to talk about this?" I keep my voice low. "There's a time and a place. Not now."

Everyone's eyes are on us, Gio's standing by like he's ready to step in if needed, but I can tell he doesn't want to. It's a wonder who he'd hold back, which side he'd choose.

None of us ever thought we'd be split up like this. Our group was tight, nothing could have come between us, until something did. Someone.

"I don't wanna fucking talk—" he shoves me for the third time and I stumble back into a fold up chair, knocking it over.

"If you don't stop putting your hands on me, Diesel, I swear."

His arms fling into me, but I stay solid. Only moving an inch from his force. "What? You gonna tell my mom? I mean, we all know you've been fucking her, right?" His hands jet out at me again and reflex forces me to grab him by the front of his sweatshirt, the cloth bunched up inside of my fists.

"We can do this somewhere else," I rasp. And then I release him with a rough shrug.

"Nah, we can do this right now." Diesel removes his hoodie and I rub my tongue over the front of my teeth as I see it drop to the ground. Everyone steps back, their phones out and ready to hit record as soon as arms start swinging.

"I'm not going to fight you, man. Stop," I warn, but Diesel's stuck in attack mode. His fists clench and he's seething through every breath. His glare is dark, and meant to be menacing, but I'm not afraid of him. He's pissed at me and I'll admit, he has a right to be. He has every right to be.

"Then just fucking stand there while I beat the shit out of you then! I don't care!"

"Dees, relax man." I shake my head, my jaw tightening as I see him prepare for his first punch. The rest of them cheering him on like a bunch of wild animals.

"You were supposed to be my fucking friend!"

He's right. I was something to him before I was anything to Aubree. That should have meant something. It should have meant he came first, but I let her take priority and now I'm sorry.

If Diesel wasn't ever my friend, I'd fuck him up without even a second thought. But he is and I betrayed him. I did the one most lethal thing that would break us. The only thing he could never forgive, and now I deserve everything that's coming to me. "I fucked up. I know, but we don't have to do this."

"Fuck him up, Diesel! What the hell are you waiting for?!" Manny shouts.

"Shut the fuck up!" My body livens at the fact that he's finally came this way and I remember why I'm here. "You fucking piece of shit!"

"You shut the fuck up, motherfucker!"

I charge him, Gio ramming his body against mine before I can go any further—probably because he knows I may kill him. "Stay the fuck away from my sister!"

"No problem. I got what I wanted from her anyway." He holds his arms open like he's inviting me to fight him, yet he keeps backing away. I want to tear off his smug smile and shove it down his throat.

"Gio, back the fuck up!" I finally shout, moving him out of my way. With a clear path to the guy, I storm toward him, my fist strikes him right in the stomach without anyone even having time to prepare for it.

Manny bends over, his breath leaving him in a desperate gasp before I straighten him up to get another couple of hits in.

His blood's puddling in droplets onto the pavement, my fist feels drenched in it, but it's not stopping me.

I didn't even realize the music had turned off and everyone's cries of excitement and gasps of horror replace the sound. Voices in the crowd beg me to stop, but all I can hear are my sisters cries. I see the red hand marks wrapped around her wrists, the bruises from where his fingers pressed into her skin and marked her in him.

In the next moment, I'm on the ground. Diesel's fist pummels into my side, and as I endure the shooting pain, I raise my arms to cover my face just like we do every birthday.

I take it.

I take every hit, bracing myself for the next, counting each one as they exceed eighteen. I know I deserve it all.

TWENTY NINE

Trenton

I CAN'T SAY I DIDN'T KNOW AUBREE WOULD BE THE ONE THAT'D drive a knife through my heart and twist it until it's drained dry. I knew that the moment I first looked at her.

I can't say I didn't know I'd fall for her as hard as I did, because I knew that the first time we kissed.

I can't say I didn't know I'd be okay with it all as long as she gave me a chance to really know her, even if it was short. What I didn't know was how low I'd feel when I heard her say she'd never choose me, even though I already knew that too. The pain is unbearable, and I finally get it.

I get why my parents acted like maniacs when they were going through their divorce, I get why Mom is always so miserable. She always loved Dad so much more and she was the one he never chose.

Diesel hasn't talked to me since we fought and it sucks, but I wouldn't have it any other way. He won't be my friend if I have her and I won't sneak around behind his back again just to have her back. I'd rather have nothing if I can't have both.

He glares at me every time we cross paths at work and I have to find time to hang out with Gio when he isn't with him, which leaves me alone most times. But I've fixed that by taking up more hours at work, even going as far as to work a few hours overtime just to keep busy. It tires me out so much that I knock out as soon as I get home, which is good because then I don't have much time to think.

Except for today, when my boss forced me to take a day off after

I tried working three weeks straight before he caught me. He said he'd love to let me continue working, but doesn't want to get into any legal trouble because of it, so now I'm in my room with all the lights out, watching true crime stories on my phone.

"Trenton?" Mom's voice speaks closely to the door.

I pause the screen on the mugshot of a man who'd murdered his whole family for no apparent reason. "Yeah, Mom?"

She forcefully opens the door before flipping the light on, and then she stares at me pitifully in a way that makes me pull my blanket over my face.

She snatches it off of me as she sits down on my bed. "What's going on with you?"

"Nothing. Just enjoying my day off."

She blinks at me like she knows more than she wants to let on. "I wasn't born yesterday. What's eating you?"

I sit up, swinging my feet off the bed and locking my phone before running my hands through my hair. "Nothing, Mom. I swear." I smile at her and it feels like my face is going to crack.

She exhales, crossing her arms over her chest. I know she doesn't want to let this go. I've been plainly moping around the house for about a month now. I'm here but not here. They only ever really see me in the dark because I leave early in the morning and come home late at night.

"You've lost weight, Trenton."

I look down at myself. My stomach's a little thinner, but I feel like my muscle tone is only more prominent from working so hard.

A sudden thought prompts me to stand up and go over to my backpack. I pull out a wad of cash and count out eight hundreds to hand to her.

"What's this?"

"Rent—I don't know, whatever you need it for."

"We already talked about this, son." She shakes her head. "You've helped me back on my feet and I thank you, but now it's time for you to start saving your money."

My hand recoils and I return the money to the stack of bills.

She stands up in front of me. "You work so hard and you've really proven yourself to be such a mature young man, Trenton. I'm so proud of you." Her hand drops on my forearm. "I think it's time you started looking for a place of your own. I've tried to keep you here too long and that was wrong of me. I've burdened you for the past five years over my finances and I don't want you to worry about me and your sister anymore, you clearly aren't happy here. If you need to go, then go."

So I did. Little did she know, I had a ton saved. I took her advice and found an apartment not far from home, just a few miles south in a nice area that wasn't so reminiscent of my old life.

I'm starting over like I never met her. Like Aubree's just a painful figment of my imagination again. She's unreal and out of my reach. The one thing I wanted most in my life that I couldn't have.

All that time spent at work led me to Isabel, the office clerk who works right under my boss. She's got short brown hair cut bluntly to her shoulders, green eyes, and freckles. She's even almost as tall as me. She's everything Aubree isn't, and that's what I need because I can't handle any reminders of her.

I've taken Isabel out to dinner tonight, I let her pick the place because I just don't care. I'm only glad for the outing.

"I was really surprised when you asked me out," she admits, playing with the straw in her cup.

We're at a Mexican restaurant downtown. I'll admit, I was relieved when she asked if I liked tacos. I haven't been near a pasta noodle or a red sauce since me and Aubree went to dinner for the first and last time.

"Yeah, me too," I say, distractedly. "I mean, I didn't think you'd say yes."

"Duh, have you seen yourself." She chuckles, using the straw to spin the ice cubes in her drink. "I don't even know how you're single —unless you're just like, really picky or a dick or something."

I let out a weak laugh, only hearing half of what she's said as my attention's grabbed by the group of singing waiters who've gathered around a table on the far end of the room. One of them sets a big, comical sombrero on a grey haired man's head as they sing happy birthday in Spanish.

I can't understand what they're saying, but it still reminds me of how I spent my eighteenth birthday at Aubree's house, looking up at her window all night. Hoping she'd come out and talk to me because I felt like shit and knew she'd change that instantly with just a smile. With just a hello.

Earlier that day, my mother wished me a happy birthday, hugged me, told me she loved me with tears in her eyes and then handed me a white envelope.

I almost didn't take it from her. But I also almost snatched it from her hands and tore it to shreds. Instead, I took it with haste. I couldn't open it in front of her, though. She seemed to understand that I wasn't going to and left me alone in my room.

Just like the letter I'd gotten on my sixteenth, I had to mentally prep myself for the moment I opened the card, but an eager knock on my door quickly made me back track and hide it behind my back.

"Ha—ppy...BIRTHDAY!" Joselyn shrieked, busting through my door. She ran into me, tackling me in a big hug. Our twice a year hugs that only happen on our birthdays, not including the occasional forced one that Mom makes us do on Christmas. Otherwise the only contact we have is pinching, smacking, or when her foot hits my shin when my leg jets out in front of her after she goes to take a step.

I'm immature, I know. But only with her.

"Thanks, Jos." I crumpled the envelope behind her back, but the paper was so thick, she heard it and broke our hug like she already knew what I was holding.

"You got a birthday card?" Her eyes watered as they set on the envelope in my hands. "I didn't...get one...I—"

Joselyn never received a thing from our father after he left. No one knew why, maybe he didn't feel close to her since she was so young, maybe he thought she didn't care or remember him. I don't know. But she always looked at me like I had some special relationship with him because I was the only one he did try to contact a few times.

"I'm not opening it."

"No." She swallowed. "Open it. I want to see what he has to say to you."

My sixteenth birthday card didn't have a word written in it. Not a *love, Dad*, not an *enjoy your day*, not even a damn *yours truly, Franco*. It was blank besides the generic hallmark message printed inside. But that time, on my eighteenth, it felt different.

I'd sat down next to Joselyn on my bed. She peeled open the white paper, quickly slipping the card out and revealing a colorful design on its front.

"*You're eighteen today...*" she read before lifting the page. "*Which means you're now legally able to do everything you've already been doing since you were fifteen.*"

"Like he'd fucking know," I muttered.

I expected that to be the end of it, until I realized she was silently staring at the card. Silently reading his handwritten words.

TRENTON,

THIS IS YOUR YEAR. THE YEAR YOU GRADUATE FROM HIGH SCHOOL, MAYBE EVEN THE YEAR YOU MOVE OUT OF THE HOUSE. MAYBE THIS IS THE YEAR YOU MEET SOMEONE WHO MAKES YOUR LIFE MAKE SENSE. WHO KNOWS. THE FACT IS, THIS IS THE YEAR YOU HIT ADULTHOOD. THE YEAR YOU BECOME A MAN. BUT YOU'VE BEEN A MAN SINCE THE DAY I LEFT, HAVEN'T YOU? FROM WHAT I'VE HEARD, YOU'VE OUTDONE ME. GRANDMA HAS KEPT ME UP TO DATE ON YOU TWO.

I KNOW WHAT YOU LOOK LIKE THESE DAYS, I KNOW HOW KIND AND CARING YOU ARE, I KNOW WHAT YOU'RE INTO. I HEAR YOU DRINK LIKE I DO AND IT WORRIES ME, BUT I PRAY YOU SEE THE SIMILARITIES AND HATE ME ENOUGH TO STOP. PLEASE REALIZE IT DOESN'T KILL THE PAIN, IT ONLY MASKS IT UNTIL IT KILLS YOU. I KNOW JOSELYN IS GOING TO START DATING SOON AND I PRAY THAT SHE DOESN'T ATTRACT A MAN LIKE ME WHILE TRYING TO FILL THE VOID I CREATED IN HER.

I PRAY THAT YOU ARE BOTH BETTER THAN I WAS, AND I KNOW YOU WILL BE BECAUSE YOU'RE DOING BETTER WITHOUT ME. ONE DAY, MAYBE YOU'LL UNDERSTAND WHY I'M NOT AROUND. ONE DAY, MAYBE YOU'LL BE GLAD I WASN'T. BUT IF THERE'S ONE THING YOU CAN BE CERTAIN ABOUT, IT'S THAT I'M SORRY. IT'S THAT I REGRET MY DECISION EVERY DAY. I MISS ALL OF YOU, EVERY DAY. MY ADVICE TO YOU, SON, IS TO GO FOR WHAT YOU WANT. DON'T HOLD BACK.

YOU CAN HAVE WHATEVER YOU WANT IN THIS LIFE. <u>YOU CAN BE WHOEVER YOU WANT IN THIS LIFE</u>, AND I KNOW YOU WILL BECAUSE I SEE THAT YOU'VE ALREADY BECOME EVERYTHING I'M NOT. YOU ARE SO DETERMINED AND DRIVEN AND I'VE ALWAYS ENVIED THAT ABOUT YOU. SON, YOU MAY HAVE LOOKED UP TO ME FOR A SHORT WHILE, BUT I'VE ALWAYS LOOKED UP TO YOU.

TAKE CARE OF YOUR MOTHER AND SISTER AND DO SOMETHING EXTRAORDINARY.

I'LL BE THINKING OF YOU,

DAD.

I still rack my brain as I think of that card and the way it made me feel. It pissed me off. It made me sick to my stomach, because for the first time I'd read something and it sounded like the old dad I used to know.

Isabel's bright eyes jet up at me. "So, what do you do? Are you in college, or do you just work for PKG?"

Much like my dad, I've found myself wallowing in the wreckage

I'd made. I ruined what I had with people I loved, and now this new life is a fresh start. Isabel is a clean slate, but I only crave the dirty, complicated one between me and Aubree.

"I just work for now." I flip my hand in a small gesture. "I've been saving up and just moved into my own place a couple weeks ago."

"Oh, awesome. I've been trying to move out of home, too. It's hard. Clerks don't make much."

A waiter serves us our plates, lingering by to ask if everything looks okay and if we need any extra utensils, but I simply shake my head and smile.

My phone's burning a hole in my pocket and I pull it out to glance at old messages while we eat. I've barely brought myself to look at my text thread with Aubree just a couple days ago. I never deleted anything even though I told her I would. I just couldn't.

"Are you okay, Trenton? You seem kind of, down?"

"I'm sorry, I just—I kind of just got out of a relationship."

"No it's cool." She sucks a glob if salsa off her thumb. "So did I. I was with this guy for four years and then suddenly I wasn't." Her eyes drift away like she's thinking back to it, but not like it's a painful thought. I envy her for that.

"Did you love him?"

"I don't know. I was young when we got together. I'm eighteen now, four years ago I was like, fourteen. It's like when you've been around someone for a long time, you can't really tell how you truly feel anymore because you get so comfortable it's almost like you've just become numb to everything they do, you know? I think I was just going through the motions and he was the only one smart enough to finally cut the cord."

I nod, taking a bite of my taco.

I can't really relate to that, but it makes me wonder if Aubree was simply going through the motions with Roger. She had to be at this point. Just so comfortable with him that she settled, because it's easiest that way. To turn a blind eye to his ways to keep Diesel happy.

And why are we all trying so hard to keep Diesel happy? He needs to grow the hell up and stop trying to dictate what his mom does and doesn't do.

"Trenton..." I hear beside me before a couple stops at our table. I look to see a pair of hands linked before my eyes rise up to the familiar blonde tresses, finished with a braid pinned around the crown of her head. "Oh my God, it's been forever!"

I can't help the small bunch in my brows upon first seeing her. "Marina." I blink, taking a moment to glance at the guy she's with. He's tall, brown hair, brown eyes. Nothing extraordinary about him. "Hey."

I haven't forgotten what territory we'd left off on. It's weird between us. It's not friendly, and the way she's acting right now doesn't mesh with our current relationship level, at all.

"Hey, yourself." She grins, glancing at her date. "Danny, this is Trenton, the ex I was telling you about."

"No, I'm not—"

"I'm Marina." Her hand juts out at Isabel who's looking completely caught off guard.

This is new for Marina. She suddenly seems self assured like the shy girl act has vanished for good, but I don't buy it for a minute.

"Hi, I'm Isabel."

They shake hands.

"Trenton's girlfriend?"

Isabel looks at me, and not like she's looking for my acceptance over the notion that she's my girlfriend, but because she's probably feeling attacked.

"She's my date, Marina." My face hardens. "It was good seeing you, but if you don't mind..."

"Oh." Her brows raise. "Right. Well I'll let you get back to that then. Nice seeing both of you."

As she's guided away and out the door, we linger in an awkward silence until Isabel says, "That was weird." *Weird indeed.*

The rest of the date went okay. I realized we like the same kind of music and she also used to play basketball at her high school, so that was cool.

I drove her home and we sat in front of her house talking about nothing important. She filled me in on a lot of work gossip which was interesting, but ultimately I could've done without it.

"You should come inside." She looks at me, hopeful, her hand on my arm in encouragement.

I smile at her without showing my teeth and kindly refuse her with a slow head shake. "I would, I just have to be up early tomorrow. I go in at five."

Her mouth twists, but she leans in and kisses me like she accepts that and even respects me for it. I keep my senses wide open while her lips set on mine, hoping to feel a tingle, a vibration—anything to give me hope that I can move forward with someone else, but nope. Nothing.

I smile at her like I enjoyed it anyway, and as she leaves my car, I let her hand slide from my fingertips.

As she disappears behind her front door, I let out an agitated groan and bang my fist on my steering wheel. I'm completely hopeless.

THIRTY

Aubree

Two months later

"ROGER?" I ROAM THROUGH THE HOUSE, SEARCHING FOR HIM ALL downstairs. I'd spent all morning decorating the backyard in baby blue streamers and confetti and matching blue and white striped table cloth to drape over all six of the fold up tables I dragged out of the shed by myself.

He'd slept in all morning despite me telling him how important it was that he be up and ready to help me get everything set up for the shower this afternoon.

We've been rocky lately—more so than usual. When he came home three months ago, swearing he was going to be a different person, that things made sense, that we would fix our family, etcetera etcetera? That wore off in only a couple months. Now he's back to stomping around like a mean giant, sleeping in, laying around, bossing me and complaining about the nit-pickiest things.

And Diesel absolutely hates me, but there is no way around that one. He looks at me like I attempted to murder him. I've tried to talk to him, but he doesn't want to hear a sound from me. He brushes me off, stays feet away from me at all times.

That's why today is so important.

This shower needs to go well, Diesel needs to see that I'm putting in an effort in his life. I'm doubtful this'll make a difference. I'm really just grasping at straws to get his attention. My regret and guilt over the way he caught us has been the only thing keeping me from thinking about how badly I feel about Trenton.

Their friendship is over and it's all because of me.

"Roger!" I call, swinging my head in through the garage door. He isn't there either. I hike up the steps, wondering if he's in the master bathroom and I missed him when I checked earlier, but he must have heard me coming up because he steps out of his office with a stone look on his face.

"Are you going to help me outside? I need you to grab the ladder and—"

He holds up a pair of black panties that make my heart pound in my throat. "What the fuck were these doing shoved under my desk, Aubree?"

"I don't know—I must've dropped them in there when I was doing laundry."

He stares at them, held tightly in his palm, then shakes his head. "You don't need to go into my office when you're doing laundry. You have no reason to go into my office, period."

"I cleaned up in there months ago, I—"

He draws his arm back and chucks them full force at the wall before going back into his office and shutting the door.

I shut my eyes tightly, covering my face in my palms as I recall Trenton's graduation night. When Diesel came home, we panicked and I only grabbed what I could see. "Oh my god…" It had to be then. Any other time we'd done it in there I was already naked.

I continue up the steps, side eyeing my panties on the ground before I knock gently on Roger's office door. He opens the door so quickly, air whips me in the face as he yanks me inside by my arm.

"Sit the fuck down." He paces to the window, the blinds are open, giving us a shuttered view of the street. "Who is it?" Roger pivots around, then slams a hand on the desk. "Who did you fuck in my office, Aubree?"

"Roger, I didn't—"

"Bullshit! How long have you been bringing men into this house, hm? My house." He tilts his head. "While I'm hard at work, jet lagged to pay for everything we have, you're here fucking in my office!"

I stare up at him, my lips held tightly together.

"That half-assed excuse about the birth control...*I'm regulating my cycle,*" He mocks before blowing out a hard breath.

I'm speechless.

I'm caught, again.

"Any day now, Aubree." He smiles, impatiently. "Explain yourself."

"You're a hypocrite."

"But I can afford to be. I make all the money here, that's my job. Your job is and has always been to take care of my son, not have sex under my roof with anyone that isn't me."

I cross my arms over my chest. "While you get it from anyone who isn't me, right?"

"That was the deal we made, Aubree." He points a menacing finger at me, reminding me of the mistake I made when I was a timid teen who didn't have a clue. "This is the life we agreed on."

"I agreed to do the right thing, but allowing you to freely cheat on me in exchange for a wedding ring wasn't that. I was a fucking kid. I wasn't fit to make an agreement like that, let alone consent to sex with an asshole like you."

"Oh!" His brows raise. "So now you're feeling ballsy enough to call the breadwinner of the household an asshole? I'd watch my fucking mouth if I were you!"

"Why don't you just admit that you hate me, huh? You've always hated me. You don't respect me as a mother. You've never treated me like a wife, you never wanted me to be your wife—"

"Because you ruined my life, don't you get that?!" He shouts at me unapologetically, leaning forward over the desk. "The least you could do is abide by my rules in my damn house! Is that such a hard concept for you to grasp?!"

His voice echos in my head long after it's stopped and he waltzes around the room until his hand swings across the top of his bookshelf and knocks off a collection of decorative knickknacks I'm sure were gifts from his mother. Some clink as they hit the wall and others only tumble onto the floor.

"When does this ever end, Roger?"

"Why would you want it to?" He speaks more calmly, staring out at the street again. "You've got it made here. I pay your way, you have access to all my money. Why leave unless you're interested in starting over with someone else?"

The room's so quiet, I can hear my spit go down as I gulp.

Besides get as far away from Roger as possible, I don't know what I want to do. I've always wanted to get a job, go to school, explore hobbies and have a life, but he's kept that from me and I blindly went along with it. Thinking this was the best I could do, that this was what was best for me and my son. Roger's the worst thing to ever happen to me and if I really ruined his life, I'm glad because he ruined mine.

"I don't want this life anymore," I croak out the words I never thought I'd have the will to say. Realizing beneath them that I have nowhere to go, that my son will never forgive me and always blame me for this, that I don't know what my future looks like on my own, but that I also don't care. I can't take the abuse anymore. This was never love and I didn't know that until Trenton came in and showed me why it wasn't.

I have to go.

"You already know what happens if you leave me, Aubree, I'll never speak to you or Diesel ever again." He talks at the window, his breath fogging up the glass. "Diesel will never speak to you again."

"Diesel has nothing to do with this." My voice breaks. "Leave him out of it, please."

He turns to look at me. "He has everything to do with this. He's the damn reason we're here. He's the fucking plague that killed us both before we even got a chance."

"He loves you," my voice wavers as I fight the tears choking me.

He shakes his head and huffs out a chuckle. "And that's why he'll hate you if you're the reason I leave. If I show him this..." He pulls out his keys from his pocket and unlocks the top drawer to his desk, unveiling an old friend. My biggest regret yet, just looking at it after so many years makes my stomach tense.

The diary I'd written in religiously since I was thirteen. It has everything in it. My rawest, truest feelings. Things I wrote while going through the toughest time of my life.

I stare hard at the book, seeing him flip through the pages like he's about to read me a bedtime story. "I'm sure you remember this old thing, huh?"

"Roger…"

"I mean, who could forget? I know I can't. The number of times you called me a mentally abusive husband, a self centered, egotistical prick—and my favorite—the biggest mistake you ever made. I love that one."

I snivel into the back of my hand as he continues skimming through the pages.

"*May 5th, 2001…I'm going to do it. I've decided I'm going through with the abortion—*"

"Roger, please, I'm begging you!"

He holds a firm finger up as he struts around his desk. "*I can't let my mistake become a reality. When I stopped to look at things clearly, it wasn't a hard decision. It wasn't hard at all. It was as easy as asking myself, do I want to ruin my life or not? I choose not. I choose me.*"

"I didn't mean any of that. I changed my mind an hour after writing that."

"Then it shouldn't be a problem if I show it to Diesel."

"He won't understand."

"I think he'll understand that perfectly. That, and all of the other entries you'd written just like it after he was born."

"Just let me go, Roger." I sob. "I'm miserable with you. We're miserable together."

He walks back to his desk, hopping up and sitting on its top, right where Trenton sat me down on multiple occasions. "You know I need you. I can't show up to company Christmas parties without my wife, how's that going to make me look?"

"Fine, if I'm not your wife anymore."

"Divorce isn't an option, Aubree. Not in this family."

I drop my eyes from him. I hate him. I hate the hold he has on me, the fact that he keeps me both secure and insecure. There's no way out, there never has been.

"Who was it?" He licks his lips.

"Does it even matter anymore?" I drop my face in my hands.

"Why aren't Diesel and Trenton friends anymore, Aubree? And why does he suddenly seem to despise you even more than usual? Why are you suddenly groveling at his feet? Running around the house to put together a baby shower he couldn't give a damn about?"

I raise my head slowly.

"That little fucking punk that's always drooling over you, you fucked him." He says it like he's just put it all together, eyes narrowed to slits like he's concentrating hard on me. Like he's hoping to drag the confession out of me. "You did, didn't you?"

I swallow, shaking my head. My hands have began trembling and I feel like I'm going to puke.

"You're sick." He laughs. "You were that desperate for some attention that you opened your legs up to a teenage boy?" He wipes his eye like he's swiping away a stray tear from laughing and then spits out the words, "Pathetic. You've always been pathetic. Do you really want that to get out? Do you want to humiliate your son with the fact that you cheated on me, his father, with a teenager?"

I didn't answer him. I couldn't answer that, not even in my head.

All I've wanted the past seventeen years is to keep my family together. To give my son as normal of a life as I possibly could, to keep him from wanting anything, but all he's done is want more and more until all that was left to want were things I could never give him. A happy family. Parents that genuinely loved each other. A father that doesn't blame his son for his mistakes, but owns up to his own.

I got up fast and left him there.

Roger left shortly after that. I'm not sure if he'll be back, he clearly doesn't care about anything and never has. I just want to get through today for Diesel. I need to put on a nice face, and get dressed like my life is perfect. Nothing different from what I normally do. I've faked it all for as long as I can remember.

My face required more makeup than usual to hide the dark circles underneath my eyes, and the burns from not being attentive enough while curling my hair, due to my thoughts being all over the place.

I put on a nice dress and heels and and smiled in front of the mirror to see if it would be believable.

It isn't, but I've gotta make this happen anyway.

One thing I am happy with is how well the decorations came out. Chloe showed me a whimsical sky theme months ago. I agreed it was a cute idea, so last night with Lyssa's help, we made mini hot air balloon centerpieces and strung together an archway of white balloons in different sizes to give them a cloud like appearance. Stuck gold glittering stars all around them, complete with a gold moon on the snack table. I even hung some teddy bears dangling from balloon bouquets to make it look like they're floating into the sky.

I'm happy a new life is coming into the world. If anything, I look forward to that. Meeting my *grandson*. I still can't believe it. Me. A grandmother.

It seems unnatural.

The guests trickled in, the music played, bottles popped, and food was served. Solana stuck by my side, keeping me cool. Cracking jokes, keeping my mind off things. She knew about Diesel catching me in the act, that was the last I'd told her. But I have a new bomb to drop and I need to tell someone before I self implode.

"Roger found out." I look at her, my voice hushed and spoken close to my cup. "He found a pair of my panties underneath his desk."

"Aubree." Her eyes widen at me. "Well, what did he say? The *D* word?"

"No, actually. He doesn't want that at all."

"What?"

"He wants me to stay with him. He wants me to just forget about everything and continue doing what we've been doing. Leading this fake life, except now it's going to be worse because the truth's come out. No more faking. Everything's wrecked, Sol." My voice breaks and I turn to the side to keep anyone from noticing the tiny tears I can't suppress. "It's all ruined."

She grabs me by my wrist and pulls me all the way to the side of the house where we keep the bins, staring me dead on and holding me by my shoulders. "Don't stay, Aubree."

"I have to."

Her face tightens. "What do you mean you have to? Roger's a fucking gaslighting dick and this is finally your opportunity to leave him. Go. Run."

I shake my head, my eyes tracing the grooves in the fence.

"Aubree, talk to me."

"He's going to show Diesel things I wrote about him when I was a kid. It was all wrong. I didn't mean any of it, but I wrote it down anyway and now Roger has it. Every negative thought I ever had, every time I regret him, every time I wished I could start my life over, it's all in that book. He's been holding it against me all these years, it's the main reason I stayed. He's going to show Diesel that diary, and when he reads it he'll never forgive me."

Her eyes examine my face, she's probably realizing she's never seen me this way before. Completely broken down.

"He's already said he hates me, and I don't know…maybe he can hate me more than he does now."

"He doesn't. He doesn't mean that, he's just hurting. He needs you and you need him. I don't care about what's been said today or written years ago, Diesel's your son, he will always love you unconditionally, no matter what he claims."

"I don't know."

"Talk to him, and when you're done I've got a guest room with your name on it. Get away from Roger, Aubree. He's terrifying."

I blinked at her, hearing her words. Stunned by them. I'd never heard her refer to Roger as terrifying before, but he is. He really is.

We returned to the party after she lent me her bottle of eye drops. I guess she was no stranger to faking a calm face, too.

Diesel still blew past me like a plastic bag in the wind whenever I was near.

Solana's right. I need to talk to him. I need to tell him his father knows what went on, but he also needs to finally know the truth about his father as well.

Diesel thinks Roger can do no wrong. His father's always been his hero, and I've always been too scared to crush that image for him. But by withholding the truth, hiding Roger's wrongs, I was made the bad guy.

How am I going to tell him that everything he once thought about his father was a complete façade? That our entire relationship was a cover up for the truth?

"I didn't know if you'd be able to pull it off, but everything looks great, Aubree," says Lyssa.

"Thanks for the optimism." I chuckle.

"You know I mean that in the most loving way." She smiles, glancing around at everything and everyone. "But seriously, you may have a future in party planning. You know, I always thought if I had a second pair of hands, I'd be able to take it more seriously and expand."

"Well, keep me in mind because I may have some free time on my hands in the near future."

She looks at me perplexed, but Chloe swoops in with a habitual hand held over her belly and ends the conversation before I have to explain my life to Lyssa.

Her pink dress is beautiful, it's floor length with sleeves that drape off her shoulders. She grins at me, completely floored. "Mrs.

Cooper, this is perfect!" She walks into my open arms, her belly creates a barrier between us and we can only hug so close. "Thank you so much for everything, I love it."

I pull back to look at her, our hands linked together. "You're very welcome, Chloe." I can feel my eyes watering and smile through it, but her face sinks and her smile fades.

"Mrs C.?" She frowns at me like she doesn't want to blatantly ask if I'm okay, but I know she's wondering.

I move my hands to her shoulders and nod. Diesel walks by and I excuse myself to go after him.

"I need to talk to you," I say as he stops in front of the buffet table, reaching for a paper plate.

He doesn't respond and instead serves himself a grip of tortilla chips with a pair of tongs.

"Diesel." I watch him lift the lid off the pot of hot cheese and pour a spoonful over the chips. "Your dad found out," I mumble, but the words make him freeze and for the first time in months, look at me.

"You guys finally breaking up?"

"I don't know. Maybe."

"Good. Let Patrick sign for the apartment, we can all go our separate ways." He snags a cookie from the dish of dozens. "Just like you wanted."

"What are you talking about?"

"You think I don't know? You think I never knew what was going on all this time? Unlike you, Dad never hid anything from me, he was open about everything. You never wanted to marry him, you never wanted me, you hate your life. If you want to leave Dad so bad, go ahead, but don't drag my friends into your mess. Don't drag me into it either." He shrugs and my mouth jumps open to argue, but he waves his hand and says sternly, "I'm not talking about this here."

He walks away with his plate as the pieces all fall together for me. Diesel doesn't hate me for no reason. He hates me because Roger wanted him to hate me. Roger's been feeding him lies for who knows how long. He's groomed him to believe that I'm the the cause of all the problems. If I leave, it'll just be me striking out once again.

THIRTY ONE

Aubree

WHEN THE PARTY ENDED, I WAS ALL ALONE.

Solana offered to stay, but I told her to go. That I'd be okay and really just needed time to think.

Roger did pop in earlier with a big *look at me* sort of gift, only to further convince Diesel that he's the good guy despite him not contributing a thing for this party.

He left as quickly as he came, and before he was gone he made sure he kept up his front as the *Pleasantville* husband by leaning in like he was going to kiss me on the cheek, but instead murmured the word *Pathetic* in my ear.

I stood in the middle of the backyard watching the last few guests leave, thanking me for having them as they all trailed out the gate. I shut the music off and spun around to look at the aftermath. It'd take me hours to put everything away, but I kicked off my heels and began folding up chairs, carrying them to the shed, trip after trip. I folded up table cloths, carried leftover cookies and food inside and set them on the island, and then I took a seat.

I sat down on the sofa, realizing how exhausting that was. How exhausting it is to smile at everyone when you feel like shit on the inside.

Roger's voice still echos in my head. *Pathetic.*

I can't do anymore today. I don't want to be a wife anymore.

I run up the stairs, changing into a pair of leggings and a t-shirt. I put on my comfortable white trainers because I'm tired of heels. I'm tired of dressing like a professional model. I'm tired of being told I need to be made up all the time because everyone Roger works for or is friends with needs to know he has a trophy wife who never has a single hair out of place—and that's only because he sets and pays for my bi weekly hair appointments.

I throw my hair into a messy bun and snag my bag before shooting out the door.

This is crazy. You're crazy, I think as I cruise down the street. Chasing a boy. Being in love with a boy.

Insanity.

But Trenton isn't a boy anymore. It's been so hard to wrap my head around that, yet it's the simple truth.

And I shouldn't be ashamed of my feelings for him, I shouldn't feel pathetic for being in love with Trenton because Roger says I am. I shouldn't let him feel like he's second best when he's been the first and only thing on my mind.

I love him.

And he needs to hear it again because I can't let another minute go on with him thinking I don't.

My hands are shaking around the steering wheel as I pull up to Trenton's house. His car isn't here and my mind automatically reads that as a bad sign, but I pick up my phone and call him anyway.

I listen as the line trills and eventually goes to voicemail. I call again and the same thing happens. Did he block me?

I push the lock button on the side and tap the edge of the phone to my chin as I muster up the courage to knock. But before I even step out of my car, the front door opens and a girl steps outside.

She's got earphone cords dangling from her hands and when she gets closer, I realize it's his younger sister and she's coming right up to the car.

She bends down to speak through the open window. "Mrs. Cooper, I thought that was you."

"Hi, Joselyn…I'm looking for your brother. Is he home?"

She purses her lips curiously and then shakes her head. "He

doesn't live here anymore."

"What?" I frown, but then realize I need to tone down my disappointment. "Oh, well…where does he live now?" *Please don't say he did something crazy like leave the state.*

"He got his own apartment a few months ago. He lives in South Ridge, if you know where that is."

His own apartment? He must be doing well—I'm glad he is, that's what I wanted for him.

"Yeah, I know where that is."

"Why are you looking for him?"

My lips part as I think up a lie, but the way she's smiling at me lets me know she knows much more than she should.

"He's in love with you, you know? Total mess before he moved, it was kind of a relief when he finally left. He was so depressing to be around."

My face sinks and I stare down at the empty passenger seat between us. "He told you?"

"I got it out of him." She shrugs, proudly. "I'll give you his address."

I copy down the address in my phone's GPS and head over. It leads me to some beige colored apartments with nice, up kept shrubbery and patches of pretty colored flowers lining the walkways. Vibrant pinks and purples, edging along the pale stone.

I park in the visitor parking and take a moment to stand beside my car, wiping my hands on my leggings because they're seeping nervous sweat.

I don't really know what brought me here, I don't know what I'm going to say. I don't know if he's going to welcome me, or shut the door in my face.

But I still take the steps to his apartment and knock in the most uncertain way, contemplating running back to my car as my knuckles hit the door.

I hear footsteps behind it, but it doesn't open, so I brave up and knock once more. Harder this time.

The door swings open and he stands in front of me, tall, handsome, and shirtless with an expression that I'm unable to read. A mixture of confusion and shock. He looks bigger than I remember, like he's been a regular at the gym.

"Aubree." His voice is thick and his throat bobs as he swallows, but he just stands there, looking me up and down like he's seeing me for the first time.

"Um...I..." I begin, but shut my mouth when I notice movement behind him.

"Babe? Have you seen my pink sweatshirt?" A feminine tone asks, voice adrift, like she's walking from room to room. "I can't find it anywhere!"

My chest tightens and I drop my head. *What was I thinking?*

"I'm sorry, Trenton. I—I'm clearly an idiot." I turn to walk away, scolding myself in my head. Embarrassment flushes my face while jealousy kicks me in the belly.

"Aubree, wait," his voice is so strong and pleading I stop in my tracks and turn to face him. "Talk to me."

"There's nothing to say, this was a mistake."

"Yeah, you said that last time."

I shake my head and a short haired girl steps out of his door, staring at me curiously with her bright green eyes, wearing a pink sweatshirt that I'm assuming is the one she was looking for.

"Trenton, aren't you going to introduce me?" she asks.

He shuts his eyes and quietly hums like he hates that I've caught him like this. "Yeah...Isabel, this is my friend's mom, Aubree. Aubree, this is my...girlfriend, Isabel." He hangs his head and I reach out to shake the girl's hand.

My chest aches violently, but I mask it with a smile like I always do.

"Nice to meet you." She grins before wrapping her arms around his torso. Almost like she's staking her claim over him.

Hope you're enjoying everything I taught him, I think as I fight back the urge to glare at her.

"Same here." I purse my lips together, watching her kiss his bare arm, leaving what looks to be an intentional pink lipstick mark on his skin. His brazen stare on me makes me wonder if he's angry that I've come or that he's still just upset with me after the way we left things.

"I'm going to finish grabbing my things," she tells him before skipping back inside.

Trenton wipes off the kiss print she left him as soon as the door shuts.

He opens his mouth like he wants to explain himself, but I shake my head. Nothing needs to be explained. He's moved on, he's got a whole new life and I'm here stepping on it with my dirty shoes.

"I shouldn't have came. I'm sorry."

"Aubree."

I continue toward my car, hearing his bare footsteps follow after me but I don't stop. I unlock my car with the control in my hand before his hand curls around my arm.

"Aubree," he pleads. "You didn't just come here to remind me everything was a mistake."

"I don't know why I came here." I shrug. "I shouldn't have."

He shakes his head like he's dismissing everything I'm saying. "She's leaving. Just, wait here. We'll talk."

I get into my car and sit there, watching him jog back to his apartment. I very seriously consider driving home to finish cleaning up, but then he walks his girlfriend outside and sees her to her car. I notice him lean down before shutting the door and although they're out of view, the idea of him kissing her makes my throat knot.

He stands under the parking stall with his hands in the pockets of his sweats, watching until her car disappears out the front gate and then he jerks his head toward his apartment as if that's my cue to come inside.

Warily, I leave my car and follow after him.

He has a few pieces of furniture in the living room, but not much. A small couch, recliner, television mounted on the wall, and a game system on the small, bare entertainment center beneath it. The room even still has the fresh paint and new carpet smell.

He stands against the wall, eyes on me like he's waiting on me to explain myself.

Maybe I would if his body wasn't so damn distracting.

"You look…" *Hot as hell.* "Really…fit."

"Yeah, I've been going to the gym. I have to, or else work would kill me."

I rip my eyes from his glorious torso and return to scoping the place out. Admiring the faux marble counter tops and black cabinetry in the kitchen. "This is nice."

"I know you didn't come here just to check out my apartment." He blinks at me. "How'd you find me?"

The unfamiliarity in his voice is disheartening. Like after everything, we're strangers. I'm not even Mrs. Cooper, I'm just his friend's mom. Virtually nothing.

"I stopped by your Mom's. Your sister gave me your address."

He drops his head and slightly smiles like he knows that's something she'd do.

"Your girlfriend's pretty," I say, staring out the window like she's still out there. "How long have you been dating?"

He shrugs a shoulder, eyes almost rolling. "What'd you come here for, Aubree?"

It's suddenly harder to speak and I'm struggling to gather words.

He pinches my chin and lifts my head so that I have to look at him. "Is it that hard to just say you missed me?"

"Yes." *Because I see you moving forward, doing well, and who am I to get in the way of that? Of you having a normal life, dating girls your own age, reveling in the excitement of having your own space?*

"I missed you. I missed you so fucking much," he whispers. "Why'd it take you so long to come find me?"

I fall into his arms like melting butter and he tightens around me.

I don't have an answer to that question. I guess I just spent more time trying to keep him off my mind, trying to convince Diesel I was sorry, and trying to convince Roger I was still the same woman he married.

We stand there in the middle of his living room, holding each other. I count his heart beats, listening as his breathing loops over and over, his warm body reminding me he's with me. Confirming that I'm where I need to be.

And then we finally sit down on his couch, it's slightly stiff, but I'm sure that's just because it's brand new.

"We just had Chloe's baby shower earlier today."

"Oh yeah? That means she's about ready to pop then…"

"Yeah…one more month to go." I nod. "They're naming him Aiden."

He huffs under his smile, I can see how much he misses Diesel. I know the feeling is mutual, because when I do see Diesel, he's quieter, he's blander. He's just not the same without him.

"Look, Trenton, I didn't mean to come here and disturb your life, especially since you're doing well—"

"Doing well?" He scoffs. "This is desperation, Aubree. I've been miserable the past three months. I did all of this just to try and take my mind off it all. Off Diesel, off you. I've flipped my whole life around and it still didn't change anything. I still think about you every fucking day."

I've been absolutely miserable too, I've missed you every day, I think to myself, but my lips don't move to expel the words even though I know he wants to hear them.

"So, I'm curious. What made you finally crack? I knew that was all a lie, about you using me. I meant something to you."

I stare down at my hands. *You meant everything to me.* "Well, Roger found out. He figured it all out on his own."

"And you're leaving him?" He says it like he's challenging me.

That's Trenton's favorite question. But I guess it's always been mine too. It's always been a small voice in the back of my head that only grew louder the longer I stayed with him.

I open my mouth to speak, but can't force out another sound.

"Dammit, Aubree," he speaks into his hands in frustration.

"I just, I can't."

"You have to." He stares daggers at me. "Do you know how long me and Diesel have been wondering when he's going to finally snap and hurt you? You know he's capable of that. His hate for you is that strong, I've only been waiting on the day."

"I don't think he would ever—"

"Stop looking for good in evil. There's nothing good about him, you've gotta get away from him before he fucking kills you." He stares straight across the room.

"You don't understand."

"I want to, Aubree! I've been trying to understand it, but I can't if you don't tell me anything!" He takes a breath. "We're alone. No one's here to interrupt us, and I don't know about you, but I've got all night. Let's hear it."

I stare at him scraping my mind for an explanation that could get me out of this, something that makes enough sense but doesn't expose me for the person I've been trying to hide.

"Why do you stay with him? What does he have on you, Aubree?"

He will drive my son away from me and I couldn't live with myself if Diesel knew my truth.

So I lie. "I don't have anywhere to go, Trenton."

He huffs like he knows that's bullshit, but seems too tired to really argue against it anymore. "Your parents? A friend? I'm sure Solana will let you stay with her if you explain everything."

I scoff at the fact that he isn't mentioning himself and he catches it quick.

"You broke me, Aubree," he says flatly. "I fucking love you, but I can't be your last resort. I can't be second best to that fucking dick you married. We both know you'll probably run back to him. You always do, and I can't be the one you leave behind when it happens."

"You aren't a last resort, Trenton. Never."

"Then why does it feel that way? Why'd you even come here? To cram yourself back in my head? To try and trick me into thinking you're finally going to do the impossible, only to change your mind for the tenth time?"

I rise from the sofa, covering my tired eyes with my palms. "This was a huge mistake."

"Everything's always a fucking mistake to you."

"I'm sorry I came." I make my way to the front door. "Goodbye."

"Aubree."

I hear his voice behind me as I jog across the street to my car. From behind the wheel, I can see him standing in the walkway in front of his door.

I take off, and as much as I don't want to look back, I glance up at him in the rear view mirror, watching him gather himself back inside.

THIRTY TWO

trenton

AS SOON AS SHE STEPPED OUT MY DOOR THAT DAY, I KNEW I fucked up. I knew I'd regret letting pride get in the way, but I couldn't succumb to groveling at her feet even though I felt seconds from dropping to my knees the moment I saw her at my door.

But now she's gone again. And although at the time I felt like I told her all the right things, it feels all wrong now.

I always hoped she would come to me when the time came— then the time came and I turned her away. I had to. I just knew if I gave into her, it was all going to backfire on me.

I'm stronger than that—or I'm trying to be.

I'm making a life for myself. A life where I don't have to settle for the scraps she gives me the way a dog laps up crumbs out of a dish.

Isabel's been a good girlfriend. She's funny, she's caring, she makes breakfast every morning after she stays the night. She does little things, like packs my lunches, or rubs my shoulders after a long day. She's lighthearted and kind and she isn't ashamed of me.

There's nothing in our way.

No numbers between us. No husband between us. No weird history. No jealous ex. Nothing.

I'm moving on.

I stare at myself once more in the mirror, feeling like a different person. I'm not at all the kid who was in love with a woman almost twice my age. I'm an adult. I'm a man who gets things done. Who sticks to his word. Who makes sure his family is okay all the time as

246

opposed to just popping in for dinner sometimes without a clue of what's really going on in their lives. I have a normal relationship that I don't have to hide anymore. Friends who are on the same track as me. Friends who don't spend every night of the week partying in backyards until they're blackout drunk, only to wake up under the sprinklers. Friends who don't have a grudge against me.

Clean slates.

Isabel is due to show up any minute, we've gotten into the habit of having pizza and a movie every Friday night in my living room— Of course that's code for pizza and sex while a movie is playing, but either way it makes for a decent night.

I try not to compare sex with Isabel to sex with Aubree, if I do I'll just be setting myself up for disappointment. It's not bad, just different.

The door bell rings and I come down the hall, adjusting the hem of clean shirt I'd just put on.

I swing open the door and to my surprise it's not Isabel at all. Diesel's staring me in the face, hand held on the door frame like he's entitled to a chance at speaking to me after everything that's gone down.

He is. I open the door wider and he comes inside.

"This is nice..." he says, looking around the exact same way Aubree did. "How much do you pay to live here?"

"Uh," I scratch my head as I shut the door. "Twelve hundred."

"One bedroom?" He peers down my short hallway.

"One and a den."

I could have chose a regular one bedroom, but when I picked this layout, I had Aubree in mind—even though she'll never stay here.

He nods, walking over to the television, glancing behind it like he's checking the mount.

"What's up, Diesel?" I quickly get us back on the important subject: Why he's here.

"I want to know everything." He takes a seat on my couch.

"About what?"

He takes a breath. "About you and my mom. The fuck do you think?"

My mouth twists and I keep my arms crossed tight as I sit in the small recliner beside him. "It's over. There's nothing to know anymore. It was nothing."

"I'm not playing games right now, Trenton." He stares at me. "Were you guys just...fucking...or..."

"Pretty much."

"How long?"

"A couple months." I stare down at the floor. "How'd you know we were there, Diesel?"

"A little birdie told me. I got a text that morning..."

Marina's a fucking bitch. I had a feeling she was the one making Diesel sprint home at weird hours, but I didn't want to believe she'd be that low to actually do it. To rat me out to Diesel. To fuck everything up.

"It was vague. They just asked if my dad was home because his car wasn't, but that some guy was walking around in her room. I didn't think it would be you."

I purse my lips, trying to ignore the short instance of silence between us.

"Did you...get close to her?" he asks. "Did she tell you things?"

"Like fucking what?"

"Like personal things. Like about her and my dad."

I bite my tongue, my mind feels like toes hanging off the edge of a cliff as I think about what I do know.

"I'm at a point in my life where I'm realizing there's a lot my parents kept hidden from me, and I have a feeling you know way more than I do."

"I don't know much."

"Bullshit."

"I don't, Diesel. All I can say is you hated the wrong person, man. Your dad treats her like shit, but she tolerates it all because of you. There's no love there for her. She only stays with him *for you*."

"Did—were you in…love with my mom?" He asks the question like his throat's constricting. Like it's hard to ask.

"I was." *I am.* I nod. "I never wanted to be…but fuck, I really was."

His face balls up in disgust. "That's my fucking mom, man."

"I know and I'm sorry. Look, as soon as it got to the point of actually fucking up my relationship with you, it was over. We took it too far…but it's done and it's been done since you found out."

I flinch as his fist knocks into my shoulder. "You fucking asshole."

"What? I did the right thing. I cut it off."

"Why didn't you tell me?"

"I couldn't tell you I was pursuing your mom. I mean, look at how you flipped when you found out."

He squints at me like I'm speaking another language. "I just… yeah, you're right."

"Well, lucky for you it's over. We don't have to talk about it ever again."

He stares at me like this isn't the direction he wanted the conversation to go in, but I don't care. I don't want to discuss this. It's honestly hard for me to even look at him.

"Alright." He shrugs. "I didn't just come here to talk about my mom, though. I came to tell you that Chloe's due any day now and I can't imagine doing this without you. You were always supposed to be Aiden's godfather and nothing's changed."

I blink at him, but he's dead serious.

"Look, I'm sorry for everything, but I think we're even now."

I chuckle, thinking about how I let him beat the shit out of me in someone's back yard a few months back. And yes, I let him. It took everything I had not to flip the script—everything and the fact that I couldn't lay an honest hand on Diesel even if I wanted to.

He holds his hand out for me and I stare at it for a second, wondering if I can even stomach being his friend again. If I can handle being around him without having her in my life.

In haste, I shake his hand. An apology, a confirmation, and a truce without any words exchanged.

I glance at my apple watch for the time, remembering Isabel's still on her way. "Alright. Well, time for you to go."

"What the fuck? I just got here. Let's check out this flat screen." He reaches for the remote on the small end table.

"My girlfriend's coming over." I chuckle, quickly grabbing his attention.

"Girlfriend?"

"Yeah. You know Isabel, from work."

"That shit's not gonna last, bro." He takes his time getting up.

I grab him by the shoulder and guide him to the door. "Well, I'll enjoy it while it does."

"Let's hang out this week."

"Alright, I'll text you when I'm not working."

He nods and we shake hands before I shut the door. It feels a lot less heavy knowing that we're okay, but I'm still unsettled.

THIRTY THREE

Aubree

I'VE AGREED TO EVERYTHING, JUST AS I ALWAYS HAVE.

I've agreed to allow Patrick Hanes to co-sign for Diesel and Chloe's apartment because I know how much it means to him. Looking at it now, it's probably their best bet at starting this off right and making it work.

I've also agreed to stay in this house because Roger's right. I don't have anything else going for me. I've wasted the most important years of my life with a man who thinks more of the dirt underneath his nails than of the woman he's married to. I don't know why he wants this kind of control over me, but he has it. My life's purpose has been to make sure my son is happy, and if my happiness is compromised in the process, so be it. Anything to soothe the ache of guilt for what I'd written in those pages.

I don't know what's stronger. That ache, or the deep longing I have for Trenton. I haven't stopped crying since that day I visited him. I break down every morning because he's in my dreams. He's in my head. He's like a ghost in this house. I see him everywhere, but he's simply not here. And it hurts because I know it's only best for everyone if I just let him go.

"So you're just going to keep doing this then?" Roger stands in the open doorway of the den. "Sleeping on the couch?"

"Why would I sleep with you? You hate me. You think I'm to blame for why your life is such a *failure.*" I fluff my pillow,

251

straightening up the blanket I've just pulled out of the dryer. "I don't get why you feel that way. In reality you have your own personal slave. I think you have it pretty well."

"Slave? Please. Besides picking up a broom or the handle of a pot, you hardly lift a finger around here. I've given you everything you can possibly want, so stop being like this and come to bed."

"I want a husband that loves me, Roger. That's the one thing you never gave me."

"Well I also want things I can't have, but that's life. I'll fucking get over it."

"No you won't. You'll say you'r over it and you won't be. It's exhausting watching the door everyday, wondering if you're going to hate me or not."

"So what then? You want to leave? You want to just leave me for some little boy who's going to be over you by next week? I remember being that age. I went through women like I went through socks."

"See, that's not normal. This isn't a normal marriage, Roger. You having all the women you want while I'm stuck under lock and key after being blackmailed into staying with you, it's not okay."

"But I kept my end of the deal. I never got sloppy. I never brought any of them home, I never gave them the number to the house. They didn't know where I lived. You didn't know what they looked like, their names—"

"But I knew they were there! I knew someone was with you whenever you weren't with me. I sat at home with our son, knowing you were out. Knowing you were sleeping with them and were coming home to me after you were done." I drop my head.

"You were here writing horrible shit that I think Diesel deserves to know about." He cocks his head. "Don't you think Diesel deserves to know how you really felt about him all this time?"

"That's not how I really felt."

"Then why'd you hide it? It wouldn't have been necessary to hide it unless you meant everything you said and didn't intend on anyone reading it."

"I don't know." I don't know why I did it. I don't know why I scribbled out horrible things on notebook paper, but it felt good while I was doing it. It was an outlet. A way to get out all of the nasty things I kept bottled up inside me. They were just words. Words I'd arranged in my head, words that crossed my mind.

And maybe I did mean them at the time, but I never meant them all the time.

"It's too late for all this now, Aubree. Like I've told you before, nothing can fix all the damage there is between you and me. But you have a life here. A life, and a choice."

"I've never had a choice."

"You do now." He leaves me on that note.

Alone with the thoughts of the past swirling in my brain. Thoughts of all that I put up with just to keep him. I don't know why I did it all. Naivety? Foolishness? The desire to be loved?

Roger shook his head, frowning at me with his arms crossed. "I told you to put on the blue one."

I glanced down at the maroon fabric encasing me. A spaghetti strapped dress with a classy draped front. I wore it to my high school graduation and it became a favorite of mine. "I just…I thought this one was more appropriate for a work party—"

"I said the fucking blue one, Aubree. Hurry up."

I began slipping the straps down my arms as he shut the bedroom door. The blue one he was referring to was busty and short. I wasn't comfortable in things like that, especially around Roger's parents, but I was even more uncomfortable arguing against him. He both picked it out and bought it for me. I felt I shouldn't.

I heard the boys downstairs giggling and probably running rampant around the house, but that was the babysitters' problem. Worrying about not further ruining this night was mine.

As soon as everyone found out I was pregnant, Roger's father hired him on to the family company. His parents were wealthy enough to have bought us our house and everything inside without making a dent in their finances, but they're old fashioned. They wanted Roger to earn his own way. Probably their idea of a punishment for getting a young girl pregnant before he'd even finished high school.

Roger's father wanted him to work for him eventually, anyway, so I saw it as no harm done. Roger saw it differently. He had hopes to be scouted, to eventually make it into professional football, but then I came along and made that all vanish with one little act of harmless sex on his parents' living room sofa.

"Trenton?" I click-clacked through the house, following the giggles that lead me to the backyard.

He was a good boy, he'd always come when I called, unlike Diesel who'd pretend he'd suddenly gone deaf any time I was looking for him.

Trenton came to me with his cute little smile, his chubby cheeks slightly pink from all the activity. His hair messy and skin slightly bronzed and dirty.

"Your mom's on her way to pick you up."

He drew his head back and groaned. "Can't I just stay? We were playing nicely."

"Yeah, we were playing nicely," Diesel echoed, peeking his head out from behind the shed.

"I know, but it's getting late buddy." I placed my hand on his head. "You got all your things together like I asked?"

He nodded.

"Alright, good job." I winked at him. "I know I can always count on you, unlike someone we—"

"Lets go, Aubree," Roger barked behind me. "We're already late enough because of you."

I sucked in a breath, playfully widening my eyes at Trenton. He giggled as I mouthed the words, So bossy *while I squeezed his shoulder.*

"Bye Mrs. C."

"See you later, Trent." I rustled Trenton's mousy brown hair. "Diesel, come say bye, please!"

Silence. He'd tucked himself behind the shed, and knowing him he wouldn't be coming out. He'd also shoved a ton of toys back there that we'd been asking him to clean up, which he always rudely refused with his tongue stuck out. Neither I, nor Roger could get to them because we couldn't fit, and he knew it.

Anything to be a pain, I guess.

I took a few steps closer to the shed. "Diesel!"

"Aubree, let's fucking go!"

I dragged my feet. The babysitter—who we went to high school with—was sitting at the outdoor set while on her phone, and glanced up only to give me an awkward smile as I followed Roger out. He roughly snagged me by my wrist like I was a child, shoving me into the passengers seat of his Benz.

"Simple things, Aubree." He began backing out of the driveway. "I ask you to put on the blue dress, you put on the blue dress. I want your hair curled and pinned to the side, you curl your hair and pin it to the side. I ask you to be ready by seven thirty, you be ready by seven twenty-nine. Why the fuck have you been so defiant lately?"

I sat silently, staring out my window.

"Answer me!"

I jumped from the volume of his voice. "I don't know. Sorry."

"You know, you're lucky. You're lucky I stay and put up with your bullshit, Aubree."

"All because of a dress?"

"Don't fucking try me tonight," he warned.

"I just think—"

He grabbed a hold of my wrist and squeezed it so hard I gasped. His nails dug into my skin, causing a sharp sting. "I SAID SHUT THE FUCK UP!"

"You're hurting me!"

He let me go as soon as he realized he'd lost his temper completely and I stared down at my throbbing red wrist, his hand print still visible.

Roger didn't say a word the rest of the way. I took his silence as recognition of his wrongdoing. Either that, or an effort to keep from leaving more angry evidence on my skin.

We'd spent the entire night with his arm linked to mine, which could have been a sweet gesture if not to hide the slowly purpling mark he left me. People made comments on how in love we appeared and how he seemed like he couldn't keep his hands off of me.

Maybe they weren't wrong.

It scared me, the way Roger could act like two different people. He was one man at home and another to the world and I'd never before encountered someone who could possess that ability. It frightened me.

He didn't speak to me on the drive home and we both did our own nightly routines in silence. I washed off my makeup and changed into pajamas while he flipped through channels on the television. On nights like that, I didn't stay in his space much. I'd go down to the den and write, but not until I knew he were sleeping or that he wouldn't be coming back down for a while.

I'd write most nights. I'd go downstairs and dig up the diary I kept hidden in my old high school backpack, shoved far in the back of the linen shelf, behind blankets and towels and things that only I ever really reached for. I'd tiptoe back to the den, leaving the doors cracked because shutting them called for too much noise, and then I'd sit in the corner of the couch and write.

One night, not long after the office party, I was really upset. I'd had enough of Roger and waited all day for the after hours when I could just blast my thoughts down onto paper and shove them away when I was done.

JULY 12TH, 2008

I HATE MY LIFE. I HATE ROGER. I HATE LIVING HERE, BEING STUCK IN THE CONFINES OF A BEAUTIFUL HOME THAT'S BECOME NOTHING MORE THAN A BEAUTIFUL HELL. WHEN DOES THIS EVER END? THE RECURRING NIGHTMARE WHERE I WAKE UP, DAY AFTER DAY, PAINTING MY FACE SO THAT IT RESEMBLES ONE OF A HAPPY SUBURBAN WIFE. THE ONE WHERE I'M THE PERFECT SIZE ONE WOMAN THAT ROGER STILL DOESN'T LOVE, DESPITE HER BEING SO PERFECT.

HE'S GETTING WORSE. HE'S SO CONTROLLING, SO MANIPULATIVE. HE'S THE DEVIL HIMSELF AND IT SEEMS I'VE SIGNED MY LIFE AWAY TO HIM FOR THE SAKE OF A RING. I WEAR THE TITLE OF WIFE, BUT THERE'S NO REAL MEANING BEHIND THE WORD. I'M NOT A WIFE. I'M A HOUSEKEEPER WHO CLEANS UP AFTER ALL OF HIS MESSES, A LIFE SIZE DOLL FOR HIM TO DRESS HOWEVER HE WANTS, A LIVE IN NANNY TO LOOK AFTER HIS SON, AND THE WOMAN HE HATES SO PASSIONATELY, H—

"What the hell are you doing?"

I clutched the book to my chest, feeling like my tongue had lodged itself down my throat. I couldn't even speak. Roger barged in so quietly, it was like he knew I'd be down there doing something I didn't want him to know about. Like he'd been waiting on the right time to sneak up on me, and that was it.

He snatched the book from my grip, eyes dancing over the words freshly marked in ink as I began to tremble violently.

"What the fuck is this, Aubree? Is this how you really feel about me? Is that what this is?"

I cowered beneath him, afraid of what he may have done to me. I still couldn't find any words. There was nothing I could say to clean that up.

"You hate me?" His forehead ridged as he looked down at me. "You fucking hate me? I give you everything and you hate me?" He threw the book at me and I jerked when it hit me solidly against my chest before falling onto the floor, pages spread. I reached for it with shaky fingertips in an attempt to keep him from wanting to read any more.

"I don't go to work all day for you to sit at home and write that kind of bullshit, Aubree!"

I slid to the ground, my body almost paralyzed like if I'd stay still the problem would resolve itself. But he wasn't satisfied with that at all. He roughly pulled me up from the ground, the book falling out of my hands, but it was the least of my concern as he shoved my back to the wall.

His mouth opened to shout at me again, but we both looked beside us when our attention is snagged by something small moving outside the doorway.

Roger dropped his hands from me and I wiped my eyes before going toward the door to look out.

Trenton had backed himself against the hallway wall, eyes wet and a scared pout on his face. "Trenton, why aren't you asleep?"

My hands went to his shoulders to comfort him while Roger stomped up the stairs, my eyes peered up at him until he'd locked himself up in his office.

Trenton hugged me without warning and I held him back, rubbing his back as if to apologize for waking him. For scaring him. For probably traumatizing his young mind with the sight of what just happened.

Of what he was seeking to escape from his own home.

I stayed awake, but he soon drifted back to sleep. He kept clung to me the rest of the night in Diesel's bedroom and he gave me what my son refused to at the time. He'd let me brush my fingers through his hair and pat his back until he fell asleep.

He let me be a mother. He let me love and feel loved.

And I learned something that day. Roger wouldn't dare act that way in front of the boys. That made me feel, safe.

THIRTY FOUR

Trenton

THE BEST THING TO COME OUT OF MY MISTAKE IS THE FACT THAT Diesel's forgiven me. Our friendship is still viable and that just proves to me that I can move forward after all. It'll take a while for me to get over Aubree—if I ever fully can—but getting Diesel back is the biggest relief.

"If someone told me a year ago I'd be sitting in a tiny bedroom with you guys, putting together baby furniture on my day off, I wouldn't have believed it," says Gio, prompting mine and Diesel's laughter.

I'm in the middle of screwing in the final screw to the crib. I stand up, grabbing the bars and jiggling it to make sure it's all tight.

"If someone told me a year ago that I'd be having a baby soon, I would have told them to fuck off," Diesel mutters, working on the expensive looking dresser that's soon to be a changing table on its surface. They got a lot of gifts from the baby shower, so many, I don't even feel so bad for missing it.

I stretch my arms above my head, twisting my torso as I glance around the room. When I said he and I were on good terms, I meant it. He and Chloe chose to move into my building, well Diesel chose, and Chloe went along with it because she's been a lot more lenient now that she's days away from giving birth. They opted for a two bedroom which is a little more costly than mine, but with the Hanes family paying partial rent, I'd say it was a great deal.

They both turn their heads to me, looking at me like they've asked me a question I didn't answer.

"Your turn, T," nudges Gio. "If someone told you a year ago dot dot dot…"

I purse my lips, setting my hand on the crib rail. *If someone told me a year ago that I'd be heartbroken over ~~my best friend's mom~~ Aubree, I would have believed every word.*

"Nothing. My life's been pretty believable."

They both scowl at me.

"I got one," says Diesel, setting down a screw driver and turning to face me on his knees. "If someone told me a year ago that Trenton Laguna would end up being the most responsible guy I know, I definitely wouldn't have believed that shit."

They both laugh and I let out a sigh of relief over the fact that he didn't mention the obvious. The most unbelievable thing is that I fucked his mom and I'm glad no one wants to joke about it. I guess it finally isn't funny anymore.

We finished moving in and setting up in only a few hours.

According to Diesel, Chloe's been really on edge about having everything set up at the apartment as soon as possible because she's already been having pre labor pains the past couple of days and wants to be able to come straight to their new home right after birth. What kind of friend would I be if I didn't spend all day helping him move and assemble furniture? It was my pleasure.

It was also worth it to hang out and smoke in his private patio afterwards, too. Like old times. Felt nice.

Felt like nothing ever came between us. Like Gio wasn't pulling Diesel's bloody fists away from me a few months back, like I didn't drive home drenched in my own blood. Like I didn't accept it as punishment for being so selfish.

I let my wants get in the way of the essential order of things. Diesel's mom could have never been mine. It's just unnatural. Sometimes I wonder if it is just a fetish. Something that I only enjoyed so much because it was so wrong. We want most the things we can't have, and I can't have Aubree. At least not in this lifetime.

I sucked the end of the blunt, resonating in my own thoughts. Not realizing I'm in a total daze until Diesel's snapping his finger in my face.

I blink before my eyes slowly shift onto his face.

"I told you this shit's good," he says with a chuckle as he snatches it from my fingertips.

"Fatherhood…" Gio begins, his back presses firmly to his chair. We brought a few fold ups from Gio's house in anticipation of doing this after everything was done. "Man, I can't wait to see you as a dad."

"Fuck you." Diesel laughs. "I can't wait to see *you* as a dad."

"Fuck that. I'm holding off till I'm forty."

Diesel throws his eyes at me as smoke seeps through his smile. "T, I'm expecting you to babysit when me and Chloe go out on date nights."

I rub my chin, smiling slightly. I'm not in the mood to mess around, to talk shit to each other and joke. I haven't been in a while.

Gio laughs, rocking his chair. "You guys don't even go out on dates now, what makes you think you're gonna do that when a kid's in the picture?"

Diesel wrinkles his chin like he's realizing that's a true assumption, and then he digs in his back pocket for his phone which I can't tell is vibrating until he has it held in front of him.

I watch his face transform into something I'm not used to. A look that's border-lining both stunned and anxious.

"Chloe just checked into the hospital."

"So?" Gio says, holding up a hand. "When my sister was pregnant she was in and out of the hospital cause she thought she was having contractions when she really wasn't. That doesn't always mean the baby is coming now."

Diesel's still staring at his phone. "It does when her water already broke…I think."

We all glance at each other without a clue of what to do or say. We're all high as hell and shouldn't really drive, so we split a Lyft and head to the hospital.

It's exciting, actually. I feel like I'm having a baby brother or something. A new member of the family is due to arrive and all I can do is sit and wait with my best friends. It's a good ending to a good day.

But Diesel is nail biting and trancing out, small beads of sweat mist his forehead despite it being that cool, drafty, start-of-fall weather that you expect in mid September.

Gio and I stay behind in the waiting area of labor and delivery as Diesel rushes to Chloe's room. I've never seen him like this in my life, but it's very becoming of him. I'm almost convinced he cares for Chloe more than he wants us all to believe he does.

We sat and waited, talked aimlessly, bought snacks from the vending machine, watched Chloe's mom come and go. And then Diesel returned to us, looking slightly calmer than before.

"So?" I say to him as he sits down on the edge of the grey seat next to Gio.

"I don't know what the fuck they were talking about—a bunch of numbers and diameters and weird bullshit—but they estimate that he'll be here by morning, latest."

Gio knocks his knuckles into Diesel's shoulder. "Fuck yeah!"

"You guys don't have to stay." He shrugs. "It's late and who knows how long it'll really take. I get it if you guys want to go home and sleep and just come back tomorrow."

Gio and I exchange a glance, but it's clear we're thinking the same thing.

"Nah man, we'll stay," I answer. "We don't got nothing better to do."

"Yeah, it'll be fun. I can't remember the last time I pulled an all nighter sober," says Gio.

His optimism makes me chuckle and although Diesel would never admit it, there's an ease brought to his face.

"Cool." He smirks, standing from his seat. "I'm gonna go call my mom."

And then it occurs to me. Knowing Aubree, she'll get here at the drop of a hat once she receives that call. We'll be forced to be near each other, to share this night together. Right when I was starting to get her out of my head.

Yeah right. Don't downplay it. She still takes up every corner and crevice of your mind and you know it.

Gio's looking at me like he can see what I'm thinking, but again he doesn't say a word and I'm grateful for that.

The more I don't acknowledge my feelings, the easier it'll be to pretend there are none.

Gio's finally stopped talking and has his feet propped up on the chairs in the adjacent row. A small impulsive smile curves his lips as he stares at his phone's screen. He looks comfortable.

We've only been here for forty five minutes and I'm already uncomfortable. The chairs are hard and have no support for the neck or upper back, but I'm sure they aren't really meant to be sat in for long durations.

I feel like I've just signed my whole night away to being tormented by Aubree and she isn't even here yet. She hasn't walked through those doors, but my body still responds like she's standing right in front of me. That deeply disturbed feeling that makes my whole body feel numb and my brain feel like it's on fire. I'm nervous as hell.

Nervous because I'm still so stupidly in love with her that I may say something to reel myself back in.

Gio laughs at his phone and slaps his thigh, momentarily giving me a brief distraction from my thoughts. And then my eyes are drawn to the doors as they glide open again. I hadn't looked up the several other times they'd opened before, but this time I knew it was her. I felt her.

She rushes through, her hair flying back as she whips the wind with her powerful walk. She breezes past us and it isn't until she's out of sight that I realize I'd sat completely still as she did.

Gio's now curled up in the corner seat, his head resting on an armrest, and he looks content. But I'm so on edge. Wondering when she's going to leave the room and notice me, my anxiety is spiked.

I get up and go to the soda machine to grab another drink and as I press on the picture of a Dasani water bottle, I spot something in my peripheral that makes me slightly shiver under the ridiculously cold hospital air.

"Hi, Trenton," she speaks, and I'm reminded how much I loved the sound of my name on her lips. How much I missed hearing it in her tone.

I don't turn my head to look at her, instead I grab the bottle that's tumbled into the slot below. "Hi, Mrs. Cooper."

"You're here to stay?"

I nod, focusing on my shoes. "Yes."

"Great. I'll join you." She walks away and I listen for the sound of heels, but there aren't any. I turn to glance at her and she's got on a pair of running shoes and leggings and a baggy sweatshirt like she's a laid back college student. Last time I saw her, she had on something similar. I'm not used to seeing her so comfortable, but I really like it on her.

I hear her speaking to Gio as I sip my water next to the machine. I hope to calm myself down before taking a seat. I realize that wherever I sit, I'll be there until this baby comes. I just got Diesel back and I'm not messing it up again because of her. Because of me.

I sit across from her and a couple of seats down, but it still feels like she's right beside me. Her eyes are burning into me as I stare down at my phone, looking at my home screen just to seem busy. To seem too occupied for her to feel comfortable enough to try to speak to me, but it's Aubree.

She speaks to me anyway.

"So you're going to be Aiden's godfather."

I swallow before my eyes meet hers. I always thought she looked best without makeup, without the burden of putting on a face for everyone. She's gorgeous. "Yep."

She doesn't say anything in response. I've closed the conversation that way on purpose. I can't possibly sit here and have small talk with her. Aubree and I are long, deep conversations, jokes and laughter. We've always said what we were thinking and spoke only the truth to each other. But to sit and chat about the obvious or the unimportant like we've only just met makes me sick to my stomach.

This is going to be a long night.

THIRTY FIVE

Aubree

I SAT WITH MY LEGS CROSSED UNTIL IT BECAME UNCOMFORTABLE. More uncomfortable than the silence between Trenton and I. But again, I asked for this. I told him to forget about me because I was in denial of how I felt for him, I still am. I still feel guilty. I still feel unsettled, but I still love him.

I still love him and I know he still loves me.

Gio was helpful enough to fill the awkward tension between the three of us with his ridiculous banter and jokes. He got Trenton to crack a couple of smiles and every time they came, I silently melted like I always do but so much harder now that he's so distant.

Something told me I'd be most helpful if I went in and checked on the progress. I feel this is mostly Chloe's mother's territory, so I'm not going to barge in much, but I feel I have a right to check in occasionally and give some support. Let my son know I'm still here.

Roger isn't. He left days ago to Atlanta and I don't speak to him much, so I have no idea when he's returning. I assume Diesel called him and told him the baby was coming within hours, but whether he knows or not is none of my concern.

"How's it going, girl?" I ask, my mouth curved in sympathy. I remember this day when it happened to me. I was a wreck. I had no one but my mother by my side and was left to wonder when Roger would come, and if.

"It's going." She blows out a breath and I have to admire Diesel for a moment. Her hands are in his and she's leaning toward him as she rides out the pain. He's there because he knows he's supposed to be, but I also can tell he wants to be.

He's surprised me lately. I haven't interacted with him much because he's been absent from the house, but from what I have seen of him, I'm so proud that he's turned out to be nothing like his father after all.

Chloe's mother is by the window, on the phone speaking medical terms and from the sounds of it, she must be relaying the process back to Patrick.

Diesel glances at me and although his face is still, I can tell he appreciates that I'm here. It's like he's acknowledging me for the first time in years.

I dismiss myself after that, not wanting to overstep. Diesel can be easy to trigger and I take that look as the first step in a good direction.

I stroll down the hallway on my way back to my seat, my body tensing at the fact that I'm subjecting myself to being ignored again for the next eight or so hours. I wish Trenton would at least have more to say to me than one word answers, but it's not like I can really expect more from him.

Purposely, I sit in the seat directly in front of him, but not without noticing the snores coming from the corner of the room. "Is he asleep?"

"He definitely is asleep." Trenton slides further into his seat, his legs widening like an invitation for me to sit on his lap.

I miss him. I miss not only what we were, but what we became. He's right, our relationship was always different, but he made it that way. He made me love him as a friend until he could make me love him as a man, and I want that man back.

"Is this how it's going to be from now on?" I ask, prompting him to scoff and bring his head back until it's propped up against the wall.

"This isn't the time to talk about that, Aubree."

"Well, is there ever going to be a time? I just want to know that we're okay."

"We're fine." His eyes are wide at me like he expects me to believe that, but I don't because underneath them is a flicker of uncertainty.

"You know, I had high hopes that Aiden would be a girl." I stare blankly at the wall across from me. "I always wanted a girl. I asked Roger for another baby early this year, and—"

"Why would you do that?"

I drop my gaze from him and focus on the sleeves of my sweatshirt that are slid most way over my hands. "I don't know. Either way, he said no. He got a vasectomy years ago, so it was never happening anyway."

He lifts a shoulder and his eyes veer past me.

"Do you want kids, Trenton?"

He huffs like the question was slightly funny, and glances down at the space between our shoes. "Yeah. I did want them."

"What changed?"

"I don't know. That's just not a focus on my mind."

"That's good."

We sat in silence for another hour.

I watched him get up and talk on the phone, walking around the small lobby space. He'd smile, and laugh, and I just knew he was talking to Isabel. It made my stomach churn in envy.

I flipped through photos in my phone to keep my mind off of it, but I heard the difference in his tone when he spoke to her in comparison to me. I hate this.

I hate that he wants nothing to do with me, but is it wrong of me to put my family first? To put Diesel first? He doesn't know the awful things I've said that would crush me if Diesel knew.

I'm trying to get my son back, not drive him further away.

Trenton finally returned to his seat with two bottles of water. He handed me one and I thanked him, happy that I crossed his thoughts even briefly.

I watched his throat bob as he gulped it down before setting his bottle beside his feet.

"How are you and Isabel?"

He shifts in his seat. "We're fine—good." He nods. "Normal relationship. We don't have to sneak around to date, fuck, or even speak. It's great."

His words spear a hole in my chest. I knew they were *probably* having sex, but I wanted to doubt it. I wanted to believe he was still the boy who didn't want anyone touching him unless it were me.

He's purposely being spiteful now. He wants me to hurt, and I'm definitely hurting.

"That's...that's great." I swallow my pride as I speak those words. It's not great. I don't want to know anyone else is touching him. And then my lips move without my permission. "Do you love her?"

"No."

I won't say I'm not relieved to hear that. Trenton's the only person I know who clearly knows what he wants and he doesn't play with his words. He spoke it with no hesitation. A solid answer that made my heart pound.

By three in the morning, things shifted. Gio was still sound asleep and although I was envious that he'd found that kind of peace and comfort at a place and time like this, I'm not at all jealous of how badly his neck's going to ache in the morning.

Trenton's seemed to get a bit more comfortable himself. He's been eyeing me with his tired stare for the past hour and I've been sending him the look right back.

"Why isn't the sergeant here?" he asks. His head propped up on his fist. "You know, since he loves his son so much."

"Don't. Please."

"Why not? I mean he is the perfect husband. The family man, right?"

"Trenton," I warn through gritted teeth.

"Just tell me, do you really want to be his doormat the rest of your life?"

"Why do you care? I thought you were moving on."

"I'll always care."

I want to respond, I want to tell him I hope he does. That I hope he never stops, because I won't. I want to tell him I only want the best for him and that's why this has to happen. That that's why we could never continue this. There's no loophole for us, there's no way out. We can't move forward unless our lives take five steps back. That's it.

But then I spot someone standing in my peripheral, and before I can go to look, Trenton's already turned his head.

Diesel's standing there awkwardly, like he was watching us speak that entire time. Like it was out of his comfort to try and interrupt.

"Diesel, what's going on?" I ask, eagerly. "How's she doing?"

He sits beside Trenton. "Good, I guess. She got the epidural, so it's a lot less intense now. She's taking a nap, but I guess she's almost there."

I smile at him but it doesn't reach my eyes. Probably because I'm that tired.

"Thanks for being here…" Diesel mutters as he stands up and looks down at both of us. "It means a lot, you know?"

"No problem, man. Wouldn't miss this," Trenton tells him.

Gio snores loudly before adjusting between the bed of seats he's created and we all share a weak laugh.

Roger should be here. I know that's what's on Diesel's mind.

I want to ask him if he'd talked to him at all lately, if Roger even knew what was going on tonight, but I won't. The answer's written all over him.

"I'm gonna head back in, in case she wakes up soon."

Both Trenton and I nod before he goes, leaving us alone once again. I let a few silent moments breeze by while I watched his eyes flutter shut.

"I'm sorry, Trenton." I keep my voice low. "I'm sorry for everything. For making you feel like I didn't care enough about you —"

"Aubree—"

"No, let me finish." I scoot to the edge of my seat in an attempt to be closer to him. "I'm sorry for dragging you into my life. I shouldn't have. I should have never let things go as far as they did."

"So we're back to you apologizing for giving me a chance, then? That's not what I want you to be sorry for. I want you to be sorry for lying to me. For hurting me when I didn't need to be hurt, Aubree. Be sorry for choosing a shitty life over one where you'd only be loved."

"You don't understand."

"*Aaaand* now we're back to that too." His face constricts like he's dry swallowed a pill. "I wanted to understand. I tried to, but I can only understand what you let me."

"You understand how important my son is to me, right?"

He nods, clasping his hands as he leans forward.

"It all comes down to Diesel, and where this would put him. You get that, right?"

"No. No, I don't get that." He deeply inhales as his fingers mow through his thick, light brown, hair. "No, because Diesel's got his own shit going on. He's having a baby today, Aubree. He's entering adulthood. He'll be eighteen in just a month from now, he'll graduate next year. He can't keep having control over your life. He's not a seven year old kid anymore, he doesn't have unrealistic views of his parents anymore. He doesn't need you to hide yourself anymore. He can get over us being together."

"It's not all about you—us. There's more to it than that."

"Like what?"

"Like…Roger has something that will make Diesel think of me in a way that no one should think of their mother. That's what."

He doesn't question me further, he keeps his eyes on me and lets his back lay against the plastic seat.

"He's always had it and it's always been the biggest factor in why I haven't left. There's a lot more to the story that you don't know, Trenton. That's not even half of it."

THIRTY SIX

Trenton

At six this morning, Chloe gave birth to Aiden James Cooper. Nineteen inches, eight pounds, all healthy and that's all we could have asked for.

I saw a side to Diesel I've never seen before. For one, a genuine smile as he held his son for the first time. And besides that, he just looked different. Like he entered a new phase of life, like he leveled up.

An hour before that, I was sitting beside Aubree. We finally stopped beating around the bush and just talked about other things. Lighter things. I don't know what Roger's holding over her head, but I know in time I'll get her to get it out, and not for me but for herself.

We fell asleep together, and I woke up to Diesel nudging us both awake. Her head was on my shoulder and I forgot how that felt.

Gio got a great sleep in, considering he was out the entire night. *So much for pulling an all nighter.* He could lay on a bed of nails and still sleep like a baby.

When Aubree first saw Aiden she cried, and I wondered if it were absolute joy or if it were really confusion or regret or fear, or everything all rolled into one. She fell in love with the kid at first glance, and I know she's terrified of losing both him and Diesel because whatever she did in her past is clearly that bad. I've considered so many possibilities in my head of what she could have done, but I can't come to a logical conclusion. I can't imagine her doing anything crazy enough to warrant someone hating her, let alone her own son.

"Alright, well it was fun." I hold my hand out before Diesel slides his over my palm in a lazy handshake. "But I'm exhausted and you guys clearly have a lot of transitioning to do."

"Thanks for staying, Trent. Seriously."

"No problem."

We come into a hug, I slap his back as he does mine before we part. From over his shoulder, Aubree's already eyeing me like she knows I'm leaving, but neither of us say anything.

It's still not comfortable enough to act ourselves in front of Diesel, or even to act like ex's who got out of a messy break up, but it's even harder to act like Diesel's best friend and Mrs. Cooper. That's not us anymore.

I hold my hand up at her, but I don't open my mouth to say a word. I don't know when I'll see her again. I don't know if I even want to.

It hurts too much to be around her, it's too confusing, it's too frustrating.

I hear Gio's loud mouth talking as I leave the group, feeling like I've just done something wrong. The feeling you get when you think you've left a door unlocked, but can't go back to check.

Keeping forward, my hands shove into the pockets of my hoodie as I feel the cold air blow over me when the doors slide open.

And then I stand still, right there in the middle of the front entrance.

That can't be it.

We can't leave off on a note like that. That's never been what me and Aubree have ever been about, and I don't want it to be that way now.

I turn around to go back—to go after her—and as soon as I'm facing back the way I came, she's stumbling to a stop like she was looking for me. Like she knew I was looking for her.

She had a way of doing that.

"We're not done, are we?" I ask as she takes a few smaller steps toward me.

She shakes her head, her hands reach out for me as she picks up her pace and then she's back in my arms.

Meet someone that makes your life make sense.

Her head over my chest makes the most sense to me out of everything. Her and I make the most sense out of everything, it's like there's no other option but us. I can't go on without her and I don't want to, it's as simple as that.

She drove me to my apartment and came inside with me.

Once her keys were set on the kitchen ledge, I couldn't wait anymore and I kissed her. I pulled her hips into me like I didn't feel close enough and we kissed like we always had. Like we don't need air to breathe, because all we breathe is each other and I'm gasping for her.

I finally inched back, keeping her close to me and her face in my hands. "What are we going to do?"

"We'll figure it out."

"I need you to promise me something."

She nods subtly as I brush my thumbs over her cheeks.

"If you come back into my life, you're here to stay."

"I'm here to stay, Trenton. I always have been." Her eyes pierce into mine and make my heart skip multiple beats at a time. "I promise."

I pulled her back in until our lips met again. I can't get enough of her. Who was I kidding, trying to go on without her? There's no one I want more, there never will be.

"I missed you," she breathes onto my lips and I drink every word of it the same way she polished off glass after glass of Merlot.

She pulls my shirt off over my head.

"I'm sure I missed you more."

She narrows her eyes at me for a second as a smile touches her face, but then goes back to unbuttoning my jeans.

It's been months since I've had sex with Aubree and I'm so excited right now, it's like we're doing it for the first time again.

Our mouths latch back together as she yanks my pants down and

I step out of them, moving closer. Her sweatshirt comes off and I slide down her leggings so fast, I almost wonder for a second if I ripped them.

With her bare back lain against my couch, she moans as I position myself between her legs, pre-cum beading at the tip of my dick as I place the bare head at her entrance, but I don't care. She doesn't care. I don't even bother with a condom and she doesn't mention it either.

I'm too busy being hypnotized by her lustful gaze, by the way she stares up at me with both love and passion in her eyes. I hold her by her hips, sliding her onto me until there's no space between us. We're one.

"I don't want anything coming between us anymore," I growl in her ear, her fingers dipping into my bare back as I steadily thrust back and forth.

"Nothing," she breathes.

I kiss her lips to seal the deal before pressing against the couch to look at her. She's stunning. An actual angel. I've never been more in love and never will be.

I lift her hips, angling her so that I can go deeper.

She shivers beneath me, her hands grabbing a hold of my forearms as her eyes close. "Oh my god, Trenton...Don't stop."

I bite my lip, loving the way my name forms on her lips. Feeling her tighten around me, her walls pulsing rhythmically and letting me know she's already close.

"You feel so fucking good, baby."

She moans loudly. Freely. We don't have to worry about keeping quiet, we don't have to worry about anyone walking in. I used to think that turned me on, but seeing her so unconfined has me on the edge already.

She feels so wet, so warm. She feels like she's mine.

I set her down, lowering myself before lifting her leg up on my shoulder. Her eyes roll back beneath her lids and I know I've found the right spot. "I want to give you everything, Aubree."

She nods, panting and unable to respond as her senses take over.

"I want everything with you," I whisper into another thrust.

She pulls me closer until our lips have all but fused together, but I inch back before the kiss can deepen.

"I want to give you a baby. A boy—a little girl, I don't even care."

Her face drops slightly, and I slow my pace.

"I—We couldn't, Trenton—you're so young, I—"

"I've wanted this with you for as long as I can remember, baby." I cup her face in my hand and she leans into it. And then my heart speaks before my mind can censor myself. "I want you to move in with me, I want to put a ring on your finger, have a family, I want it all."

Her eyes first widen, then glisten, and then she smiles, pulling me back in for a kiss so deep, so smoldering, I completely lose myself.

Our bodies move together in a way I can't even explain. We fit so perfectly, we're so in sync.

"Mm, come all over me, baby," I tell her, noticing the way her cheeks blush as she throws her head back. Her warm cream begins running down my balls as she shudders in front of me, it's a beautiful view. My favorite, and if she means what she says, I'll get to see it front and center, every night.

I come seconds into her orgasm, my fingers grasped around her neck, her leg over my shoulder. My hips still as I release every drop of me into her without even a second thought. It's the closest I can come to claiming her as mine again.

I kiss her leg, her cocoa colored skin exciting me once more, making my dick harden while it's still buried deep. "You have the best pussy. Ever." My hand glides down her cheek as our breaths collide.

"Who are you comparing me to?"

I don't even want to say the name, and Aubree quickly drops it so she doesn't have to hear me say it, either. Isabel is gone. I just got Aubree back, why bother arguing over nothing?

We lie together on the couch, my head on her chest as she brushes through my hair, slowly lulling me to sleep. After last night,

I'd love to fall asleep right here on top of her, but I missed her so much I don't want to waste any time with her by sleeping.

"I'm not on birth control anymore."

I blink, tracing the length of her arm. The idea of impregnating Aubree makes my stomach flutter. I want that and I want her to want that too.

"But...you know I can't really let you get me pregnant, right?" Her fingers rake through my hair once more, but those words wake me up.

I lift my head to look at her. "It's a little too late for that revelation—"

"Trenton, you're only eighteen. You have a lot ahead of you, I don't want to throw you off track."

"Off track with what?" I sigh, sitting up completely. Her legs lay over mine. "What am I supposed to be doing right now besides being with you? That's all I want, to just be with you. Everything else is fine. My job, my money, my car. I won't ever be off track as long as you're here."

"I just don't want you to think this is what you want, only to have regrets about it later."

"I'm not fucking Roger." My voice comes out harder than I anticipated it to and I lower my tone. "I'd never regret anything like that, Aubree. I've loved you my whole life, I've wanted this my whole life. I used to *fantasize* about you making me a husband. A father. That's all I want as long as you want it too."

"Trenton," she says so adoringly, her eyes softening on mine. And then she laughs. "Are you even real? I've never met anyone like you."

"I ask myself the same thing about you all the time."

She gets up, kisses me and then starts toward the hallway. I can't resist tapping her ass before she goes, and I get a cute laugh out of her that only encourages me to want to do it again.

As I watch her walk away, a fleeting thought hits me. I just hope this doesn't backfire. I hope she means what she says.

THIRTY SEVEN

Trenton

"So…what's the big obsession with 'would you rather'?" She laughs, taking a sip from the bottle of pink, carbonated liquid. Aubree isn't a big drinker unless it's wine. I always thought it was cute, her pretty nails wrapped around a wine glass. Her sipping on the red drink while she read. But tonight she needed something a little stronger. Something that would lower her guard and get her to spill.

My plan for tonight was to get her to talk about some things I know are hard for her, so earlier we went and picked up some drinks just to hang out on my living room floor.

Honestly, this feels the most intimate we've ever been. Her sitting directly in front of me, both of us slowly letting the alcohol lower our inhibitions as we talk about whatever is on our minds. The room is dim and the only noise filling it is our voices and laughter. It's perfect.

"I mean, every damn party in my backyard was Gio shouting something like, *would you rather fuck Mrs. Brown from English, or give head to Principal Thompson?*"

I laugh because her impression of Gio is spot on, also because of the fact that Principal Thompson's this long haired *Fabio* type of guy and Mrs. Brown is like eighty, so that's definitely something he's probably said.

I run my hands up and down her thighs. "Damn, I didn't know you heard all that, you little eavesdropper."

"It's not eavesdropping when it's my house." She shrugs with a pretty little smirk. "But I did. I heard it all." Her eyes narrow at me and something reminiscent of a smile tugs on her lips. "Even the few times I was a choice in the game, and you picked me without any hesitation."

"Of course I did," I tell her. "They all thought I was joking—I said it like I was, but I meant it. I'd always choose you."

She huffs a laugh, placing her bottle against her lips before the liquid seeps into her mouth.

Marina: It's not going to work out. You can't possibly be with her.
Marina: I don't know what you expect to come out of this.
Marina: You're only setting yourself up for pain. She's going to hurt you.
Marina: I'd never hurt you.
Marina: I just don't get why you went back to her. She doesn't love you.

Aubree clings to me. "Who's been blowing up your phone all day?"

"Mm, Pinot Grigio..." Aubree smirked at the bottle in her hand.

I crinkled my nose at her. "No, no wine. We need something a little stronger."

"What, like Mike's hard?"

I laughed, my arm sliding around her hip. "Oh, you're so fucking cute. Mike's hard," I mocked, kissing her temple three times before she grinned at me.

"Don't make fun of me! I don't drink this kind of stuff. I'm classy."

"Oh, so I'm not classy?"

She shook her head, biting her lip.

At that point, we were shameless.

We'd still glance down the aisle to see if the coast were clear enough to hold hands for a moment, for me to swat her on the ass, or for her to hug the back of me. But it was still tricky to be affectionate in public because anywhere I'd turned, I was worried I'd see someone I knew or that she knew. Then the secret would be out sooner than we wanted and I didn't want anything getting back to Roger or Diesel before we even have a set plan on how we wanted to come out to everyone. But being seen together wasn't such a big deal to her anymore and to me, that meant Aubree was serious about me. She wasn't trying so hard to hide me or deny me. And everything felt natural.

"Well, I want you to be anything but classy tonight," I growled beside her ear, pulling her closer until she reached my lips. We slow kissed in the middle of that aisle.

Maybe shameless was an understatement.

Aubree was kissing an eighteen year old in the liquor aisle at Ralph's—not even ten minutes from Roger's home—and I had two handfuls of my best friend's mom's ass in my grip.

We clearly didn't give a fuck anymore.

When we parted, I opened my eyes and immediately they locked with Marina's. She was standing at the very end of the aisle, the push bar of the shopping basket held so strongly within her fists, her hands lost their color.

I could've jumped away from Aubree, I could've let her go. But why pretend at this point? Marina already knew, and Aubree was still cuddled into my side as her eyes glazed over the bottles on the shelf. She didn't see her watching us and had no idea Marina knew a thing about us being together and I wanted to keep it that way, so I shot her a look that was meant to be a reminder of the night we spoke in the yard.

Plainly, stay out of it.

"No one. That was a phone bill notification." I shrug.

I don't like lying to her, but I don't want her to know Marina's been acting like a raging psycho ever since she saw us at the store earlier. If Aubree finds out that she knows, she's only going to freak even more and I don't need anything in my way of getting to the bottom of this.

My best bet is to just ignore her messages and hope she chills out soon.

I slide my phone underneath the couch and let my back lean against the recliner behind me, pulling her foot up onto my lap before gently kneading the skin just below her pretty, pale pink painted toes.

"Let's play."

Her brow quirks at me. "Would you rather?"

"Yeah." I bounce my shoulder and she nods at me like she's ready. "Would you rather…redo high school all over again, or redo your entire childhood?"

She purses her lips and hums, staring at her bottle like she's measuring how much is left in it. I can see it's hitting her a lot quicker than three bottles of wine does. "High school."

"Why?"

"That's where everything fucked up for me. If I could go back, I'd steer clear of quite a few people the second time around."

I nod subtly. This is all an attempt at working my way into the bigger issues. I'm afraid if I ask her straight up before she's good and comfortable, I may scare her away like I have the past couple of nights she's been here. She'll shut down completely at any mention of talking to Diesel, or of Roger's leverage against her. This has to be done gently.

"Your turn." She blinks at me. "Would you rather have the power to control minds, or be able to read them?"

"Isn't that the same thing?"

"No. One is controlling what a person thinks, the other is just listening in. Which would you rather have?"

"You're good at this game…" I mutter to myself, smiling as I tilt my head back. "Fuck it—mind control."

"Why?" She grins.

"Because I don't think I'd want to know what everyone really thought of me…but if I could control those thoughts, they'd all be good ones, whether they liked me or not."

"I don't think there's anyone on this Earth that thinks badly about you."

"I do." I shrug. Our eyes roam over each other freely. I take note of her glossy stare, her beautiful eyes seeing only me. I feel so lucky and still so nervous. Nervous because with Aubree it feels like I'm on thin ice and it's cracking beneath my feet.

I take another sip of my beer, my eyes not leaving hers when I say, "Let's say you're on a plane. You know it's going down, you have no chance of surviving the crash, but you have time to make one last phone call, who is it to?"

"Uh, that's easy. Diesel."

"Diesel never answers you!" My arms playfully flail in frustration. "Why would you waste your last call like that?"

We both laugh, my hands find her bare legs again because I can't keep my hands off her longer than a few seconds.

"Well who would you call?"

"Honestly, probably Joselyn. She's always on her phone so I know she'll answer. I'll leave her some instructions on what to do with my valuables. Probably apologize for being a shitty brother." I chuckle. "My mom's always at work so I wouldn't even bother calling her."

She blinks at me, biting down her smile. "Okay, I change my mind. I'd call you."

"You can't call me."

"Why not?"

"I'd be on the plane with you." I raise my eyebrow. "You're not traveling without me, it's too risky. If you die, I'm dying with you."

She giggles and I slide her into me, pulling her by her thighs so that we're face to face, clasping my arms at her back.

I watch her hold a mouthful of Smirnoff in her cheeks while holding back from smiling. It's infectious. I don't think I've stopped smiling all day.

"Would you rather, I kiss you here..." She lays her lips on mine, then hovers to my neck. "Or here..." She kisses me on my jugular before lowering herself. "Or—"

I bite my lip, pulling her back into me as I remember the end goal: Getting her to talk about Roger. As much as I'd love to see where her lips travel to, this is important.

"Aubree, wait..." I hiss, fighting myself for control as she slides her hand down my abdomen and grabs a hold of my rock hard dick through my sweats.

"What?" Her hazy eyes raise to mine.

"Can you tell me about Roger now?"

She sighs, and I feel her disengage from our embrace, but she doesn't leave.

"I know you don't want to, but we have to talk about it at some point, babe."

"You're right, I don't want to. I wish he wasn't even a part of my life. I wish it was just you and me."

"He won't be for long." I tighten my arms around her and she places her hands on my shoulders. "Just, tell me what Roger has against you that you think is going to hurt Diesel?"

"I *know* it will hurt Diesel."

I lift her face by her chin and her eyes are hesitant but they follow.

"I used to have a diary...I'd write in it a lot, but mostly when I was upset. It's full of horrible things that I'd never say out loud. Things I never should have even been thinking, and that's why Roger's used it to keep me around."

"A diary? That's it?"

"It's not just a diary, Trenton. You don't get it. It's a weapon now."

I sigh. It seems like she's making it into a bigger deal than it is, but then again she's right. I don't get it, I only know Diesel to an extent. I'm not his mother, I'm only his best friend.

"You know I'm going to help you out of this, right?"

"How? How am I going to convince Diesel that I didn't mean what I said when I was in my teens and twenties and just mad at the world?"

"Well...what did you say?" I stare at the side of her face. "I bet it's not as bad as you think."

"It is." Her throat bobs as she swallows, dropping her eyes to the anklet she's wearing. "I...said things like...I wish he were never born, I wish I would have aborted, I wish he weren't such a bad kid, that I hate his father—"

I click my teeth. "Aubree, he's not going to hate you over that. I mean, I'm sure he can understand that you were young and just trying to handle a very adult situation. That's just teen angst at its finest."

"But I don't know if he will. He's sensitive and stubborn, he'll take it to heart and he'll never get over it."

I kiss her cheek, seeing her lashes bat shut as my lips press against her skin. "I'll talk to him."

"I don't know…"

"I think tomorrow we should just tell everyone."

I feel her body tense within my arms, but I mean it. We've let too many days pass without coming to a conclusion on how this is all going to go down. We need a plan. I can't go another day with the uncertainty, wondering if she's going to suddenly decide it's best to leave me alone again and crawl back into that jail cell of a house.

"Everyone?" she echos.

I nod. "Diesel, my mom, my sister. Everyone that matters. We can figure out Roger when the time comes, but I think it would be best if we got to Diesel before Roger found out you're leaving him. Explain to him who Roger really is, what he has on you, and why it doesn't matter because none of it's true. You didn't mean any of it."

She nods, her face solid with contemplation. "How do you think your mom is going to take this? She doesn't think very highly of me already, she never has. I don't see it going well."

I shrug, linking our hands together before bringing her fingertips to my lips. "She doesn't have a choice, does she?"

She stares at me as I kiss her fingers. I can't get enough of her.

"I didn't want you to know this, Trenton…but I knew Roger was cheating on me. I've known for years, and I thought if I told you, you'd think I was an idiot for putting up with it."

"No. Not an idiot, I just thought you were really dependent on him, but he made you that way so it isn't your fault."

"Except, it is my fault."

I frown at her, clutching her hand to my chest.

"I grew up in an average home, in an average family. Money wasn't always there, but we lived an average life. My parents were averagely religious, averagely strict, kind and caring. There was value in getting along with my siblings, respecting them and myself as well as everyone around me. My mother taught me that I was better than allowing some boy to manipulate me and use me, but as soon as I had the opportunity to hook up with the guy I'd been crushing on forever, everything she ever instilled in me went right out the window."

"Happens to the best of us." I shrug.

She tilts her head and raises her eyebrows as if to say she begs to differ, but continues. "When I got pregnant with Diesel, Roger's parents made me a proposition. They told me if I aborted the baby, they'd both pay for the procedure as well as give me some money for going through with it—as long as I stayed away from Roger. The deal was tempting, They were the only one's who knew I was pregnant at the time and the amount of money they were offering wasn't small, so I really considered accepting it."

"Well, clearly you didn't."

"Clearly. And that's because I quickly became overwhelmed, went to my parents, explained to them everything including the disgusting deal Camille Cooper made with me, and they assured me I didn't have to do anything I didn't want to do. They were against abortion, but they said I could do whatever I felt was right and that they wouldn't hold it against me." She picks at her fingers held in between us. "I don't know if that was right either, giving a fourteen year old girl a choice that would affect not only her entire life, but also the possibility of her unborn son's...but they made me feel like I should keep the baby, so I did. I did and when I denied the deal with Camille, she gave me a new one."

I watch her eyes shift around as she speaks like she's replaying it all in her head for the first time in who knows how long.

"Roger was furious, his family was upset—and not with him, but with me—they all thought I was a *leech*. They called me that word, both in front of me and behind my back. I was the poor, young girl who was after him for his money—which I didn't even know anything about until I ended up pregnant and had to meet his parents."

"So what was the new deal then?"

"That I marry Roger to spare his family some embarrassment. That we play house, permanently. Put on happy faces in public and act like we were only ever madly in love—versus a couple of kids who had two minute sex on his parents living room couch."

I shake my head to myself. I had a feeling something shady got her to marry Roger, I just didn't know it was that deep.

"I accepted the new deal, but Roger didn't. He didn't want to marry me. He wanted nothing to do with me—but just like me, he didn't have a choice either. His family wouldn't stand for us to go unmarried with a child. Roger Cooper Sr. was and still is an important business man. He owns the entire company Roger works for, and besides wanting to keep his son from looking like the scandalous pervert he was, he explained that it would compromise the family's integrity to have a reckless son who became a teenage father with no intent on marrying the girl.Said it made Roger look *undisciplined*, but he was. Roger was a spoiled, entitled, brat. They forced him to marry me." She shrugs. "The only way we convinced him to go through with it is if I promised him he'd keep his freedom. Meaning, he could have all the affairs he wanted and in turn, my son and I would be taken care of. I don't know what I was thinking at the time, but I remember thinking it was a fine deal. Eighteen years later I now know it was the biggest mistake I ever made."

"Aubree, you were young. You were too young to have made a decision like that, it's not your fault things turned out this way. Roger took advantage of you. He's a fucking pig."

"But it still feels like everything's my fault. I've felt trapped for so long, the idea of finally getting away from him is terrifying." She frowns, blinking away tears. "Diesel has every right to hate me, and if Roger gives him that book—"

"He won't." I shake my head at her. "Because we're going to get it first."

THIRTY EIGHT

Aubree

I TIPTOED OUT OF BED TO GET BREAKFAST STARTED BEFORE Trenton woke up. It took everything in me to let him sleep and not wake him up with a morning blow job like I have been, but I didn't. I can't do that every day. And today I want to do something cute.

He doesn't know how to cook, so having me here is really doing him some good. If it weren't for me, he'd be eating a whole lot of junk and work would be hell for him.

I scrambled some eggs, made some toast, cut up some fruit, an avocado, and poured some orange juice.

Today is Trenton's first day off this week, and Roger is due back home in a couple of days. He called me yesterday while Trenton was at work and said he was just checking in with me. I didn't mention the fact that I hadn't been home in a week and he blamed poor cell reception as his reasoning for not responding to Diesel when Chloe was in labor.

I hummed and breathed into the phone, spent the majority of the call messing with my cuticles. It's official, I feel nothing for Roger anymore and it never occurred to me before Trenton that I never did.

I always knew I hated him, but there was still some desire in me. Something that kept me pleading for him to notice me.

I craved attention from a man, but not necessarily him.

Trenton gives me everything I need and more, and this week has been the happiest I've been in years.

I know now that I am going to move forward with him. It still sounds crazy and feels crazy, but I am going to leave Roger for

Trenton. I don't care what Roger thinks, I don't care what Lyssa thinks, Martha, my parents, the neighborhood. I only care about what Diesel thinks and unfortunately that's the one thing that may stop me.

"My beautiful baby." Trenton comes into the kitchen and like magnets we come together into a hug. His arms wrap around my shoulders, my face into his bare chest. He smells like me, I smell like him. This apartment smells like us. Being here feels right on all levels, but as soon as we step out the door it's the complete opposite and that's why I'm dreading today.

He kisses the top of my head, rocking me in his arms like he hadn't just held me the entire night as we slept.

"I made you breakfast," I sing as he releases me.

He looks at me with his goofy little smile, the one that's just for me. The one that reminds me of the little boy that looked up at me with pure adoration in his big eyes. The little boy that always strove to make me laugh because he knew I'd been crying all day.

I've never seen him smile like that with anyone but me.

"I see that."

I turn the knob on the oven before reaching for the oven mitts. Trenton doesn't have a lot of appliances here. There's no coffee maker, blender, or toaster. I had to make do with what he does have, meaning I just made toast in the oven. It reminded me of living at home again in my parents little two bedroom house that only had enough, but nothing more.

I swallow as I set the hot tray on the counter, staring blankly at it while removing the mitts.

"Hey." He pinches my chin, dragging my face toward him and I see his frown. "You've got that face."

"What face?"

"That thinking face. That, *you're thinking about something I don't want you to be thinking about,* face."

I purse my lips to try and morph that face into something else. A less obvious one. Of course I'm thinking. Roger's coming home soon, he's going to be completely blindsided when he finds out that I'm leaving him for the one person he'd never have expected.

"Today will be fine, Aubree." He leans against the counter. "They're all going to have something to say about it, but none of it matters. The only thing that matters is you and me, unless...*unless* you're changing your mind."

He looks at me, pleading. Hoping that's not what's on my mind.

"No." I shake my head, grabbing his hands. "I want to be with you regardless. I don't care about Roger or your mom or whoever..."

He stares into my eyes and I shy away.

"See, no. Something's wrong." He releases my hands. "What are you worried about? Tell me, please. It'll help me to just know what's bothering you so that I don't go crazy wondering what it is."

"It's just, this is a big move. I've never done anything like this. I've only ever really been with one person and I never thought I'd ever leave him, so the fact that I am, it's just something I'm still getting used to."

He looks at me like he's slightly let down. I don't mean to think that way, but it's the truth. I'm afraid. And although I know I want this, I don't know if I can handle what comes with it.

He holds my cheek and leans down to plant his lips on mine. "I get it." He begins serving the plates beside me, suddenly quiet. Like his personality has been muted and I don't like it.

"I'm not leaving you, Trenton. I'm not changing my mind."

He glances at me, peppering his eggs. "Okay."

I turn his head toward mine. "I love you."

"I love you."

As soon as we got into the car, my hands trembled the way they do when I haven't eaten and am running on wine alone, except with much more anxiety. Trenton noticed and held my hand during the drive, but that didn't calm me down. I only felt more nervous with every turn that brought us that much closer to the Laguna house.

I'm insane. Clearly. I've lost my mind and Roger's driven me to this point.

I look at Trenton's perfect side profile, admiring his sharp jaw and the stubble that'd began coming in like a direct result of his new found manhood. He's gorgeous.

But he's young. Too young, the small voice in the back of my head says.

This'll never work, Aubree.

A young man like him, as handsome as he is. He'll dump you like yesterday's trash soon enough, then you'll be all alone.

No one to love you. Not even your son.

If you think Diesel will accept this love, you've got another thing coming.

That voice torments me. Day in and day out. The fear of being alone. Of not having my son. Of having no one, not even the measly little fraction of Roger he's given me over the years.

And then Roger's voice blares in my mind like a siren. *Pathetic. You're so goddamn pathetic.*

I let out a breath through my mouth, slowly counting to three before I pause and inhale through my nose and repeat a deep exhale. Maybe that summer yoga class was good for something after all.

Trenton pulls my hand to his lips before placing a kiss to the back of my palm. "Let's do this, baby."

I nod, my bottom lip tucked into my mouth.

Trenton's happy because this will mean *we're official.* The more people know, the more we're really together—but I'm afraid, because this will mean *we're fucking official.* The more people know, the more I'm hated, the more I'm judged, the more I drive everything I've ever known away from me.

The more I drive Diesel away from me.

Trenton lets go of my hand to shuffle through his keys.

I follow him in, keeping a short distance behind in the hopes that I can either hide or just prolong the inevitable.

Once I'm completely inside and notice Martha's voice isn't already blaring off, asking a million questions, I take a look around the room.

Trenton puts his arm around me. I'm sure he can see the panic in my eyes as they dart over each wall. This house is exactly as I remember it. I've only been here a few times when picking up Diesel or dropping off Trenton, but being in here is nostalgic.

She even still has photos of Trenton's father hanging up. She never moved them. She never got rid of them.

I hear a door open and turn my back to the noise, almost tucking myself under his open arm. His arm tightens around me like he knows I'm completely wimping out and he's so sweet for allowing me.

"Big brother…" *It's just Joselyn.*

Not threatened by her, I turn around, watching her take slow, dramatic steps toward us. It's Martha that scares me. Normally she doesn't, I just feel like her disapproval is inevitable. Trenton's not like Diesel. I know his mother's opinion means something to him and I don't know how he'll respond if she doesn't approve of us.

Will he listen to her? Will he change his mind? It's one thing for me to have second thoughts considering everything I have to deal with, but Trenton's been one hundred percent in this since we started and if anything makes him rethink his commitment to me, it'd crush me.

"Hi, Mrs. Cooper." She grins, her eyes focusing on his hold on me.

"Hi, Joselyn." I babysat Joselyn a few times when she was around elementary school to middle school age. I never got very close to her. She always stayed underneath her brother. Following him like she's his shadow. He spoke for her, he fed her, he made sure she did her homework and she aways did what he said. I thought it was sweet the way she trailed behind him like a baby duckling, even if he didn't see it that way back then.

"Mom's in her room." Her mouth twists as she leans against the wall. "She's in a great mood."

"Good," says Trenton.

"Not for me since you're about to ruin it like always."

I bite my cheek, my chest tingling like someone's blowing hot air over my skin.

"No offense," she adds.

I look up at Trenton, and he stares back at me before brushing his thumb against my jawline.

I can feel Joselyn's eyes on us and I hate that we're just some kind of freak show. Is that what it's going to be like, being with him? People eyeballing us, not because we're an attractive couple like Roger and I were, but because they're trying to figure out how old we are or what our relation to each other is?

Trenton's looking at me like he can see every thought I'm having, as if the words are flashing across my eyes like the marquee board outside of their high school.

We're probably going to fight about it tonight because in his all I see is, *I'm not letting this go.*

Another door opens and I step back from him, letting his hand fall from my face.

"Aubree." Martha smiles as Joselyn scatters to a seat on the couch.

"Martha." I take a breath. "It's been a while. How are you?"

"Good, good." She nods, then looks over at Trenton and back to me like she's waiting on an explanation as to why I'm here with her son. "Did something happen with Diesel or something?" She clasps her hands together.

"No, Mom." Trenton gulps, suddenly looking nervous as he glances at me, giving me a pointed look like he'd like me to take over.

My lips part in response, but I have no words. Martha's looking at me suspiciously. Who are we kidding? She had an idea this was going on, but never said a word because she didn't *know.*

She looks like she's boiling, like she's going to bubble over if one of us doesn't finally speak.

"Alright!" Joselyn hops up from her seat. "Trenton and Mrs. Cooper are dating." She raises her eyebrows, eyes shifting over everyone in the room. "There. I said it."

Mine dart onto Martha, trying to get a reaction from her, but she's only staring at her son in complete shock. Hands still firmly clasped together, but much, much more tightly now.

Trenton rolls his tongue between his lips. "Mom."

"Wh—wh,…what do you mean, dating? What does she mean?"

"Dating, meaning…" He glances at me. "I'm in love with her." He shrugs boyishly and I can't help but to swoon over his words.

Martha's shaking her head at him, she hasn't even looked at me. This is all about Trenton, it always has been.

"You don't know anything about love, Trenton," she snaps before finally looking to me. "And you! You're a predator! Did you prey on my son, is that what you did?! How long have you had your eyes on him, huh?! How long have you been grooming him into thinking that he's in love with you?!"

"Mom!" Trenton warns, his hand on the back of my neck.

"How long, Aubree?"

I shake my head, my will to speak has vanished completely. My legs are threatening to walk me out of here—or run.

"It's not like that, Mom."

"Then what is it like?" Her arms cross tight over her chest. "I mean it all makes sense now. The reason she dresses like she's some little teen herself. It's all been to grab you young boys' attention—"

"I can't." I hold my hands up. "I'm not going to stand here and be insulted," I mutter, stepping out of Trenton's grasp.

"I'm the one who's insulted! You've been seducing my child!"

"I'm not a child!"

"You are, Trenton! I don't care how much of an adult you feel like you are, or are trying to be, you are still just a teenager!"

I rush out the door, not wanting to hear another accusatory, belittling word from her mouth.

Not long after, I can hear Trenton's steps coming quickly behind me.

"Trent, I am so sorry," I speak with tears in my eyes.

"You don't have anything to be sorry about." He pulls me into his arms. "You didn't do anything wrong."

"Then why do I feel like shit?" I dab the corners of my eyes. "Why do I feel like all I'm good for is ruining things? Ruining lives? Breaking families apart?"

His arms tighten slightly as he rocks me in his embrace. It calms me down significantly, feeling like I'm untouchable when shielded by his strong arms. Breathing him in.

"No, you didn't ruin anything," he says, gently. "That was nothing. You should've seen her when I crashed the old SUV."

I find the will to chuckle, despite the quickly running tears down my cheeks.

"She wasn't going to be okay with it, we already knew that." His chin bounces on top of my head as he speaks. "We aren't doing anything illegal, we aren't doing anything wrong. People are going to have their opinions on us, they're entitled to them. But we're entitled to not giving a damn because we are so fucking happy together—we're so fucking in love that none of that matters."

My tears stream violently, forcing me to shut my eyes tight as I drench his shirt.

"I love you so much, Aubree. Nothing's going to change that. We're in this together."

"I love you, too. I love you so, so much." So much it's crazy. I can't even believe it. I've never had someone fill me with so much love and confidence and strength.

He pulls back, holding his hands on my cheeks, and for a moment I'm embarrassed that he's seeing me this way. I'm an emotional wreck.

"I know, baby."

"So, this is really what's happening then?" Martha comes outside with a slight change in tone. She looks us over and it makes me feel like a teen again. She's got both judgement and concern in her eyes and it reminds me of my own mother. "You love my son?"

"I love him, Martha. I didn't want to—I tried not to—but it happened," my voice wavers and Trenton kisses the top of my head.

"And…your marriage?"

"It's over." I gulp down those words. "It will be." It still doesn't feel real to me, leaving Roger. He's all I've known for so long, I couldn't ever imagine life without him, until now.

She nods affirmatively, her eyes still studying us. "I'll be honest, I don't like this. If you came for approval, I can't give you that…not right now…but I do support whatever makes him happy," she tells me.

"I am happy, Mom."

"I've never seen you this way before—a man." She reaches out and places her hand on his arm. "Just, take care of each other."

A sheen comes over Martha's eyes and I think she's finally doing it. She's finally letting him go.

Trenton hugs her, a small smile places on his face before they release each other.

She frowns. "I love you, Trent."

"Love you too, Mom."

I look by the door and see Joselyn peeking out at everyone with her phone in her hand. I wave at her and say goodbye to Martha, wondering if there will ever be a time that she doesn't actually resent me.

THIRTY NINE

Trenton

"THAT WENT...BETTER THAN EXPECTED," I SAY, BUT NOTICE Aubree's quietly sitting with her averted gaze angled at the window.

That was by far the hardest thing I've ever had to do. I won't lie, my mom's reaction to us stung. Seeing Aubree freeze up was scary. I thought for sure she was slipping out of my grip again, but luckily Mom realized I was serious. That we were serious, and that I'm an adult and can make my own choices in this type of a thing.

Aubree isn't convinced, that's for sure. She hasn't said a word since we left. I was going to try and get her to go to Diesel's afterward, but now I'm thinking that's enough for today. What's important now is just getting this diary of hers. I hope that's all it takes to get her to finally relax and realize that everything will be fine.

I put the car in park, stopped right at the curb in front of what's soon to be just Roger's house.

"A predator?" she finally utters. "Is that what people are going to think of me? That I was plotting on having you from a young age? I'm not—"

"I know that, baby. If anything, it's backwards. I'm the one who's the predator here. I've been preying on that ass for years."

I expected to get a laugh out of her, but she glares at me like it doesn't help.

"Aubree, it doesn't matter what she thinks. It doesn't matter what anyone thinks." I take her hand in mine, swiping my thumb over her fingers. "You're worried about what Diesel's going to think, aren't you?"

"Yes."

"Well, he already knows we were fucking. He got over it."

"But did he? I mean, he forgave you—of course—but that's probably only because as far as he knows it's over."

"Well, at least it won't be such a shock this time."

"Shock aside, he's going to look at me like I'm the bad guy. Like I'm the one who's trying to take everything he cares about away from him and I'm not doing that with you. I don't want to take you from him."

"You aren't." I scrunch my brows together, adjusting so that I'm facing her as much as I can while in the drivers seat. "Me and Diesel are tighter than ever, Aubree. I'm not leaving him unless he tells me to."

"I know that, and that's what I'm afraid of. That he won't accept us and that he won't accept you anymore if you're with me."

"If that's what has to happen—"

"Do you hear yourself? That's your best friend and you're just okay with him possibly kicking you out of his life?!"

"Of course I'm not okay with that! But I love you and I've been in love with you for as long as I've known Diesel, so there's no competition there." I shake my head. "None."

She bites her lip as the first tear falls since twenty minutes ago. I swallow hard, enduring the sharp sting that pierces my chest at the sight of her so upset and anxious, although her tears do make her eyes look more beautiful in a way.

I open my mouth to speak, unsure of what's about to come out, but I don't get a chance to say a word because she leaves the car before I can get one in.

My phone vibrates for the hundredth time today.

Marina: *I hope you know this is all going to blow up in your face.*

She's been non-stop sending me weird messages like that. I don't know if I should take them as threats, or brush them off as Marina just trying to get me to notice her.

I erased the entire thread before finally blocking her number and running up to the house. I can't entertain her anymore. I tried being nice, I tried letting her down easily, I tried being her friend. Now I'm done.

It's already blown up once and I'm going to make everything right before it can happen again.

Aubree

We head straight up to Roger's office. I don't want to be in this house any longer than I need to. Roger isn't even here and it still feels like his black, beady eyes are on me.

I go right around the desk, my hand reaching for the handle on the drawer just to double check that it's locked when Trenton pats its flat surface.

"Hello, old friend," he mutters, prompting my glare.

"No jokes right now."

"You're right, I'm sorry. I was just trying to lighten the mood." He tilts my head up by my chin and plants a soft kiss that surprisingly does ease the tension. Even if only slightly. "So, where's it at?"

"In this drawer where it has been, forever. I don't know why I never thought to do this before, I'd have way less problems if I'd just burned that book a long time ago."

"Don't worry, we're getting it now. That's all that matters." He kneels down, takes my hair pin and sticks it in the key hole, jiggling it in confidently. Maybe I was wrong about these boys. Maybe they were the ones breaking into everything on our block. I wonder if Diesel knows how to pick a lock, too. He's hacked into Roger's laptop so many times, I can only be certain.

In only a few short moments, it clicks unlocked and he glides the drawer open like he didn't just break into Roger's desk with the same ease as slicing butter with a machete. It was kind of sexy—but I almost wonder if that's just because this desk is tied to so many orgasmic memories.

And it's open. My freedom is just one reach away.

The relief that came over me was nothing compared to the dread that knocked me in the chest when I shuffled through paper work, sticky notes, and manila file folders and came up with absolutely nothing.

"It was in here. It's always been in here. I saw him put it back and lock it." My breath shudders as I panic, on the verge of crying. "If the book isn't in his drawer, then…he…he probably—"

"Diesel doesn't have it. Don't worry, Roger probably knew you were going to try and steal it back and moved it."

"Well, then it could be anywhere. It could be with him in his suitcase halfway across the country or—"

"Why don't we just try to talk to Diesel, Aubree. Talk to him and tell him everything before Roger does come home and gets to him first."

I nod. He's right. I probably should have just went to Diesel first. I should have never tried to hide anything else from him. He deserves to know it all. The good and the bad.

"Okay…Let's tell him tomorrow."

"You're running low on time, babe. Roger's coming home in just a couple of days."

"And I'll tell Diesel tomorrow," I say, sternly. I really just want to get out of this house. I can't wait until the day I never have to return.

The next day, I woke up on Trenton's chest. Sometime during the night, every night, one of us will reach for the other and that results in us waking up swaddled in each others arms. It's something I'm still getting used to, but I love it.

By the way the sun is coming through the blinds, I know we over slept a bit into the afternoon. We were up late last night talking and then eventually having round after round of mind-blowing sex—the details of which are slowly coming back to me as I blink my eyes.

I watched him sleep for a moment, waiting on the will to break away from him to kick in so I can get the day started. Lately I've been spending most of my time looking into schools and jobs. I've put in applications, hoping someone will look over my sad excuse for a resume and give me a chance.

I've always wanted to do something in the medical field. Specifically, sonography or something along those lines, but being in Roger's clutches only deterred me from doing the things I always wanted to do. From having the life I always wanted to have, with hobbies and passions and exploration. He's made me this shallow human being who let all of her goals go once he slipped that ring on her finger.

It was like I didn't need them anymore if I was going to be with Roger. Why have any when he gave me everything?

I take a breath as I gently slide out of Trenton's arms, grabbing my phone from the nightstand to begin my job browse until he wakes, but the screen is already lit up like I've just received a notification.

My heart stops.

My screen is full of notifications and all are from Roger.

Angry text messages with capital letters and profanity and exclamation points, and the most recent are missed phone calls and voice messages. My hand shakes as I lift my phone to my ear and get ready for the inevitable to blare from the speaker.

"Yeah, I came home early. Something told me I should…and what a surprise it was when I saw that you weren't there." He chuckles. *"A girl came to the door. One of Diesel's friends—Lyssa and Scott's daughter. She told me all about how you were just here last night with Trenton."*

I gulp, his voice making me vibrate like I'm being stuck by needles.

"How he left her for you and how close you two looked at the grocery store. She said you two didn't stay long and I knew why. You didn't find what you were looking for, did you, Aubree?" He pauses and I can hear the constant winding sound like he's on the road. *"That's because I have it. I know you better than you know yourself. You can be in denial all you want, but no one will ever know you the way I do. I gave you everything and this is what you want to do? Leave me for some little tween boy like he'll be able to take care of you any fraction of the way I coul—"*

Trenton groans, rolling over and I stop the message with the press of my thumb in a panic.

Roger: *You made the biggest fucking mistake of your life, Aubree. Your past is finally coming back to bite you.*

I gasp and as soon as I do, Trenton sits up.

"What? What happened?" He scoots toward me, looking at the phone held in my hands.

"Roger's back. We have to go to Diesel's."

I jumped into a pair of jeans and a tee shirt and Trenton did the same. Luckily, Diesel wasn't far. He was only steps away. Minutes.

I spotted Roger's car parked in the car port in front of his apartment and my chest throbbed. Trenton grabbed me by my hand and led me the rest of the way because I was so physically numb, I couldn't even think straight, let alone tell myself to walk.

Those messages were sent over an hour ago. Diesel's probably read everything.

He finally knows my secrets. The hideous thoughts I never wanted him to know even entered my mind. That I hated parenthood. That I hated my life because of it. That it not only made things harder, but it made things worse. It made my life bleak, dark. Oppressive. I felt hopeless.

I was hopeless.

Looking back on that now, it wasn't true. It wasn't parenthood that did that to me, it was Roger. Too bad I never got to write that down. I never got to write one positive thing in that book, and I wish I had even one sentence that didn't sound so miserable.

Something tells me to try the knob and I do. The door is unlocked and as I swing it open, I see Roger's brooding stare already on me like he were only waiting on the moment I walked through that door and saw my worst fear playing out in front of me.

Diesel's sitting on the edge of the couch, my diary open and my dark smudgy writing all over the page. The pages look brittle, slightly yellow. He's reading silently, and all I want is for him to stop. I want that book out of my life. I want it burned.

I want my past to finally be just that. In the past.

"Diesel…I didn't mean any of that. I don't know why I wrote it, I don't even remember writing most of it. None of it was never meant for anyone to read, ever. Especially not—"

"Is this true, Mom?" Diesel's voice is dull, almost a murmur and I can tell he's still reading beneath it.

"No, no it's not true!" The words jump from my throat as I come toward him. "I never regret you, I never hated you, I never didn't want you—"

"But about Dad? About Dad cheating on you all this time and marrying you just because Grandma and Grandpa made him do it?"

"Yeah…that's—"

"That's not true, Diesel," Roger says, his eyes widening slightly.

Diesel scowls Roger's way. "So suddenly it isn't true, even though just an hour ago you handed me the book and said, *the truth about your mother is all written in her handwriting?*"

"I wanted you to see how twisted she is, Diesel. She made up all those things about me. None of that happened. She wasn't forced into marriage, there's no proof I was cheating, and I definitely didn't force her to sleep with me in order to conceive you. She made it all up in her head! She's crazy."

"You're a sadistic son of a bitch, Roger!" I swallow, shaking my head. "I wish it didn't have to come to this for me to finally leave you, but it is what it is."

"I told you, you had a choice and this is the one you chose! The one where you're exposed for who you are." He points his finger at me, almost snarling and I can feel Trenton beside me, ready to block if he takes even one more step.

I think Roger sees it himself and instead, turns his focus back to Diesel. "I have my own faults, but that's not why we're here. I gave you this book because I wanted you to see who she really is. I wanted you to know that your mother didn't have a happy thought proceeding your birth. She didn't want you, Diesel. She never did."

The look in Diesel's eyes makes me want to run toward him, to wrap my arms around my baby and tell him again how far from the truth that really is. I've always loved my son. Through both the good and the bad, Diesel has been the absolute light of my life. There isn't a thing I wouldn't do for him. There isn't a person I'd choose over him. There isn't a person I wouldn't kill for him—and right now I want to murder Roger for even speaking those kind of lies to him.

"But, did you, Dad? Did you ever want me? Were you ever happy about me being in this world at all? I'll be honest, when I found out about Aiden, I wasn't happy. I felt a lot of the things Mom wrote in this book. I was scared, I was mad, I had a lot of regrets, but as soon as I saw him it all changed for me. Did it change for you?"

"Of course it did, son. Of course." Roger scrunches his nose. "That's why I'm still here. That's why I've tried to make it work with your mother. She's the one who's been making it impossible—"

"You tried to make it work by cheating on her since before I was even born? By making her agree to a marriage with infidelity? You took advantage of her."

"She's not innocent here," Roger snaps. "She's been fucking your best friend for who knows how long—Did you know about that?"

I watch Diesel pinch the bridge of his nose and shut his eyes.

"Why don't you just tell her the truth for once, Dad?" He speaks in that way he does when he sounds like he's been talking too long and has grown tired of repeating himself. "Just tell her."

"Tell me what?"

Diesel looks at me, his brows fallen over his eyes. I can just barely see the familiar *sleepless nights* look in them.

"He hasn't been leaving on business trips. He hasn't been leaving at all." He looks at Roger. "Have you, Dad?"

Roger's jaw flexes and his nostrils flare, but he shakes his head and gives in. "Fine. No, I haven't been."

"Where have you been going, then? You're gone for weeks sometimes, where could you—"

"Visiting my daughter in Santa Monica. Seeing her only on some weekends wasn't good enough. The mother threatened to take it to the court, and I couldn't risk either of you finding out that way."

"Santa Monica?" I echo. "Your daughter? How…" I sigh, my face falling into my hands. "How do you have a daughter, Roger? You had a vasectomy years ago, unless—"

"She's five. She was born before I decided to get the vasectomy— she was the reason I got the vasectomy. Sadie was unplanned and I never wanted to have another unplanned child again."

"So I have a sister, hm?" Diesel scoffs, making Roger glare at him but he doesn't say a word.

"How did you know about that, Diesel?"

"I didn't know all that, but I followed you one day. Some things you said didn't add up for me, I had my suspicions."

"So where do we all go from here then?" Roger raises his hands. "Is this it? You're going to leave me for him?"

"I'm leaving you for me, Roger. I should have years ago…I want a divorce." And just like that, the white flag is finally waved. I've finally said the words I've only screamed in my head a thousand times.

Roger's face puckers like he's eaten something foul and then he throws his hands in the air. "Fine. Fuck it. Fuck what everyone else thinks, who fucking cares about all the shame you'll be putting on this family."

"Shame? Cheating on your wife for eighteen years doesn't shame this family? Having a secret love child no one even knows about—do your parents know?"

Roger's silence confirms my assumption that they have no clue. His father may remove him from the brand all together once this gets out.

"You're lucky I'm not vindictive enough to send out a mass email," I say. "And I'm sure Camille would love to hear from me."

He shakes his head like he knows it's better not to add more fuel to the fire and he leaves out the front door. He's not worth my time, and apparently I'm not worth anymore of his.

"I'm sorry, Diesel. I never wanted you to find out about any of this, all I ever wanted was for you to have a good life. To have a normal life. I'm just sorry we hid so much from you."

He shakes his head. "Don't be sorry, Mom. I'm sorry." Diesel speaks with a small glisten in his eyes like he's holding himself together. "I...I should have told you about Dad as soon as I found out...I just, I didn't know what to do. I was confused. I always thought it was you that was dragging us all down—because that's what he wanted me to think—but now I understand. I get it."

"The diary—"

"No, I know. I was an asshole as a kid, I would've hated me too."

"I don't hate you. I never hated you." My eyes widen at him.

"I know. I know that, but I'm still sorry for always treating you the way I have. You didn't deserve it. You've always been a pretty good mom."

A pretty good mom. I'll take it.

For the first time in years, I hug my son.

With my eyes shut and my arms around him, I'm hit with a rush of memories. His sweet face looking up at me the moment he was first placed in my arms. His one year old toothless, chocolate covered grin. His five year old first day of kindergarten tears. His sleepy smile greeting me on Christmas morning as he held out the gift he picked for me. His excited chuckles as I let go of the bicycle seat and let him soar down the pavement. Waving at me during his basketball games as I watched him from the stands, hoping he knew how proud of him I was.

"Diesel, you will always be the center of my world, I always understood even when I didn't and because of that, I've never held any of it against you. I love you."

"I love you too, Mom."

When I release him, he immediately takes Trenton by the shoulder and pulls him out to the patio, shutting the screen door behind them.

I almost forgot. The other reason we're here, his best friend and actual love of my life.

"So, what is this?" Diesel's finger points from me to Trenton.

"Diesel…" Trenton sucks in a sharp breath. "Like I told you before…I'm in love with your mom. I know I made a lot of stupid ass jokes, but it's always been love. I just want to make her happy— She deserves to be happy, and for some crazy reason, she's happy with me."

Diesel stares at him and I'm not sure if he looks like that because he wants to attack him for saying those words, or because he's probably remembering the morning he caught us in the shower.

"I swear I have nothing but good intentions with her. You're my best friend, I'd never—"

The rest of the conversation is mumbled and they glance up at me every once in a while with the most serious looks on their faces.

"Mrs. Cooper…" Chloe emerges from the hallway with Aiden wrapped in a blanket and held against her chest. The awkward look on her face shows she heard it all and now she's the last to find out about Trenton and I.

"No more Mrs. Cooper, Chloe. Call me Aubree. That name isn't me anymore."

A solemn smile appears on her face as she gently pats Aiden's back.

I can finally let out the breath I'd been holding when the boys clasp hands and hug. Was it really that easy? Was I worried for no reason at all? Diesel has proven once again not to be who I thought he was, but maybe that's because I was basing him off of his father and never off of himself. But I never really knew who Diesel was, he'd never let me. Now I'm seeing it first hand.

He's strong minded, he's assertive, he's loving. He's a provider, a fighter, a young man, a father. He's maturing.

Roger's gone, just like that. My old life as a fake wife is finally over. The only life I ever knew, but for the first time I feel like I can breathe. Like I'm not shackled to one spot, being told what I can and cannot do. I'm free.

Or I will be as soon as I burn that book. I Don't even want to touch it, but I take it from the couch anyway. It's the last bit left of my past and I can't wait until it's gone.

"One more thing." Diesel sets his hand on Trenton's shoulder. "Is it okay if I call you Dad?"

"Shut the fuck up." Trenton laughs and I gauge Chloe's reaction, which is hardly a reaction at all. She's smiling at the two of them and I'm convinced she already knew. I'm convinced she's just happy for the peace. That Diesel has his best friend again, that Diesel has his mom again. That he's no longer in the dark.

"Well, *Dad*. I'm gonna need a monthly allowance of five hundred bucks. Non negotiable." And for once Diesel smiles genuinely.

It's not altered or weak from being insanely high or bordering-alcohol-poisoning drunk, he's been taking care of himself. He's been taking care of his family.

All I ever really hoped for for my son was that he walk away learning something from me and his father. That he take all of our mistakes and do the opposite. He definitely did, and he definitely learned. But it was me who learned so much more.

FORTY

Aubree

Two Years Later

"CHLOE, CAN YOU PLEASE HAND ME THE SPATULA—OH, AND THE
icing." I pull the cake from the freezer, running back to the island
while multitasking by grabbing a couple of sprinkle shakers I picked
up in a rush today.

I should have just ordered a cake, but sometimes I forget I have
connections for all of my party needs right in my phone—thanks to
Lyssa hiring me.

Trenton found out I was planning this party a week ago. I was
bummed that he ruined the surprise—and shot it down by proposing
to do something with just the two of us instead—so I cancelled it.

After a lot of contemplation, I decided the party is back on.
Why? Because I love him and I know he'll be happy to see his friends
and family after having his head buried in books the past couple of
weeks for midterms—while also working for PKG. I'm just glad he's
finally gotten a better position at work. I always worried that working
on the floor was going to kill his back, even though it did do wonders
on his body.

"*Of course,*" Chloe sings, handing me the cake spatula. She whisks
little Aiden into her arms, not without him whining and kicking his
feet as he's suspended into the air, though.

He's been such a handful, and I'm sort of glad Diesel's finally
getting a taste of his own medicine with that one. He's his father

times ten. A natural born menace, but only with his parents. With me, he's an absolute angel.

While scraping the white icing until it's perfectly flat, spinning the plate to smooth out the edges as well, I glance out the window at Diesel. He's grilling the burgers while chatting with Joselyn as she prepares the utensils and napkins beside him.

Gio and Martha look to have just finished draping the tables in dark blue table cloth and I'm just hoping everything's set by the time Trenton walks through the door. Not like he'll really care if it isn't. He'll come in with a big smile either way.

There's a knock on the door, then the bell rings.

"Chloe—"

"I'm on it." She jogs to the door, Aiden bouncing in her arms as I write Trenton's name on the cake in blue icing. The good thing about the party business is that I've picked up a ton of tricks. Business has been so great that Lyssa and I have been able to work this job full time. We're hoping to go on to wedding planning soon, depending on how everything goes with our first client, Marina.

She's getting married in the fall and we're currently drafting plans for something pretty in the mountains. I'm happy to give her the wedding of her dreams, because that just confirms she's finally over Trenton. He's mine.

I hear a deep voice speak and soon after, the man it came from appears in my kitchen, holding up a gift bag in one hand and the hand of a young girl in the other.

"Aubree." Roger smiles at me.

He and I were finally able to come to terms with everything last year. It was actually easy. I've been so happy living my own life that forgiving him for everything he'd put me through was just the last step in freeing myself.

If it weren't for him, I couldn't be in this position. I wouldn't be.

Trenton's the absolute love of my life, and although my past with Roger was filled with trials, it was all necessary in guaranteeing me this level of happiness.

"Roger." I huff out a laugh—finally removing my hands from the cake I was sure wouldn't be ready when Trenton got home—and dust my palms on the fronts of my jeans.

I take the bag from his hands and then we come into a hug. It's different. It's like we never were in love—because we really weren't. We are just Diesel's parents and that's all we've ever been.

"Hi, Sadie." I kneel down to her level, she's always firm at Roger's side and it's beautiful. He looks at her in a way I've never seen before, and I'm happy for him. I'm happy for her. She gets to have her father all the time, in a way Diesel never had him.

She pulls her finger out of her mouth and smiles. Waving at me, although I'm right in front of her. She's a shy little thing.

I give her a hug before coming back up to a stand.

"Diesel's out back," I say to her.

"Why don't you go out and say hi to your brother, sweetie." Roger tilts his head at her. "I'll be out in a minute."

She peeks out toward the sliding glass leerily, but nods and heads outside.

We watch until Diesel spots her and lifts her off the ground into an overenthusiastic hug. I can hardly hear him through the window, but her giggles are unmistakable. I always knew Diesel would make a good big brother.

"You look good Aubree."

"As do you." I nod, taking note of how casually he's dressed. I didn't realize how used to seeing him in suits I was until we finally were apart. I grab as many beers as I can from the fridge and set them on the island before sliding one to him. "How's Lydia?"

"She's great, just been wondering why she hasn't gotten an RSVP from you."

Just to prove how much of a hypocrite Roger had been, Lydia, his soon to be bride, is not only twenty six, but had Sadie when she was only bordering nineteen. Just to add the cherry to the pie, she's Roger Sr.'s business partner's *daughter.*

I blow a short puff of air past my lips as his bottle pops open, remembering the invite I'd gotten from them weeks ago. "I'm sorry, I forgot. We'll be there, though—of course."

He nods, taking a sip. His hand slips into his pocket and I briefly watch him stare out at the kids playing in the back yard. A backyard that is nothing like the one he and I used to own.

When we were going through our divorce, I didn't want that house and neither did he. He sold it and we split the money. Thanks to being Roger's wife, my credit is exceptional and I was able to find a new house. Something brighter, something smaller. More modest. And without all of the baggage the old house had.

I look back at him after feeling his eyes on me and we share a laugh.

"What?" I ask. "Do I have something on my face?"

He shakes his head. "Just pregnancy glow."

"What?"

He laughs, his head dipping back. "You're fucking pregnant as hell."

Solana saunters in with her empty glass in her hand, most likely about to pour her fourth cup of our latest shared fetish—Rosé. "That's what I've been saying!"

"I am not."

"Look at your flawless skin, your smile. You are so pregnant," he insists.

I shove him, Solana squeezing past me and back into the living room before I walk back over to the cake to move it to a safer location. Call it mothers intuition, but I can already see someone running in here and knocking it off the counter.

More specifically, Aiden. Even though he is only three feet tall, I know he'd find a way to stick his tiny fingers in the icing.

"Does he know?" Roger asks while my back is turned.

"I don't know what you're talking about." I smile to myself before checking my watch. He'll be here any minute.

"Hey Dad," says Diesel, with Sadie trailing in after him.

"Hey, yourself." Roger scowls at him. "What's with you not returning my calls, lately?"

Diesel bunches his brows, then raises them like he's thought of something. "I got a new phone—new number." He goes to the fridge, grabbing a couple of capri suns and hands one to his sister. "Aiden flushed my old one down the toilet—or tried to."

"Telling me would have been nice."

"I told Mom." He shrugs, popping the straw in the pouch.

Roger scoffs, but I laugh. Diesel and I are closer than he and Roger ever were. He comes over all of the time with Aiden and Chloe, and Roger is totally jealous.

I'm finally in the loop. I'm finally the favorite parent. The reliable parent. The one who gets all the invites and first phone calls.

Only thing that isn't funny is that Aiden hardly knows Roger, but there's no one he can blame but himself for that.

"Thanks for letting me know, Aubree." Roger squints at me.

I chuckle, arms raised. "How's it my responsibility?"

The sliding glass opens, interrupting our family tiff as Joselyn pokes her head through the opening. "He's here!" She speaks in a sharp whisper, and I hear the garage rising on the west side of the house.

Diesel runs his sister into the living room and they find a hiding spot behind the sofa. The others rush in and all take cover wherever they possibly can.

Solana tucks herself behind the kitchen wall, sipping on yet another freshly poured glass of wine. Poor Gio decides to lay flat on the floor and it makes us all laugh, only wrecking the surprise element because Trenton opens the door to our unapologetic chuckling.

"Surprise!" The lights flip on.

He smiles at us all as we rise up from behind the furniture. "Aw man, I said I didn't want a surprise party!"

"But it's your birthday." I grin, coming toward him and not stopping until his arms are around me. "I had to."

We all head back outside, everyone makes their plates before picking seats. I value this time like no other and I feel so fortunate that everything went better than it ever could have. Diesel's a great dad, a great son. A *fiancé*. Roger's a great friend. Solana's the greatest friend.

Martha finally came around a year ago when she saw that nothing was changing between us, that I wasn't going anywhere and neither was Trenton. She's so accepting of us, she sometimes shows up without warning. We go to dinner, and even sometimes have pamper days with Joselyn.

Everything fell apart just to come together in a way greater than I could have ever imagined it would.

"Think about it, man," says Gio, "you can get into any casino, any club—you can drink legally, smoke legally—"

Trenton raises a hand to interrupt him. "All things that I either don't do anymore, or don't really care about."

"But you can now do it, *legally*."

I see Trenton's phone light up beside my plate.

Dad: *Happy Birthday, son. I'll try to be in town by nine tomorrow morning. Did you decide where you want to eat? I was thinking the three of us could have a birthday breakfast, but I know how Jos is about sleeping in.*

"Is no one going to mention the fact that I've been eighteen for a whole month?" Joselyn sasses. "Who cares about Trenton turning twenty-one?"

"Eighteen doesn't matter," Gio goes on, waving a hand at her. "You're a small fish. You can't even buy a pack of smokes."

She narrows her eyes. "I don't smoke anyway."

"Good, keep it that way." Trenton points a stern finger at her and it makes my heart jump. I love when this side comes out in him, I just know he's going to make a great father.

He's begged me for a baby ever since we made things official, but I am so glad that I returned to birth control and convinced him to hold off. Of course I want another child, despite my only son already being twenty years old. I just think it would have been selfish of me not to push Trenton to do more for himself. To go to college, to save his money, to have fun and just enjoy his freedom. He did. *We* did.

He's been in junior college for two years and will transfer out in three months, his car is paid off, his savings account is phenomenal, his credit is excellent. We went on a couple of vacations out of the country last year, and he has guys nights with the boys every once in a while, but none of that held him off long before he was back on the baby train, asking me if we were ready yet.

I didn't think we were, but apparently someone else did.

Trenton looks at me with a small smile, he has been for the past few weeks. I swear he knows. Or maybe I've already given it away by just being me.

"What?"

"You gonna explain why you suddenly look extra beautiful?"

"I do not. This look is courtesy of a whole day of procrastination."

"I love it. Procrastinate more often."

I chuckle as he pulls me into him and kisses my cheek.

Aiden's running around the yard, Diesel hot on his heels but keeping enough distance to make him think he can actually outrun him.

"But seriously though, Aubree." He pulls back to look at me, I can feel his arms linked around the small of my back. "You look different, you seem different. What is it?"

I purse my lips as a smile begins and it prompts him to do the same. *He knows! How does he know?!*

"I heard you this morning. You sounded sick, but don't seem sick at all." He raises his eyebrows as the back of his hand grazes my temple. "What's going on?"

I open my mouth, but a shy sigh comes out instead of words. This isn't how I wanted to tell him. I had a whole plan, a cute, intimate dinner, and then I'd give him a positive test in a nice box.

Maybe I'd fold up a stupid tee shirt that says *Worlds Best Dad*, or something, but looks like that's all up in flames. He's got me cornered.

"Baby." He sighs with an ounce of hope in his eyes. "Are you…."

"If I tell you…"

He stands still, and with urgency and question in his tone he says, "Aubree, come on…"

I nod. "Yeah…I'm pregnant."

His smile widens and his cheeks tinge in pink before he slides his hands up to my jaw. "Really? You're—you're not playing around?"

That was only once last April fools day and I realized it was a terrible joke as soon as I saw how excited he was—as soon as the first of a few tears were shed.

He stopped talking to me for a few hours afterwards. I learned my lesson.

"No, it's not a joke. I'm seven weeks, Trenton. You're going to be a dad."

He laughs, but I can see his eyes glossing over as his thumbs brush over my hairline. I hold his arms in my hands, loving the sight of his smile and seeing him this happy over having a baby. With me.

He kisses me twice quickly, then once deeply before pulling away and staring into my eyes like he's in total disbelief.

"I love you so fucking much, Aubree." He pulls me into his arms. "You make…my life make sense."

I hear him sniff in my ear and pull back. "Trent?"

He turns his face away from me and everyone else, wiping his eyes to hide his reaction. Seeing him so emotional jump starts my hormones like nothing else, causing a tear to run down my cheek without me even realizing it.

"What's going on over there?" Martha says from the table, clear concern in her voice.

Trenton and I chuckle, feeling like two emotional idiots, but it doesn't stop him from smiling over at them and saying the words, "Nothing crazy. I'm just gonna be a dad."

"I knew it!" Roger speaks like he's just won a bet, slamming his fist in his palm. Joselyn awes and giggles in her seat beside him. She'd been egging on pregnancy for a couple of years now and so has Martha. I always felt ganged up on whenever I was alone with the two of them.

"Whoo!" Diesel raises his arms. "Please be a brother!"

Sadie scoffs, crossing her arms and we all laugh.

With Trenton in my life, I laugh everyday. I love everyday, and I'm loved everyday. I couldn't imagine living any other life than the one he's given me.

EPILOGUE

Trenton

Six Months Later

"WE HAVE TO GO OUT THERE." SHE LAUGHS. "THEY'RE ALL waiting!"

My hands continue pulling up the back of her dress. It's pink, soft, strapless, stops at her ankles, and I would really prefer it bunched up on the floor.

I place my lips on her bare shoulder and she bites down a moan, which only serves as a delicious indication that she's seconds from giving in to me. She's always been easy like that.

I love her pregnant. Not only is she even more curvy and beautiful, but she's always horny and so am I.

"It'll only be a minute, baby," I speak onto her neck before biting the soft skin. She climbs into bed, propping her hands up on the headboard, getting into position as I slide her panties down her thighs. "Or not. This is our party, they can wait."

She begins to laugh and probably protest, but I slide into her so quickly, not expecting her to be that wet for me already and she drops her head instead. "God, Trenton…why do you feel so good?"

"Because I was made for you, baby." I smile to myself, holding her by her hips as I thrust in and out of her, feeling her constrict around me as her orgasm brews closer.

Her fingers run over the base of my dick before she grabs a hold of my balls and begins working them the way I like. The way she knows will get me to come at her will.

"Harder," she breathes, rubbing me rougher in encouragement. I do as she asks, my thighs slamming into the back of hers, her ass bouncing and mesmerizing me with each hit.

I feel her walls tighten around me. Similarly her fingers tighten around my balls, and on the other hand, around the bedpost she's holding onto.

"You're squeezing the shit out of me." I still inside of her, biting down on my lip as I talk myself out of coming this soon. Her glowing bronze skin so beautiful, so enticing. Her dark curls running down her back. Her body moving and quaking beneath me. I could come by just looking at her. She's the only one who can get me there this fast. Who can make me beg both her and myself not to let go.

"I'm so close, Trenton." She sighs as she wriggles in front of me, her hips pleading for me to keep going as she rubs her ass against me, despite me holding her tight so that I don't blow. "I'm so close, I just need to feel you come inside me."

And for me that's all it takes. Just hearing her beg for what she wants. *Me.* I still can't believe it sometimes.

I grab a firm hold of her ass and fuck her roughly, mercilessly. The sounds coming out of her root me on toward my climax.

"Fuck, I love you," I groan, seeing how her back arches when my dick disappears inside of her, glistening in her sweet juices when I all but remove the tip from her core.

I see a smile begin to curve her lips, but then stop right as she loses it. Her cheek presses to the headboard and I fill her up while she spasms around my cock, moaning my name like it's the only word she knows.

"I love you, Trenton," she finally says, breathlessly, while I pull her hair away from her neck. Gently, I run my fingers up her sides, making her shiver before trailing kisses across her shoulder, inhaling her sweet scent.

"I know."

I button my jeans and then help her off the bed, steadying her on her feet before she goes to the bathroom to clean up..

Peeling the curtains back, I look out our bedroom window, staring down at our backyard full of our family and friends.

Decorations that we all spent the morning putting up together.

My Mom, my dad. Cousins and coworkers. Diesel and Gio, fully animated and in the middle of what looks like a funny story.

My sister standing beside Gio, looking at him with the same stars in her eyes that have always been there, and I only watch with the same anxiety in mine because that's always scared me. But then again, Gio's my best friend and I trust that he'd never cross that line with her. *Knock on wood.*

Even if he did, I'd only be a hypocrite if I stepped in or tried to stop it, but damn how could a person not?

That's my little sister.

I still see a complete baby when I look at her. The one who used to hold her arms up to me and ask to be picked up all the time and who'd cry and pout if I didn't share every single thing I had with her. When it comes to Joselyn, I completely get why Diesel did all but kill me when he found out about me and Aubree. I'd do the same if anyone posed a threat to my sister.

The bathroom door opens and I turn around to look at Aubree. I'm taken aback by her beauty every time I see her. Like she gets better every day, if that's possible.

My fingers tuck into my back pockets, but my right hand stops before it can slide all the way in. Blocked by what I'd put in there this morning. I'm not sure if that's a sign or a reminder—or both.

"Ready to shower this baby?"

I go to her, admiring her in all her entirety. Her dark eyes stare up at me sweetly like she has no idea. She has no clue just how lucky I feel being with her, how happy I am being with her. *How blessed.*

How amazed I am by her. By how much I love her and this other person she's growing inside of her.

I wish she could know.

I tuck her hair behind her ear, completely ignoring what she's just asked me. "Aubree Maharaj, will you do me the absolute honor of being my wife?"

I've asked her this before multiple times and her answer has always been the same.

"Duh. That's the plan, right?" She takes my hands in hers and I just watch her speak. "Eventually I will be a wife again. A real wife. Your wife." She huffs at the thought. "Just wait until baby girl is out."

"No. Not eventually." I reach in my back pocket for the ring box, taking a knee. "Be a real fiancée. Be my fiancée."

She covered her face with her hands before I could even finish speaking and broke down. "You asshole! I wanted a pretty proposal with dinner and a nice dress—where I wasn't huge and pregnant!"

"I know, but I couldn't wait anymore. It was burning a hole in my pocket." I look at her sideways. "And you just look so beautiful, I had to ask you now."

She nods, wiping her eyes with one hand and holding her other out to me while I slip the ring on her finger. We laugh as I pull her into my arms, kissing her lips a million times because they're officially mine. She's all mine and I'll never let her go.

One Month Later

"If someone would have told me four years ago I'd be putting together baby furniture for my baby sister—who also happens to be Trenton's daughter—I would have knocked them out." Diesel's laying on the floor after declaring he's on a break only two minutes ago, while me and Gio are actually working to get some of this stuff done. "One hit, uppercut right to the chin."

Gio laughs, but I hardly think it's funny. Not that it isn't, I'm just too stressed to laugh. We didn't think Aubree would go into labor this morning, but I still shouldn't have waited this long to get everything in order.

She was working with Lyssa this morning and her water broke. I only found out a few hours ago that she'd been admitted into the hospital.

After dialing Aubree's number, I wedge the phone in between my shoulder and cheek as I continue assembling this black crib. "Hey baby, how are you doing?"

"I'm…hanging in here." She chuckles weakly and I admire her for trying to sound strong for me. "I forgot how brutal labor was."

"Do you want me to just come now? I can finish everything up when we get home."

"No, don't worry, Trent. I'm only at a four."

"A four? Like on a pain scale? That's not too bad."

She laughs. "No, dilated."

I'm quiet a moment as I'm still not following.

"*Meaning*, I probably won't have her until tomorrow morning, if that."

"Oh, okay." I nod, the guys both looking at me like they're waiting for me to get off the phone. "I just…I think I should be there."

"I want you here, but I also want everything ready for the baby so just please get everything ready at home. I'll be fine."

"Okay." I nod, swallowing as any mention of the baby makes me nervous as hell. I'm about to be a dad in just a few hours from now. I thought I was ready, but I don't know.

Define ready.

Emotionally ready? Mentally ready? Whichever one I don't think I am anymore.

"I'll finish up here as fast as I can, Aubree. Let me know if anything changes."

"I will. I love you."

"I love you." I end the call, my eyes linger on my phone screen a moment as another wave of anxiety washes over me. My biggest fear is that the baby is born and I'm not there because I'm putting together a fucking crib, or some type of emergency happens and I wasn't there, where I should be.

"T, why don't you go to the hospital. We'll finish up." Gio looks over at Diesel and he nods at him like it's a fine plan.

"Yeah, man. Go." Diesel shrugs. "You're clearly more useful there. We're almost done, anyway. Don't even worry about it, I'm a veteran at this kind of thing."

So I did. I got changed into something that hadn't soaked up buckets of nervous sweat, and drove to the hospital.

The look of relief on Aubree's face when she saw me made me glad I came when I did. Even if it were just to hang out overnight until our daughter finally arrived.

I kiss her on her lips before she lays her head back and shuts her eyes. I see the pain in her body language and it makes me feel helpless.

"See, this is why I didn't want you here." She sighs. "I knew you were going to look at me like that."

"Like what?" I grab her hand, placing her fingertips on my lips before kissing them. "Like I missed you?"

She smiles, but it doesn't reach her eyes. If she weren't hurting so much, I'm sure it would have. "No, like a one-man pity-party."

"I'm just, concerned. I wanted to be here. I need to be here through all of it."

And I was. I hardly kept my hands off of her, unless she told me not to touch her, which she did a few times during some bad contractions. It got easier when she got the epidural and then she fell asleep at some point, and as much as I wanted to rest, I couldn't. I stayed up, I waited. I paced the room.

Diesel, Gio, and Joselyn came and kept me company around one in the morning and they didn't leave me alone. I never knew how nerve wracking awaiting the birth of a child would be, but I'm as excited as I am nervous.

"Look at you, Princess," I whisper to the baby in my arms. She's bundled in a white blanket with pink and blue footprints all over the cloth.

Her eyes are closed, but her tongue's poked out at me sporadically since I've picked her up.

This morning at five A.M., Aubree gave birth to our daughter. She came into this world healthy and loved beyond belief. A ton of hair, dark like her mother's and I can already sense an attitude to match.

"You're just perfect," I tell her, hoping she can understand. Hoping she knows just how much I love her only minutes after meeting her the first time. I look over at her mother, the woman of my dreams who's watching me like the feeling is mutual. "Aubree, she's perfect."

"Let me see her."

I lay the baby in her lap and see her eyes brighten.

"Oh, she's so beautiful," she breathes like she's border-lining speechless. "And she's ours."

"She's ours." I kiss her forehead, sitting beside her. "And you're mine, and I'm yours."

"Forever," she whispers as she leans against my shoulder, kissing my arm.

I watch her admire our baby who's perfect in every way. I'm already angry at every boy who I'll have to fight away from her, and even more so at the few that will break her heart. The rest of my life will be dedicated to making sure she's always smiling and I'm okay with that.

"She looks just like you, Trent."

I huff at the thought. "You think so?" She looks a bit wrinkled and her face is a little squished and chubby, but she's the most beautiful thing I've ever seen so I have no choice but to take it as a compliment.

"Mhm, she's got your lips and nose." She nods before brushing her hand over the baby's cheek. "Trinity Grace Laguna...What do you think?"

Naming our daughter has been the source of all our arguments for the past four months. We couldn't seem to settle on a single name and it'd gotten to the point that we just opted to leave it open until this day. But now, seeing her darling little face, it's almost like she's named herself.

"I love it." I chuckle as Trinity pokes her tongue out again and then her eyes open and they're a gorgeous green like I've never seen before. My heart melts and it's like falling in love all over again. "God, I love her so much already."

I hear Aubree's soft sniveling and it removes me from the gripping trance my daughter put me in when we made eye contact for the first time.

"Trenton, I know I don't say this a lot, but I am so grateful for you. You've always been there for me, even in the smallest ways and you were always right about, everything. We were always bound, we were always meant to be...I know that now."

I look her over, her dewey complexion, the twinkle in her eyes, her hair still runs majestically down the sides of her face. She's just as beautiful as she always has been.

We thought we'd flipped each others worlds upside down, but looking back on it now, nothing was right side up until we knew we loved each other. We needed each other in order to be right with the world.

I kiss her temple, our daughter cooing in her arms. I have perfection right by my side. I have everything I'll ever need.

My impossible love was possible.

AUTHOR'S NOTE:

I just wanted to take a moment to thank you readers and supporters. This story was so fun to write, came so naturally and so impulsively that Aubree and Trenton have marked a special spot in my soul after really challenging me to stop censoring myself. With this story, I wanted to open up. I felt my debut was so bottled up. Although I was happy with how it turned out, I do feel that it could have been so much more had I really dug deeper.

This time around, I wanted to lift my own personal boundaries while pushing those of my main characters. It was a real learning experience writing my first forbidden tale and I hope you enjoyed it as much as I did putting it together.

As always, reviews are so welcome. As a new author, I appreciate any reviews received, good or bad. Thanks so much!

Cheyenne xx

Other Works

All of Us Series
Between Us
Beyond Us
About Us

BadLuckBrides Series
The Window Seat (#1 - A Novella)

Keep Up With Me...
www.cheyennecierrabooks.com
Instagram - www.instagram.com/authorccierra
Amazon - www.amazon.com/author/cheyennecierra
Blog - www.cheythenobody.wordpress.com
Pinterest - www.pinterest.com/authorccierra
Find me on Goodreads!

Made in the USA
Monee, IL
10 April 2021

65372767R00204